'TIL DEATH

CONVERSION
BOOK THREE

S.C. STEPHENS

Edited by Debra L. Stang

Cover photo © Toski Covey Photography

Cover design © Sarah Hansen, Okay Creations

ISBN-13: 978-1496112699

ISBN-10: 1496112695

Dedication

Thank you to all the original fans of this series who begged for the trilogy in print, and thank you to all the new fans, who took a chance on my "little bit" vampires. I hope you have enjoyed reading their journey as much as I have enjoyed telling it!

I cannot thank enough the people who have helped and supported me throughout this crazy process of writing and publishing. I could not do it alone! Well, not with my sanity intact, at any rate. A behemoth-sized thank you to Lori, Becky, Nicky, Sam, and Nic, for taking time out of their busy lives to read all of the massive stories I send their way. And a huge thank you to Debra Stang, for her mad editing skills, Sarah Hansen for her amazing covers, Toski Covey for the beautiful photography, and Julie at JT Formatting for making my life easier and my ebooks stunning.

Chapter 1 – My Family

My heart was racing. It was hammering in my chest like it was about to break free of my rib cage. My breath came fast through my parted lips and my body was on fire.

I was sprawled across the longest, softest leather couch you could possibly imagine, and my arms and legs were tangled around the handsomest man you could possibly imagine. His body pressed against mine in a teasing, rhythmic pattern, reminding me that it had been quite a while since more than just his rough denims had rubbed against me. His breath was equally fast in my mouth, and his heart, if it still had a beat, would have been racing as well, I was sure.

But it had been a long while since his heart had beaten its last beat. Almost five years to be exact. And while his skin was cool and his tongue was icy, he was masterful with both and more than made up for the temperature difference.

The harsh roughness of his stubbled jaw brushed against me and I contained a moan. I loved that. My overly sensitive skin could feel and hear each grain of coarse hair; it electrified me. His cool lips shifted to my neck, and his fangs pricked against my skin. I almost begged him right then and there to do it, to pierce my flesh and taste my blood. He would have loved it, I would have loved it, but I resisted, and only squirmed with growing desire.

A cool palm ran up one side of my body, up my hip and along my breast. His thumb circled over a nipple and my head dropped back as I contained another groan. I could feel his lips curve into a smile as he pressed them into the indentation of my collar bone. His hip digging into my thigh made his readiness for me all too obvious, even if I'd only been a standard human.

But I wasn't a standard human, not anymore, and he had never been one to begin with. He was a vampire, or as he'd first told me, a "little bit" vampire. Born into the life, it was just the way he had always been and would always be. Me? I'd been bitten by some jerk-off vampire with an attitude problem. The man currently running his nose up my jaw was the man who'd saved me. My husband. Teren Adams.

After the attack, Teren had given me his blood. He'd only been trying to heal me, but what he'd ended up doing was changing me. Now I was a "little bit" vampire, just like him. It was an odd, complicated process that others far more knowledgeable about vampire anatomy understood, but for all intents and purposes, I was vampire *and* human, a mixed breed. I enjoyed sun, mochas and silver jewelry. I moved blindingly fast, had hearing that was almost too good at times, and most of all, I loved blood. No, *love is too insignificant a word.* I wasn't out killing people for it or anything, but if I was forced to choose a last meal, that would be it.

But I had a heartbeat and I was still alive.

I also had fangs, just like my husband. Releasing the hold on them that I had to constantly maintain, I let them drop down into the position they always wanted to be in—drinking position. Shifting my head, I dragged my teeth along Teren's neck. He loved that, too.

He sucked in a quick breath and let out a small groan. "Stop that," I muttered. "We're being discreet, remember."

"Sorry," he breathed in my ear.

One of his hands pinched my nipple and I bit back my own moan, stopping it just short of making a noise. He chuckled as he lowered his lips to mine, and that marvelous tongue made it hard to remember why I couldn't shift his hips over just a smidge, so he was in a much more satisfying position.

One of Teren's hands, the one not actively caressing my body, was making a repetitious pattern through the air: lift, stop, pull back, extend. He did it over and over again. The move would seem pretty strange, if you didn't understand what he was doing. I contained a laugh as I thought about what he *was* doing. To an oblivious set of toddlers, he was idly playing catch while simultaneously making out with me. Multitasking at its finest.

His hand was coming up, catching a sloppily tossed ball, and chucking it into the other room, where two sets of feet shuffled off for it, giggling the entire time they raced to beat the family dog to the favored object. Teren used his super acute hearing to track the ball, and the sense in our blood to tell him exactly where the children were. Since he didn't need his eyes, lips, and one of his hands for that, he was focusing those parts of his body on me.

We reveled in soft, heated kisses while I mentally tracked how many minutes were left until bedtime. More than a few, less than too many. Our two miracle children—miracle that we'd conceived them before Teren's aforementioned heart had stopped, and miracle that we had found a way to keep mine from stopping before they were born—were laughing as they played with Spike and Daddy.

Nika and Julian, the other two loves of my life. They were perfect, precocious three-year-olds.

Suddenly the children grew tired of their game with Daddy and decided to crawl up his legs. He broke off from kissing me and looked down at them. Laughing, he shifted his position, so that he was nestled in-between me and the couch. That signaled an end to the foreplay, for now, until we had a more private place to explore each other.

As he reached down for them, they giggled and crawled up into our arms. Sighing contentedly, my passion faded and an overwhelming love swept in. Teren sighed in a matching way as he slid one arm underneath me and wrapped the other one around Nika and Julian on my chest.

Listening to my heart, Nika giggled. "Mommy, you're loud." Squeezing her tight, I laughed and gave Teren a wry smile. He suppressed a laugh with a twitching grin.

"I know, sweetheart." I kissed the top of her head, and the scent of baby shampoo filled me. "That's Mommy's heart."

Julian peeked up at me. "How come Daddy doesn't have a heart?" I looked over at Teren with a sigh. Our children had our senses. Just as they could hear that my heart was pounding, they could hear that his was not.

Teren stared down at his son. Brushing a lock of hair out of his eyes, he said, "I do have a heart, Julian. But…we're vampires and when we get old enough, we don't need our hearts anymore. We're magic." Teren grinned, and his blue eyes sparkled. Then he brought his finger to his lips. "But you can't tell anyone. It's our secret, okay?"

Julian nodded, his little face serious. "Okay, Daddy."

I shook my head and held them tight. It was sort of amazing how easy it could be to explain things to a child. They accepted everything so readily. If you told them the sky was blue because a paint can on the clouds had spilled over, then that was what they believed. And for now, it was best if their own could-be scary conversions were introduced to them as "magic."

Nika frowned and sat up on her elbows. "Is Mommy not magic?" She pouted, like this was a tragedy to her.

Teren let out a soft laugh as I reached up to stroke a lock of Nika's silky hair. "Thanks to Grandpa Gabriel, Mommy gets to have her magic when she wants to. Maybe, someday, the two of you will as well." I looked over at Teren and he smiled softly at me.

When I'd been close to death, on its doorstep as they say, Teren had done the only thing he could think of to save me. The result had shocked everybody. When I'd awakened, dazed and hurting, my heart was still beating away and the twins were safe and sound. No one had known what that meant. None of them had ever tried to change someone. None of them were even sure if it was possible for their mixed blood to do it. The only thing we'd been certain about was that a human body couldn't handle the strain of being pumped full of vampire juice for long, and mine *was* going to give out, it was just a matter of time. That had left us with two important questions. Would I come back as an undead vampire? And would I die before the twins were ready to be born?

Those questions had driven Teren right to the brink of madness. He'd become obsessed with finding more of his kind in the hopes that they'd have an answer for him. Since he couldn't find mixed, he'd found purebloods. And he'd done anything he could to get them to talk—*anything*. His poking and prodding eventually got the attention of Gabriel's group in Los Angeles. A prissy vampire named Starla had arrived on our doorstep one day and changed everything for us once again.

She'd taken us to see her "father," a man who really wasn't related to anyone in the area, but was embraced as such because of his generosity to vampires in need. He'd amassed quite a following of loyal mixed and purebloods. It was almost cultish, and some of their practices, like catching hunters and locking them up for bloodthirsty mixed vampires going through the conversion process to kill, were not desirable to me. Even though I understood the reasons why they did it, and even though I had done it myself for Teren, when I'd essentially fed him a hunter, I didn't like it.

But Teren and I kept our feelings to ourselves on the matter, because Gabriel was also a genius, and had concocted the drug that was keeping me alive. In fact, because of Gabriel, I was having my thirtieth birthday in a couple weeks. A fact that most women don't celebrate, but as there was a time when I wasn't sure I'd live long enough to see twenty-six, much less thirty, I celebrated every birthday.

The twins both smiled and giggled as they looked at each other. They had a soft spot for the ancient vampire, calling him Grandpa because he was around a lot, and was sort of…involved…with Teren's Great-Grandmother, the only full vampire in the Adams clan. They'd started a romantic relationship back when we'd first met Gabriel. Halina tended to move fast if it pleased her, and Gabriel had definitely pleased her. But the surprising thing was that they were still together, and from what I'd heard, Halina was actually *not* sleeping with anyone else. That was sort of shocking to me.

But I had my reservations about Gabriel, as did Teren. I genuinely liked him. I mean, he saved the lives of my children, how could I not adore the man after that? But, he was also a scientist, and tended to look at my children with appraising eyes rather than loving ones.

Twins were rare among mixed. The circumstances surrounding the twins' birth was pretty rare too, what with me starting the pregnancy as a human, but ending it as a mixed vampire. It also didn't help ease Gabriel's curious nature when it had been discovered that our children were…special. Now, I know that every parent thinks their child is special, but for Teren and me, that was actually true. Aside from the traits that we all shared—fangs, speed, and super hearing—our children had an extra bond. A seventh sense, if you will, if the blood bond between us all, that allowed us to know each other's locations, could be considered the sixth.

It had taken Teren and me over a year to spot it. Really, until they'd started talking, we hadn't noticed, or we'd brushed it off as a "twin" connection, but it wasn't. It was so much more. See, some human twins claim that they can sense what the other is feeling. For instance, cases have been made of one twin feeling ill or pained, and the other, thousands of miles away, will have been suffering from a sudden case of appendicitis or something. Our children had that, but to the tenth degree.

Our children, literally, felt what the other was feeling. Not that they felt it for themselves, if one was happy, the other could still be sad, but they were aware. Julian knew exactly how Nika felt about watching butterflies in the pastures, because he felt it. Nika knew exactly how much balloons terrified Julian, because she felt it. If he stubbed his toe or fell down and bonked his head, she'd cry. Not because she was hurt, but because she felt his pain. If Teren tickled her into a giddy ball of laughter, Julian would laugh too, because he felt her joy.

It was like they were empaths...but only with each other.

Gabriel had never seen anything like it, and aside from his fondness for Halina, I think it was a large part of why he came around so often.

Spike barked, distracting the twins from their conversation, and they hopped off our bodies to go ruffle the patient collie's fur. Holding the prized ball in his mouth, he wagged his tail as he stared at Teren, eager for his master to throw it again. The kids attached to his sides, Nika burying her face in the fluff around his neck.

Luckily for us, Spike adored the children. He'd even tolerated months of being yanked and pulled and poked without ever yelping or biting. Sometimes, when the twins had been infants, he'd made a sound that I could have sworn was a sigh, and then he'd look up at me with those large, tired puppy dog eyes. I'd had to laugh at the poor canine. Sure, dogs couldn't emote, but at those times it was obvious that he'd been wishing for the tactile stage of the kids' development to end.

Teren sat up, shifted my body so my legs were over his lap, and ruffled his dog's fur. "Hungry, boy?"

Spike thumped his tail against the floor as he sat down. The kids giggled as they adjusted to the floor with him. Dropping the ball, he barked again. Teren smiled. "All right, let's get you something to eat." He looked back at me on the couch. "I could use something too, how about you?"

He smiled at me, and I took a second to appreciate the beauty of him before answering. Teren had eyes the color of a perfect spring morning; they were the warmest eyes you'd ever see on a person. Whoever created the image of vampires as soulless, bloodthirsty creatures had clearly never met one. They were people, same as any other people, and while some were bad, as wicked, sick, and twisted as any human could be, some were good, exceptionally good. Teren...was exceptional.

"I would love some, thank you."

Knowing my husband only tolerated an all-plasma diet, I knew he meant blood when he spoke of food. Dead vampires couldn't handle anything else. It wasn't just that their bodies couldn't digest it; eating wasn't something they could do for show then cough up later. No, their bodies rejected food like it was poison. It was extremely painful and uncomfortable for them. I'd seen Teren do it once. I never wanted to see him do it again.

He nodded at me, his black-as-night hair shining in the fading rays of the sun. Returning his attention to Nika and Julian, who were now showering Spike with kisses, he leaned forward. Once he was closer to their level, he asked, "What about you two? Who wants some blood?"

As a young person, the thought of what you will be like as a parent occasionally crosses your mind. It certainly had for me when I'd been plowing through my job, wondering who I would eventually marry, and fantasizing about how many of the imaginary man's kids I would have one day. But what I'd never envisioned, ever, was hearing myself or my husband ask those delightful little beings if they wanted a steaming glass of cow's blood. Those are just words you never expect to hear spoken to a child. But then, when you marry a vampire and have vampiric children, it just sort of comes with the territory. Besides, it *was* the best meal on the planet, and what parent would deny their child the most delicious thing on earth?

They both agreed too. Julian and Nika loved and craved the nutrient as much as any vampire I'd met. Although, for them, it wasn't as high on the list of snacks as it was for us. Truly, they got more excited about getting cotton candy at the fair. But…it was right up there.

Jumping up and down, they both started saying, "Me, me, me!"

Teren laughed as he extracted himself from my body so he could prepare meals for everyone. He loved to take care of people. It made him a pretty fabulous companion since, from the very beginning of our relationship, he'd spoiled me with homemade dinners; he usually even cleaned up too. That was just his way. And he was equally attentive to the kids, even going so far as to cut their sandwiches into fun little shapes. He was sort of, well, Mr. Mommish. I was a very lucky girl.

Followed by a pair of eager toddlers and a hungry dog, Teren walked out of the living room into the kitchen. I stayed where I was on the couch, smiling as I listened to a family that I could hear, but no longer see. With my blood sense though, I knew exactly where they were. That was such a comfort to me, knowing exactly where my children were. I couldn't imagine not knowing their location at every point of my day. I couldn't bear the thought of leaving their sight and not knowing, with every fiber of who I was, where they were. I thought I would worry myself into insanity if that were the case. Honestly, I didn't know how human mothers did it. They sort of amazed me.

Listening to my husband pop open the fridge, I heard my children start to play with the magnets on it. While Teren grabbed the pitcher of plasma in there, he helped them spell words, calling out different letters so they could arrange them into the words that they used most often—mom, dad, dog…blood.

I smiled and shook my head when he spelled out that last one for them. That probably wouldn't be in a normal three-year-old's vocabulary, but it was one of the first words they'd said, right after Dadda, actually. They could even say it in Russian, along with a few other simple phrases. Teren was teaching them as they grew, so I was finally starting to pick up a few things too. I liked that soon I would be privy to the private conversations he sometimes had with his family. I hated being kept in the dark, even if it was unintentional.

While he warmed the blood in the microwave, he sped away to

get the dog some food. He was back before the fifteen seconds had gone off on the timer. Nika giggled at the display. "Again, Daddy." Teren chuckled, and I heard him place a kiss on her head. The kids loved the blurred visual of us moving fast. They could do it too, in very short bursts, but it generally led to one or both injuring themselves, so Teren and I tried to dissuade them from doing it. Plus, that was something they could absolutely not do around humans. We drilled that into them constantly.

In fact, just after I thought it, Teren reminded them that that was something that only happened at home with family. They both automatically replied with, "Okay, Daddy," as Teren set the blood for another warming cycle.

Smelling the warmth of that blood drifting out to me, I inhaled deep. My smile was a satisfied one. My stomach, less satisfied, even after the chicken and vegetables the kids and I had eaten earlier, let out a loud rumble. Everyone in the kitchen laughed, clearly having heard me.

"Mommy's noisy," Julian gigged.

Sighing at my super-hearing family, I stood and shuffled off to the kitchen, enjoying a languid stretch with each step. Teren smiled at me as I stepped through the archway into the room. "Yes, Julian, she sure is."

He raised his eyebrows suggestively, and I bit my lip, knowing he wasn't talking about what Julian thought he was talking about. Being that there were impressionable little vampires in the room, I couldn't even smack him for his dirty talk. I settled with discreetly pinching his butt.

"Am not," I muttered as I kissed his neck.

The kids clamored around our legs while Teren tested the blood, then poured some into two sippy cups. "Are too," he muttered back, adding, "and it drives me crazy."

I pinched him a little harder.

He chuckled but didn't act like I was hurting him in any way. Nika looked up at him, her dark brown eyes a mirror image of mine. "What's cr..a..zy?"

Teren laughed as he handed her a bright pink cup. "Nothing, sweetheart. Drink up, it's almost bedtime."

She grabbed the cup and eagerly swished it back. Teren handed a light blue one to a similarly eager Julian and the both of them were silent for a moment as they enjoyed their dessert. Teren made tall glasses for us and we romantically clinked them together before tipping them back as well.

The smell hit me first—heavenly, heady, life-giving. Then the taste—sweeter than you'd think, like candy, but with an interesting tang to it. The vampire in me growled in contentment; the same noise echoed from Teren. Pausing in my drink, I watched him. His fangs had dropped down. Noticing me staring, he took a second to flick his tongue over one. It was unbelievably hot, and I had to look away.

Glancing down at our kids, I watched their little fanged faces. Julian smiled around his cup as he looked up at me. His fangs were tiny, little more than slightly elongated and sharpened canines. I shifted my gaze to *my* carbon copy. Nika's hair was lighter than my dark shade, but my mom assured me that my daughter's sandy brown hair was exactly the same color mine had been at her age. She smiled up at me too. Opening her mouth with a long "aw" sound, she showed me the red blood on her tongue and her small, dainty fangs.

It had surprised me, but their fangs had been their first teeth to come in, and they'd come in as a matched set, both breaking through the skin at the same time. For a couple of months, they'd both sort of looked like snakes. It had been pretty humorous and I'd often wished I'd been able to take a picture of it. But, until the other teeth had dropped down around them, it had been too obvious what they were.

I grabbed their cups as they finished them, rinsed them out, and then put them in the dishwasher. Teren kissed my neck. His still extended fangs grazed the tender surface, making a shiver run down my spine that had nothing to do with the chill of his lips.

Giving him a warning glance to behave himself, I watched him chuckle at me and slip his teeth away. My now normal-looking husband scooped up a child in each arm, and plopped them over his shoulders. They laughed at first, then started to squirm in protest when they realized that he was getting them ready for bed. I kissed each pouting face before he shuffled off with them.

At the stairs I heard, "No, nigh-nigh, Daddy," from Nika, and, "I want Mommy," from Julian.

Teren calmly replied with, "If you two are really good, I'll tell you stories."

They instantly quieted. "Mommy and Daddy stories?" Nika asked.

I heard Teren set them down upstairs, heard their soft feet scramble to find their pajamas. "Yep, Mommy and Daddy stories."

I finished cleaning up the remnants of the day in the kitchen, then lickety-split cleaned up the rest of the house. Picking up broken crayons, missing puzzles pieces, and small piles of goldfish crackers was quick work when you could move at nearly the speed of light.

As I was putting the tricycle back outside for the hundredth time, I heard Teren trying to convince the kids that brushing their teeth was fun. Laughing at his attempt, I slowly made my way upstairs. By the time I got to the bathroom, he'd convinced Nika to give it a try, but Julian had clamped his mouth shut. They didn't like the brushes sweeping across their sensitive fangs. I understood. Even retracted, they were more attuned to vibrations and movements than the teeth around them.

Shaking my head at Julian, I squatted in front of him. "I know it feels weird, honey, but it's important." Raising an eyebrow, I very seriously added, "You wouldn't want your fangs to fall out, would you?"

His little eyes opened wide, and his mouth soon followed suit. Teren gave me a wry smile as I scrubbed Julian's teeth to a pearly white.

As soon as we were done, they thundered off to their room. Since birth they'd shared one, at the far end of the hall from ours. We'd talked about splitting them up, but they preferred to be together for now and we let them. We were pretty sure that they would let us know when they were ready for their independence from each other. And surely, by puberty, they would want some space from each other.

Following them, we entered their jungle play land bedroom. While I'd been recovering at the ranch after having them, Teren's mother and grandmother had snuck over here and decorated the place. And while I loathed painting, and had no artistic abilities whatsoever, those vampire girls were incredible at it. They had turned the room into a work of art: light green rolling hills, blue sky with fluffy white clouds, huge trees with branches that extended from one corner to another. And living in the world they'd created, was just about every jungle animal you could imagine—elephants, tigers, and the kids' favorite, monkeys. It was amazing, and that was just the walls. They'd completed the look with toys, curtains, bedding, lamps, play rugs—everything a child's dream bedroom needed.

I was seriously considering telling Alanna and Imogen to forsake the family business and go into interior decorating.

Teren settled on the floor with the twins while they begged for the tales they wanted to hear. Teren loved to tell them bedtime stories and he usually told them things that had actually happened to us. Of course, he would turn our scary stories into fairy tales, so the children wouldn't have nightmares—the evil troll stealing the valiant prince and the brave princess, the jealous monster putting the princess into a deep sleep, and the prince awakening her with a kiss. But the family stories he told just as they'd happened. And the twins' favorite story was one that I sort of wished Teren had never told them. It was kind of an embarrassing moment for me. But Teren had a thing for the memory and repeated it often.

"Five years ago, on a beautiful, sunny spring day, I met the most beautiful creature on earth. She had the longest, prettiest dark-brown hair. It glowed in the sunshine, like she was an angel. Her beauty stole my breath. I'd never seen someone who looked so…perfect. Her eyes were a warm, deep brown and, as our gazes locked on that busy sidewalk, it took me exactly one second to fall madly in love with her."

He paused dramatically, and the twins, already knowing what was coming, started giggling. I contained a sigh. "Then…one second later, she smashed right into me, pouring her boiling hot coffee down the front of my shirt."

A chorus of laughter went around the room and I rolled my eyes and shook my head at my husband. He laughed with the twins as they sat on either side of his lap, all of them thoroughly enjoying the story that he'd told them umpteen times before—the story of how we'd first met.

He glanced at me, leaning on the doorframe with my arms crossed over my chest, and smiled. It was one of those half-smiles that spoke volumes of how much he adored me, regardless of his never-ending teasing about our first encounter. I pursed my lips at him, feigning displeasure. He grinned even wider, seeing right through it. He knew I loved the image of him sitting with our children, sharing our history with them. And with our sometimes terrifying history, my moment of clumsiness was a preferable memory for him to share. Some stories just couldn't be watered down into fairy tales.

Nika's little hands came up to clutch his face, forcing his attention back to her, where she preferred it. She was Daddy's little girl, down to the core, and she had him wrapped around her finger so tight, I didn't know how they'd ever separate. Her shoulder-length hair shifted around her as she leaned up and gave him a quick kiss on the nose. "Then what, Daddy?"

Teren nuzzled his face against hers, and the scruff of his stubble made her giggle and flinch away from him. On his other leg, Julian clapped his hands together. "More, Daddy!"

Teren turned his head to his son, and in that instant, as I studied them, it was like watching Teren look into a mirror. With pale blue eyes and thick, black hair, Julian was so much like Teren that it hurt my heart sometimes. My eyes, being slightly more enhanced than the average human's, could see the miniscule variations that made Julian different from his father, but to everyone else they met, they were near twins. Or would be one day, when Julian grew into a man.

But right now, he was his daddy's little boy, and he and Teren shared a look that only a father and son can share. As he rubbed Julian's back, he continued with his tale. "Well, as my chest was burning, the most beautiful woman in the world began to try and clean up the mess with the one lone napkin she had in her hand. It was much too small to do anything, but she had the most adorable look on her face that I had no choice but to let her keep feeling like she was helping. It's always nice to let others feel helpful."

Looking up at me, Teren laughed. Julian and Nika looked up at me too, while Teren said, "The woman looked so upset that she'd lost her favorite treat." He gave me a wry smile as the twins giggled and cuddled into his side. Enfolding them both in a hug, he added, "And she looked horribly embarrassed that she'd run into me."

Nika peeked up at him. "What happened next, Daddy?"

Teren smiled down at her and kissed her head. "You've heard this story so many times, you probably know it better than I do. What do you think happened?"

Nika sat up straight, clasped her hands together, and held them to her chest. "You kissed Mommy!" she exclaimed with a soft sigh. I couldn't help but laugh and shake my head at her. Just a few months shy of being four, and she was already a romantic.

Teren laughed too and was about to comment, but Julian across from her piped up. "No, Mommy ran away." Julian smiled, looking happy that he'd remembered the story correctly.

I raised my eyebrows at Teren, who laughed at my expression. "Well, I wouldn't say she ran away, but, yes, she left in a hurry."

Smiling, I looked at the floor as I remembered that day. So much had changed after that afternoon. I learned that vampires were real. I fell in love with one and decided to stay with him, regardless of the drawbacks, because he was worth every single one of them. I decided to try and have his children, before it was too late for him to create them. I stayed by his side as he prepared to changeover from a living vampire to a dead one. I even killed for him, to help him complete his conversion and to save us both.

Then things had settled. We'd had a dreamlike few months, where nearly everything was perfect. We discovered I was pregnant, with twins no less. We got married in an ideal ceremony at his parents' place, a ranch where the vampires could live in peace, without fear of being discovered. Teren and I had anxiously been awaiting our new arrivals, when quite unexpectedly—as most tragedies are—I was attacked by that jerk vampire who'd felt slighted. He'd bitten me for no better reason than to hurt Teren, because he'd felt Teren had been inhospitable to him, by not allowing him to "hunt" wherever he wanted.

That vampire had irrevocably changed my happy family. But I suppose, in a way, since everything had worked out, that strange man had completed our family too, giving us the chance to spend the rest of our unnaturally long lives *together*.

Nika, remembering how the story went now, looked over at me reminiscing by the door and clapped her hands. "Mommy had a magic card for Daddy."

I smiled at my daughter's fanciful imagination and Teren grinned. "I suppose it was magic, because when I called her, and asked her if I could get her another treat, do you know what she said?"

Julian piped up, raising his hand in the air, his pale eyes joyous that he knew the answer. Much like his father, Julian always liked to have the answer. "Yes!" he pronounced.

Nika giggled. "And, I love you."

Teren laughed and rustled her hair. "No, not yet, sweetheart."

Leaning into her, he peeked up at me; his eyes were overflowing with warmth and love. "The most beautiful woman I'd ever seen agreed to meet with me, agreed to have dinner with me, and over time, agreed to marry me." He smiled widely as he whispered that.

Nika and Julian, both recognizing the end of Teren's story, clapped their hands and squealed. "Again, Daddy!" they said at the same time.

Teren laughed as he began shifting children off his lap. "I've told you that story at least ten times this week. Aren't you sick of it?"

When he set Nika on the floor, she grabbed his hand and shook her head. "Again, Daddy."

Teren stood up after setting Julian beside her, and Julian grabbed his other hand. "Daddy, again!"

Teren looked over at me. Smiling at him, I walked into the room and placed a loving kiss upon each tiny head. Standing in front of Teren, who now had a child attached to each leg, I whispered, "Go ahead. I'll just be waiting for you…in bed…minus these." I suggestively pulled at my clothes.

Teren groaned and eyed me up and down in a way that made my heart race. He groaned again, hearing it. Shifting his attention to the miniature beings attached to his body, he patted their backs, and quickly said, "Okay, one more and then it's bedtime."

He gave me a devilish smile while Julian and Nika dashed to their side-by-side beds. "Mommy and Daddy need to snuggle," he murmured.

I chuckled and gave him light, teasing kiss. He closed his eyes and his breath was faster when I pulled away. Smiling to myself, I turned my back on him, tucked my pajama-clad children under their covers, washed them in kisses that had them squealing in delight, and then left him to his story telling. I was fairly certain that this time he would breeze through the story without letting them participate.

Teren's deep voice filled the room as I left it. Looking back at the trio, I smiled at Nika and Julian holding hands across the short distance between their beds. It wasn't unusual for them to fall asleep that way and on occasion, they were still like that when they woke up.

After giving myself my daily shot, a sting that I was completely used to now, I got ready for bed. Sliding under our cool covers, I kept my seductive promise and didn't bother with pajamas. Teren and I didn't get to have "snuggle" time as often as we preferred, but we tried to make it work. Having children with super hearing could put a damper on your love life. Now that they were more aware, we generally avoided doing anything while they were awake.

Especially after that one particularly embarrassing time when they *had* heard us…

They had been about two and a half, and we hadn't thought much about plopping in a movie for them and disappearing into our bedroom for a little…reconnecting. We thought about it after the movie though, when Nika and Julian both had concerned and slightly scared looks on their faces. They'd run up to me after I'd gone in to check on them, and wouldn't let me go. It had taken some deciphering of their disjointed language, but I'd finally understood that they'd heard everything, and they'd thought I was in pain.

Yeah, that sort of killed the mood for me for a long time. Of course, Teren thought it was hilarious, and didn't see a problem with just explaining to them what we'd been doing. I...just could not do that yet.

We eventually came up with the compromise to at least hold off on being intimate until after they were sleeping. And really, since their language skills had improved dramatically in the year since that encounter, I really didn't need them telling any of our family members that Mommy made funny noises in the bedroom with Daddy. Just the thought of them saying that to Halina made my cheeks heat.

A cool body blurred into bed with me. Chilly arms wrapped around my waist and a stubbled jaw nestled against my throat. I sighed contentedly as I twisted my legs up with his; he was just as bare as I was. The anticipation of where this was going started surging through me, but the two toddlers talking through the walls helped contain my fire.

Teren's cool palms slid over my skin, sending a trail of goose bumps across my flesh. "We could try being quiet," he murmured in my ear, his voice low and husky.

I knew by "we," he meant me. I bit my lip and considered it. Silent lovemaking wasn't impossible, just really, really difficult, especially when the object of my affection was a super-hot vampire. There was just something about that combination that evaporated any thought of holding back. Plus, I had my own vampiric impulses to consider. I didn't think I could keep a low growl from rumbling up my chest, and who knew what the kids would think about that.

Sighing, I pushed him back. "They'll fall asleep soon," I whispered, my hand cupping his cheek.

He grinned at me and shook his head. "While I wish we had more time together like this...I do love that you *know* you'll be uncontainable." He raised his eyebrows. "Knowing that makes the wait worthwhile."

Laughing, I squeezed him tight and pressed my lips to his...carefully though. The man was a fabulous kisser and I didn't want to get carried away just yet. "Well, I'll try not to fall asleep before they do," I murmured against his lips.

He made an amused noise in his throat as his hands ran over my hips. Teasingly, I refrained from pulling us together.

Sighing as his chest started to warm against mine, I pulled back to gaze at him. "Do you have to keep telling them that story?"

He smiled and relaxed back on the pillows. "It's a good story. They love it."

I rolled my eyes. "It's embarrassing."

Twisting back to me, he ran a finger through a long strand of my dark hair. "Nothing about you is embarrassing." His eyes flicked down the silhouette of my body under the sheets, and the phosphorescent glow highlighting the whites of his eyes traced every contour of my body. It made my heart beat faster, made my skin ignite.

Hearing me, he returned those glowing orbs to mine. He'd told me once that a vampire's glowing eyes were to help subdue their prey, as if they needed the extra help, and staring into them, gave me a calm, almost hypnotic feeling. Watching his face being highlighted by the glow of my own eyes, I wondered if he felt that too.

At first, I'd been worried about the glow. It's not something you can shut off, and I'd inherited it along with my teeth, hearing and speed. But it was only evident in perfectly dark places, like our bedroom. In the outside world, it was masked by the light pollution in the sky. It was the only time, I'm sure, that pollution of any kind came in handy.

I smiled as I let his peace absorb into me. Hearing the children repeat Teren's tale with their own twists to the story, mainly a dog who could fly and a mailbox that talked, I considered the fact that their eyes hadn't shown any trace of a glow yet.

We'd tested them right away, walking into the darkest room in the house with them in our arms. I'd felt like I was nine again, testing out my glow-in-the-dark t-shirt, but as we'd stared down at them with our own headlights, nothing had shone back at us. The women all assured me that Teren's glow was instant, and that the trait must not have carried over to the twins. They were all extremely excited to see an aspect of the vampirism fade from the lineage. That was what they were striving for—full humans. We knew that was a goal that would probably take several generations, but just the fact that my children's eyes were perfectly normal made it seem like an attainable one. But really, as a mother, I was just grateful that they had one less thing to worry about in their lives.

Teren leaned in to restart the soft kissing. "You're beautiful, Emma, and I want our kids to know how I see you." His speech against my lips vibrated my sensitive skin. I nearly tasted the words.

Running my hands through his hair, the sound of the sliding strands clear, even under our quick breaths, I murmured, "You amaze me, how you see me."

Into my ear he breathed, "And I see better than almost everyone, Emma."

I bit my lip to contain a groan. Pushing him back so I could stare into his calm-inducing eyes again, I listened for the telltale sounds of sleep coming from down the hall—all I heard was a chorus of ABCs. Sighing, I ran a finger across his lips. "Well, I at least appreciate how romantic you make the story." I shook my head. "It's not nearly that romantic in my memory."

He sat back on his elbow. "Nearly every memory I have of you is romantic, in some way."

I sat up with him as well. "Even when I'm chucking things at you?"

Grinning, he leaned in to kiss my collar bone. "Especially when you're chucking things at me." He raised an eyebrow before trailing his lips up my neck. "You're hot when you're feisty."

I exhaled in a way I shouldn't as his cool breath washed along the vein in my throat. "You make me feel like the most beautiful woman on earth," I whispered.

He stopped sucking on my earlobe to look at me. "Good, because you are." Not really caring anymore that my kids were still awake, and had moved on to practicing their numbers, I leaned over to kiss him. He spoke before I could make the connection. "Well, almost."

I pulled back and cocked an eyebrow at him. He laughed at the look on my face and then shook his head. "I think our daughter may surpass even you one day." He smiled at the thought, a look of pride on his face.

A sudden rush of emotion hit me and I felt my eyes sting. "Not surprising…since she's half you."

I swallowed back the sudden lump in my throat while he cupped my cheek. "I love you, Emma. For always."

I could only nod and find his mouth, needing that connection to temper the overwhelming emotion that I felt for him. Some couples claimed that having children dampened the love they felt for their spouse, but it had had the opposite effect for Teren and me. If possible, I loved him even more now. So much so that I couldn't believe I'd ever been okay with his one day living without me. Maybe it was selfish, but I didn't ever want him to be without me.

As I melted into his arms, I finally heard loud yawns coming from the twins' room. I smiled into Teren's skin; his body was lukewarm now from so much exposure to mine. Yawning was the precursor to sleep for our children. And their sleep was the precursor to our awakening.

As Teren rolled me to my back, propping himself on top of me, I heard a sound that I heard every night. And every night, it made my heart expand in a way that seemed physically impossible, like surely that frail organ should have busted wide open from the level of warmth and tenderness that rushed into it on a daily basis.

From down the hall, my vampiric ears clearly heard my children saying goodnight to the day, and goodnight to each other. As always, it brought tears to my eyes.

"Night, Nick, love you."

"Night, Julie, love you too."

Chapter 2 – Supernaturally Normal

I dreamt of my children as I slept, of what their futures might be like. I imagined the partners that they'd meet and fall in love with. I imagined Gabriel supplying them with as much life-suspending juice as was necessary for them to continue as living vampires for as long as they wanted. Unlike us, our children could take their time having their own kids. It delighted me to no end that there were no biological alarm clocks hovering over their heads. They could have children whenever they wanted, or never at all. I was fine with that too. Just so long as they were happy…and safe.

I was picturing an adult Julian standing beside an adult Nika, on what looked like her wedding day, when a harsh scraping along my neck brought me back to awareness. Groaning as my body fought against stirring to consciousness, I brushed the irritant away.

Teren laughed in my ear. "Wake up, Emma. Time to start your day."

I flung an arm over my head, sort of hating my husband at the moment, even though he was nicer to wake up to than an alarm clock. He laughed again at my displeasure, and ran the back of his finger down my cheek. "You're going to be late, sweetheart."

Peeking an eye open, I cringed as the bathroom light he'd left on hit me in the face. "Tell me again, why I went back to work?"

He smiled and shrugged. "Glutton for punishment?" Twisting my lips at him, I narrowed my eyes. Chuckling, he shook his head. "Because you are an intelligent, beautiful, confident business woman who loves her job and loves to feel good at it." Raising an eyebrow, he waited for me to object to his summation. When I didn't, he added, "And you like turning me on in those hot little lacy camisole things you wear."

I moved to smack his chest but he'd already blurred away from me. Smartass. At least that was one thing that hadn't changed since the very beginning. Teren was still a playful little tease.

Sighing, I tossed off the covers and stood up. Since I still wasn't wearing anything, having immediately fallen asleep after our passionate session last night, his eyes widened and he stopped smiling. Loving that my body still affected him, even after being as huge as a house with two children inside of me, I sashayed in front of him; he didn't even bother to pretend that he was interested in my face. I loved that too. "Fine, I'm up," I husked.

He finally peeked up at my face then; the grin on his mouth was devilish. "I think I'd prefer it if you were back down."

His hands ran over my flat stomach and for a moment, I felt worshipped by his caress. I'd worked hard after the twins to get my regular body shape back, hitting the gym every chance I got. And having vampiric speed and strength, let me tell you, getting in shape was harder than I thought it would be. I had to constantly remind myself to run at a normal pace. And since weights did nothing for my enhanced muscles, I'd had to do yoga and Pilates to firm myself back up. But eventually, all of the effort had paid off and my curves were even tighter than before. I loved knowing that if and when I ever decided to stop taking Gabriel's shot, my body would be fit for eternity, much like Teren's.

Just as his hand on my stomach delved lower, I twisted away and blurred into the bathroom. While turning the water on, I clearly heard, "Hey, I wasn't done!"

Laughing, I muttered, "Yes, you were. I don't want to be late, remember?"

Hearing that, even over the forceful flow of water beside me, Teren stepped into the room and leaned on the doorframe. "I believe I've told you this before, but, I can be really fast."

I threw him a smirk and shook my head again. Men. Even though Teren was more romantic than most, he'd still chuck it all out the window for a quickie. A super quickie, no less.

"Tempting...but no." I quickly stepped into the shower before he decided to throw the charm back on. If he really wanted to, he could have me laid across our mammoth bed with just a few whispers of devotion, both of our jobs be damned. Teren grinned as he watched me through the glass, like he was well aware of the power he held.

Shaking his head, he let out a dramatic sigh. "Fine. I'll see you tonight. Tuesday dinner, right?" He cocked an eyebrow and I paused in wetting my hair. It was so sexy when he did that. Clearing my head, I nodded. "Yep. Mom will bring the kids."

He nodded, waved goodbye, and then headed downstairs. I tracked him while I went about washing my hair. A long time ago, I had ditched the fragrant shampoos. They were way too strong now. My replacement shampoo was technically considered unscented, by human standards anyway. To me, it smelled like a fresh sea breeze. It was a soothing scent, since I had lived near the ocean my whole life, so I'd readily adapted to it.

As I scrubbed up some bubbles, I felt Teren leave the house. A slight pull of sadness swept through me as he engaged the tension in our bond. As creator and child, although I hated thinking of myself as Teren's child, we had a bond that was unique to us. In the beginning, it had been a nearly primal need to be together. Embarrassingly strong, and at times, inappropriately graphic, the bond was designed to keep sires near their newly created vampires. The intensity of it varied, depending on the connection in place before the turning. Since Teren and I had been married, well, it was like a four alarm fire being kindled every time we started coming towards each other.

Luckily for us, the bond had eased up considerably over the years. Now, it was more a feeling of warmth and love, and less a feeling of, *Oh God, I need in your pants right now.*

I smiled as I rinsed away the lightly scented suds. I did sort of miss the passion, but I definitely didn't miss ripping off my shirt in front of innocent bystanders...like Hot Ben. On my top ten list of the most embarrassing moments in my life, that one was right up there.

It had happened not too long after the twins had been born, when Teren had been spending the day with Ben. They'd gone fishing together and when Teren had tried to return Ben to his car, our bodies had had other plans. We'd ended up having sex in the front of Ben's SUV. He'd barely run out of there in time—he'd almost accidentally witnessed the whole show. He had not been happy with us, although, months later he'd confessed, to my horror, that he *had* liked the peep show.

Shaking my head at how crazy that intense pull had been, I stepped away from the shower and turned the water off. I heard each lingering drop fall as I wrapped a warm, plush towel around me. I also heard the beginnings of rustling, as the other two members of the house also started stirring.

After drying and curling my hair, I dressed in my favorite work outfit. Apparently it was Teren's favorite as well. Adjusting my trim pantsuit and the clingy, plunging camisole underneath my jacket, I felt my husband's presence stop moving away from me. He was at work, probably sitting down at his desk to pop out another fantastic article on the highs and lows of city life in beautiful San Francisco. If only Gate Magazine was aware of how undead their life and style writer was. The irony of it always brought a smile to my face.

After I stepped into my shoes and made last minute adjustments to my hair, I put on the locket that I always wore to work. Teren had gotten it for my birthday, right after we'd learned that I would survive long enough for the twins to be born. The gold heart folded out into four pictures, the two of us and our two children. I loved having the reminder of my family around my neck during the times when we were apart. A visual reminder to go along with the physical reminder constantly binging their position to me in my head.

As I smiled at the tiny, sleeping infants in the locket, I heard Nika yawn and say to her twin, "Morning, Julie."

He in turn yawned as well. "Morning, Nick."

I smiled at the nicknames they'd given each other. They'd started doing that nearly from the first time they'd started speaking. It was such a personal thing between the two of them, that no one else in the family used the shortened names. That was something just between them.

Standing in my empty room, I said, "Good morning, children. Hurry and get up so we can go to Grandma's."

There were excited squeals and a flurry of movement as they rushed to do what I'd asked. They loved visiting my mom and she insisted on having them. A traditional daycare was out of the question, since the twins were still learning to hamper their abilities, so my mom had stepped up. Teren and I had both told her repeatedly that Alanna and the girls would watch them at the ranch, but she'd bristled at the idea of us driving so far each day, when she was right here in town. And since she'd retired, just so she could be available to watch them, it sort of made it hard to say no to her offer.

But she was so great with them that mainly, it was a relief. Someone I loved and trusted was taking care of my babies every day. That was such a burden lifted from my shoulders that I thanked her every time I saw her. Teren did too, although I think he was also compensating her monetarily for her time. My suspicions were all but confirmed when I noticed her brand new flat screen TV. But I didn't say anything about it. Teren's family had money and if he wanted to share some of that with my mom, as a thank you for protecting and caring for our brood, I wasn't about to question him.

Feeling the pressure of time ticking away in my head, I blurred down the stairs to get the children's breakfasts ready. Thankfully, I'd perfected speed movement, and no longer tripped on my lightning fast feet. When I was done, I dashed upstairs to check on the kids' progress.

As I entered the room, I saw Julian attempting to get a shoe on Nika's foot. They'd been practicing dressing themselves and were sort of getting good at it. Nika had chosen a bright pink and yellow striped dress with a pair of teal and orange, polka-dotted pants underneath it. The dress was on backwards. Julian had gone for a button-up shirt, but he'd only gotten one of the buttons fastened—the bottom one to the top one.

Chuckling at them, I kneeled down by Nika and pulled off the outrageously clashing pants. Twisting her dress around, I finished putting on the little black Mary Janes that Julian had been trying to mash on her foot.

Julian frowned at me as I fixed his shirt. "Nick liked the dot pants, Mommy."

I looked back at Nika, and she had a sullen, disappointed look on her face. As she watched me watch her, a genuine pout graced her lip. It was one of those pouts that only toddlers could make adorable. Containing a prideful smile over the fact that Julian had stood up for her feelings, since he had felt them himself, I tilted my head at her. "Do you want to wear those today, honey?"

She nodded, her pout growing larger. Shaking my head, I put the pants back on her. Sometimes, you just had to let children feel like they were in control of their own lives; it was good for their self-esteem. I'd read that somewhere.

Finished with the dressing portion of the morning routine, I quickly got them to eat their breakfast, and then we were out the door. Strapping them into the back of my cheery, bright yellow VW bug, I pulled out of the driveway. As our warm, comfortable home faded from my view in the mirror, I listened to my children sing a Russian nursery song and smiled. Halina had taught the song to the twins, and they loved practicing the strange enunciation.

I found myself humming along to the song, which I believed was about a boy drinking vodka, no joke, but I ignored that as best I could since even English nursery rhymes weren't exactly innocent. Jack and Jill falling down a hill? Humpty Dumpty breaking beyond repair? Ring Around the Rosie was said to be about the plague for goodness sake! But the Russian tune was catchy, and by the time I stopped the car, it was completely stuck in my head.

A flood of homecoming hit me as I stared up at my mom's place, a cute little one-story rambler that she used to share with my sister, Ashley, before Ash moved into my old place. Even though my mom's house wasn't technically my childhood home—that one burned down when I was young—this place had memories of Mom, Ashley and me, and now it had memories of my children. That firmly cemented the building into my heart.

Unfastening the kids, I popped Julian on my hip and grabbed Nika's hand. At times like these, I was grateful for my enhanced strength. Without breaking a sweat, I could have held both of them, the bag of all their stuff, my overloaded purse, and probably, if I had another arm, the family dog. That sort of strength was a little suspicious though, so I kept it to one child at a time.

Mom greeted us at the door. Her plump face was alive with joy at seeing her two favorite little people in all the world. I handed her Julian as I picked up Nika. Wanting to be in Grandma's arms too, Nika squirmed but I held her tight. Mom could definitely only handle one at a time.

"Morning, Mom," I said as I stepped inside.

"Morning, honey," she replied, nuzzling Julian's face. He smiled and feeling how much her brother liked it, Nika giggled. I set her down and she blurred to her grandma's side. I shot a glance at the door behind me, but I'd luckily shut it automatically. Squatting down, I looked Nika in the eye. "Not so fast, Nika."

She looked down, her expression guilty. Teren and I urged them to use human speed all the time, so she knew better and felt bad for it. Feeling her guilt, Julian reached down to pat her shoulder in sympathy. "I sorry," she whispered.

My mom harrumphed at me. "It's just me here, Emma. It's fine."

I sighed and rolled my eyes at her. Once she had accepted the oddness of my family, she'd fully embraced my children's gifts. While she understood the importance of secrecy, she was also a proud grandma, and wanted her grandchildren to exalt in what made them unique.

"Mom, you know they need to be careful about stuff like that. Please don't let them do it."

She placed a kiss on Julian's head before setting him down and picking up Nika. With a little effort, she lifted and squeezed the beaming girl. "I know. I just hate that they can't be as…special as they are."

I sighed as I watched her cuddling with vampires. "I know…but it's for their safety." A slice of fear ran through me as I thought about the assortment of different people in the world who would harm these two beautiful specks of sunshine if they could, just because of what they were.

Prejudiced bastards.

After seeing Mom struggle with Nika's weight, and then eventually set her down, I frowned. "Your leg still bothering you?" She'd been having problems with her leg going out on her. She swore it was nothing more than the aging process, but it worried me anyway.

She brushed aside my concern with her hand. "Completely normal getting old stuff." Mom gave me an odd look. "Nothing you'll have to worry about, I suppose?"

Mom and I had never talked about all of the side effects of what Teren had done to me. She generally didn't talk about it at all, and we'd never sat down to have the "my heart is going to stop, but I'll be fine" speech. That day wasn't here yet anyway, and I wasn't ready to have that conversation with her. I'd become much more sympathetic to how hard that conversation must have been for Teren when he'd had to tell me.

I looked over to my children darting off to watch cartoons and ignored her comment. "Yeah, well, let me know if they start to be too much." I returned my eyes to hers, concern in my voice. "I know they can be…challenging, because of what they can do…"

She gave me a proud smile. "I'm happy to do it, and I'll keep at it as long as I can. As long as I can still chase after them, I want to be the one watching them."

I gave her a tight hug. She inhaled a bit and I relaxed my super-strong grip. "Well, thank you so much. It means the world to Teren and me that they have somewhere safe to go."

When I pulled back from her, she shook her head. "The two of you are so wonderful with them. You are doing such a great job." Her brown eyes glistening with unshed tears, she softly said, "I'm so proud of you, Emma. Both of you."

I nodded, my eyes equally moist now. "Thank you." I sniffled, then flicked a glance at my children laughing at the Count on Sesame Street. Naturally, he was their favorite character. "I should get to work."

Mom hugged me again, then with one last quick hug for my kids, I walked back to my car and left them for the day.

That had been a hard thing to do when I'd first gone back to work, but I'd wanted some part of my old life back. Work, while at times boring and monotonous, was also my final connection to normalcy. At my job, I wasn't Emma, the mixed vampire married to an undead vampire, trying to raise two partially vampiric children with no one finding out. No, at work I was just Emma—super employee.

And that was what I had become. One thing I'd discovered early on was how beneficial my new skills were at my job. No one in the office could type faster than me. No one in the office could pull reports faster than me. No one in the office could do *anything* faster than me...literally. To them, since returning from my maternity leave, I'd become this indispensable worker bee who everyone relied on to get things done.

As I pulled into the parking lot of Neilson, Sampson and Peterson, the prosperous accounting firm that I worked for, I remembered my first day back after the twins. As my old boss, Clarice, had warned me, she'd filled my position and I'd had to start again at the bottom. Grudgingly, I had gone to my new spot...in the mail room. I hadn't been there two months before my reputation for quickness started to precede me, and I was quickly promoted out of there.

Of course, my super hearing also played an invaluable role. I'd sort of become known as the "psychic" one, since I had an uncanny knack for bringing people what they needed, before they'd even asked for it. It was one of the few benefits of being able to hear almost every conversation going on in the building.

Once I'd learned how to shut out the pockets of conversations that I didn't need, I found that I could hone in on the conversations that I wanted to hear. Say, Mr. Peterson muttering to himself that he needed a tax statement on an important client. I could then walk in and hand it to him, explaining that I knew he had a meeting with that client later and I figured that he would need it. Moves like that tended to impress bosses, and within the year, I was back to my old job.

Well, no, that wasn't exactly true. What with my super efficiency and my uncanny "psychic" abilities, I was no longer the secretary's secretary. I was no longer underneath Clarice. I was Mr. Peterson's *second* executive administrative assistant. I was her equal. She hated that.

Smiling as I walked down the corridor to my new office, an actual room instead of a life-draining cubicle, I waved at my friends and coworkers. Pausing beside one of the cubicles, I looked down at my assistant. Yeah, I had my very own assistant.

"Good morning, Tracey," I brightly told my friend.

She smiled over at me as she stuffed her purse in the tight desk drawers; I constantly delighted in the fact that I now had a closet for my behemoth of a bag. "Morning, Emma. How are those adorable kids of yours?"

Pausing, I took a second to mark where I felt their presence in my mind. Imagining them climbing all over my mother made me smile. "They are wonderful, perfect little angels."

Tracey twisted her beautiful pixie face into a pout. "I miss them. Ben and I need to come over soon and spoil them rotten."

I had to laugh at that. She and Hot Ben had made a real go of their relationship. Tracey even had a full carat sparkler on her ring finger to prove it. I'd had to feign ignorance when she'd told me that he'd proposed. As he'd been talking with Teren about it for over a month, I'd known exactly where, when, and how it was going to happen. I'd even been the one to suggest the place—the diner where they'd gotten back together after momentarily splitting up for the second time.

The separation had been brutal on both of them, and was sort of Teren's and my fault. Ben had walked in on an....intimate moment and had discovered what Teren was. The constant fear of unknown monsters that may be lurking in the dark had eaten Ben up inside, and he'd distanced himself from the love of his life. At that diner, he'd opened up to her and they'd gotten back together. Sure, he'd been lying his ass off to her about why he'd been distant, but she didn't need to know the real reason for his turn around.

But, regardless of the reason behind the split and make up, the memory of that afternoon was a big one to her, a wonderful one—one that she still mentioned to this day. I knew that Ben proposing to her there would be perfect.

"Yeah, we'll have to arrange something really soon." To her, I only smiled with contentment, but in my head, I was making a list of all of the preparations that would have to happen before someone not in the loop, like Tracey, could come over.

The kids were sat down individually and warned about what they could and couldn't do, and what they could and couldn't say. It was exhausting for them, it was exhausting for us. When they were younger, we wouldn't let anyone come around unless Halina was there. Since she could do adjustments to people's memories, one perk of full vampirism that Teren and I didn't have, she eased a lot of the tension in the air. And if something weird did happen, she could evaporate the memory in the blink of an eye.

Hot Ben was handy, too, when it came to distracting Tracey. When she'd commented on something weird she'd seen once, he'd expertly shifted the conversation around to their upcoming nuptials. Any memory of the kids doing something strange was immediately lost on the bride to be. After that moment, we'd all agreed that Ben would come with Tracey whenever a visit with the twins was in order.

Waving goodbye to Tracey, I headed over to my desk to start my day. As my office was situated directly in front of Mr. Peterson's office, I shared it with Clarice. And of course, she was already there when I breezed through the door. Maybe wanting to feel secure in her own job, she had started coming in fifteen minutes before me, and leaving fifteen minutes after me. It still didn't help; I got more done in a day than she ever could.

As I waved at the sour, rotund woman, I felt a little bad for her. I did have a supernatural advantage that she'd never have. But then I remembered all of the years of abuse I had suffered under her scowling, disapproving eyes, and I let the guilt slide right off me. What was that saying? Karma is a bitch.

She adjusted her June Cleaver pearls while I tucked my satchel into my closet. "Good morning, Clarice. How are you on this fine day?" I tried to keep the smirk out of my voice but it was just so hard not to tease her.

"I don't have time to chit-chat with you, Emma." She raised a penciled-in eyebrow at me. "Some of us have work to do around here."

Nodding my agreement, I sat down at my wide-open, spacious desk. Clarice grabbed a stack of papers from her inbox and marched them out to the cubicles, where I knew her assistant was about to be loaded down with copying and collating in triplicate. Poor thing. The woman who had my old job was a slip of a girl, not really cut out for the harshness of this environment, especially under Clarice's dictatorship. I gave her another six months before she cracked, tops.

Smiling that I no longer had to fake my cheeriness at being here, I listened for my boss through his door while I rapid-fire read through my emails. When I heard him muttering that he was dying for some coffee, and that he really needed to be looking at the Johnson report, I chuckled and went about getting both for him.

Yes, sometimes being a vampire was exceedingly handy.

Feeling a prideful sense of accomplishment after I completed my work day, I hopped into my car to meet up with my family. The Tuesday night dinners had kept going after the twins' births. If anything, they had felt even more important after that event. We were all so busy now. It was a good way to put the brakes on the world and reconnect with each other, if only for an hour or two.

Driving over, I popped in a CD that I couldn't listen to when I had the kids in the car. Not that the music was dirty or anything, but the song did have a couple of F-bombs in it, and I didn't need three-year-olds repeating that kind of stuff. I mean, at least not until they were petulant teenagers and truly understood the swears they were spouting at their overprotective parents. God, I was *not* ready for that day. I didn't think I would ever be ready for that day.

Pulling into the cozy little café that was an extended home for me and my family, I smiled at seeing Teren's Prius already parked in the lot. I wasn't surprised, since I knew with absolute certainty that Teren was in the far corner of the café, not moving, and that our children were about a mile away, closing fast. No, what had me smiling was the peace that had started spreading throughout my body when I'd started moving in his direction.

Our bond was like a warm fire after being out in the cold all day, or like stepping down into a hot tub for the first time—that warmth soaked into every muscle, down to the bone, relaxing every part of me, parts that I hadn't even realized were sore. No matter where it happened, our reconnection always felt like coming home.

I felt Teren's direction shifting towards me, most likely coming over to meet me at the door. Languid contentment seeped throughout my body as I walked towards him. Warm and soothing, all I felt was peaceful joy. When we met now, it was usually with a mellow kiss and whispered words of affection. I was grateful that the dial had been turned down from boiling to simmer. While the smoking hot connection had been electrifying when we could ride its coattails to multiple satisfying releases, it had, more often than not, been annoying.

The very first time we'd all attempted to get back together for our dinners, Teren had been running late from a meeting with his editor. Everyone at the diner who had gotten to know my family over the years, had oohed and aahed over the babies when I'd brought them in, and had virtually ignored me and any oddities that I might have had, like, say, a fang elongating when I accidently relaxed my hold on them for a micro-second while cooing at my son.

We'd gotten the twins' car seats safely propped up on wooden high chairs, and were all watching them stare at the toys dangling in their faces. I was watching Julian's pale eyes track a black and white ball when I'd felt my husband draw near.

Knowing that I couldn't lose control in the middle of the restaurant, I'd begged my sister to start talking about something, anything. Noticing and understanding my condition, she'd started rambling about her schoolwork and how she was inching her way up to the top of her class. I'd struggled to ask intelligent questions, but I'd had to sit on my hands to stop myself from tearing the table apart.

Because I was noticeably breathing heavier, my mom had asked me what was wrong. Since I couldn't talk long enough to explain, and since Mom knew what I was anyway, Ashley started filling her in on my situation. Mom thought it was weird. I agreed.

I had whimpered and bit my lip when I'd felt him in the parking lot. Ashley had held my arm tight at her side as I sat beside her. She looked like she was afraid I was going to blur out of the room to get to him. Honestly, I'd wanted to, and since I was sitting on the edge of the bench seat, I could have. That would have been complete chaos if the diners had seen me rushing by them in a streak of light. I had shifted my gaze to my children then, to distract my body from my growing desire. I wouldn't risk them by exposing myself. Not for this. I was stronger than that.

When I had finally felt him walk into the café was when things had gotten embarrassing. He'd speed walked over to me and I'd dashed out of my seat to crash into his arms, like we were lovers reuniting in some sappy home-from-the-war movie. Then we'd started ravishing each other right there beside the tables, while shocked patrons gawked at our fondling hands and eager mouths. My mom had sputtered reprimands, and my sister had had a serious attack of the giggles, but it was eventually our longtime waitress, Debby, who had pried us apart with threats that she would ban us if we ever did that again.

Laughing at the memory of that passionate greeting, I watched Teren gallantly swing open the door for me right as I approached it. His timing would have seemed miraculous, if anyone had been there to notice. "Thank you, sir." I paused to place a light kiss on him before sweeping past.

"You're welcome, my lady," he laughed back. Grasping my hand, he led us to a corner table in the back.

The memory of our embarrassing encounter fresh in my head, I flushed when Debby popped over to say hello. The waitress had probably forgotten the odd greeting, but my vampiric mind held onto stuff like that. Teren's expression was curious as he examined the rush of blood to my face, but he didn't say anything. I shoved the lingering uncomfortable emotion aside and warmly greeted her. Teren and I really had done the best we could with that intense connection.

Squishing close together in the semi-circle bench seat, I leaned against Teren's cool side and focused on feeling my children approaching me. Teren kissed my head and whispered that he missed me. I clenched his hand and whispered that I missed him too.

Resting my eyes, I let the sound of the world flow through me. But for the low, even breaths that he was faking, Teren was silent as he rested beside me. The others around us were not. Clangs and curses streamed from the kitchen, laughter and whispered conversations echoed from the other customers, and the hostess at the door was commenting to her friend about how nicely shaped Teren's backside was. Teren chuckled at the same time I did; he'd heard her too. I twisted my head and smirked at him. He only smiled and shrugged his shoulders.

Then the conversations shifted to hushed mutterings of, "Oh, wow," and, "Look at that." Some asshole even murmured, "Ugh." A low growl rumbled from my chest before Teren jerked my hand and shook his head. I forcefully stopped the reaction, but I knew who the comments were about, and it boiled my blood.

My sister had just entered the café, and she always garnered a reaction from people. Having been caught in the fire that had destroyed our childhood home, Ashley was horribly scarred. The burns had been so bad that she'd had to have several painful surgeries to heal properly. As a result, her body was blanketed with overlapping skin graft lines. She was a patchwork of imperfection, and in a society that placed a lot of emphasis on external beauty, she stood out.

Of course, not everyone who saw her reacted negatively. In fact, most people ignored her, were sympathetic, or commended her for her bravery. But the negative ones were the ones that I honed in on, since they bugged the hell out of me. I was tired of my sister being considered different, just because of her appearance. It had bothered me so much at one point that I had asked Teren to change her, just to heal her. I knew how stupid and dangerous that request was now, having gone through such a change myself, but I just wanted her to be able to walk down the street without a thousand stares following her.

But as Teren had told me once, she was happy, and as she bounded to the table, a slight spring in her hobbled walk, I thought she looked happier than usual. Curious, I asked her about it while she carefully sat down and scooted around to sit beside me. "You seem extra chipper, something up?"

Ashley shook her head; the half of it that could grow hair swished around her shoulder. "Just had a good day at work. You should see the way this little girl there idolizes me." Her eyes teared up as she thought about it. "I give her hope."

That made my eyes get misty too. Ashley had finished school. Being in the top of her class, she had gotten the dream job she'd wanted in the burn unit ICU at San Francisco General Hospital. She was more than just another nurse there, she was a living, breathing example of what the patients there could be, if they just plowed through the horrible fate that they'd been given. I couldn't have been any prouder of my sister, and once again, I wished to be just like her when I grew up.

"That's amazing, Ash. You're amazing." I reached around her body, hugging her to me, and felt Teren wrap an arm around her. He adored her too, and completely understood what it was like to feel different.

Ashley laughed and flushed under my praise. "Yeah, well…" Her brown eyes perked up when she spotted who I'd already felt. "No…they are the amazing ones."

I released her and looked over at the two boisterous toddlers clutching my mom's hands as they came up the aisle. The trio was a happy sight. Nika was still in her mismatched outfit, and Julian's mouth was covered in some sort of chocolate treat. I shook my head at the spoiling grandmother that my mom had become, then smiled when my children let go of her to get to me.

"Mommy! Daddy!" they both exclaimed in unison. Teren laughed as they hopped up on the seat and crashed into his side. Nika squirmed over his lap to sit in mine. Throwing her arms around me, she showered me with kisses. Laughing, I kissed her back. I loved how kids could make you feel like you'd been away from each for decades, instead of just a few hours.

"Oh, I missed you guys," I said, giving each of them sloppy kisses. Teren tickled Julian with one hand while wiping off his mouth with the other; Nika laughed at Julian's joy. "Any problems today?" I asked my mom after she sat down next to Ashley.

Smiling, she tucked her chin-length hair behind her ears. "Of course not. Those two are perfect."

"Perfect little monsters," Teren chuckled, tickling Julian until he squirmed and tried to get away from him. I elbowed Teren in the ribs for his comment, but everyone at the table laughed, entertained by the fact that technically, in the eyes of most people, they really were monsters.

Chapter 3 – Forever

A few days later, we were packing up the kids and their things for a weekend at the ranch. We tried to go out there most weekends, especially when they were in-between busy times and the hired help wasn't around. Then the toddlers could frolic and play uninhibited. When they were safe at the ranch, we let them play to their full capacity. They loved the freedom of not having to rein in anything.

Personally, I loved it too. It was frustrating to have to walk at a normal pace when you were in a hurry to get something. It was so hard to not blur down to the espresso stand on the corner and then blur back. I knew I could do it in the same amount of time it would have taken me to brew a pot in the break room, but I wasn't going to blow my cover for coffee...even really good coffee.

Pulling out my daughter's favorite fuzzy pink blanket and my son's must-have fire truck, I shoved both coveted items into an overnight bag for them. I followed that up with about six pairs of clothing; the kids got incredibly dirty playing in the countryside.

Teren slipped his arms around my waist and kissed my neck. I shivered as his cool breath tickled me. "You know, we could always leave them overnight and go on a date."

I twisted to look back at him. "An overnight date?"

Nodding, he held me tighter. Cocking an eyebrow, he added, "You wouldn't have to worry about being quiet."

I smacked his chest, then thought about it. We hadn't spent a night apart from the twins since they'd been born. Sure, we'd gone on dates—a movie here, dinner there, drinks with Hot Ben and Tracey—but we kept it to a three or four hour maximum. Maybe it was because they were so young, maybe it was because I missed being with them for the bulk of the day while I was at work, or maybe it was just because I was a first-time mom, but the thought of them being gone an entire night tightened my stomach.

Biting my lip, I shook my head. Tears were stinging my eyes at just the thought of not hearing them say goodnight to each other. Teren cupped my cheek as he watched the emotion flood my face.

"Not yet…they're not ready. They're still too young."

He gave me a knowing smile; he knew what I really meant was *I* wasn't ready, but he didn't call me on it. Instead, he only kissed me. Our tender moment was interrupted by a set of giggles at the door. We twisted to look at the children we knew were there, watching.

Nika held her hand over her mouth while she laughed. Julian tilted his head, curious. Smiling at them, I asked, "Are you two ready to go?"

Julian dashed off to their bedroom, but Nika stayed and pouted. "Can we bring Spike, Mommy?"

I walked over to her with a frown. Explaining the situation to a toddler was tricky. Halina had a thing for dogs. I really didn't want to freak out my daughter by telling her that, though. She loved Spike. She loved Halina. Just as I was about to tell her that Spike would want to stay at home, Teren walked over and squatted in front of her. "Do you really want him to come?" he asked, tucking a strand of hair behind her ear.

She nodded, cupping her hands together in a prayer position. "Please, Daddy?"

I glanced over at the big bad vampire melting into a pile of putty for his daughter. Grinning, he ruffled her hair. "I think we can do that."

She squealed and flung her arms around him. From down the hall I heard Julian hoot his agreement, exclaiming, "Thank you, Daddy." Nika repeated the sentiment and dashed off to join her brother in gathering the rest of their treasures.

As Teren stood, I put my hands on my hips; a playful smirk was on my face. He looked over my expression and shrugged. "She did the hand thing. How am I supposed to say no to that?"

Shaking my head at him, I slung my arms around his waist. "You are the biggest softy."

He leaned down and kissed me. Grinning against my lips, he whispered, "Quiet, you'll ruin my reputation."

I pulled back and cocked an eyebrow at him. He actually did

have a reputation in the vampire community, one that, if it weren't for Gabriel and his influence, might have been an issue for us. Not so long ago, he'd provoked and even interrogated several nests of local vampires. That sort of thing had repercussions.

We had been approached by a pissed off vampire before. Luckily Halina had been with us at the time. She'd flung the vamp into a wall, warning him to get over himself. Not really wanting a fight, the man had run off and we hadn't heard from him again. I had the distinct feeling that Halina had gone to her boyfriend afterwards and the two of them had "taken care of it." I'm not sure how. I didn't ask about stuff like that.

After that moment, no other vampires bothered us. Gabriel had only said that, at Halina's request, he'd put the word out that we were untouchable. The word gave me pause. Untouchable? It made him seem like some vampiric crime lord. But, regardless, he was a good person, so I tried to ignore the power he held. And his power stuck; we hadn't been bothered again.

Shaking my head, I changed the channel of my thoughts. "Are you sure about bringing Spike? What about Halina?" I whispered that, even though the kids could hear me anyway.

He looked down the hall towards their room, but they were busy laughing and picking out toys that would never all fit in their bags. Looking back to me, he whispered, "She won't do anything that would make those two cry. She won't touch Spike."

I couldn't help the thought that Spike was also...untouchable.

Sighing, I shrugged and tossed my arms around Teren. "You're right."

He kissed my nose. "Aren't I always?"

I burst into laughter at his comment; he frowned which only made me laugh harder. He pulled away from me when the tears started stinging my eyes. "It wasn't that funny," he murmured.

The giggles overtook me at the look on his face. I couldn't help it. There were so many times when he had been so incredibly wrong...it was just funny to me now. Holding my stomach, I watched him cross his arms over his chest. It was clear he was not amused in the slightest.

I tried to control my giddiness, but I had entered into that everything-is-funny stage and his expression was only making it worse. As his hands went to his waist and he actually started tapping his foot, I had to double over, the reaction was so strong. I was quickly joined by two tiny, curious youngsters looking up at me. They laughed right along with me, not really understanding what was so funny, but eager to join the fun. Teren sighed in exasperation.

Knowing that I was pushing the limits of his tolerance, I scooped up a child in each arm. "Let's go get Spike," I told their excited faces.

We hurried out of the room. Teren was shaking his head with his lips pursed when I looked back at him. Still chuckling as I walked down the stairs, I tossed a, "Sorry," over my shoulder.

The only sound that answered me was something similar to, "Uh-huh." I smiled and shook my head. I could make it up to him another time.

Later, as the car made its way around the last turn in the Adams' super-long driveway, I inhaled a deep breath. The midmorning sun glinted off of the red Spanish tile, a visual reminder of the one thing that coming here afforded a family of vampires. Blood. Very, very fresh blood. And practically as much as we wanted, since they kept the "open-air" pantry pretty full.

The kids squealed upon seeing the house, announcing our arrival verbally, since our approach had already been felt. I leaned my head back on the seat, enjoying the way my enhanced eyes saw the beauty of this ranch. The sharp points of the white stucco walls were easily apparent to me. The seamless wall of flat river rocks encrusted into that stucco finish along the bottom of the home seemed even more impressive. My eyes could see the mortar holding each stone in place, could see the way they lined up perfectly. I could even see faint cracks in the rocks that I'd never noticed before.

And that was from the parking lot-sized driveway.

The rest of the home was no less impressive. Expansive glass windows shifted colors in the sunlight, showing me the rainbow gleam of freshly applied cleaner. The ancient logs, both structural and decorative, released a scent that carried through the confines of the car. It reminded me of summer camp.

As Teren opened the door to get out, the other smell that was abundant at this place hit me. Cattle. Lots of cattle. Even to human noses that smell wasn't always a welcome one, but as I opened my door and stood up, I inhaled a deep breath, savoring it. Somewhere in all that mess of animal was the tang of a wounded one. It smelled incredible.

Looking over at Teren as I opened Julian's door, I noticed his brows were furrowed as he scanned the fields of long, waving tan grass. He smelled it, too.

"Everything all right?" I asked, unbuckling Julian from his restraints.

Teren glanced down at me, then moved to open Nika's door. He nodded and shrugged. "Yeah, probably. That's just a weird place for the smell of blood to come from, and there's a lot of it. We've had cougar attacks down there before." Tilting his head, he indicated a stream running between two low hills.

Unbuckling Nika's seat, he pulled her out; her tiny arms instantly closed around his neck. "There may have been an attack last night. I should let my dad know," he said with a frown.

I frowned too. The cattle were important to the Adams for more reasons than just the vampire's survival. They were also the primary source of the family's wealth. Although, they seemed affluent, even for successful ranchers.

Julian hopped out of his seat and darted off to the massive oak overhang covering the front door. Nika squirmed as she watched him run, so Teren set her down; she was instantly on her brother's tail. Spike, having fallen asleep between his two favorite people, woke up and chased after them.

As I watched the trio approaching the entrance to the warmest home I'd ever been to, the massive double doors opened at just the right moment to let them all rush inside. Spike barked and sniffed everything while Nika and Julian leapt into the awaiting arms of their grandmother, Alanna.

As she knelt in front of the door and hugged them tight, her sky blue eyes looked over to her son. Teren's mother was like all of the vampires in the family. Well, all of them except Nika. Alanna had the trademark straight, jet-black hair, crystal clear blue eyes, and the youthful appearance that belied her true age. She looked no older than Teren, and a bit younger than me. That made calling her "mom" feel a little odd, but I did it, to please her.

"Good morning, my lovelies," she said, kissing each grandchild on the head.

Teren and I waved our greetings to her then grabbed the various bags that accumulated whenever you went anywhere with kids. It wasn't as if the ranch didn't have every toy or luxury they could have asked for, but try telling that to a three-year-old who needed to bring *his* set of army men or *her* plastic ponies. It was a good thing for Teren and me that we had super strength.

As we walked to the house, fully loaded down, Imogen greeted us through the walls. The kids broke off from Alanna to go say hi to their great-grandma, or Grandma Immy, as they called her. They were flying up the duel staircase that lead to Imogen's rooms when we walked into the entryway; Julian tripped halfway up the stairs and Nika paused to help him.

Dropping my bags, I hugged the woman who had brought my husband into the world. "Hi, Mom," I warmly said as I patted Alanna's chilly back.

"Hello, Daughter," she replied. When we separated, she drifted over to Teren and squeezed him tight.

He laughed and tried to hug her back around his armful of bags. "Morning, Mom. Does Dad know about—?"

Straightening, Alanna cut him off. "Yes, I told him about the blood when I woke up and smelled it. He's out examining the herd now." Stepping away from her son, she folded her arms over her chest. "We don't usually have a predator problem, but with Grandma gone…" She shrugged.

I let my senses pinpoint the location of the one vampire who wasn't with us. It being daylight, I knew Halina was sleeping, but she wasn't at the ranch. She wasn't even in the city. She was down south, way down south, in L.A., where she was visiting her sort of boyfriend. Her location had been down in that direction all week. Since she was a night owl and a hunter, she'd naturally kept the property clear of threats, being the biggest one herself. Her absence had let a little bit of bravery seep into those hungry creatures.

Teren looked over at where we'd smelled the blood, then back to me. "I should give him a hand cleaning up."

Smiling, I nodded. I loved how he turned into a rancher anytime he came here. It was sexy.

He crooked a smile, like he was aware of my thoughts, then he grabbed the bags I'd dropped on the floor and blurred away upstairs. Once he was back down, he paused to kiss my cheek, then he darted out to help his father. I felt him leaving in my head as the distance between us lengthened.

Alanna laughed and shook her head. "For someone who refuses to seclude himself here, he sure does love it." Her smile at her son's opposing attitudes about his life was amused. Mine was too.

But, she had a point. Teren lived in the city so he could feel like a part of society. The vampires here mostly stayed to themselves and kept contact with the outside world at a minimum. Teren enjoyed feeling as normal as he could, and he refused to hide away. Of course, he also had the least amount of side effects from his condition, so he could do that pretty easily. Assuming he didn't have to eat in front of anyone and no one lovingly rested their head against his silent chest. No one but me, that was.

But when he was at the ranch, you had to wonder why he went through all the effort. He obviously loved it here, and the lifestyle was completely natural on him. But for his stubbornness, he could easily stay and run this place with his dad…and be perfectly content doing it.

Spike sat at the floor near my feet, thumping his tail on the cool marble floor of the entryway. Not bothered in the least by his presence, Alanna reached down and ruffled his fur. "Would you like something to eat, boy?" she cooed, just like she would have for the children. Spike thumped his tail harder and Alanna's ice eyes flashed up to me. "What about you? Hungry, dear?"

I shook my head with a smile. Alanna never stopped trying to do things for people. She was the mother I hoped to be one day. Patting Spike's back as he started walking towards the kitchen, I wondered when and if I'd see the full vampire. Maybe we hadn't had to worry about Spike's safety after all. "Is Halina gone to Gabriel's all weekend then?" I asked, curious if she'd be back, but also wondering how that pair was doing.

Alanna looked at me with a small smile as we walked down the hallway. "She's coming home tonight. She wants to see the kids." Her eyes flicked up to where they were playing in Imogen's room; leapfrog by the sound of it. Smiling wider, she returned her youthful face to mine. "She wanted to leave last night, but I guess she got…distracted."

She shrugged, and I knew exactly what had distracted her. There really was only one thing that would keep Halina away from a grandchild visit and he had a powerful demeanor and startling emerald eyes. I grinned and shook my head. "Well, the kids will be happy to feel her closer."

That was one question we'd had to endure all week. "When is Grammy Lina gonna move?" We told them all the time that she was with Grandpa Gabriel, but, really, that didn't stop the questioning, it only added, "Is Grandpa Gabby gonna be there?" Even though we visited the ranch nearly every weekend, it was always quite the event to our kids, nearly rivaling Christmas.

Entering the kitchen, I watched Alanna open one of the deep mahogany cabinets and pull out a can of dog food. The good kind, too. I smiled. Alanna was prepared for everything, even random visits from grand-pups. Taking in the tidy opulence of the master-chef quality kitchen, I asked, "Is Gabriel coming back with her? I'm sure the kids would love to see him too."

I frowned after my question, not displeased if he showed, but not entirely pleased either. I always felt like we should all be sitting under a bright light with a giant magnifying glass over our heads whenever he visited.

Alanna popped the gooey dog food out of the can. The mush made a sucking noise as it released. The smell was atrocious, but Spike attacked it like she'd just poured a liter of blood into his bowl.

Looking back up at me, she shrugged. "I don't know." Shaking her head, she sighed a little. "It's hard to tell sometimes what's going on with those two."

I leaned back against the counter opposite her; the granite was cool under my fingertips. "Do you think she actually loves him?" I raised an eyebrow. It seemed such a foreign word when put together with the seductive, carefree Halina.

Alanna cocked her head, thinking. While she debated, we both heard Imogen say from upstairs, "I think Mother does love him…not that she'll ever admit it. She plays it off as just a physical relationship, but I've seen things."

It made me cringe how open the mother and daughter were with each other, but, in the beginning, all they'd had was each other. I supposed that had bonded them in a way that was much closer than the average family.

With a smile, I shook my head. "Halina in love…what is the world coming to?"

Both vampire women laughed. My children joined along, even though they didn't understand what they were laughing at.

A few hours later, after running through every room in this massive spread, my breathless children ran up to me in the living room. Relaxing with a glass of wine in my hand, and my feet nestled in Spike's fur as he stretched out in front of the enormous fireplace, I smiled at them as they crawled all over me.

Julian sat in my lap while Nika grabbed my face. "Mommy, can we go see Daddy?"

Feeling that Teren was close to the house, and no longer near the place where the "incident" with the cows had happened, I nodded that they could. Julian squealed and then they took off, running out the backdoor to where they could sense him. Spike lifted his head as they darted between Alanna's legs, but then rested back down, too comfortable to chase after them. I felt the same way.

Alanna smiled at my contentment, patted my shoulder, then went on maintaining the luxurious home she lived in. Closing my eyes, I offered to help, but she only chuckled and told me to relax as she moved from the main building to one of the side buildings.

Settling back into the couch, I felt my family reunite. I smiled at the image of Teren and his dad greeting the kids. Teren's dad, Jack, adored our children and doted on them nearly as much as the women. It would be a miracle if I could raise those two without them getting spoiled to pieces.

Setting my empty glass on the coffee table, I drifted in and out of alertness. My hearing and sense of smell drifted in and out as well. I could make out Imogen and Alanna talking to each other, even though they weren't anywhere near the other. I could smell the roast Alanna had cooking in the kitchen, along with the hint of fresh blood that was still wafting in from outside. I could hear Spike's breathing, slow and steady, as he started drifting off to sleep.

It was some time later when my eyes popped open and alertness slowly returned to me. Spike was wrapped around my feet, and he groaned when I stretched out and moved him. Mentally rolling my eyes, I wondered why this ranch constantly wore me out, even when I hadn't done anything. Maybe it was just so comfortable here that it lulled me into submission. I think I preferred that thought.

I yawned as I sat up. Glancing out back, I saw the bright rays of afternoon sun glinting off the water in the pool, and felt for the other vampires.

Imogen was in her room, waiting out the remnants of day; her knitting needles were clacking away. Alanna and Jack were in the kitchen talking about the animal attack; apparently a mountain lion had taken down two cows, one with child. Both Alanna and Jack were upset about it. While Imogen offered to stay out during nights Halina was away, to spook off any would-be predators, I felt for my children.

They were still outside with Teren, playing in the pastures. While Alanna and Imogen worked out a plan to watch-guard the property when their nocturnal predator was away with her boyfriend, I stood. I felt bad that I couldn't help. But seeing as how I could barely keep my eyes open here during the day, I knew I wouldn't be very helpful on guard duty. Plus, I knew they wouldn't let me do it. Not while I was alive. Not when I didn't have the super healing attributes that they all had as undead vampires. They'd keep me away from danger just as surely as I kept the kids out of danger.

Quietly leaving them to their conversation, I went to go find my darlings. As I stepped into the bright California sunshine, Alanna addressed me. "Emma, tell the kids I have some fresh cow's blood for them."

I shook my head at her thoughtfulness. "Okay, thank you, Mom."

"You're welcome, dear."

As I heard the conversations shift back to the cows, I blurred across the fields to find the hearts that lingered outside of my body, beating or not. Streaking to the very east fields, I slowed to a normal pace.

As I walked into the empty pasture, where I could sense Teren and my children, I came across a scene that made my heart jump into my throat. My husband was playing with them in the way that most men played with their offspring. He was laughing as he tossed them into the air. I was fine with that. Children, for some odd reason, loved being chucked around. What made my heart surge though was the fact that Teren was chucking them "vampire style."

He would toss one in a sideways arch, the child laughing and giggling as they flew through the air. Then he would blur to where they were going to land and catch them. It was like he was playing catch with himself...with my children.

The toddlers squealed, giggled, and begged him for more. Their little faces were alive with love, joy and complete faith that their father would never let them get hurt. They probably didn't even comprehend the meaning of the word. Daddy had them. They were safe.

I had a little more understanding of just what could go wrong with Teren's little game. Blurring over to him, I grabbed his hand just as he was about to fling our giggling daughter. "Teren Nathaniel Adams! That's enough of that!"

He looked over at me with a huge grin on his face as he swayed Nika back and forth in his arms, still prepping to launch her. "What? They love this. They've been asking me to do it all day." He turned to

Julian sitting on the grass beside us. "Right, little man?"

Julian grinned and clapped his hands; his fangs were extended in his merriment. He was clearly enjoying himself. I sighed. Teren took my moment of indecision to chuck our daughter into the air. I gasped as I watched her tiny limbs flail about. He'd thrown her pretty far, and my heart started to race. He was already speeding over to her, but what if he missed? The ground wasn't exactly a soft cushion. She'd break something for sure and with her mixed blood, we couldn't take her to a doctor.

Just as my hands were coming up to cover my face, Teren caught her in a bucket scoop, twisting his body with the movement so the landing would be a gentle one for her. Nika laughed and threw her arms around his neck. "Again, Daddy!"

The vision of them together was heartwarming, but there was no way I was letting this continue. My heart couldn't take it. Blurring over to Teren, I grabbed Nika. Scooping her up, I rested her on my hip. Julian blurred over to us, tripping once halfway through the field, but I grabbed his hand before he could reach Teren.

"Me, Daddy. My turn!"

Teren reached down for his son, but I pulled them both a step away from him. He glanced up at me and a slow grin spread on his face. "I think Mommy's had enough of our fun for today."

Clutching my children tight, I pursed my lips at him. "I wish you'd keep in mind that they don't heal like you do. They're mostly human, you know."

He put his hands on his hips. "Do you really doubt my abilities? I wouldn't let them get hurt. Ever."

I stifled a sigh. I knew he meant well. I also knew that sometimes things happened that were beyond your control. Our entire family was sort of proof of that. "I trust you with them, Teren. I just can't handle the what-ifs."

He gently shook his head. "Still the worry-wart."

I laughed in spite of myself. "One of us has to be."

The kids started complaining once they realized their vampire games were over. "No! More, more, more!" They chanted in unison, while their hands reached out for Teren. Sometimes I cursed the fact that we'd ever taught them to speak. It was so much easier to redirect an infant who couldn't talk back.

Turning towards the house, I pulled Julian's arm and held Nika tighter. Both were trying to escape from me to get back to Teren. "Nope, fun's over for now."

They started crying in earnest and Teren laughed. Rustling Julian's hair, he patted him on the back. "Go with Mom." Ducking down to Julian's height, he added, "We'll play again later."

Julian smiled, and his devilish grin was identical to the grown man's before him. I gave Teren a scathing glare as he stood, but he only laughed at my look and shrugged. "What?"

Groaning in frustration, I tugged Julian's arm. He willingly went with me, since Daddy had promised him more flying later. "Come on, kids, Grandma has some blood for you, and it's getting cold." That immediately got their attention, and squealing in delight, they both jerked away from me.

Setting Nika down and letting Julian go, I watched them streak off to the house. I completely understood their enthusiasm; I was getting a little thirsty myself.

Teren walked up to me and grabbed my hand, and I looked over at him. The sunlight bounced off his dark hair, creating a ring of light. It highlighted his pale eyes, showcased the sexy stubble on his chin. Even though I didn't want to, I found myself responding to just looking at him. He smiled wider when he sensed where my mood had shifted. Grabbing my waist, he pulled me into him. "They're fine, but I'll stop if it really bothers you."

His hand started rubbing a circle into my hip. It made a jolt of desire flash through me. He leaned in and inhaled deep. "Yes, please." I wasn't sure if I was responding to his statement, or the question our bodies were starting to ask.

Alone time with the children was a tricky thing. Especially when those children were super-fast and had amazing hearing. Plus, they always knew where we were, thanks to the bond, and since we were their favorite people to be around, that usually meant...they were around. It had been a while since Teren and I had been truly alone. And since they were currently preoccupied in the house with the other vampires, we had a bit of time.

A growl came out of Teren's chest as he pulled our hips together so they were touching. I could feel his desire now, too. My breath came in sharper pulls as my arms laced around his neck and my fingers twirled in his hair. Our lips met, soft and searching. He sucked on my lower one, gliding his cool tongue over me. I groaned and grabbed his backside. Grinning, he adjusted his mouth to fully enclose mine.

As that miraculous man's mouth made every fiber of my body burn with the need for more, he reached down, picked me up, and wrapped my legs around his waist. Within seconds we were flying, traveling farther away from where our kids were. I wasn't worried, though. Alanna was with them, probably feeding them and telling them childhood tales of Teren.

After we stopped, I briefly looked around. He'd taken me to one of his favorite spots here. It was a wide, slow-moving creek winding its way through a low spot in the hills. Long tufts of grass lined the banks and the water sparkled like tiny diamonds under the perfect, azure sky. It wasn't a childhood haunt, since he hadn't grown up on this particular ranch, like I'd once imagined, but it was idyllic and lovely, and I liked to imagine a young Teren here, lying out under the stars.

He knelt down by the edge of the creek with my legs still wrapped around him, and then he laid me back in the tall grass. We'd made love here before, what seemed like a lifetime ago, when we'd been trying to conceive those little miracles he'd been tossing around earlier. The spot held a warm place in my heart. It was not the only spot on me that was currently warm.

Laying his body along the length of mine, his tender kiss picked up intensity. My legs around him ran down his calves as my fingers tightened in his hair. God, it had been a long time since we'd let ourselves be consumed by each other. He groaned, his hands as eager as his mouth as he started unbuttoning my blouse. When he finished, he pulled back to gently take the shirt off of me. I wasn't so gentle as I stripped the t-shirt off of him. My hands slid down his perfect chest while his eyes raked over mine.

Needing so much more, I reached behind myself and unclasped my bra. I chucked it over my shoulder somewhere and pulled his head to a breast. He pushed us both back down to the grass as his mouth worked over a nipple. I exalted in the chill of his breath, his tongue, his hands. Everywhere he touched ignited me.

While he worked one breast, then the other, my fingers found his jeans. As deftly as I could, I popped them open and unzipped them. Since we were holding each other so tightly, I could only slip my hand inside the fabric. He hissed when my fingers touched him. He was so hard, so ready. I was equally ready. I wanted him so badly I lost control and my fangs extended.

He paused with his head resting on my chest. Breathing heavy, he murmured, "God, you feel so good around me. Your hand is so warm."

The clear desire in his voice made me groan. I grabbed his cheek and pulled his face back to mine. Gently squeezing, I hungrily kissed him. He ignored my fangs and returned my eager kiss. The smell of grass wrapped around us, followed by the scent of clean water and the faint smell of animals. Somewhere in there I smelled my own desire, and with the sun beating down on our bodies, I swear I could smell the rays too.

Smiling at how beautiful it all was—his words, his body, this peaceful location—I breathed, "I don't need any more, Teren. I'm ready for you, for us, I'm so ready for this." He pulled back to look at me, his eyes hooded with lust. "I just want you inside me," I whispered to him.

His eyes widened and there was a flurry of movement as the rest of the barriers between us were stripped away. When he finally resettled himself between my waiting thighs, he paused; the cool tip of him just barely pushed into me. Searching my face, he panted, "I love you."

I smiled, meaning to say it back, but then he pushed deep and the only thing that left my mouth was a stream of groaning, incoherent consonants. My body wrapped around him. His back was slightly warmer from the sun heating it. With long, slow strokes, we both enjoyed our rare moment of togetherness.

We shared breathless kisses, and his tongue occasionally flicked a fang, sending a jolt straight through me. As his groans deepened and his hips rocked faster, I could feel the buildup starting. I was torn, wanting that euphoric release, but never wanting this connection to end. Dropping his head to my shoulder, Teren grunted in a way that I knew meant he was close. I wondered if he was torn too. We both wanted to hold out as long as possible, since who knew when we'd get a chance to be this free with each other again.

As I started moaning louder, the approaching climax too much to contain, I felt his fangs prick my shoulder. Gasping, I tilted my head and exposed my neck. "Yes, oh please, Teren, yes, bite me." I was a little embarrassed to beg, but really, I hadn't had that in a while either.

He groaned as his cool lips came to my neck, then shifted to my shoulder, just above my collar bone. As our hips continued our escalating rhythm, he licked the skin he was about to pierce. That almost ignited my orgasm. His next words nearly did too. "Bite *me*," he whispered, moving his shoulder so I could sink my teeth into the same spot on him, just reversed. "Bite me, too."

Groaning, and cursing with the eroticism of it all, I shifted my head and body so I could bring my lips to him. A low growl came from us both as we sank our teeth into each other simultaneously. His cool blood poured into me—tangy, sweet, tasting of his scent— and combined with the fire in my body. Pure bliss. I heard him groan as my blood poured into him. I had to imagine I tasted equally good, just warmer.

The blood hitting my tongue, his teeth sinking into my skin, his manhood thrusting into me again and again—it was too much. I came hard and clutched him tight as I sucked deep. I recognized the sound of him releasing and knew he was coming at the same time. We were so in sync right then, we might as well have been one person.

As our bodies slowed, Teren's teeth eventually pulled out of me. I could feel him start to lick the wounds closed, his tongue languidly sliding over my skin while a content rumble escaped his chest. Knowing his body could handle it, I left my teeth in him and took a few last draws as the ripples of a great release washed through me.

Adjusting his body, he gently pulled out of me and shifted to my side. He quietly ran his fingers through my hair, letting me take his nourishment as long as I wanted. Feeling full and satisfied on every level, I finally retracted my teeth. I licked away the few red streaks on his skin, but the actual wounds closed right before my eyes.

Twisting to his back, he pulled me into the crook of his arm. Sighing with a contentment that matched my own, I felt him kiss my head as the warm sun caressed our spent bodies. Propping myself up, I watched him close his eyes and smile. I nudged him in the ribs. "No you don't. Don't you dare fall asleep on me."

Eyes still closed, he laughed and shook his head. "I'm not…just relaxing."

I snuggled into his side, enjoying the cool length of him under the warm sun. Clutching him was like having my very own ice pack. "Good, because I don't want to waste our free time unconscious."

He laughed again as he peeked an eye open. "Did you have another idea?"

His eyes drifted down my body and even spent and satisfied, I responded. His smile turned a little cocky as he sensed it. I pushed him away and stood up. Propping himself up on his elbows, he watched me as I looked down at him. "Where are you going?" he asked, his cocky smile twisting to a frown.

Not answering him, I twisted and darted into the water. I splashed in, then dove under the surface. When I came up again, I screamed. It was freaking cold, even for someone who was used to being wrapped in coldness.

Teren stood and moved to the edge of the wide, slow river. Laughing and shaking his head at me, he managed to get out, "Makes me seem warm, doesn't it?"

I laughed through my shivers, then splashed him with the frigid water. "Get in here…warm me up." It made me smile that his body probably would be warmer in comparison.

He watched me in the water for a moment longer, his face holding an expression of pure love and devotion, then he blurred into the stream with me. I giggled as his arms and legs wrapped around me. I stopped giggling when his weight pulled me under the water. He instantly let me go, since out of the two of us, I still needed air, then he slowly popped up beside me, his blue eyes playful. I splashed him as I grabbed a quick gulp of oxygen, then I wrapped my freezing body around his.

Eventually I adjusted to his temperature and then the water's temperature. Running his fingers up and down my back under the water, he held me in place in the chest-deep creek. I smiled down at him, as I ran my fingers though his dark, wet hair.

"Forever?" he muttered, adoration in his eyes. I shook my head, not understanding. A small smile crept into his reverent expression. "Do I really get you forever?"

With a sigh, I rested my head against his. "No."

Pulling back, his brows narrowed to a questioning point. I gave him a half smile as I wrapped my arms around his neck. "*We* get forever," I clarified.

Smiling, he leaned up to kiss me. "Good. I won't settle for anything less now."

The water licked my shoulder blades. Some of it splashed over my collar bone to run over the twin wounds, soothing the very slight ache. Smiling at my romantic husband, I laid my head on his shoulder; my cheek rested above the perfectly healed spot that I'd torn into earlier. Clutching him tight, I watched the sun glint and shine off of the diamond ring encircling my finger; the blood-red rubies around it deepened in color as I shifted my hand. The symbolic representation of eternity, and our undying love for each other. Only for us, it wasn't symbolic. We really would get forever. This love and joy would last for so long that it was sort of incomprehensible to me. Closing my eyes, I felt that love physically wash over me.

Forever…I wouldn't settle for anything less either.

Chapter 4 – It's Okay to Be Happy

After our dip in the stream, Teren and I took our time walking back to the ranch. We stopped to watch some cattle munching nearby. None of the docile beasts seemed worried at all about the mythical monsters just a few feet away from them. We held hands while we strolled along, just enjoying the quiet of being together. For a minute, we shut off that portion of our minds that were constantly in parent-mode, and we were just a husband and wife.

By the time the gleaming red tiles of the ranch came back into view, Teren's wet hair was mostly dry. Mine was just a little damp at the ends. Our toddlers rushed out to see us, while Alanna watched them from a shaded corner of the building. Since our children had our level of limitations, or lack thereof, they enjoyed the sunshine just like any human. Alanna hadn't ended up so lucky in that department, and while she could be in the sun for short doses, it bothered her after a while.

When our children reconnected with us, jumping into our arms, Alanna waved and headed back into the house. She had a small, knowing smile on her lips and I was pretty sure that she knew exactly what we'd been doing during our extended absence. I tried to not be embarrassed about it. She knew what we were going through, having had a superfast, super-hearing toddler herself. Plus, Alanna would never make me feel uncomfortable about all of the things she had seen or heard, which was unfortunately quite a bit, since she'd been present for the beginning of the creator-createe bond. She was very gracious in that respect. I adored her all the more for it.

Dinner was at dusk, when Imogen could freely and painlessly join us. Pleasant conversations and warm laughter filled the spacious dining room and it seemed a little miraculous to me that there had ever been a time when tension and turmoil had filled this room. But back when Teren and the others had been desperately searching for a way to save me and the children from an unpredictable fate, there certainly had been.

As everyone but Jack enjoyed a little plasma refresher, my happy and healthy children ducked out into the ski lodge-like living room to play. I felt an odd tension start to build as we leaned back in our chairs. Looking at Teren's parents, my enhanced sight saw a slight furrow in each brow line. "What is it?" I hesitantly asked.

Imogen sighed and I shifted my attention over to her. "We need to prepare you for something that will be happening soon."

Knowing how quickly life could shift, I instantly felt ice flood through my veins. Hearing my own heartbeat pick up, I looked between all of the loved ones seated around the table.

Teren put an arm around my shoulders, silently comforting me. "Is it time…already?" he asked quietly.

Alanna and Jack gazed at each other for a moment before Alanna swung her eyes over to her son. "Another year, maybe two, but there are preparations to make, as you know."

Teren nodded, then looked down. Confused and a little annoyed at what they all knew that I didn't, I felt a pout form on my lips. Knowing I was probably a mirror image of my daughter, I shook my head, and said, "What are you talking about?"

Teren looked up and squeezed my shoulder. "They need to leave this ranch."

My mouth dropped open as my gaze flicked around the room, taking in the beauty of it. I'd gotten so used to them being here that a part of me couldn't imagine them gone. But I also knew that as a part of their never-ending charade to pass as human, they had to move around, so the girls' unchanging appearance was never questioned.

Even as secluded as they were, people talked, and Alanna and the others, would soon attract attention for their seemingly unending youth. Naturally, the vampires tried to avoid attracting attention, and so Jack moved with his "new" bride and her sisters to one of several similar ranches they had around the country. Teren was still young enough that his appearance wasn't an issue…yet.

"Oh," I whispered. "Where…will you go?" I couldn't imagine them all being far away from me. I was too used to being just a short drive away.

Alanna gave me a sad smile. "The next ranch in rotation is in Utah."

Nodding, I looked down. As a moment of strained silence fell around the table, I felt Teren give me a comforting squeeze. They were all so close, it was difficult to imagine them breaking apart. But, all families eventually had to, I supposed.

Jack sighed and reached over to pat my arm. "Don't worry about it yet, Emma. We're not going anywhere for a while. We just have to start preparing the new home and shifting some of the herd. It takes time to move a working ranch. We just wanted to let you know."

I smiled at him, then pushed it to the back of my mind. They'd said a year or two. Since I didn't want to spend that much time fretting over it, it was best to shove it into a far corner of my brain, to be looked at and examined at a later date.

After lighter conversations returned and our drinks were finished, we all retired to the living room to watch the children play tag—super-speed tag. When their energy finally wore down, Teren and I got the yawning twins ready for bed. Nika wrapped her arms around her father's neck, and her small head flopped onto his shoulder. "No, Daddy. Grammy Lina's coming."

When I picked him up and kissed his head, Julian sighed his agreement to his sister's statement. "We want to see her."

Teren and I exchanged glances. The sun had set hours ago and we could both feel Halina moving towards us. She was approaching fast, but she had driven a car and her speed was more a normal one, although I was sure she was driving at about twice the legal limit. She could have run the distance and gotten here faster, but it was exhausting to maintain the super-speed for that long. It was much more effective in short bursts, especially for mixed vampires like us. Full vampires could hold the burst longer, but it still came at a price. Halina tended to only run great distances if it were an emergency, like when Teren had been going out and getting into all sorts of trouble without her. She'd done a lot of running when he'd been searching for other mixed vampires.

Teren sighed and kissed Nika's head. "Sorry, sweetheart, she's still far away."

Nika lifted her head; her eyes were brimming with tears. In my arms, Julian sniffled. "I want Grammy Lina." Seeing her lip start to tremble in the telltale sign of an exhausted breakdown, Teren soothingly rubbed her back and encouraged her to lay her head back down on his shoulder.

I mimicked the action with Julian. Since he felt Nika's disappointment through their bond, he was beginning to share her emotional reaction. Kissing his head, I told them, "She'll come in and see you when she gets here."

Nika looked over at me. "Promise?" she asked, a tiny tear dropping to her cheek.

Walking over to kiss away the moisture on her skin, I nodded. "Yes…I promise."

Imogen, her long, black hair neatly pulled up into a bun at the nape of her neck, walked over to them and simultaneously rubbed both of their backs. "I'll make sure that she does."

The twins tiredly nodded as they slumped against our bodies. "Goodnight, Grammy Immy," they muttered together.

Imogen shook her head. Amazement and pride were clear in her grandmotherly eyes. "Goodnight, my angels." She smiled as she watched their eyes start to close. "Sleep well." Clasping her hands in front of her, she sighed in contentment.

Alanna stepped up to us as we started leaving the living room. "Teren?" she quietly asked. He twisted back to his mother, and she glanced at Nika in his arms; her breath was low and even as she drifted in and out of consciousness against Teren's chest. Looking over at her husband, Alanna shrugged. "Can Jack and I put them to bed?"

Jack's eyes were on Nika as well as he smiled at his son. His hair was more silver now than when I'd first met him, and his stomach was a touch more padded, but his eyes were warm and alive. The mind behind them was still young at heart, if not in body.

Stepping forward, Teren slightly extended his arms out to his father. "Of course."

Jack's smile grew as he gently took Nika's huddled form from Teren. She stirred a little as she was jostled. Blinking, she looked up at Jack as he enfolded her in his arms. "Hi, Grandpa," she muttered.

Twisting, she clung to him as surely as she'd been attached to Teren.

The burly man sniffed back his emotion as he kissed her head. Jack got a little uncomfortable showing what he was feeling, but it was obvious to just about anyone that he adored his grandchildren. Rubbing her back, he nodded a goodnight to Teren and me and started to head out the glass double doors that led to the staircase.

I watched him leave with my daughter, then turned to Alanna and handed her my son; her cool arms brushed against me as she took him. Julian looked up and yawned as she effortlessly shifted his weight over, then he closed his eyes and snuggled into her body. I smiled at the comfort and love between them.

Alanna closed her eyes and laid her cheek on his head. Her loose hair washed over Julian's back, and his dark hair blended seamlessly into her ebony strands. Watching them, I instantly saw how Alanna must have looked when she'd cuddled with a young Teren. Since Julian was a carbon copy of my husband, and Alanna looked the same now as she did then, it was like I'd just rewound into the past. It brought tears to my eyes.

Eyes still closed, Alanna followed the path that her husband had taken with Nika. As I watched them leave, my heart expanded even more. Teren put his arms around my waist, pulling my focus back to him. "Aren't you supposed to be less emotional now that you're no longer pregnant?" He smiled wryly at me, then tilted his head. "You're not pregnant again, are you?"

Laughing, I smacked him in the chest. "No. Your little swimmers are good, but not that good."

He chuckled and held me tighter. Imogen softly laughed at us, then left us to our privacy. I heard Alanna giggling upstairs and felt my cheeks heat. Even though I could hear so much better now, sometimes I forgot just how good their hearing was.

Teren's thumb came out to stroke my flushed cheek. "Sometimes I wish we could have more."

He shrugged, then sighed. I sighed too. We hadn't been sure whether or not Teren's body would be able to produce viable baby-makers, now that he was dead. A candid conversation with our vampiric scientist had confirmed what we'd been afraid of—he couldn't. That life-giving part of himself was over with. But that was okay. We had our two miracles, and they were enough.

Smiling, I said, "That's because you didn't have to carry and birth them. You'd feel differently about having more if you had been the one shoving bodies the size of watermelons out of an opening about half that size."

Every single vampire laughed heartily at my statement, my husband included. Shaking his head, he laughed out, "You have a point."

Wrapping my arms around him, I laid my head on his heartbeatless chest; his laughter echoed in my ear. I heard Jack ask his wife what was so funny, and my children yawn and mutter, "Quiet."

"Yeah, sometimes I wish that too," I said with a sigh. I looked at Teren. His handsome stubbled face was slightly orange from the light of the fireplace. "But I have you, and I have them. It would be selfish to ask for more, when I already have everything."

Smiling wider, he kissed my nose. "Agreed," he whispered.

I felt Halina return to the property a while later, when Teren and I were kissing in the hot tub. Busy straddling my husband's lap in the near-boiling water, I only half listened to the roar of her sports car as it peeled into the drive. Teren chuckled beneath me as his warm hands slid up and down my back. Being exposed to this temperature for so long warmed every part of him. For the next several hours, he'd be just as toasty to the touch as me. "She's back," he muttered, his lips moving to my ear.

I made some sort of noncommittal noise as I sucked on his neck. Laughing a little more, Teren grasped my hips and pulled me into his body. A light groan escaped me at the feel of him so close under the scant material of our swimsuits. I regretted that groan about ten seconds later when Halina breezed out to us.

"God, don't you two ever stop procreating? It's a little pointless now."

I hadn't been expecting her to immediately rush over to us, and she startled me. With a squeak, I slid off of Teren's lap and slipped into the deeper section of the hot water. Halina sniggered while

Teren scooped me up and set me on the rim of the hot tub. Once I was back on dry ground, he sat down beside me. As steam lifted off of my skin, I glared at the teenage vampire in front of me; she only laughed harder.

"You're one to talk, Halina," I muttered under my breath.

Halina, having the best ears of all of us, and that was saying a lot, cocked an eyebrow at me. I generally avoided back-talking to the pureblood vampire, but she had sort of scared the crap out of me; I could even still hear my heart racing. Besides, I did have a good point. Aside from Teren and me, she was the most sexually active vampire I knew.

Perhaps amused by the fact that I'd talk like that to her, she ignored my comment. Her pale, slightly glowing eyes shifted to Teren. "I have another batch of vials for you in the car; about three months' worth."

Teren smiled and glanced over at my chest, like he was listening to my thumping heart. "Thank you, Great-Gran," he said politely, looking back up at her.

She shrugged, like it was no big deal to her either way. And I supposed it wasn't. Whether or not I kept aging, whether or not my heart kept beating, my overall fate was the same as any other mixed vampire's. She probably didn't see the point in prolonging it. Sometimes I didn't either, but waking up and thinking—*today is a good day to die*—never actually happens. It was human nature to want to live, and I was still very human.

"Thank you, Halina." Her ancient eyes swept over my bikini-clad body, making me extremely self-conscious for a second.

She shrugged again. "It gives me a good excuse to see Gabriel, at any rate."

An odd expression passed over her face. Almost grief, if I didn't know any better. But Halina, while not exactly happy with the hand that fate had dealt her, was rarely sad about it. I'd only seen her emotional a few times, and that was generally when she was reminiscing over the loss of her husband, the human husband who she had inadvertently killed after her conversion.

The youthful face turned away from us. Halina was wrapped in a dress so tight that a human wouldn't have been able to breathe in it. I was pretty sure it was leather. It matched the thigh-high boots she preferred to wear. But the evocatively dressed vixen that she usually played so effortlessly seemed cracked to me as she slowly moved back towards the house.

Actually feeling concerned for her, I called out her name. "Halina?"

She stopped and looked back at me. Her ageless eyes seemed tired, as her black-as-night hair billowed around her in the slight breeze. "Emma?" She raised her lip in a smirk after she said my name, almost daring me to call her on her mood.

As Halina could still intimidate me, even after all these years, I shook my head and motioned upstairs. Completely changing what I had been going to say, I sputtered, "We promised the kids you would see them when you got in." Smiling softly, I added, "They miss you."

A genuine smile broke over her face as she looked up to where they were. "I've missed them, too," she said before she streaked away.

I blinked at the afterimage of her glowing eyes still in my vision. She was fast, faster than everyone. Teren's arm, delightfully still warm, came around my shoulders. I sighed, and cuddled into his side. Dangling our feet in the steamy water, we listened to Halina greeting our children in Russian. They instantly awoke at hearing her voice, and laughter and the sound of soft kisses filtered down to us.

The various sides of Halina marveled me some. She could be a cold, ruthless killer, a sexed-up male fantasy, or, as she was being now, a devoted grandmother, cooing and coddling our children like they were her own. A part of me understood why she amused Teren so much. The majority of me was careful to never piss her off. Unless she really, really loved you, you probably wouldn't survive making her angry.

When our children's laughter turned into quiet yawns, Halina started singing them a lullaby. It was naturally in her native language and was remarkably beautiful. But as I leaned against my husband, I heard the melancholy in her timbre, the sadness in her words.

Looking up at Teren, I quietly asked, "Is she okay?"

He furrowed his brow, like he didn't know who I meant. Not wanting to get her attention by saying her name, I flicked my eyes up at where Halina was singing to our kids. Teren looked up at the window where the twins' bedroom was and then back down to me. "Sure, she seems fine."

I pursed my lips and shook my head. As perceptive as Teren could be at times, he was still a man, and the male species sometimes had to be hit over the head with things, since they tended to lack the ability to pick up on subtleties. He furrowed his brow at me. "What?"

I shook my head again and rolled my eyes. He hadn't seen the emotion in Halina, but I had, and it worried me. "She just seemed...off."

He kissed my head. "I'm sure it's nothing. Maybe she's just thinking about the upcoming move, too." He pulled back and raised an eyebrow at me. "It will put her that much farther from Gabriel."

He shrugged and my mouth dropped open. I hadn't thought of that. Of course that would be upsetting to her. I shook my head again. And just when I thought my husband was oblivious. He furrowed his brows again. "What?"

He laughed at the look on my face and I joined him. Leaning up to kiss him, I murmured, "Nothing, you just amaze me."

He laughed a little more while we kissed, then he pulled back. "I should go get those vials from the car." His eyes flicked down my body and I felt the unasked question in his gaze—*How much longer are you going to use them?* I only smiled and nodded at his remark. I didn't have an answer to his question yet. I wasn't sure.

He stood up. The beaded water ran down his chest and dripped off his shorts. I bit my lip as I studied the pleasing shape of him. He smiled as he studied the pleasing shape of me. Raising an eyebrow, he softly said, "I'll be back for you in a minute."

I laughed as I sank back into the searing water. I felt Teren causally walk away from me, not in any rush, just enjoying the evening. Closing my eyes, I felt the heat of the tub. I could almost feel it entering my body, soothing my muscles, warming me to the bone. The scent of chlorine was overpowering, but it was worth it, for the comfort.

I listened to my children wish each other goodnight again as I felt Halina move away. Then I felt her presence lift higher into the air. Confused, I opened my eyes and looked up to where I felt her. Above the two-story main building, there was a belfry. Okay, it wasn't actually a belfry, but I preferred to think of that way, since the whole home kind of had a castle-like feel to it. There was a raised section of the roof there though, like a covered patio.

I could see Halina standing up there, still and silent with her back to me as she looked out over the hills of Mount Diablo. As I sat up and got out of the water, I watched her. She appeared to be deep in thought. Being pure and not mixed, Halina was different from the others. Not looks-wise. She had the same dark hair and pale eyes, although her skin was snow white with no trace or hint of any sunlight ever having hit it. No, it was more her attitude that was different.

She had a presence about her, a lethality under the surface. She struggled less with the ethics of being a natural born killer. She would do it, if she wanted to, although, she did still have a moral code she followed, and she only killed those who she felt deserved the death. But the reluctant vampire had admitted that she felt foreign, that she no longer felt human, and that foreignness was evident in her at times. She could, at first glance, seem cold and standoffish, but I'd seen her heart and I knew she still had one, beating or not, and I knew something was wrong.

My concern for her overriding my common sense, I wrapped a fluffy robe around my body and walked over to the edge of the main building.

Wondering how the hell I was going to get up there, I looked around for a ladder. There wasn't one. I sighed as I realized that this was a private place that only the vampires went to, and vampires had no need for ladders. Hoping my enhanced body was enhanced enough, I took a few steps back and made a running leap for it.

I realized just how stupid my attempt was when I caught the lip of the roof. For one, I hated heights. For another, as I was constantly telling Teren, I was mostly human, and couldn't heal like the rest of the vampires around here. If I fell...well, it would suck.

"Shit," I muttered as my fingers started to slip. Cool hands wrapped around my wrists and deadweight lifted me into the air.

Holding me dangling over the edge, Halina cocked an eyebrow and asked, "What are you doing, little heartbeater?"

At the same time, I heard Teren's panicked voice calling my name. Looking down at just how far the patio cement was beneath me made me shiver. I looked back up at Halina with wide eyes. "Put me down...please."

She smirked and set me down next to her. Relieved to be back on solid ground, I closed my eyes. The stronger wind up here whipped around me, instantly chilling me, and I held my robe tighter as I answered Teren; he was asking me in a worried voice if I was all right. "I'm fine...just sightseeing with Halina."

He sighed while Halina's smirk widened. "Emma...good lord, you just about gave me a heart attack." I bit my lip to not nervously laugh. Teren couldn't have a heart attack anymore, but I'd nearly given myself one; my ticker was even still beating extra hard. I felt Teren's location shift back into the house. "I'll be in our room...when you come down." I heard him muttering something about how maybe my worry-wartness could start including myself as he walked to our bedroom.

Halina crossed her arms over her chest as she listened to Teren complaining about me. She was leaning back on one of the wooden beams holding up the raised roof section and she didn't seem worried in the slightest about the drop-off behind her. As I moved to stand in the center of the tiled square, she asked, "What are you doing up here?"

Wondering that myself, I shrugged. "You seemed...down. I thought you might want to..." I let my thought trail off and I wondered just what I'd expected to happen up here with the generally closed-off person in front of me. A heart to heart?

Instead of giving me the biting remark that I expected from her, she shifted her gaze back to the view. The wind blew strands of dark hair across her cheek as she looked south, towards Los Angeles. She sniffed. "I smell death in the air...some cows were attacked while I was gone…" Looking back at me, she raised an eyebrow just like Teren sometimes did. "Weren't they?"

I nodded, my brows furrowing that she'd be so upset over that. She frowned and shook her head as she looked out over the fields again. "I should have been here. My job is to protect the family, and that includes protecting the food supply." She paused, and just when I thought to tell her that it wasn't her fault, she added, "I've been too distracted lately…with Gabriel." She bit her lip, then nodded. "I'm thinking of breaking things off with him."

Surprised, I took a step towards her. "Why? Because of a couple of cows?" While I didn't quite know what they had together, they both seemed happy, and it seemed wrong to sacrifice true happiness over a few easily replaceable cattle. "This doesn't have anything to do with cows…does it?"

Looking back to me, she tucked the hair across her cheek behind her ear. "No, not really." She shrugged in a casual way. "But Gabriel and I have run our course. Besides, I'm not used to being with just one man. It feels…restrictive." Her voice warbled and her eyes reddened before she looked away. I knew she was lying.

"Halina…" I said softly, walking up and putting a hand on her chilly arm. I made myself ignore the fact that nothing was behind her but open air; standoffish or not, she'd never let me fall.

When she looked back to me, her eyes were definitely moist with blood-red tears. "I enjoy the company of men…but I don't *ever* feel for them and I'm starting to feel…." She shook her head as a bloody tear dropped to her cheek. "I cannot fall for him. It's wrong."

Amazed at the depth of feeling she was showing me, I brushed away her tear. Or I tried to anyway. Mainly, I smeared it across her skin. "Why not? Isn't falling in love a good thing?"

She cringed at the word love and stared at the floor. "No…no, I can't. I'm…I'm betraying Nicolis…and I've already done so much to betray him."

When she looked up at me, there was so much guilt in her face, my heart constricted for her. Nicolis was the husband she'd killed, the husband she still mourned. Swallowing the lump of emotion in my throat, I stroked her arm. "Oh, Halina, no…he would want you to be happy."

With a sad sigh, she looked over my shoulder. "Would he? He died because of me."

I stepped into her line of vision, bringing her glowing eyes back to mine. "What you did to him wasn't your fault, Halina. You didn't ask for this. You didn't know what you were or what the urges you felt were. You couldn't possibly have stopped yourself." She started to look away but I held her gaze. "I watched Teren go through it, and even knowing what he was, he could barely stop himself."

Her eyes drifted over my face for a long moment. Just when I thought our bonding was over, she quietly said, "I almost killed Imogen too. If my anger hadn't surfaced, I think I would have." She looked away from me, and the rage she'd mentioned suddenly became apparent in her features. "I've held onto that anger for so long. It's how I survive. It's how I get through…the day."

Moved and emotional, I leaned in to hug her. She instantly stiffened and I stopped. Maybe she wasn't ready for that. Instead of wrapping my arms around her, I moved a lock of hair from her eyes. "Nicolis would want you to release that anger. He would want you to be happy."

Her eyes narrowed as she locked gazes with me, and the anger in the blue depths was still apparent to my enhanced sight. "Would you? If Teren had killed you, would you wish him peace with someone else?"

My stomach tightened at the thought, but my answer was instant. "Yes." A sudden chill ran down my spine, and I wrapped my arms around my body.

Watching me, Halina pushed away from the supportive beam. Taking long, languid steps, she walked around me with appraising eyes. "So, when you agreed to a relationship with Teren, knowing full well his fate and your own, you didn't want him to mourn you for eternity in solitude?"

Shaking my head, I twisted to keep my body facing hers. "No, no I never wanted that." A little surprised that she would think I'd wish that on a loved one, I whispered, "Did you think I wanted him to be alone? Crying over me every day?"

Just as I was feeling a little dizzy, she stopped her endless circling. "He openly admitted that he'd never love anyone else. I didn't want my life for my grandchild," she whispered.

Stepping up to her, I placed a hand on her arm. "I didn't either. I kept myself from thinking about it for the most part, but when I did...it killed me." Sighing, I looked down at my bare feet on the tiled ground. "If my fate were a regular human's, I'd want him to move on. I would wish him love." I peeked back up at her, and her youthful face seemed torn by my words. "A life alone...is no life at all."

Her anger seemingly diminished, she placed her hand on my shoulder; the act surprised me. "I never wanted him to fall for a human. I only ever wanted a receptacle for a grandchild. When it became apparent that he had fallen for you, I may have resented you a little." She tilted her head and sighed. "I'm sorry, I just didn't want him to grieve you." She closed her eyes, and a long tear dripped down her cheek. "I watched my daughter go through it, and Alanna will someday with Jack. It's not easy, being in love with a human..."

Her words tore at my heart. Peeking up at me, she whispered, "I couldn't stand the thought of Teren going through that. He looks so much like... He reminds me so much of..." She swallowed, and another blood trail left her eye. "While I never would have wished vampirism for you, I am glad that Teren won't have to live without you."

Nodding, I threw my arms around her. I didn't care if she was ready or not. *I* needed a hug. Darn emotional vampires. Halina awkwardly patted my back, while I sniffled; her body was nearly as chilly as the wind.

Pulling back, I dried my eyes. "You deserve that too. You have been alone for so long. Nicolis would wish you peace and I think Gabriel gives it to you. Doesn't he make you happy?"

She looked down, her expression guilty, but she nodded. "Yes," she whispered. "Although, we're complicated. He has his own nest, his own family. I won't leave mine, he won't leave his..." She shrugged.

I found myself cupping her cheeks. I think that surprised us both. "So your solution is nothing? Halina, he's over six hundred years old, you're just over one hundred. Think of how long he's been alone. Do you really want to end up like that? Do you really want to be alone for the next five hundred years?" I searched her face as she let out a forlorn sigh. The joint glow of our eyes lighted the space around us. "It's okay to be happy," I whispered.

She closed her eyes, then slowly nodded. I pulled her in for another hug, and this time she warmly returned it. Then, almost as if a switch had been flipped, she pulled back and narrowed her eyes at me. "Don't think we're suddenly best friends or anything." Releasing me, she crossed her arms over her chest. "I won't be braiding your hair or exchanging recipes with you anytime soon."

Eyeing me up and down, she stepped to the edge of the raised platform. I smiled as I stepped up to her. "Don't worry, I never thought that would happen."

She twisted her lips into a wry smile, then grabbed me blindingly fast and hopped off the roof. I started to scream but the motion of my stomach lifting into my throat halted any noise I might have made. She was laughing when her feet lightly hit the ground of the parking lot. She adjusted her skintight dress after setting me down. "Thank you for the conversation, but I need to go kill something now."

My eyes opened wider as I considered what she might mean by that. She shook her head though. "Relax, I don't feel like human tonight." She crouched down in a predatory way as she muttered, "I think I'll find our little cow killer."

Happy that at least the murderer dying tonight wasn't my own species, I clapped her on the back. "Have fun."

A devilish smile appeared on her lips as she glanced at me from the corner of her glowing eyes. "I always do." She streaked away, and the rush of her leaving sent a shiver down my damp back.

I was blown away by the complicated, forever teen vampire. The farther she streaked from me, the more my earlier exhaustion hit me. All I could hear were the sounds of sleeping humans so I figured I was the only one at the ranch still awake. Shuffling upstairs, I checked in on my angels. They shared a bed here and even though they were nestled around the huddled lump of Spike, they were still holding hands. Smiling, I silently closed their door and headed to my own. Yawning, I prepared for bed, then slid under the cool covers.

Nestling my back into Teren's lukewarm-from-the-tub chest, I exhaled in contentment. As Halina's comments drifted through my mind, I was immensely grateful that her fear for Teren's future wasn't happening. I didn't want him to be alone, but I really didn't like the thought of him moving on either. I wanted him like this, with me.

He sighed and clutched me to him. "I love you, Emma. A life without you…is no life at all."

I smiled in the darkness. He'd heard that entire conversation with his great-grandmother.

Chapter 5 – Grandpa Gabby

Giggling woke me up. Giggling and my feet being licked. That woke me right up. Jerking my knee forward to avoid Spike's early morning affections, I ended up smacking into Teren's unmentionables. That woke him up, too.

As the twins clambered onto our bed, Teren rolled onto his stomach. Groaning, he murmured, "Emma… I know I'm a tough vampire and all, but some things still really hurt."

Even though his voice was pained and irritated, I couldn't stop the chuckle. "I'm so sorry, babe," I laughed out loud, genuinely feeling bad, but amused by his tone.

He peeked an eye up at me; he wasn't sharing in my amusement. Nika threw herself on his back and a smile finally broke out of the tight line of his lips. "Morning, Daddy!" she yelled, chipper as could be.

He gently shushed her, then twisted around to hug her. "Good morning, sweetheart."

A shaft of light fell across the two of them, highlighting the close-knit pair. Julian crawled into the space between Teren and me, and snuggled his warm body into mine. "Hi, Mommy," he yawned. He wasn't quite as awake as his sister. I wrapped my arms around him, savoring the snugly affection of my little boy. Kissing his head, I laid my cheek on his hair and glanced at Teren tickling Nika. He met my gaze and smiled at the image of his wife and his son.

As Julian started to fall asleep again in my arms, Nika stopped giggling and looked down at him. "Julie likes that, Mommy." Curious, I studied where her eyes were watching my hand rub circles into Julian's back. I hugged him tighter, feeling more connected to him through my daughter.

"Thank you, Nika," I told her.

She smiled bright as she bounced on Teren's stomach. "Daddy, can we go help Grandpa outside?"

Teren chuckled, then halted her continuous pounding on his

body. "Of course." Raising an eyebrow, he added. "I don't think Grandpa can run this place without us."

Nika nodded and leaned down, like she was telling him a secret. "I know, Daddy. He needs our magic."

A look passed over Teren's face that I knew was grief. He knew his father was aging, they all did, but there was nothing that could be done about it. He was human, his life was finite. Teren successfully turning me had been a miracle. Gabriel had confirmed it. Most mixed turnings were fatal to the human. And Halina wouldn't bring someone into this life as a full vampire, not that Jack wanted that life. He'd made peace with his fate long ago, and while he grieved for the future loss that Alanna and Teren would have to suffer through, he had shown no desire to live for all eternity. It was sad, but it was also a part of life.

Teren's face regained its warmth as he held his daughter. Our new lives helped dull the sting of old life passing. "You're right, sweetheart. We'll go help him after breakfast, okay?"

She gave him an eager nod as she bounced on his chest again. I felt Alanna exit her room and head downstairs. Nika felt it too and she turned her head to look at the wall separating us. Twisting back to Teren, she kissed his nose. "I'ma go help Grandma." She scrambled off his body while he nodded.

I watched her skip out the door. Shaking my head at her brightness, I looked back to Teren. "She gets her morning peppiness from you, you know."

Teren, looking thoughtful as he stared out the door, blinked, then looked over at me. "What?" he asked, clearly distracted.

Carefully shifting my sleeping child to the pillows, I sat up on an elbow and placed a hand on his arm. "Hey, you okay?"

He sat up on an elbow too, then looked down at Julian resting between us. "I was just thinking about what Nika said about my dad."

His voice was quiet, speculative. Downstairs, I heard my daughter loudly proclaim her greeting to Alanna, who feigned surprise at her entrance. Cupping my husband's cheek, I brought his gaze back to mine.

"I'm sorry," I whispered, knowing that there was nothing either one of us could do about it.

He nodded in my hands. Swallowing, he added, "What you and Halina talked about last night…her being afraid to move on, her worried that I would be alone forever…" His eyes drifted to the floor, to where we could both feel his mother. "She *is* going to have that future. And I can't do anything about it."

I swallowed the sudden lump in my throat and leaned over to kiss him. "No, you can't, Teren, but that's life, baby. That is the way nature intended us to be." Pulling back, I shrugged. "Well, for humans, that is."

He looked away from me, then pulled my hand from his face. "Don't hate me for this…"

Not sure what he could possibly be referring to made tension seep into my body. "For what?"

With a sigh, he met my eyes. "I want to move with them. I want us to go to Utah."

My mouth dropped open nearly to the sheet. I stammered for something to say, but really, I was too stunned to say anything coherent. I'd just assumed that the vampires would leave without us. Truly, I hadn't even considered moving with them, not that I'd had long to think about it. I guess, since Teren and I had jobs here, and my family lived here, it had just never occurred to me that *we'd* be moving.

Teren still looked his age, and he would look his age, or close enough to it, that moving wasn't necessary yet. Staring at him though, watching him bite his lip as he watched me shuffling through my thoughts, I clearly saw the desire to leave, the conflict of being separated from his own kind. Even if Teren desperately tried to live a life of normalcy, he still needed them.

I sighed as I rested my hand on my son's back. "But…my family…?" I let that trail off, knowing I couldn't argue my family's importance over his own. There was just no way to do that.

He looked down; he understood that as well. "I know." He

peeked up. "We could visit…constantly."

I looked down to the end of the bed, where Spike had decided to rest while he waited for us to get up. "If we left, would everyone here be wiped?"

When I glanced back at him, he slowly nodded. "Yes. Not your family, of course, but everyone else…yes. They would still remember you, vaguely, but not anything about you being with me." He shrugged. "I'm sorry."

I lay back against the pillows again and tried to imagine every friend or acquaintance I knew only sort of remembering me, and probably not remembering my name. I tried to imagine leaving my mother and sister behind, only to see them on holidays and special occasions. I couldn't picture it. Being on "bed rest" had been hard enough, and that had only been a few months. A long term separation…would be painful. Feeling the tears sting my eyes, I unfairly muttered, "But your family is immortal…mine isn't."

"My dad isn't." He grimaced, like he knew it wasn't a fair argument either.

We both sighed at the same time, and I had a sudden appreciation for spouses who met and married great distances from each other's families. You pretty much had to choose which side to go over to, and there was no way to really fairly decide that.

Looking glum, he whispered, "We've always moved together…" He let that trail off as he looked away from me.

I could see the guilt there and hated that he felt that way. He shouldn't feel guilty for wanting to stay near the family he loved, the same as I shouldn't feel guilty. Pushing aside a decision that was still, at the minimum, a year away, I brought my fingers to his stubbled jaw. He looked back at me with sadness in his pale eyes.

I gave him a reassuring smile. We could work this out. The two of us being together was the most important thing anyway. Smiling even wider, I stroked his cheek. "We have time to think about it. We have time to decide what we want to do…and we'll decide together, okay?"

He smiled softly, then nodded. "Together…I like that."

I laughed. His words were reminiscent of a conversation held between us a long time ago, a conversation regarding the two miracles we'd brought into this world. He laughed with me, then leaned across Julian's body to give me a soft kiss.

Julian stirred between us; a shudder ran through him at the feel of Teren's chill. I bundled him up next to me and pushed Teren away. "Why don't you go keep your promise to your daughter, and go help your dad."

Teren's eyes flicked over my face for long seconds before he stood up. I silently watched him as he stripped off the clothes that he'd slept in, then dressed in rugged jeans and a button-up shirt. He was so damn attractive, and I wished for the millionth time that he had a cowboy hat tucked away somewhere. It would just complete the fantasy for me.

Once he was finished getting ready for the day, he leaned over and gave Julian and me a cool kiss. "We'll be outside, if you need us." He grinned, obviously eager to show his daughter the world he secretly, or maybe not so secretly, loved.

He ruffled the fur on Spike's head as he twisted to leave. "Come on, boy." Spike thumped his tail and hopped down to follow his master out of the room. Alone with a snoring toddler, I rested my cheek on his head and thought about leaving my family.

I was still thinking about it when I walked downstairs a while later with Julian in tow. His energy level now matched his boisterous sister's as he bounded into Alanna's arms when we met up with her in the kitchen. Laughing, she effortlessly picked him up. The sight of them, so similar, so perfectly natural together, made me think of my own mother, bad leg and all. Alanna turned to me as she held Julian on her hip. "You all right, dear?"

Her voice was quiet, subdued, like she knew exactly what thoughts were tumbling through my head. And I supposed she did, since she'd heard Teren's and my entire conversation. Lack of privacy was something you got used to when you were around vampires.

I shrugged. "Just torn, I guess."

Alanna rustled Julian's hair then made a bowl of cereal for him. She set it in front of a stool, beside a granite island in the center of the room, and I watched him scramble up to his breakfast.

"Don't let Teren's concerns for his father override your own," she replied.

I looked up at her, surprised that she wouldn't immediately side with her son. Surely she would want him to stay close? Noticing my reaction, she shrugged again and shook her head. "Jack will be around for several more ranch shifts. Teren has nothing to fear yet."

Her smile was sad, and I wondered for a moment if she really believed that. Forcing happiness back to her expression, she rested a cool hand on mine. "We've already done so much to you. We won't ask you to give up your life here." Her eyes flicked to the scar on my neck. A scar I tried to keep hidden with my hair, but one their super sight could see no matter what I did. The place where I'd been bitten, where my life had turned a complete one eighty.

I looked down, troubled that she felt responsible in any way for that. It really hadn't been anybody's fault. Well, except for the prick who'd actually done it. Him I blamed wholeheartedly. "Well, we haven't decided yet either way and we have time?" I peeked up at her and she nodded.

Releasing me, she went about prepping some food for her mother, tucked away in her darkened bedroom. As I watched the eternally youthful caretaker warm up a container of blood, I wondered how she'd get through the torment Halina and Imogen had both suffered. I wished beyond anything that I could spare her that pain.

"Alanna…will you be all right?"

When she looked back at me, her timeless eyes seemed worn. "Of course, Emma." She turned, leaned her back against the counter, and let her gaze wander outside to where I could hear Jack whistling a soft tune while he worked.

The edges of her lips curled into a small smile. "He's the love of my life. He's given me so much joy and happiness. He accepted me for what I was because he loved me. He let go of every friend he'd ever had to be with me. He deals with the gossip of being called a cradle robber, every time we start up somewhere new. He watches me kill. He watches me drink blood. And he watches me stay young…while he ages."

Her eyes came back to mine; soft pink tears were in them. "And he does it all without complaint, because he loves me, and he doesn't want to be apart from me." She shook her head, and the tears fell from her eyes. "He is my everything and I will take each day that I have with him, each memory that we make together, and I will cherish him for all eternity, whether he's beside me or not."

She shrugged while I sniffled. "But I won't condemn him to Halina's life, nor does he wish to be condemned. I will respect his wishes, by letting him die. In the end, that is the best way that I can repay him for the sacrifices that he has made for me over the years."

I nodded, hating that I understood. A part of me wanted them to be together forever, like Teren and I would be. But Jack was happy as a human, and he wished to stay that way. Alanna wouldn't have him changed for her own selfish reasons, and she was right, being with vampires was sometimes a sacrifice. I could see that as I contemplated my own future. Jack had already given her so much, and all he'd asked in return was a normal, typical death. While sad and horrible, it was also the cycle we all lived by, even long-lived vampires, eventually must die.

Walking up to the woman, I engulfed her in a warm hug. "You will never be alone, Alanna. We will never let you be alone."

I pulled back from her, and my cheeks were disastrously wet. She smiled as she wiped them dry. "I know." Inhaling deep, she glanced over at an oblivious Julian. "My family is what makes it okay for me to let him go."

The blood warming on the stove filled the air with a warm, refreshing scent. It was better than cinnamon on a chilly day. Alanna smiled as she poured some into a thermos for Imogen. "And I *will* let him go…just not today." She winked at me and then turned to go take care of her mother.

I shook my head in awe as I watched her walk out of the room. The women in Teren's family continuously blew me away.

A few days later, when we were back at home, Alanna's words

were still tumbling through my mind. Even though I had an ample amount of time to decide, I was torn over which direction to take my life. Thinking of everything that Jack had sacrificed for Alanna, willingly, without complaint, made it feel a little selfish to do anything other than give Teren exactly what he wanted.

But I couldn't really compare the situations. Jack might have had no better option to him than his life with Alanna. Maybe what she deemed a sacrifice really wasn't one in his eyes. Mentally, I made a note to sit and talk with Jack. Even though he wasn't the type to open up with his feelings, he'd surely have some insight for me on life with a vampire spouse.

As time went on, I thought to talk to Teren about it again, but Teren didn't seem to want to think about it again yet. No, Teren had started to fixate on something else entirely.

"So, what do you want to do?"

I sighed as I set my mammoth bag on the couch. Julian and Nika immediately started going through it. Watching Nika grab my cell phone and start to pretend that she was talking to Julian on it, I said to Teren. "Why do we have to do anything? Can't we just have a quiet night in?"

He smirked and walked up to me while I pouted. Slinging his arms around my waist, he shook his head. "You only turn thirty once, we should celebrate in style." He ducked down to meet my eye. "We could get that overnight sitter?"

His attempt to get me alone for a while made me smile, but then I shook my head. "I think, just this once, I'd rather have a quiet night at home with you and the kids. Maybe watch a movie?"

Teren chuckled, then pulled me into his body. "All right. I guess I should cancel the clowns and pony rides."

Nika dropped my phone and stared up at us starry-eyed. "A pony?"

Julian peeked up too, but he had a frown on his face. "No clowns, Daddy." Clowns came with balloons, so naturally Julian didn't like either one. He brightened instantly as he asked, "Can we have a pony?" Then both kids were wrapped around our ankles begging for horses.

Teren laughed and I poked him in the chest. Some things you just didn't say around kids. "Pony" was one of those things. Looking down at the twins, I sighed. "No, Daddy was teasing, nobody is getting a pony."

They both groaned in unison, and still chuckling, Teren said, "Sorry, guys, no ponies this year."

They groaned again, then twisted to storm off upstairs. Teren tightened his grip on me and whispered in my ear, "I might still get the bouncy house though." He gave me a devilish smile as he said it and my heart beat just a smidge faster.

From upstairs, I heard, "Yeah, bouncy house!" I rolled my eyes and sighed again. Darn super ears.

Teren laughed and was about to respond when we both stopped and tilted our heads. A car was crunching to a stop in our half circle drive. Our house was well spaced from our neighbors' homes, so it was pretty easy to tell when someone was pulling into our drive. Thinking it was my sister, I smacked Teren on the arm and disengaged myself.

As I started walking to the door, I heard a voice I knew pretty well, a voice that did not belong to my sister. "Ugh, I hate San Francisco…it stinks of salt."

Wondering what Starla was doing here, I walked over to the door and immediately opened it. In front of me was the blonde, spoiled, princess of a vampire, who Teren and I tolerated with as much grace as possible. Starla had been the one to find us when we'd both needed her the most, so we sort of owed her.

"Hi, Starla," I said.

Smacking on an annoyingly loud piece of gum, she popped off her bug-like sunglasses as she brushed by me to walk into the house. "Hi-ya," she replied.

I was just about to ask her what she was doing all the way up here, when the door on her BMW opened. My jaw dropped open when Gabriel stepped out of the car. It wasn't that I was shocked that he was here—Gabriel came up a couple of times a month to see

Halina and visit with the kids. But seeing him here, in broad daylight, was a little disorienting.

"Good afternoon, Emma." He walked up to me, imposing, powerful, and extraordinarily beautiful. His emerald eyes glinted in the sunlight; they seemed more like jewels than eyes in that moment.

"Good afternoon, Gabriel," I stammered back, looking up at the sky.

Gabriel was in Alanna's generation. He could tolerate small doses of rays, but not hours of it. When he did visit, he always made the long drive at night. Tinted windows, while effective in blocking out the harmful effects of the sun for humans, just weren't enough for vampiric skin. Some of them preferred the privacy and mystery of dark glass, but really, it was just aesthetics for them.

I felt Teren walking over to me while I heard Starla plop down on our couch, making herself at home in our home. "You guys have cable?" she called out. Ignoring her, I fixated on the ancient mixed vampire in my doorway.

"Gabriel?" Teren asked, extending a hand to him. "We're honored to have you, but...how are you here during the day?"

He looked up at the sky too, and Gabriel chuckled at the both of us. Smiling languidly, he indicated our house through the open door. "It is bright out here. May I come in?" he politely asked.

I felt myself flush, irritated at myself for not immediately letting him in. Gabriel wasn't as self welcoming as Starla. "Of course, please, come inside."

Both of his feet had barely hit our threshold before he was practically tackled by two tiny beings.

"Grandpa Gabby!"

Nika and Julian each attached to a leg while I closed the door behind him. The children had shortened his name early on. They spoke well for their age, or so I was told, but Gabriel was a mouthful, even for our precocious little miracles. Gabriel found the nickname charming and never corrected them.

A wide smile on his handsome face, he ran an ageless, lineless hand through their hair. "Teren, Emma…my, how you've shrunk."

The twins giggled and looked up at him. "No, it's us, Grandpa Gabby."

He squatted down to their level; genuine happiness was on his face. He might be scientifically curious about our children, but he cared for them too. "Well, so it is. Nika and Julian. You look so much like your parents, I didn't recognize you."

I heard Starla on the couch sigh as she started flipping through television stations. She wasn't much for coming up here, since the drive was a long one. She also had a decidedly snobbish view of her home town, and saw just about everywhere else as being beneath it, although, she did like our home in San Francisco much better than the dirt-filled ranch.

Ignoring Starla's barely contained displeasure, I watched Gabriel as he scooped up a child in each arm. He was eyeing them closely, like he was mentally tallying their weight, height, and general health. Looking outside at the bright, early-evening sunshine, I again wondered how he'd managed to come up all this way. As our group walked into the living room, Teren asked him that very thing.

"How did you make it all the way up here, Gabriel?" He shook his head as he took a seat on the couch. Gabriel plopped down with his arms still loaded up with giggling toddlers. "Aren't you in pain?" Teren asked softly, not wanting the question to bother the kids too much.

Gabriel smiled at Nika bouncing on his knee and answered Teren's question to her. "Well, I discovered something…neat, and I decided to test it out." Nika giggled at the word neat, and Starla tore her eyes from the mindless program she'd found and raised an eyebrow at him. Gabriel was well over a half century old and some words just sounded really strange coming from his mouth.

Teren and I looked at each other while Julian repeated, "Neat."

Curious, I asked, "You discovered something?"

Gabriel ran a hand back through his light, sandy-brown hair. Smiling, he nodded. "Yes, a compound that blocks the effects of the sun." He shifted the children off his legs and leaned over his knees, going into teacher mode. His face animated, he started telling us the specifics of what his brilliant mind had conjured up.

Splaying his hands out over his knees, he said, "I've been working on a way for early generation mixed to enjoy a more normal life. None of us should have to hide from the sun." Gabriel's lips twisted into a sad smile. For a moment, all of his vast years were apparent on his face. He'd had to do a great deal of hiding throughout his life.

Now that the kids were no longer the center of Gabriel's attention, they started climbing over Starla. She groaned, but did nothing to stop them from snuggling in her lap.

Before I could ask Gabriel just what he'd created, he told me. "I made a breakthrough in a compound that I've been struggling with. I bonded it with glass and had it installed in Starla's car." He smiled as he glanced out our window. "The sun would normally have me needing a break from it after several minutes," he looked back at us, "but I was in it for hours, protected under the coated glass, and I didn't feel any hint of the pain that I would have normally felt."

Obviously pleased with himself, he smiled in a satisfactory way as he leaned back on the couch. Nika abandoned Starla to nestle into his side and he ran a hand over her tiny shoulders.

Teren next to me shook his head. "That's amazing, Gabriel. Can you do the same thing for full vampires?" I saw a gleam of hope in his eyes that maybe his great-grandmother could finally get to see what she'd longed to for so long.

Gabriel's smile faded as he looked over Teren's eager face. Slowly, he shook his head. "I'm sorry, Teren. Believe me, I would like to give that gift to them, too." He smiled with one side of his mouth. "I've recently had a certain...personal desire to see that happen." Sighing, he shook his head. "But a full vampire's physiology is so different and complex. I just haven't been able to successfully create a coating strong enough for purebloods." He shrugged with a smile on his lips. "It is on my to-do list though."

That made me laugh. Gabriel's to-do list probably involved things that most humans wouldn't ever accomplish in their lifetime, even the most brilliant humans on earth. Aside from the fact that

Gabriel was a genius and wouldn't ever naturally die, so time wasn't really a factor, I was pretty sure that he'd have completed everything on his list anyway. He was just determined like that.

Gabriel watched my face for a second, then shifted his emerald eyes to Teren. "I've created enough to have your parents' home refitted with the new glass, so your family will feel more at ease there. Especially your grandmother. Imogen shouldn't have to hide in just a few tiny bedrooms. People should feel comfortable in their own homes."

Teren's mouth parted in surprise, and I swear his eyes watered. I was pretty shocked too, and for a split-second, I wondered if Gabriel had done that out of compassion for the first-generation mixed, or if some part of him looked at Imogen as a step-daughter.

Reaching out, Teren clasped his arm. "Thank you. I...my family..." He looked over at me, then back to Gabriel. "We just can't thank you enough for what you've given us."

Starla snorted and popped her gum, but Gabriel ignored her as he focused on the two of us instead. When Julian gave up on Starla as well, preferring to snuggle with Grandpa Gabriel too, he looked down on the twins. "I'm sure you'll find some way to repay me," he quietly said.

The inquisitive look in his eyes was unsettling, but I pushed back the pang of fear in my belly. Gabriel would never hurt our children and even though he might be monitoring them, he would never test them without our permission. Halina would have his head if he did.

Finding comfort in the teenage vixen's protective nature, I asked Gabriel, "Why is the sun harmful to vampires anyway? I've never understood that." That one myth had always seemed a little odd to me. What about being undead made the sun off limits?

Gabriel looked up from where my kids were listening to his silent chest. His face returning to scientific impartialness, he asked, "Have you ever heard of Solar Urticaria?"

Frowning, I looked over at Teren. He was frowning too. "Um...no."

Gabriel smiled, like he wasn't surprised. "That is understandable.

It is rare for humans." He leaned forward again; the kids on either side of him mimicked his posture. "It is a condition in which exposure to ultraviolet radiation, and in some, even rarer cases, any form of light, induces a case of hives all over the skin."

He spread his hands out. Julian and Nika mimed the motion. "All pureblood vampires suffer from a form of this condition…but a hundred times over the human variation. To them, any exposure is fatal. The irritation ignites the skin." He shrugged, and my kids followed suit. Starla looked over at them with amusement on her lips. Gabriel smiled, then continued, "In mixed, the effects are diluted, and usually fade by the third generation. In first, it is the most severe, causing immense pain and discomfort, even from indirect light. In second, like myself, the sun can be tolerated in small doses."

He leaned back, watching his tiny copycats as he did so. Smiling at them, he added, "Much like with the human version of this condition, no one truly understands why." A small smile was on his lips as he shook his head. "The body, vampiric or otherwise, is a miraculous and complicated thing." He smiled wider. "Solving that puzzle is also on my to-do list."

I laughed a little as I leaned into Teren's side, both grateful that neither he nor I, nor our children, suffered from the rare trait that the other vampires did; it pushed us all that much closer to the normal end of the spectrum. Watching Gabriel take a moment to explain to the children how their hearts worked to pump their slow-moving human blood, I was also grateful that the vampiric community had this brilliant man among them, striving to solve their limitations.

Looking out our wall of windows that faced the Pacific Ocean, offering a sunset to die for, no pun intended, I also considered the flip side of Gabriel's research. If he did succeed in blocking limitations for vampires, they would be more prevalent among the human race. And the human race, like it or not, was right at the top of their dinner menu. A shudder ran through me, but I was warmed by the idea that the vial that was keeping me alive had been a five hundred year project for Gabriel. It could be several centuries before vampires roamed free under the sun, maybe a few millennia even.

Gabriel and Starla stayed until the magnificent sunset filled the living room windows. They sat on the couch and talked with us while we all enjoyed a plasma nightcap. Starla winced over our blood choice, preferring wild animals to "tame" mindless cattle, but Gabriel sipped his respectfully, while asking our kids a wide variety of questions.

He fixated most on their ability to feel each other, asking one child what the other liked or disliked. When Julian would heatedly tell him that Nika hated broccoli, Gabriel would smile and shake his head, amazed by the connection that they shared. It made me a little uneasy, watching him run a mini-experiment right in front of me, but he wasn't hurting or bothering them with the questions, so I let it continue.

Once the sun was nearly extinguished from the sky, he rose. Starla rose with him, muttering, "Finally." Gabriel raised a pale eyebrow at her, his face stone-like in its disapproval. She instantly bowed her head. It was a little submissive for my taste and the feminist side of me wanted to tell Starla not to do that. He might be her elder, but he wasn't her master. The L.A. group all deferred to Gabriel though, calling him Father. And even though Starla could be stubborn and childish at times, she clearly worshipped the man and knew her place. I had the horrible feeling that if he commanded her to kneel and kiss his feet, she would.

He didn't, though. He only turned away from her silent chastisement and gave us a warm smile. I let the knowledge of his power fade as I shook his hand. He wasn't one to abuse his position. He never insisted on people calling him Father, he never asked for adulation. All he seemed to ask for from those around him was a level of respect, for him and for others. The odd cult-like glorification seemed to come more from his followers, than from Gabriel himself.

The world was lucky that Gabriel didn't desire it. Given the proper incentive, I was sure this powerful mixed vampire could do just about anything.

Clasping Teren's hand, he warmly said, "It's been a pleasure speaking with you again, Teren. I always look forward to our visits."

Teren smiled as he returned the firm shake. "As do I, Gabriel."

Gabriel shifted to me, and his eyes ran up and down my body. It wasn't sexual in any way, he was merely a doctor surveying the health of his patient. Cocking an eyebrow at me, he asked, "Any side effects from your daily dosage?"

Knowing that he meant the life-giving shot I gave myself in the hip each day, I shook my head. "No, I feel great." I patted my chest, over my heart. "All is well." He nodded at hearing my heartbeat, not looking surprised by my answer.

Starla shifted impatiently, obviously eager to leave what she clearly considered a dump. Knowing that Gabriel wouldn't leave the city without dropping by the ranch to see Halina, I bit my cheek to hide my smile. I had to imagine that Starla would be doing a lot of sighing and eye rolling this evening. That was the price you paid when you chauffeured your father around.

Nika and Julian started to yawn as their long days caught up with them, but they stubbornly clutched Gabriel's legs. "Stay, Grandpa," Nika whined.

Julian immediately chimed in with, "Stay, Grandpa, stay."

Gabriel smiled and rumpled their hair. "I wish I could, children, but your grandmother is waiting for me." He raised his eyebrows as he stared down at our miniatures before him. "I wouldn't want to disappoint her, now would I?"

Sighing, both children finally let him go. They whispered soft goodbyes that almost had a tearful tone to them. I scooped them each up in an arm, the weight almost unnoticeable with my strength, and kissed each soft head.

Gabriel smiled at them, then he and Starla both headed to the door. Starla looked like she wanted to blur right through it. Teren and I said our goodbyes again, our children softly mimicking us, and Gabriel paused with his hand on the doorknob. Looking back at us, he locked his gaze on Teren.

"Before I forget, Halina had me looking into finding someone for you. She was a little difficult to locate, living in a rather isolated rural area, but I did and I've sent her to you." He looked up at the sky, almost like he was searching for this person in the minute cracks of our ceiling. Dropping his gaze back to Teren, he shrugged. "Assuming all went well, she should be getting on a plane sometime this evening."

Teren's brows drew into a point. Mine did, too. I had no idea who he was talking about. Teren, following my mental path, asked, "Who are you talking about?"

Gabriel straightened as he released the door. Starla sighed, her perfectly styled, chunky-haired head falling backwards with a light groan.

Ignoring her, Gabriel took a step towards us. "Miss Davids...Carrie. I found her, and had her sent to you."

My heartbeat increased as that name passed his ancient lips. Teren instinctively reached out for me, his arm encircling my waist. I hadn't heard that name in a while, and the shock of it still stung a little. Not that there was anything wrong with the woman herself—I'd only met her once, and she'd been perfectly pleasant about the whole thing—but she had an intimate history with my husband. A history that she still remembered. She remembered everything about him, right down to the pale eyes, dark hair, and love of writing. No one was allowed to remember my husband that clearly, but because he'd hidden her from his family, she did. And he'd hidden her...because he'd knocked her up. It still surprised me sometimes that Teren had almost been a teen father.

We'd struggled to conceive in time and he'd already successfully done it once. But she'd lost the baby and they'd split apart. The part of me that could look at the situation objectively saw how much the entire incident had hurt Teren. He'd lost the first love of his life because she'd been stolen away from him. They'd never really had their moment of closure, just a tragedy that hadn't ended well for either of them. I think that was the real reason Teren wanted to find her; he wanted closure. And he wanted to tell her the truth about what he was. Before he had her mind wiped of all trace of him, he wanted to finally confess what he had hidden from her for so long. He needed that moment of release, and I was going to let him have it.

While I watched the emotion slide over Teren's face, I thought about Gabriel finding her. Then I thought about his last comment. Shifting my gaze back to where Gabriel was intently watching Teren, I asked, "What do you mean, you had her 'sent' to us?" How exactly does one send a person?

Gabriel's perfectly green eyes swung to me. "I had her compelled to go to Teren." His gaze returned to Teren. "You did need to see her, correct?"

Teren nodded, then frowned. "You had her compelled? By a vampire?"

Gabriel nodded, like it was no different than having takeout delivered by a restaurant. "Yes. I knew one in the area, and had him pay her a visit."

Teren stepped forward, concern clear in his features. "A visit?"

Gabriel furrowed his brows and crossed his arms over his chest. "He was under instruction not to harm her, if that is your concern." Gabriel almost seemed offended that Teren would even consider that possibility.

Teren shook his head but Gabriel beat him to it. "The vampire was a friend, and trustworthy. I told him to send her to your address as soon as possible." His eyes swept down to the children laying their heads on my shoulders, both nearly asleep as I held them. "I did not think you would want to fly to the northeast corner of Maine." He looked between the both of us with inquisitive eyes. "I suppose I could have her turned around, if you'd rather go to her?" He tilted his head. "Perhaps I could watch the kids for you…while you're gone?"

Starla popped a bubble, breaking the sudden tension in the air. Gabriel twisted his lips, then held his hand out to her. She sighed, but immediately put her gum in his palm. Teren shook his head. "No, no, she's already on her way." He put on a strained smile. "I'm just…shocked, I guess. You caught me by surprise, that's all."

Gabriel relaxed his position and nodded. Smiling, he said, "Well, I wouldn't worry about her safety. I can nearly guarantee that she wasn't harmed in any way." Nodding at us, he twisted to open the door. "Enjoy the remainder of your evening, Teren…Emma."

Fixated on the word "nearly," I nodded and unthinkingly said, "You too, Gabriel."

A wry smile lit his beautiful face. "Thank you, Emma. I plan on a very…enjoyable evening."

I flushed when I remembered exactly where he was going.

Gabriel chuckled as he exited our home, taking the complaining Starla with him.

Chapter 6 – Letting Go

Teren checked the flight times between Maine and California after we put the kids to bed. There was nothing direct, and with multiple layovers, and the hour or so flight from L.A. to San Francisco, the earliest she could show up was six or seven in the morning. But we really didn't know how long the vampire Gabriel sent would take to find her and compel her. And we didn't know if he'd told her to go home first and get some stuff, or if he'd just run into her on the street and told her to leave town. Hopefully the man was nice enough that he let her make some arrangements before she left. I'd feel really guilty if she lost her job because some vampire compelled her to haul up and abandon her responsibilities.

Teren wasn't happy that she had been "forced" into making such an arduous trip, but now that she was on her way, he was ready to get this over with. I suppose he was probably curious about her too. While I'd briefly met her a few years ago, when I was pregnant, Teren hadn't seen her since high school. He was anxious to put this piece of his past behind him, yet he was dreading it too. What he had to talk about with Carrie wouldn't be easy for him, or her. The meeting was going to be an emotional one, I was pretty sure of that.

Sighing, he snapped his computer shut and tossed it on a chair. "It would be nice to know exactly what flight she was on, so we could meet her at the airport. I wish Gabriel had just told me that he'd found her instead of ordering someone to collect her. I could have made arrangements, given her time to request a vacation, paid for her plane ticket. I mean, what if she loses her job over this? I'd feel awful…"

I rolled over onto my side, and placed a hand on his stomach; the muscles under his shirt were tense, even relaxing in bed. "It will be okay, Teren. Whatever Gabriel had to do to get her here, we can fix it later. We can even get her job back for her, if we need to." If a vampire could compel her to up and leave her job without any warning, then the least they could do was compel her boss to take her back when she returned. Hopefully Gabriel's vampire friend had already thought of that.

Teren looked over at me with apologetic eyes. "I'm sorry you have to go through this."

I sat up on my elbow. The long strands of my hair curved around my arm and he reached up to stroke one; I could hear the hair sliding along his skin. "You're sorry for me? Why? This is going to be hard on you...not me."

His eyes searched my face. I could see the guilt in his features as I stroked my thumb over his shirt. "The first woman that I ever slept with, a woman that I accidentally got pregnant, is about to walk into our home and sit down at our dinner table. I can't imagine that you're thrilled about that."

Pulling back, I twisted my lips. "Well, when you put it like that."

He turned his head from me and flopped his arm over his eyes. "Exactly. I'm asking too much of you."

Turning his face back to me, I removed his arm from his eyes. "I was joking. I know what this means for you, how difficult it is. I'm not going to let some petty jealousy stop me from being there to support you."

Shaking his head, he relaxed back onto his pillows. "I'm still sorry. I should have taken care of this years ago, before I met you."

My hand drifted to his chest, lingering on his silent heart. "Yes, you should have." He frowned and I quickly added, "But I understand why you didn't." Sliding close to him, I brushed the hair from his forehead. He smiled and slipped a cool arm around my waist. "You wanted someone important in your life to remember what you had together. That's very...human of you."

He smiled wider as he pulled on my back. "You're all I need, Emma. You're the only one I need to remember me."

Grinning, I lowered myself to his lips. He immediately shifted into I-want-sex mode. Gently grabbing my head, he angled me so our kiss was a heated one, then his other hand ran down over my backside and squeezed. I wrapped my legs around him, and he groaned when my hips pressed into his side. Then he shifted my body and pulled me on top of him. His breath heavier, he muttered, "God, I love you."

His hands pulled my ready body into his ready body and I

groaned. Hearing the breathy sounds of slumber coming down the hall turned me on even more. I wouldn't need to tone this down quite as much with our super-hearing children asleep. Grinding my hips into his, I mumbled, "I could never forget you. I *will* never forget you, husband."

We panted as we simulated what we were both yearning for, and a light whimper escaped his lips. Frantically pulling down the light sleep shorts I was wearing, he whispered, "Emma, I want you, right now."

Hearing the desperation in his voice, I helped him slide off my underwear. Not even bothering to shut off the light on his nightstand, we pulled off his pants and I settled myself over him. The word "please" passed his lips as his eyes closed in anticipation. Watching his face, I lowered myself onto him. I groaned with relief when his coolness filled me. Even after all this time, it was still an incredible sensation. And so was my heat closing around him.

The desperation in his face relaxed, once we were connected. The rigidness in his muscles relaxed as well. I leaned over his body as we began moving together. His eyes still closed, his face euphoric, his hands clenched and released my hips at a steadily increasing pace. Understanding what he was silently requesting, I matched my hips to his rhythm, clenching him internally as I did.

His head dropped back and he made a noise that I hoped our sleeping children didn't hear. Attaching my lips to his neck, I whispered, "You like that, baby?" His only response was a quickly sucked in breath through his teeth. I let out my own groan that I *prayed* our little angels couldn't hear.

Feeling my husband's need beneath me made me feel even more connected to him. It was like our bodies weren't separate forms, working together for a common goal. No, for that moment we seemed like one body. That feeling got especially intense when his hands came up my back and clutched me to him. I wrapped my arms and legs around him, and held him just as hard. Then we both buried our faces in the other's necks and cried out in unison as we came together.

Like most things with Teren, it was intense and emotional, and it made me feel like everything was going to be okay, because we had each other.

Softly panting into his friction-warmed body, I listened for any noise from down the hall. Not hearing anything out of the ordinary, I smiled and kissed his neck. I left my legs wrapped around him as I slid over to his side. A content smile was on his face, as he peeked over at me. "I love you. Thank you."

"You don't have to thank me for that, Teren," I said with a soft kiss.

He shook his head and tucked some loose strands of my hair behind my ear. "I'm not thanking you for sex, although, that was pretty amazing." I rolled my eyes and he laughed. His expression softening, he murmured, "I'm thanking you for being so understanding...about Carrie. I don't think most women would be so gracious about their husband's ex."

I kissed him again, loving how my enhanced senses could pinpoint the very flavor of his skin. "I just understand *you*." He smiled as he held our faces together. I smiled at the peace I saw on him. Shrugging, I added, "Besides, I haven't told you all of my skeletons."

"You have skeletons?" He grinned at me in such a way that I nearly wanted to crawl on top of him again.

Placing my lips against his, I murmured, "I have a myriad of secrets that you don't know about."

He chuckled against my lips. "I'm intrigued...do tell."

I smiled, then sighed. "Well, I never told you about the gang member that I dated briefly. Or the package that he had me take to a friend of his in Vegas, which I'm pretty sure held some illegal stuff in it." I twisted my lips and shrugged. Yeah, that relationship hadn't exactly been wise...or long lasted.

He pulled back, surprised. "You were a drug runner?"

I laughed at how he made it sound. "Only once. I broke up with him after that little trip."

Shaking his head, he pulled my body flush to his. "Interesting, anything else?"

Biting my lip, I looked down at his chest. "I actually did have a pregnancy scare once." His arms tightened and I looked back up at his emotionless face. I had to imagine that if he still had a heartbeat, it would be racing. I shook my head to reassure him. "I never was. I was just a lot later than usual."

I frowned as he relaxed in my arms. "The ass freaked out when I told him, told me I'd done it on purpose." Teren narrowed his eyes, obviously irritated at my jerk of an ex too. "I dumped him and my period started the next day…go figure." I laughed, and he finally smiled at me.

Shaking his head, he shrugged. "You dated a lot more interesting people than I did. Mine mainly ran away screaming, once I told them the truth."

I raised my eyebrows. "Did you really tell them all?"

His face turned serious. "After Carrie, I made sure that they all knew, as early as I felt I could tell them." Looking down, he sighed. "After that mess, I was scared of girls for a while. I didn't date again until college." Peeking up at me, he smiled. "I think my family thought I didn't even like girls at one point."

I chuckled and ran a finger along the rough length of his jaw. "Who was the lucky girl who got you dating again?"

Smiling, he rested back on his pillows; his finger absentmindedly traced random patterns into my skin. "Her name was Gwen. We met on campus when she asked me directions to her class." He laughed lightly at his memory, staring up at our ceiling. "I had no idea where it was, but I faked it so I could talk to her."

I grinned, as I imagined a younger version of my husband trying to impress a girl. "Did you ever find her class?"

Swinging his eyes back to mine, he shook his head. "No, and we spent so long looking for it that she missed the class anyway." He shrugged. "We ended up having lunch instead."

Watching my charming husband smile at me, I thought that maybe Gwen had done *that* intentionally. I know I would have lied and blown off a class to spend an afternoon with him. "Cute. What happened with her?"

His smile faltered. "We dated for a few months...then she wanted to move into my dorm." He looked back up at the ceiling, the memory of that moment clearly not as pleasant as their first meeting. "I couldn't...without telling her first, so I did."

He pressed his lips into a firm line, and his jaw tightened. "And?" I asked, my fingers running over the curve of his arm.

He let out a soft sigh. "She ran out crying...I never saw her again. I told Great-Gran it was over and she...handled it."

I frowned at the pensive expression on his face. "I'm sorry."

He shrugged. "She wasn't the right one for me. I knew I couldn't be with someone who couldn't accept what I was, and she was only the first in a long line of girls who couldn't handle the truth." Pulling me tight, his mood lightened. "Only you handled it well." He smiled wryly. "I definitely never got to have sex with any of *them* once they knew the truth."

I smiled as I remembered the evening that he'd first told me what he was. I might have been a little...eager to be with him. Well, he was the most attractive person I'd ever seen...inside and out. "Was I the only one you told by piercing my tongue with your teeth?"

He closed his eyes and shook his head. "God, that was embarrassing. I thought it was too soon to tell you the truth. I had no idea what to tell you. I was so frazzled, I couldn't even pull my teeth back up in time." I laughed at the memory and he peeked his eyes open.

He cupped my cheek, and the cool metal of his wedding band rubbed against me, caressing me. "Yes. You were the only one who so absorbed me, I couldn't even concentrate on the one thing that was as natural to me as breathing. I couldn't pretend with you. That's how much you affect me."

I swallowed, feeling my face heat. Smiling at the color he saw there, he nestled his head in my hair. "Well...since we're having the exes discussion, I should probably tell you that I did date a vampire once."

Instantly remembering a conversation with Alanna about a

couple of visiting female vampires, I pushed him away from me. "I knew it! You did let that woman bite you!" Hearing my children stir in their beds, I quieted my voice. "Didn't you?"

His eyes widened as he stared at me. "You…know about that?"

I smirked and narrowed my eyes. "Yes, your mother mentioned it once."

He closed his eyes, then started to chuckle. "Ugh, God, I bet most men don't have to worry about their families discussing their sex lives." Peeking over at my serious expression, he shrugged. "Just once…a tiny, tiny bite." I narrowed my eyes and he grimaced. "I was curious, surely you can understand that?"

My lips curved into a small smile at the look on his face. We'd been through too much together for me to feel any jealousy over his past experiences. Besides, being a vampire now, and understanding the thrill of biting, I could see how he would be curious about what being bitten felt like. I probably would have done the same thing if I'd been in his position. Raising an eyebrow, I calmly asked, "Did you bite her? Was she better tasting than me?"

My lips twitched as I tried to contain my amusement; I already knew I was his first. Seeing the humor in my face, he pushed me to my back and hovered over me. "No one could possibly taste better than you." His eyes drifted down my body and I had the distinct feeling that he wasn't talking about my blood anymore. A different sort of flush washed over me. Sensing it, he smiled.

As his fingers slid up my ribs, pushing up my shirt, I closed my eyes. "And no, you are the only woman I've ever penetrated. The only one I ever will penetrate." He husked into my ear.

My breath picked up pace, and I ran my hands up his back, taking off his shirt. "Did you like her teeth in you?" I asked, curious if he enjoyed the sensation as much as I did.

Settling himself on me, his lips started trailing down my body. Peeking down at him as he glanced up at me, I watched the desire building in the pale depth of his eyes. Shaking his head, he whispered, "No, I didn't really care for it…until you. I definitely never asked for it before you."

He gave me a cocky smile, and his fangs slid out. Groaning, I muttered his name. Then I shut the light off and forgot all about our exes, vampiric or otherwise.

The next morning, I kissed Teren goodbye as I left for work. He'd decided to stay home with the kids, just in case Carrie showed up at the house. I hoped for his sake that she arrived later, so Halina could be on hand to instantly wipe her. And, later, so I could be there, too. I really didn't relish the idea of him entertaining his ex all day long.

I pushed it out of my head when I got to work though. He would be a perfect gentleman to Carrie if she did show up before I got home. And I knew without a shadow of a doubt that he would be faithful to me. Unlike with some marriages, the question of either one of us straying wasn't an issue. We were eternal, bonded through blood. No one on this earth could break that connection. But I did want to be there, for support, if nothing else.

Wishing I could make time blur as quickly as I could, I almost bumped into Tracey. The perky blonde grabbed my shoulders in excitement. "Get a babysitter for Saturday night. Ben and I are taking you out for your birthday."

I contained my groan. "Oh, really, I don't feel like making a fuss over this one. I just want a relaxing weekend with Teren and the kids."

She raised an eyebrow at me, her perfect lips shifting to a pout. "That is no way to celebrate turning thirty." Crossing her arms over her chest, she shook her head. "Ben and I are taking you to a club and getting you sweaty and drunk. *That* is how you ring in a new decade."

I sighed and thought to argue with her, but I could hear my boss mutter something about a report that was missing from a file. Knowing I needed to take care of that, I rolled my eyes at Tracey. "Whatever, Trace. We'll talk about it later, okay?"

Giggling, she spun on her heel. I sighed inside, knowing I was most likely going to a club for my birthday and not leaving that club until I was smashed.

Throughout the day I checked on Teren. I even texted him right in front of Clarice, since she couldn't bitch about those sorts of things to me anymore. Every time, Teren instantly responded, telling me that she hadn't shown yet. By lunch, he started getting anxious about her safety. I did my best to reassure him that she was fine, but I really wasn't sure. We didn't know this vampire that Gabriel had sent to collect her and, trustworthy or not, something easily could have gone wrong.

By the end of my work day, when she still hadn't shown, I imagined that I could sense my husband pacing. I couldn't, the distance between us kept his location more generalized—I knew what direction he was in, but until we reconnected, I wouldn't be able to feel the pacing. But I was pretty sure that was what I would be feeling when I got home—endless pacing.

That was confirmed when I pulled into the drive. His form was blurring from upstairs to downstairs and back again. I frowned that he was using so much of his super-speed around our children. We generally tried to lead them by example. In fact, I could feel them starting and stopping with their own phasing movement as they copied him.

Slamming shut my door, so he'd break out of his cycle and realize that I was home, I muttered, "Stop that...calm down." I felt his presence pause downstairs; our twins paused with him.

Over the mutual giggle of our children, who were apparently enjoying their game with Daddy, I heard him sigh and sheepishly mutter, "Sorry...I'm just concerned. I needed to burn off some energy."

Inhaling deeply, I smiled as I walked to the front door. The sense of homecoming that happened whenever I started to head in his direction crashed over me. Hoping the euphoria that I was feeling would further calm my husband, I opened the door. He was standing right there, smiling at me so warmly, that I knew he'd finally let our bond distract him from his worry.

Amid the joint shouts of, "Mommy!" he walked over to me, wrapped his arms around me, and exhaled with relief. While a twin each grabbed a leg, I wrapped my arms around him. My sigh was equally content. Into my hair he muttered, "I love it when you come home."

Pulling back to look at him, I was glad that I could give him such comfort just by approaching him. Cupping his cheek, I stroked the coarseness of his jaw with my thumb. "And I love coming home to you." I took about five more seconds to relish the completion of our bond, then my children demanded my attention, and I let him go.

Laughing, I scooped up the tiny beings trying to crawl their way up my legs. Teren started to close the door behind me, then paused. The breathing that he mimicked so seamlessly that I sometimes forgot he didn't have to do it anymore, completely stopped. Hugging and kissing my children, I twisted to look at him. He was frozen at the door, staring outside, one hand still on the frame, like he'd been struck immobile halfway through the process of shutting it.

"Teren, what is it?" I asked. Then I heard the sound that he was hearing and my breath stopped. Walking over to the door, I watched a yellow and black checked taxi cab approach our house. Even though it wasn't, the car seemed to be driving in slow motion.

Forcing an exhale from my body, I set down our kids and told them they could watch a movie in Mommy and Daddy's room. They gleefully took off to go jump on our bed with Spike. Turning back to Teren, still watching the cab, I put a hand on his shoulder. With a small, apologetic smile, he looked over at me.

Knowing he felt guilty about every aspect of this, I laced our hands together as I stood in the doorway with him. Maybe it was all in my head, but it seemed like there was a lot of tension in the air. Teren had put off doing this for a really long time.

Looking back to the driveway, we both watched the cab crunch to a stop behind my cheery, yellow car. The brakes squealed and I flinched at the loud sound in my sensitive ears. Teren didn't move a muscle; he was probably running over what he was going to say to Carrie. I squeezed his hand tighter in encouragement as the sound of a Disney movie started trickling down to me from upstairs.

We heard a woman's voice thank the taxi driver, then the back door creaked open. A light, flower scent caught the air just as a woman stepped out of the cab. She looked over to us and I felt all of my muscles tighten in anticipation. *Did she know why she was here?* I couldn't tell if she was still under the vampire's compulsion or not. I wondered what she'd been told.

Teren raised his hand from the door and waved at her. She merrily waved back, her girl-next-door face happier than I remembered seeing it the last time. Of course, the last time I'd seen her, she'd been crying…over Teren, over the loss they'd shared together.

My enhanced sight could pick out the slight moisture in her blue-gray eyes, and the perfect straightness of her slim body; while filled with life once, I was pretty certain that those trim hips had never swelled with a child. Remembering the grief that I'd seen in her eyes before, compassion filled me. A child was something that she'd seemed to really want. Maybe her fear of losing the one had made her too scared to try again? Yet another reason Teren should finally clear her.

I released my husband, so he could go and be the gentleman that I knew he was itching to be. He glanced at me, gave me a quick kiss, then started walking towards her. I leaned against the doorframe as I watched them meet in the drive. With mixed feelings, I listened to him greet her and heard her politely reply that he looked just the same. They hugged, very briefly, then Teren grabbed her bags out of the back of the cab. It made me happy that the vampire sent to fetch her had indeed let her pack some bags. I'd feel really bad if all she had were the clothes on her back.

Teren indicated the front door and Carrie looked up at me; her bright eyes were beaming. As the floral scent wafting from her strengthened with her approach, I fortified my stomach. I had nothing to fear from this woman.

She stepped up to me with her hand outstretched. Being so tall, I had to look up to meet her eye. "It was Emma, right?"

I nodded, then smiled genuinely. "Carrie. It's good to see you again." Curious, I couldn't help but add, "And a little surprising too. What are you doing in our neck of the woods?"

Teren gave me a warning glance, since we really didn't know what she'd been told. Well, really, did it matter if I spoiled the story, since we were just wiping her mind anyway? If I knew it, I could probably tell her who had really shot JFK and it wouldn't matter.

As I moved aside so she could enter the house, Carrie gave Teren an odd, appraising look, like she was shocked that Teren hadn't mentioned to his wife that his ex was coming over for a visit. I guess talking to him was part of the compulsion the vampire had used on her. Great, so I had just made my husband look like he was hiding something. Well, funnily enough, he was, just not what Carrie thought.

Shaking her head, she seemed to decide that it wasn't her place to call Teren out on his poor judgment. Meeting my eye, she said, "I was just getting into town for my two-week vacation, when my phone rang." She glanced over at Teren when he set her bags down and closed the door. He had an expertly sincere smile on his face. To the human eye, that was. I could see the slight frown line in his forehead as he listened to what she'd been forced to believe.

Smiling, Carrie indicated him with her hand. "Out of the blue, Teren calls to invite me over the next time I was in town." She shook her head, like she was amazed by life's little coincidences. "I told him I just got in, so he invited me over for dinner, and here I am!" She laughed and shook her head again.

I laughed too. Discretely watching Teren, I saw him glance at me and shake his head a little. He hadn't called her. I doubt he even knew her number. Slapping a friendly smile on my face, even as a ball of ice formed in my stomach, I gave her a warm hug. "Well, we're glad you're here."

A vampire had made her believe that she was on a previously planned vacation and Teren had just happened to call her when her plane landed. And she completely believed it. I was fairly certain that, in her mind, the memory of every piece of that story was intact. The power purebloods had was overwhelming. It was how they'd stayed hidden from the world for thousands of years. They controlled human beings like we were puppets on strings. I was immensely grateful that my children and I had vampire juice in us, and we could never be controlled like that. It also made me a little terrified for all of the people I knew who didn't have that sort of protection.

Pulling apart from Carrie, I kept all of those fears from my face. I had to keep in mind that being a vampire did not make a person evil. There was no inherent gene in the blood that instantly turned people into murdering, soulless beasts. That was still a personal choice that all vampires made on a one-on-one basis. And from what I'd seen, most were content to merely…nibble from humans.

Absentmindedly, I fixed the hair covering my scar. Most vampires…not all.

As I began showing Carrie our home, Teren quietly excused himself to make a phone call. I knew he'd spoken with his family last night and probably several times today. Halina had even wanted to stay here the night before, but Teren didn't have a lightproof area for her to hide, and she hated sleeping in the ground. He'd promised her that he would call when Carrie showed up. As the sun was still out, I figured we had a few hours with Carrie until Halina whooshed in to wipe her mind.

When he was back a few moments later, we all headed upstairs. Visiting our bedroom last, I stood with Carrie in the doorway as she looked in on Teren's children. A smile was on her lips as her hand drifted to her stomach. I watched the emotion fill her eyes as she stared at the miniature versions of a man she'd once been very close to.

When she stepped into the room, my kids tore their eyes from the TV to look up at her. Lying on their bellies with their feet clicking together in the air and their heads resting in their hands, they were the image of innocence. Having finally noticed a stranger in the house, Spike lifted his head and barked once. Guard dog, he was not.

The kids sat up as Carrie stepped up to the bed. Teren put a cool arm around my waist as he grinned at his children. Extending a hand, he introduced them, "Carrie, these are our children, Nika and Julian. Kids, this is a friend of Daddy's."

"Hi," they said at the same time. Nika blew a stray light brown lock from her face, then smiled a big cheesy grin, like she was posing for a camera. Julian, scratching his dark head, tried to watch both the movie and the new person simultaneously.

Carrie laughed at them. "Well, hello there. You are both very lucky to have such wonderful parents." She looked back at me, and her eyes were sad and happy at the same time. It made me want to hug her again.

Nika immediately nodded. "I know! Daddy's magic."

I froze, knowing what Nika really meant by that. Carrie only thought she was being cute though. Laughing, she said to Nika, "I'm sure he is."

Teren smiled at Carrie and his daughter, then locked eyes with me. His expression was full of pride and amusement for the beautiful children we had created together. Squeezing me tighter, he motioned back downstairs. "Shall I make us something to eat?" Leaning into his side, I looked up just as my stomach growled.

Carrie laughed as she looked over at me. "Oh, good, I'm not the only starving one." She shook her head. "I can't even remember the last time I ate."

I let out a nervous laugh as I wondered if she'd been "allowed" to eat on her trip here. After kissing my kids, I followed her and my husband downstairs.

When dinner was ready, we sat in the little-used formal dining room. The kids laughed as they sat across from each other and tried to kick each other under the table. I warned them under my breath to stop it, but they were having too much fun to listen to me, and Teren was too busy talking with Carrie to notice.

As he set plates of roasted chicken and vegetables in front of everyone, they caught up on their many years apart from each other. Teren listened raptly to Carrie's tales of working for a small bakery in a tiny town in the very upper corner of Maine. She lived a pretty secluded life, but she liked it that way and she was happy. She even had a secret crush on her boss, which delighted me. A crush on her boss probably meant that she wasn't secretly pining for Teren.

Teren told her several details of his life, but nothing that included vampirism. He told her about awards that he'd won for his writing, camping trips we'd taken, and his parents' ranch. I watched their easy conversations. There was a feeling of familiarity evident between them, but nothing romantic. They seemed to just have a natural friendship. One that became even more apparent when their topic shifted to their mutual childhood.

After the kids finished up and raced upstairs to watch another movie, Teren and Carrie sat back in their chairs and began to reminiscence about funny friends or sweet moments that they'd shared. I cleaned up everyone's plates—Teren's was empty, since he'd been secretly feeding the dog his dinner under the table—and left them to what would be their very last conversation. That fact hurt my heart a little as I listened to them.

Teren laughed as they talked about old classmates and what so and so was up to now. Carrie brought him to tears when she repeated a story about a field trip that had gone horribly wrong. He talked with her in a way that I routinely talked to friends that I bumped into from high school. They talked about people and experiences that they'd both shared during that eventful time in their lives. For a moment, I wasn't hearing an ex-girlfriend, I was hearing a friend. A friend that had meant a great deal to him at one time, and a friend that he was about to release from his life…forever.

I watched the sun start to set with heaviness in my heart. Listening to Teren's happiness, I wished that we could call this off and Carrie could be allowed to keep her memories of him, because I saw his point about wanting someone to remember him. It was a dilemma that I was going to have to face one day. Being alive in other people's memories was something that was often taken for granted. The desire to be remembered was an intrinsic part of being human, and Teren was, as he loved to tell me, mostly human.

As the sun set completely, I felt Halina start to streak towards us. She was probably anxious to get this over with. I sighed. Teren in the dining room sighed as well as he felt her streaking to our doorstep. He'd enjoyed catching up with Carrie.

Walking back into the room, I moved over to stand behind him. He lifted his head to look up at me, and his face was full of sad acceptance. It was time. Feeling the tension, Carrie asked, "Is everything okay?"

I placed my hand on his shoulder in support, and he reached up to clasp my fingers with a grateful squeeze. With a soft sigh, he said, "I've done something to you, Carrie, that was…unforgivable of me."

I squeezed his fingers while Carrie furrowed her brow and looked between us. She shook her head, and her shoulder-length hair swished around her neck; it brought a wave of that floral scent to me, and I was pretty sure that I'd forever associate the smell with her. A moment of realization hit her and, seeming uncomfortable that Teren was bringing up such a private topic with me here, she looked down at her lap. "Oh, Teren, that was both of our faults, not just yours."

Teren's voice was quiet when he responded to her. "I'm not talking about the pregnancy, Carrie, although that was pretty stupid of me, too."

She looked up at him, confused. "What do you mean then?"

He looked up at me, reluctance in his eyes. It was a hard thing, telling someone you cared about, all of your deepest, darkest secrets, especially if they might react badly to the truth. Moving around to sit beside him, I held one of his hands in both of mine.

Shaking his head at her, he said, "I've been a real bastard to you, letting this pain you've felt go on for so long." He looked down at our laced together hands. "I'm having a hard time forgiving myself for it."

Her look of confusion didn't ease any. Tucking her hair behind her ears, she leaned forward. "What are you talking about, Teren? What could you have possibly done about my pain?"

His eyes drifted over her face, perhaps studying the features that he'd never see again after tonight, perhaps gauging how well she'd take the news. "I could have taken it. You could have lived these past fifteen years obliviously happy…and it's my fault."

She blinked and sat back in her chair. "Who said I haven't been happy?" she whispered. Her eyes flashed upstairs though, and I clearly saw pain in them as she looked up to where I could hear my children singing along to the musical playing.

Teren's enhanced sight saw the look as well. Exhaling in a long breath, he said, "When we were younger, I couldn't tell you something…about me." He bit his lip and I squeezed his hand tighter. "I was so afraid that you'd run away from me, if you ever learned the truth. You meant so much to me and I didn't want to lose…"

He looked down, then over at me. "I have learned over the years that I can't hide who I am from the person I'm with." When he looked back at Carrie, conviction was in his eyes. "I just can't spend the rest of my life living a lie. Being with you taught me that," he whispered.

She shook her head, still confused, but Teren continued without letting her ask her questions. "Over time, I learned to open myself up to people. It was hard. It was painful. It was terrifying. But, because of what happened with us, I knew I couldn't be with someone who didn't know. Most couldn't handle it, couldn't accept me." He looked back at me, and love and devotion were clear in his eyes. "In fact, only Emma could."

As we gazed at each other for a second, Carrie popped up with her summation of his statement. "Are you...gay or something?"

He closed his eyes, and a soft laugh escaped him. Returning his gaze to hers, he shook his head. "I wish it were that simple." The poor woman didn't look any clearer on what he was talking about. I bit my lip, knowing she would very soon; Halina was nearly at our door. Feeling her as well, Teren stumbled into his next sentence. "Before we go our separate ways, I need you to know, I need you to see...what I am."

He sadly shook his head. "It might fill in some of the blanks for you...about why I never came looking for you when your parents pulled you out of school. Why I never attempted to contact you after all these years. Why I may have, at times, seemed...distant from you when we were together."

Her shoulders relaxed as she pondered their past. "Yeah...there were times..."

He nodded and I had to imagine that there had been several unexplained moments in their relationship. Knowing how secretive Teren could be with me, when I knew almost everything, I had to believe that he'd been a very closed-off person with her. She must have written it off as teenage hormones, but it was so much more than that with him.

Looking down, he peeked up at her. "I want you to know that it was never you. You were warm and sweet, and taught me a lot about the person I wanted to be." He smiled softly at her. "You were just what every first love should be."

She was smiling, but she shook her head, and her brow furrowed again. "Teren...I don't..."

Feeling him tense and Halina nearly on our doorstep, I clenched his hand tight. He squeezed me back as he kept his eyes on Carrie. "Me, all of the women in my family, my children, and recently, my wife...are all vampires."

She stared at him blankly, her face completely expressionless. I could tell she didn't believe him. She probably thought he was crazy. In the silence, the kids suddenly yelled out, "Grammy Lina!" and blurred downstairs to race to the door. Carrie had turned her head upon hearing them yell and saw the blur of their movement as they sped through the archway. Standing up, she pressed herself against the wall. Her face drained of color. She probably believed him now.

Teren stood as well, his face apprehensive. "Carrie?" he asked softly.

She started to look back at him, but Halina walked through the door and Carrie's eyes snapped to the pale white, dark haired beauty striding into the house. Halina scooped up the children and carried them into the dining room. Her face impassive, Halina gave Carrie a once over while she held the twins. She was holding them in a way that no human her size could. They were sitting on her arms, nestled on her biceps like they were sitting on swings; Julian was even kicking his legs back and forth.

Carrie's eyes widened at the physically impossible feat of strength she was witnessing. Panic was clear on her face. "What?" she whispered, looking back at Teren.

He walked over to her slowly, careful to not make her bolt. Opening his mouth, he extended his fangs. She screamed and our children covered their ears. Calmly, Halina said, "Stop screaming." Carrie stopped immediately. Her body shaking, she looked over at Halina. Carrie seemed conscious of the fact that she hadn't willingly stopped screaming; she was even swallowing like she was still trying to make it happen.

Teren stepped in front of her with a sigh. She shook while she watched him, and he smiled around his fangs. "I won't hurt you,

Carrie." He shrugged. "I'm still me."

Her shaking eased a bit as she ignored his fangs and stared into his eyes. Not removing herself from the wall, she shook her head. "Oh my God, Teren...that's not possible."

He lightly touched her arm. She flinched back from his cool touch. Maybe she was suddenly realizing why he was so cold. "I'm sorry...but it is." He removed his hand from her. "I'm sorry I couldn't tell you this back then. I think if I had, and you'd left...I wouldn't have had a problem wiping your mind."

She relaxed against the wall as that word echoed in her brain. "Wiping my... What are you talking about? What are you going to do to me?" She started to inch away from him, but that only brought her closer to Halina, so she stopped. "Are you going to hurt me?" she asked him.

Looking a little bothered that she would think that, Teren tilted his head. I stood up and grabbed his hand while he debated what to say to her. Carrie's eyes flashed between our joined fingers and his pointy teeth. She seemed confused as to how I could stand being so close to him. Just as Teren was about to answer her question, Julian beat him to it. "Daddy's nice, Daddy don't hurt."

We all looked over to him; his little brow was scrunched in a frown. I wasn't sure what my children thought of Carrie's reaction, but it was obviously upsetting Julian. Carrie seemed to realize this too and instantly slapped a smile on her face. "Oh, I know that, sweetheart. I was just...kidding around." She laughed, but I could hear the nervousness behind it.

Walking over to the kids, I picked them off of Halina's body. "If you two go upstairs and get ready for bed, you can sleep with Mommy and Daddy tonight, okay?" They both grinned and turned to run upstairs. "Remember to brush!" I called up after them.

Twisting around, Carrie looked at me with remorse. "I'm sorry. I didn't mean to scare them," she said quietly.

I smiled at her concern and shook my head. "We freaked you out, it's understandable."

Straightening, she focused on Teren. His fangs were still

extended. "You're…a vampire?"

He nodded at her while I walked up to him and wrapped my arms around his waist. Meeting Carrie's eyes, I showed her my fangs too. "We all are…and we have no desire to hurt you."

Halina snorted, but I ignored her. Luckily, Carrie ignored her, too. "But, you are going to…wipe me?" She cocked her eyebrow and looked between the two sets of fangs before her.

Teren and I slipped our teeth up at the same time. With a soft smile, he said, "I'm just going to fix a mistake. We don't let anyone remember us, and I never should have let you remember losing the baby. That was…selfish of me."

The scent of fear eased from her, as she shook her head. "I won't remember you?" She looked back at Halina. Swallowing at the blank look on the intimidating woman's face, Carrie twisted to Teren again. "But not all of you are bad memories." Relaxing, she took a step forward. "Most of you are good ones." She flushed as she glanced at me. "Very good ones," she whispered.

Remembering Alanna commenting once that sex with a vampire was unforgettable, made me really uncomfortable. I had to imagine that, even when he was new at it, Teren had been skilled. I shoved the irritating image of them tangled in a bed together from my mind, and firmly compressed my lips to stop myself from letting out a possessive growl. I could deal with this…for a little while longer.

Teren smiled and looked down like he was embarrassed. Maybe he was remembering his mother saying that as well. Peeking up at her, he softly said, "It will be easier for us both if you don't."

Shrugging her shoulders, Carrie shook her head. "Will it hurt?"

Teren gently placed his hand on her arm. She didn't flinch away this time. "No, of course not." He laughed once, as he added, "And for the first time, I actually believe that this won't hurt me either. The past helped shape me, but I'm ready to let it go." I squeezed his waist, resting my head near his silent, loving heart. Yes, I could definitely deal with this.

Teren kissed my head before returning his attention to Carrie. "You taught me so much about being careful, being cautious…about how dangerous my secret could be. But because of what we went through, I knew I had to take the chance and let Emma in. I had to let her love me, as me. And luckily for me, she did." Teren gave her a warm, friendly smile. "I thank you, for showing me that."

Carrie returned his smile, then nervously swallowed when Halina stepped up to her side. Halina tilted her head, flicked a glance at Teren, then coolly asked Carrie, "Did you tell anyone about Teren getting you pregnant?"

Carrie shook her head, her gray eyes wide. "No, aside from my rude conversation with Emma and her friend," her eyes swung back to mine, apologetic, "I don't talk about my miscarriage." She shrugged, still looking at me. "I mean, even before they passed away, I never told my parents who the father was." Her eyes shifted over to Teren. "It was...private."

Halina grabbed Carrie's arm, regaining her attention. "Good, then this will be very easy for me."

Carrie started shaking again as Halina held her gaze. Stepping forward, Teren patted her arm. "Don't be afraid, you won't remember any of this."

A tear filled her eye and dropped down her cheek. "I'll miss my memories of you."

Teren smiled sadly. "No...you won't miss anything, Carrie." I sniffled as Teren twisted to his great-grandmother. "Take it," he whispered. "Take it all."

Chapter 7 – Happy Birthday

Teren woke me up the next morning with soft lips on my neck. Murmuring good morning, he sighed a content, cool breath into my ear. I smiled and shivered, as I twisted to wrap my arms around him. Exhaling in a long, satisfied way, he squeezed me so tight I had a little trouble breathing.

Pushing him back, I laughed when I could breathe again. "Good morning to you, too." Glancing over his shoulder at his clock, I frowned. "It's so early, why are you up?"

He shook his head, his pale eyes glowing with phosphorescence and happiness as he watched me in our still dark bedroom. "I just couldn't sleep anymore."

I frowned, and my glowing eyes flicked over his face. "I know yesterday was hard for you. Are you okay?"

He inhaled a deep breath, and let it out in a rush. "Yeah, I feel great. Like a weight has been lifted, a weight I didn't even realize I'd been carrying. I feel…free." He chuckled and rubbed his nose against mine. "And I owe it all to you."

I giggled as his nose ran along my cheek, and his lips traveled up to my ear. Sliding my hands up his back, I pulled his body into mine. "I didn't do anything, Teren. Last night was all you."

Remembering his last moments with Carrie made me smile. Halina had looked her in the eye and calmly given her a new life. She'd been told that she'd never had a serious boyfriend in high school, that she'd never been pregnant before, that the name Teren Adams meant nothing to her, and upon leaving our home, she would forget everything about the man standing before her.

Under Teren's guidance, Halina then told her that she was going to stay in the city, enjoying the remainder of her two week vacation, then she was going to go home and enjoy her life. Teren also threw in that she was going to confidently ask her boss out on a date. He'd grinned after Halina had rolled her eyes and imbedded the suggestion.

I'd been a little shocked at the ease with which Halina had wiped her clean. Once Carrie had been escorted to a cab and sent to a hotel that Teren had reserved for her, I'd made the mistake of proclaiming my surprise at how simple it was for her. Halina had looked at me like I'd offended her. "You expected something…grander?"

Shrugging, I'd only managed to come up with, "Well, yeah, actually."

Her response, as typical, had been better than mine. "The human mind is exceptionally pliable. All I have to do is tell you what to believe, what to do, and you do it." Smirking, she finished with, "Truly, you are not much different than the cattle."

I was still trying to not be offended by that.

Teren paused in sucking on my earlobe. "You did so much for me, just by being there." He pulled back to look at me, and his playful eyes were suddenly serious. "I don't think I could have done it without your support." The glow highlighted our sheets as he looked down. My vamped-up vision could make out a section of the glow that was brighter, a ring directly around the iris. It was beautiful.

"I should have done that ages ago, but I was so scared to let go. But it was easier than I thought it would be." Smiling, he looked up at me and his fingers caressed my cheek. "I didn't really lose anything, because I still have you." Tilting his head, a look of pride on his face, he added, "I kind of feel like I grew up last night."

I softly laughed at his proclamation. "Well, welcome to being an adult."

Chuckling, he kissed me. "That's what I get for marrying an older woman." I gently smacked his arm and he chuckled again. "What? You *are* almost out of your twenties."

He raised an eyebrow and I smacked him again, harder. "And you already are, even if you still look perfect."

His grin turned devilish. "Perfect?"

I sighed as I looked him over. "Yes…perfect."

He looked me over as well, and his thumb stroked my cheek. "Not as perfect as you," he whispered.

I sighed softly again, placing my hand over his. He leaned in and we tenderly kissed, arms and legs and bodies tangling together. Just as I was pulling him on top of me, our light kissing getting more intimate, a foot kicked me in my rib. Breaking apart from his lips, I glanced over at my son beside me. I'd nearly forgotten that I'd told the kids they could sleep with us. Quite a feat, since I could feel them in my head. Without looking, I knew with certainty that Nika was on the other side of Teren.

He glanced over at her fast-asleep body, then shifted to my side. Grinning at me crookedly, he shrugged. "Want to go outside? It's been a long time since we've had sex in the car."

I laughed out loud, then slapped a hand over my mouth. It was too late, though. Nika immediately sat up and looked over Teren's shoulder. "Morning, Mommy!" she exclaimed brightly. Inwardly, I groaned. If it was too early for me, it was way too early for them.

"Morning, sweetheart," I whispered, hoping that at least Julian was still sleeping. No such luck.

"Quiet, Nick," he mumbled, sitting up and rubbing his eyes.

Teren smiled and rolled onto his back; Nika immediately scrambled on top of him. Looking over at me, he twisted his lips and shook his head. "Nice going...Mommy."

I rolled my eyes and smacked his shoulder. "Quiet, you. You're the one who was up before the dawn."

Chuckling to himself, Teren squeezed Nika in several short bursts, making her laugh; Julian sleepily laughed too.

Since we were all up, we decided to have a nice filling breakfast together. Humming to himself, Teren finished off the kids' pancakes by adding strawberry eyes, whip cream mouths and a blueberry nose. The twins giggled in delight at their pancake people and I smiled at the peace on my husband's face. Snipping that last piece of his childhood away had certainly freed him. He was lighter than I'd ever seen him. Well, it rivaled when the children were born, at least.

Still having to go into work before me, he kissed all of us goodbye. He lingered on me the longest. Clutching my face, he gave me an intimately deep kiss for a morning farewell. My heart was a little fast when he pulled away. Discretely running his fingers over my heart, and copping a feel in the process, he whispered, "I love that I can still do that to you."

I squeezed his bottom. "Maybe later you could do a bit more?"

He glanced over at the kids making bubbles in their milk. Laughing, he turned back to me. "They'll probably be passing out earlier than usual tonight." The edge of his lip curved up as his pale eyes flicked down my body. "I'm sure I can come up with something."

I bit my lip, but had to stop when I momentarily lost the hold on my teeth. I quickly slipped them back up before I sliced my skin, but Teren noticed the loss of control and gave me a devilish smile. I hadn't slipped up like that in months, and I was more than a little embarrassed. I smacked his shoulder, then shoved his cocky butt out the door. Laughing, he kissed me goodbye a final time, then practically skipped to his car. I smiled and shook my head at his good mood.

His good mood stayed with him throughout his day at work, where he called me and told me about Ben and Tracey wanting to take me out tomorrow night. I matter-of-factly told him that I was backing out of those plans; I didn't want to make a big deal about my birthday. A quiet weekend at the ranch with my family sounded ideal to me. With a laugh, he told me that he and Ben had already made all of the arrangements. It was a done deal. Irritated at his good mood, I sighed.

Saturday morning, Teren and I headed to the family ranch like usual, except now we had plans to leave it for a few hours in the evening. I wasn't too thrilled about that, but Teren told me that we weren't leaving until after bedtime, so I would still be able to tuck the kids in. I *was* happy about that. Smiling secretively, Teren wouldn't tell me anything else about our plans, and I couldn't help but wonder just what he had in store for me.

Shutting the car off in the drive of the palatial Adams estate, Teren laughed at the look of curious annoyance on my face. "We're here, kids," he proclaimed as he opened the door.

Rolling my eyes, I opened my door and went about the task of unbuckling the kids. No sooner were they free than they were streaking to the open front door. Alanna was on her knees, awaiting them. I blinked in surprise when I saw Imogen standing back in the recesses of the entryway. Imogen didn't come out during broad daylight. It was too painful. She was standing a ways back from the open door, and none of its indirect light was reaching her, but the home was loaded with wide windows and she was drenched in the sunlight streaming through them.

Shaking his head, Teren stared at her in disbelief. "I'll be damned," he muttered. "He did it." I glanced up at Teren's stunned face, then remembered what Gabriel had said before he'd dropped the Carrie-bomb on us. He'd developed a protective coating that blocked the harmful side effects of the sun from mixed vampires. He had offered to have the Adams home fitted with the new glass, and apparently he had. I shook my head as I grabbed Teren's hand. Gabriel worked fast; that had only been a couple of days ago.

We walked into the house, and Alanna shut the door behind us. Imogen was smiling and laughing as she chased her grandchildren around the crying woman fountain that took a place of prominence in the room. My eyes stung as I watched the bright rays streak over Imogen's dark hair. She hadn't had a moment like this…her entire life.

Alanna smiled at her mother, pink tears down her cheeks. All of us silently watched Imogen play tag, happy, content, and most of all, pain-free. Quietly, Alanna said, "She's been like this ever since Gabriel finished with the windows." Twisting to smile at Teren, she shook her head. "She won't go back to her rooms." Laughing, she wiped her cheeks dry.

Teren and I laughed as Teren slung an arm over his mom's shoulders. When the kids eventually tore off to play in another room of the house, Imogen stood up and walked over to us; her face was more alive than I'd ever remembered seeing it. "Teren, Emma…it's so good to see you out and about on this fine morning."

With a warm laugh, she embraced me in a cool hug. I laughed as I wrapped my arms around the grandmotherly woman. My joy for her made the tears stinging my eyes splash upon my cheeks. Darn emotional vampires.

"Imogen, I'm so happy for you." I pulled back from her to look over at Alanna. She had an arm around her son's waist and was standing in a bright shaft of light under a large sun-filled window. She'd been standing there for a while, perfectly free from pain as well. "Both of you."

Alanna sighed, then glanced down to where we could feel Halina's presence under our feet. Her eyes swinging back to me, she said, "Gabriel…he's done so much for our family. I really don't know how we'll ever repay him."

I swallowed a little nervously. I'd wondered that myself.

Imogen, Alanna and I spent a good chunk of the afternoon lazing in a bright patch of sunlight in the living room. Stretching languidly, I sort of felt like a giant cat sleeping in the sunshine. Both vampire women giggled and sighed with contentment. I had to imagine that the heat caressing my skin felt even better to their cool bodies, especially since they'd never really had the chance to revel in it before.

Teren laughed at the three of us before heading outside to go fishing with his dad. The kids went with him. They found it enormously funny to use their enhanced abilities to snatch up the fish bare-handed, just like Daddy.

It wasn't too much later when I felt Teren and the kids zooming back to me at lightning speed. A little alarmed, I sat up on my elbows. I was even more alarmed when I could hear my children crying. I jumped to my feet. Alanna and Imogen sprang up with me. They both looked like they wanted to rush out to Teren. Knowing he would be in the house in a matter of seconds, we made ourselves wait. Even though I only counted five seconds, it felt like five years.

When he entered the room, Teren immediately met my eye. "They're fine, more upset than anything."

Believing him, but needing to see for myself, I blurred over to Nika and Julian. The tang of blood was in the air, and my heart rate spiked. Both kids reached out for me, both crying. Smelling the blood on Nika, I grabbed her. It hurt my heart to choose, but she was the one who smelled injured. Imogen snatched up Julian though; he clung to her, sobbing as she patted his back. My heart racing as I held my distraught daughter, I peeked up at Teren. He was running a hand back through his hair, and his lips were twisted in what almost seemed like amusement.

"What happened?" I snapped out.

He started to answer me, but Nika beat him to it. Pointing at Julian, she wailed, "Julie bit me!"

Julian covered his ears and sobbed harder. Teren shrugged, and I looked over Nika's body. Sure enough, she had fang marks on her arm. I glanced at Alanna. Never having raised vampiric children before, or any child before, I wasn't quite sure how to handle this. Alanna smiled. Wisdom was in her youthful eyes as she reached out for Nika. "Come here, sweetheart. Grandma will clean you up and then we'll have a nice cup of cocoa."

Nika perked up, her sobs shifting to sniffles at the thought of a chocolate treat. She practically leapt from my arms into Alanna's. Hugging her tight, Alanna nodded her head at Julian. "You two may want to have a talk with him."

Imogen smiled and kissed his head. As Nika's emotions calmed down, so did my son's. When I could hear Nika giggle as Alanna tickled her, Julian even smiled. I figured he was probably more upset at feeling how upset Nika was. It sort of put a whole new meaning to the word guilt, when you could *feel* the pain and distress you caused someone.

Setting him on a chair, Imogen kissed his head again, then blurred into the kitchen with Alanna and Nika. Hearing them begin a conversation with Nika on biting, I started my own with my son. Teren and I squatted down in front of him. His eyes were red and watery, and a few last sniffles escaped him as I stroked his cheek. "Did you bite your sister?" I quietly asked.

He nodded, and his lip quivered as he looked between Teren and me. Teren ran some fingers through his hair. "Why?" he asked, equally softly.

Julian looked down and shrugged. "I was hungry."

I bit my lip. This was not the sort of thing that most mothers had to deal with. How do you tell a child that feeding off their sibling was not okay? Especially since it was in their nature to do so. Even if we wanted to ignore it, being attuned to blood and heartbeats was just a part of being a vampire. Sure, it was easy for an adult to make the conscious choice to not attack the meals walking past them, but three-year-olds?

Sighing, I cupped both of his cheeks. "If you want some blood, you come to Mommy or Daddy, and we will get you some." Shaking my head at him, I firmly added, "You don't ever bite people. Understand?"

He nodded in my hands, then frowned. "Daddy bites you?"

Removing my fingers, I felt my entire body flushing. We tried to keep that part of our relationship hidden, but they'd apparently caught on to that little fact. As I stammered for something to say, Teren filled in for me. "I only bite Mommy because she said it was okay. You never bite someone without their permission."

Teren's face held a calm but serious expression, and I realized that this was a conversation Teren must have heard himself as a child. He didn't have siblings to nibble on, but he'd probably been warned anyway. Julian's face got equally serious and he nodded, just once. "Okay, Daddy."

Nika laughed and told Alanna and Imogen that she wouldn't ever bite someone, that it was icky. Teren and I smirked, and Julian brightened when he saw that we weren't mad. "Can I have some cocoa?" he asked, his pale eyes hopeful.

I nodded and, giggling like his sister, Julian dashed away. When I looked back at Teren, he started laughing. "I had no idea he'd ever seen me bite you." I closed my eyes and shook my head. No, I was pretty sure regular parents didn't ever have these kinds of conversations.

When dusk settled in and our sleepy children were huddled off to bed, we reiterated that biting was something they shouldn't do, even with each other. Halina laughed for ages when she was filled in on the situation, especially after Julian repeated to her that Daddy bites Mommy because Mommy says it's okay. I wanted to crawl into the earth and never come out again.

We said our goodnights and tucked them into their joint bed— Nika's arm was thoroughly covered up in Hello Kitty bandages. Then

Teren scooped me up and told me to change into something nice. I pouted as he dragged me into our bedroom. "I didn't bring anything nice."

Grinning crookedly, he pointed over to a garment bag that I hadn't packed. "I did."

Frowning as I unzipped it, I muttered, "You all know my birthday isn't until Tuesday, right?"

He laughed as he slung his arms around my waist and kissed my neck, the unscarred side. "Yes, but it's typical to celebrate the weekend before, when the date falls in the middle of the workweek."

As I pulled out a sexy little black dress, I mumbled, "Thanks for the tip, Mr. Birthday Etiquette."

I listened to my children say goodnight to each other, then I slinked off my clothes. When I was just in my bra and underwear, I posed for Teren. Maybe if he was wrapped around me, he'd ditch this idea of going out. His eyes locked onto my body, but he stubbornly kept getting ready, buttoning up a black shirt that complemented his dark hair.

Cocking an eyebrow at me, he waited for me to cover up once he was finished getting ready. Rolling my eyes, I slipped on the dress. It fell mid-thigh and dipped so low in the back that I had to take my bra off. Removing it with sexy flair, I flung it at him. He caught it one-handed, baring a fang at me as he did. Biting my lip, I wanted to stay for another reason, but Teren slipped his teeth back in and walked over to my bag on the dresser. Rummaging for the supplies, he prepared my daily shot for me. When he had the syringe ready, he gave me a questioning look, as he always did, and I nodded.

Silently, he walked over to me, shot in hand. He stepped behind me, and his fingers ran up my thigh. I closed my eyes as his other hand rested on my hip. I could feel the desire rising in me as his hand crept higher up my leg; the syringe enclosed in it barely scraped against my skin. A low growl escaped him as he sensed it, and he dragged his teeth over my ear. "Stop that," he murmured. "We have somewhere to be."

A small moan escaped my lips as I leaned back into his body, grinding my hips into his. "Then stop teasing me…and do it."

He groaned as his free hand slipped under my dress, cupping my ass. "You're too sexy…" Then he stiffened and pushed me away from him. Surprised, I twisted to look at him; his eyes were narrowed at me. "Are you trying to turn me on, just so we won't go?"

I gave him an innocent smile. "I don't know what you're talking about, Mr. Adams."

Shaking his head at me, he grabbed my hips and pulled me into him. He injected me just as our bodies lined up. "There," he whispered, "I did it…we can go now."

Gasping as the heat of the shot flowed through my hips and desire rushed through my body, I grabbed his face and kissed him. He kissed me back just as hard and fierce as I kissed him. His hands ran up my legs, fisting my underwear at both sides. I whimpered as his cool tongue stroked over mine. Then he jerked away from me.

Blurring to the other side of the room, he panted as he stared at me. "Hmmm, you're good, but we *are* going." He raised an eyebrow, his face playful, but serious. Smirking, he put the empty syringe back with our belongings, where our children wouldn't find it and accidentally hurt themselves.

After slipping on my family locket, I took a few minutes to readjust my hair and makeup. We were still on the road to destinations unknown in no time. As I let out a resigned sigh, Teren chuckled at me. "What about this are you not looking forward to? Spending some quality time with your friends…or your husband?"

He raised his eyebrow and I laughed, relaxing. "You're right. I guess it's just turning thirty that I'm struggling with."

He furrowed his brows; his Prius flew down the road without him even looking. "You don't have to, you know. Turn thirty, I mean."

Relaxing back into the seat, I watched the headlights highlight the road before us, much like our eyes in pitch-black darkness. I knew what he meant. He meant I could stop taking the shot. I could die and stop my body from aging. I knew that, I just wasn't ready for it yet.

"No, I want to. Really, I do." I looked back at him as he

redirected his gaze to the road. "It's just the end of an era. I wasn't expecting that to bother me. I'd even been looking forward to it up until now…but, I don't know. I guess I just wanted to celebrate this milestone quietly."

Teren frowned. "Do you want me to call this off?"

I shook my head, feeling silly for objecting, now that we were out of the house and free for the evening. Putting my hand over his, I smiled. "No, I want to spend a night out with my husband, celebrating the fact that I'm still alive."

Grinning, he placed a cool kiss on the back of my hand and stepped on the accelerator. "Good, because I think you'll like this."

While I was expecting to pull up in front of some packed club or maybe a swanky bar, he ended up driving us to the San Francisco Symphony. I stared at him open-mouthed as we parked. "You got me tickets to the symphony?"

He smiled at my astonishment, then nodded. I hadn't been to the symphony since my mom had taken me after I'd graduated from college. It was one of those things that I'd wanted to do again, but it always seemed to slip through the cracks.

"I asked your mom what you might like to do and she said the last time you were here, you teared up." He shrugged. "I thought you might appreciate this more than Tracey's plan of getting you smashed and making you sing karaoke."

My eyes were already brimming. "Oh my God, I love you," I said, giving him a kiss.

He chuckled against my lips. "See what I'm willing to sit through for you." I laughed when I pulled away from him. I had a feeling that Teren wouldn't mind sitting through the symphony. He was just more open to culture than most men.

Stepping out of the car, I heard Hot Ben's grumble before I saw him. Turning around, my flirty black dress swirling around my thighs, I watched the attractive man walking up to us with his fiancé on his arm. While Hot Ben had a slight grimace on his sculpted face, Tracey was ear-to-ear smiles, eager to try something new. The perky blonde immediately engulfed me in a hug when she saw me. "Happy birthday, Emma."

The scent of freshly applied hairspray stung my nose, but I managed to hold in the sneeze. "Thank you, Tracey." I pulled back from her; my face was nearly split open with the wide grin upon it. "You realize it's not today, right?"

She shushed me in the air with her hand. "Close enough. Can you believe the guys are taking us to the symphony?"

She started going into detail about how thoughtful our boys were and how romantic the evening was going to be, but from behind me, I heard Hot Ben grumbling to Teren and I couldn't stop myself from eavesdropping.

"I cannot believe you talked me into the symphony. I mean, aren't you supposed to be a badass, soulless, bloodthirsty monster?" Sighing softly he muttered, "I can't believe I was ever terrified of you."

I inadvertently laughed, then switched it to a cough in my hand as I looked over my shoulder at Ben. He was quite dashing in his semiformal suit. His light eyes and blonde highlights made him seem more like a movie star than a substitute kickboxing instructor and former vampire hunter. He was the one human outside of my family who knew without a doubt what the Adams clan was. The only reason he still knew was the fact that he'd earned their trust. Earned it and kept it. He still hadn't told anyone what he knew, not even his clueless bride-to-be.

Ben gave me a sheepish shrug as Teren clapped him on the back. Sometimes Ben forgot just how good our hearing was. Actually, I think sometimes Ben forgot what we were entirely, a fact that made my husband exceptionally happy, as he sometimes liked to forget what he was, too.

Just as the four of us started walking towards the front doors, a familiar car rumbled into the parking lot. I heard its particular jumble and smiled at my husband. "You invited my mom?"

He smiled and squeezed my waist. "And your sister." Shaking my head at him, I leaned in to give him a light peck. Mom and Ash found a spot near the front to park. Tracey finally noticed they were there when Ashley stepped out of my mom's compact. Grinning through her disfigured lips, Ashley waved at our foursome. We all waved back, and Tracey broke free from Ben to give Ashley a sisterly hug.

Tracey had always had a soft spot for Ashley. She'd even tried setting her up with a cousin of Ben's once. The not-too-bad cousin that she'd once tried to line up for me. Apparently, he was still looking. Ashley had politely refused though, telling Tracey that she was perfectly capable of finding her own dates. I hadn't heard of any yet, but if my sister had proved anything to me, it was that she was indeed capable of doing anything. I was sure that meant finding a man too.

Wrapping her in an embrace when Tracey was finished, I ran a hand through one of the soft curls that were flowing down one side of her head. "You're beautiful," I whispered.

Ashley grinned and hugged me tight. "So are you, although..." She studied my face in the parking lot lights and for a moment I was worried that the glow of my eyes was visible. Then she grinned. "I think I see a wrinkle."

I smacked her shoulder just as my mom came up to hug me. "You're not funny," I said, breaking into laughter before I even finished saying it.

"Sure she is," Teren said, filling in for me as he warmly hugged my sister. My sister had been the first one to know about Teren. The two of them shared a certain bond. According to the world, they were both different, Ash on the outside, Teren on the inside.

As our expanded group sat in the plush box seats that Teren had procured for my birthday, I started listening to the swirl of conversations going on among the audience. As the whisperings grew in intensity, I started to worry that my enhanced hearing would be overwhelmed by the noise from a full symphony.

Teren noticed me worrying my lip and squeezed my leg. "Don't worry. Focus on one instrument at a time, until you can handle them all together."

I smiled over at him, relieved and warmed that he knew what I was thinking. Clutching his arm tight, I leaned into his side. My heartbeat slowed as peace settled through me.

When the music started, I realized that Teren was right. I had been nervous it would be too much for my sensitive ears, but I could actually hear more levels of the music than I ever could before. My attunement to sound picked up highs and lows that normal humans couldn't hear, and it added to the piece in a way that had tears ruining my mascara in no time. I couldn't help the reaction; it was the most beautiful thing I'd ever heard. Each note was distinct. Each individual instrument could be distinguished. Yet, at the same time, it was a beautiful, perfectly synchronized sound that blended together seamlessly. My vampire ears were in heaven. Glancing at Teren as I wiped my eyes, I smiled at the look on his face. His eyes were closed, and his expression reflected pure peace as he absorbed the music into himself, relishing it in a way that only we could.

Either that...or he was sleeping.

After the show, we went to a martini bar and everyone tried a different flavor. Except Teren, of course. He faked sips left and right, but never actually took a drink. And I helped with the deception, finishing off the one he'd ordered for himself...and the second round he ordered for each of us.

By what I thought was maybe my fourth martini, I was completely game for singing karaoke with Tracey, who was also feeling no pain. But our stubbornly responsible men called it a night. That was probably for the best anyway, since I had a little trouble holding my fangs in once Teren scooted me into the car. Really though, just remembering how to walk straight while tipsy was hard enough. Having to constantly hold in supernaturally long canines? Well, that was nearly impossible.

Teren expertly kept Tracey away from me as we said our goodbyes. My mom and sister only laughed, since they knew about my teeth anyway. Hot Ben laughed at me too, until I gave him a big kiss on the cheek and told him, "I love you, Ben, because Teren loves you...and that makes me love you, so I love you."

He seemed embarrassed after I slurred that out, and told me to go home and sleep it off. I gave him a thumbs up as he shut the door on me.

While driving back to where I could feel my sleeping children, I leaned back in the seat and giggled. It had been a long time since I'd been drunk. Pre-pregnancy for sure. Running my hands up my body, I stretched out my limbs. Every inch of my extra-sensitive skin tingled, especially the good spots.

"Teren...?" I mumbled, closing my eyes.

"Yes, Emma," he said, a tremor of humor in his voice.

"Can we have sex in the car when we get there?"

His laughter filled my ears, making me laugh as well. "Why would you want to do it in the car, when we have a perfectly spacious bed?" he murmured.

I looked over at him; my eyes were hooded and my vision wavered in and out. "Because you said it's been a while since we've been naughty in a car." My eyes drifted down his body and I sighed. "And you're right, it's been a while."

He smiled at me, then shook his head and fixed his eyes on the road. My light-headed mind surprisingly pieced something together while we drove along. One, we had at least a half hour drive ahead of us, a half hour in which my foggy head would begin to clear. And two, my husband knew this empty stretch of road so well that he really didn't need to see it to drive it.

Giggling at what I wanted to do, I unbuckled my seatbelt. Teren immediately looked over at me with his brow furrowed. "Emma, what are you doing?"

Still laughing, I ran my hands up my flirty dress and pulled off my underwear. Teren's eyes widened as he drove the way I knew he could, without looking. "It's my birthday," I got out around my giggles. "I want my present."

He dragged his eyes back up to mine. "And that would be...?" I laughed even more as my fingers started in on his slacks. "Oh, uh, Emma, I don't think..."

As my mouth replaced my fingers in his lap, Teren found it hard to finish that. Actually, he found several things hard...

His hand clutching my hair, he started breathing heavier. When he was as ready as I was, he moved his seat back as far as he could while still keeping his foot on the pedal. "Emma..." was all he got out before I straddled him, taking him in.

There was something about doing something highly illegal that made it all the more exhilarating. Or it could have been that the drinks I'd had were really strong and I was numb in all of the right places. For whatever reason, the feeling of him inside of me was unlike any other time before. Thanks to my mouth, he was warm, and incredibly hard. Filling the small cabin with the sound of my ecstasy, I jerked my hips back and forth over his. He laid his head back, trying not to close his eyes, trying to still drive. I wasn't sure if he would, or if he'd just pull over. I sort of wanted him to keep going, I sort of told him that too.

"Emma…"

His voice was tense with the restraint he was maintaining, while he intently focused on two opposing actions, driving and lovemaking. As I stared down at him, I watched his fangs slip out. It turned me on even more that he couldn't maintain three all-consuming activities. He sucked in a quick breath as his hand tightened on the steering wheel. I could hear the leather creaking in protest to the amount of pressure being applied to it. A part of me hoped he didn't break it; most of me didn't care.

My exhilarated body wasted no time in getting me to the good part and before I knew it, I was exploding. He groaned with me, and his free hand on my hip fisted the loose material of my dress as he released too. The car sped up and swerved, just a minute amount, before he got it under control again.

After giving him a languid kiss while we both came down off our high, I thanked him.

He laughed while he fought to regain his breath. "Um…you're welcome?"

I slid off of him, then fixed his pants. Teren groaned and laid his head back. "Oh my God." Adjusting his seat back to where it had been before, he looked over at me with a forced scowl; his fangs were tucked away again. "While I'm not complaining, remember what I said about you worrying about yourself? I could have wrecked us."

I giggled, completely satisfied with my evening. "I trust your abilities."

He rolled his eyes but gave me a charming smile. Under his breath I heard him mutter, "I need to get you drunk more often."

By the time we got to the ranch, my high had faded, but I felt no regret over my actions. Nothing I did with Teren ever made me feel anything but happy, not even when we'd christened Hot Ben's car or had sex beside a dumpster.

As we pulled up to our beautiful home away from home, a vehicle turned into the mammoth driveway behind us; I could hear its tires crunching up the road, even under the soothing low jazz playing through Teren's speakers. Halina rushed out from the main doors and listened as the car came into view. I couldn't sense any other movement in the house and figured every other immobile blip on my radar was asleep.

Teren's brow furrowed as he looked over at a black sedan with dark tinted windows pulling up beside us. He flicked a glance at me, then opened his door. Feeling my head clear in response to the tension in the air, I got out of my side as Teren walked around to join Halina. The ranch didn't often receive visitors during the day, and as it was well after two in the morning, it was a little outside of standard visiting hours.

The car's taillights brightened then blinked out as the vehicle was shut off. Just as I was planning how I would grab my kids and get out of here, if things turned violent, the sedan's doors opened. Surprise flitted through me at who stepped out. Surprise and a trace of fear.

Her face splotched from what looked like hours of crying, her eyes completely bloodshot, an obviously distressed Starla stumbled out of the door. Gabriel popped up from the other side, and a familiar blond mixed vampire who I'd briefly met in L.A. a few years ago stepped out of the driver's side. Jacen.

Looking between the three of them, I felt a sobering ice flood my veins. They all had serious expressions and glum faces. Starla sniffled. She seemed to be on the verge of losing the tenuous hold on her composure.

"Gabriel?" Teren asked.

"What is it?" Halina immediately added.

Gabriel briefly smiled at Halina before swinging his emerald eyes to me. My heart nearly stopped from all of the anticipation swirling in the air. "Emma...we need your help."

Chapter 8 – Please Help Me

Dazed, my head swam a little bit as I stepped forward. Cursing myself for getting carried away with my birthday celebration, I pressed my fingers to my temple. "Gabriel?" I croaked out, sure I was having some sort of alcohol induced hallucination.

He tilted his head at me while Halina calmly walked to his side. "Are you...inebriated?" he asked, inhaling me from where he stood.

Feeling heat flush my cheeks, I was preparing the brilliant response of, "No," when Jacen leapt forward.

"You have to help her. You owe her!" he shouted at me. Teren moved in front of the mixed vampire, shielding me. Jacen sort of resembled Starla, with a slight build, over-styled hair and blue-green eyes. Those eyes were wide and fearful as they stared me down.

I had a feeling Jacen would have flung Teren over the Prius, stormed over to where I was and lifted me into the air as he demanded my assistance for whatever Starla's problem was, but Gabriel blurred over to him before he could move. After Gabriel lightly touched his fingers to Jacen's shoulder, Jacen reluctantly straightened. In a more subdued voice, Jacen said, "Please," and slid his arm around Starla's waist.

It was a little surprising to see the affection, since those two vampires snarked more with each other than legitimate brothers and sisters did, but Starla buried her head into his chest as she stared at me, teary-eyed.

"Help her with what?" I asked, proud of the fact that I didn't sound the least bit intoxicated, although, even I could smell the alcohol on my breath. I smoothed my hands over my hair, just in case I was at all frazzled from my romp in the car with Teren.

One of Gabriel's hands wrapped around Halina when she stepped into his side, the other lifted to the open front door of the house. "May we come inside?"

Teren blinked out of his stupor. Placing his arm around my waist in a steadying way as I minutely stumbled, he said, "Of course, please, come in."

Starla sniffled again and clutched Jacen tight. The cutely similar couple leaned against each other for support as Jacen led her up the granite steps to Teren's family home. Gabriel looked down at Halina for a moment before they both followed. My head evening out in the crisp, clean, cattle-fragranced air, I took a deep breath as Teren and I followed our surprise guests.

Starla and Gabriel had both been here before, of course, since Starla reluctantly drove Gabriel up to visit with Halina sometimes. She had even spent an evening or two in the living room, playing board games with Jack, Alanna and Imogen while her "father" occupied himself with his girlfriend. But Jacen had never been here. Surprisingly though, he didn't even look around. His pale eyes were fixated on Starla; he didn't seem to notice his surroundings at all.

Concern flooded through me as Halina led the group into the comfortable living room. Whatever was distressing Starla and Jacen had to be bad. While Halina draped her body across a lounge chair, Gabriel walked over to stand in front of the lit fire. The flue behind him was encrusted with stones that were shaped into a giant flame. I'd always thought it was an exquisitely beautiful piece of art, but as I sat down, I also noticed that it provided a fitting backdrop for what looked to be a speech.

Teren and I sat close together on a long couch, staring over at Starla and Jacen on a nearby chair. Jacen held Starla tight as she gazed at the floor. She looked like she was suffering from shock.

"We are very sorry to intrude on your evening," Gabriel calmly began.

My heart rate increasing, I shook my head. "What is this about, Gabriel?" I didn't need formalities. I needed to know why Starla looked on the verge of an emotional collapse.

Gabriel's gaze drifted over to his daughter, his child by responsibility, if not blood. The aged eyes seem to tire right in front of me. "There has been an…incident, in my lab."

That surprised me. I'd been expecting something much different. Behind Gabriel the fire popped and sizzled, and the smell of mesquite swirling around the room overlapped the scent of vodka seeping through my pores. Halina and Teren straightened while

Gabriel sighed and shook his head. "We had a break-in. They destroyed...everything," he said quietly.

Starla sniffed again as she pressed into Jacen's side. Jacen, looking just as overcome with emotion as she was, leaned over to us. "She's going to die unless you do something!" he hissed.

My head felt like it was a step behind. "Die?" I glanced back up to Gabriel, who was giving Jacen a clear warning in his stern gaze. "What does he mean, die?"

Gabriel's deep jade eyes connected with mine again. Before he spoke, Teren sighed and hung his head. I guess he'd pieced together what was going on already. I felt a little out of sorts that my fuzzy mind hadn't yet.

"Emma," Gabriel began, while slowly running a hand through his dirty blond hair, "they demolished every vial of medication that I had." He shrugged. "I can make more, I even left Jordan to begin the process, but it will take months for the first batch to be ready."

As I narrowed my eyes at him, trying to picture how such a thing could have happened, Starla's small voice filled the room. "I don't have months, Emma."

I gasped as my eyes flew to hers, and icy understanding filled me. No, Starla didn't. Unlike me, who was taking the shot simply because I wasn't ready to die, Starla was taking the shot to stay alive. As she'd confessed to us once, she came from a line of "defective" mixed vampires. Her body wouldn't complete the changeover. Once she began her conversion, she would never finish it, she would simply...die.

"Oh, Starla, I'm so sorry."

She sniffled again as Jacen closed his eyes and buried his head in her neck. Gabriel sighed, dragging my attention back to him. "I have many vampires who will be converting in the next several hours, but Starla, as you know, won't live through the process." His gaze pulled away from where Starla and Jacen were cuddling, and he stared at me again. "You have the last of the remaining samples, the only supply large enough to see Starla through the interim of making a new batch. I'm so sorry, Emma, but we need your help. We need your medicine."

All of the blood drained from my face, taking any remnants of alcohol with it. I'd never felt more sober in all my life. They were asking for my lifeblood. They were asking me to give up my heartbeat, so Starla could keep hers going. As I processed that, Teren exhaled in a long, controlled breath, and Starla quietly said, "I know that you probably don't care for me. I know I'm sort of…bitchy."

Her voice cracked and as I watched, fresh tears stained her cheeks. "But this is a death sentence for me, Emma. I won't survive a conversion." Jacen kissed her head, looking like he was going to start crying too. I instantly knew that the man loved her, deeply loved her.

"Of course it's yours," I whispered.

Jacen, in his concern, didn't hear me. He looked up at me, his watery eyes fiery. "You can't condemn her to death, not when you'll survive. You can't be that selfish!"

Having heard me, Starla shushed him as she stared at me. "You'll give it to me?" She seemed genuinely surprised that I'd help her.

Jacen did too, once he figured out what I'd said. "You'll help her?" he whispered.

I looked between the two of them. "Yes, of course."

Teren lifted his head beside me. "Emma…"

When I looked back at him, his perfect eyes were torn. Lightly shaking my head, I smiled. "I won't let her die, not when I'll…survive."

Teren's fingers came up to touch my cheek. His eyes were watery now, too. "Are you sure?"

I nodded as conflicting emotions filled me. No, I wasn't sure if I wanted to die, who was ever sure of that? But I wasn't going to let another person die permanently, just so I could hear my heart beat a little while longer. Looking back at Starla, I smiled through my hazy vision. "It's yours, take it."

She started sobbing in earnest, then she tore herself away from Jacen and engulfed me in a hug. She sobbed mercilessly into my shoulder while I held her and patted her back. Jacen ran his hands back through his hair, then down his face. "Thank God," he murmured over and over.

Watching me comfort his child, Gabriel smiled warmly. Fatherly affection was clear in his face. "Thank you, Emma, for giving Starla a chance." He looked down at his daughter as she clung to me like my very presence was keeping her alive. "She's the only one that I knew for certain wouldn't survive this." As Starla sniffled and straightened, I handed her over to an eagerly awaiting Jacen. Gabriel watched the two embrace with a raised eyebrow. "I am working on her problem, but it's…complicated."

He left it at that. I watched Starla and Jacen holding each other tight in front of me, and I was glad that Gabriel was the one who was on her case. I wouldn't even know where to begin to help her genetically.

Starla smiled at me, while Jacen reluctantly eased his grip on her. "Yes, thank you, Emma," he said.

I nodded, embarrassed that they were actually thanking me for giving them back something that technically was theirs to begin with. Shaking my head, I muttered, "You don't have to… You're welcome."

Narrowing my eyes at Starla, I examined her body more closely. Even my enhanced sight didn't catch anything unusual about her. Aside from being disheveled from her earlier worry, she was picture-perfect as always. "Do you need a shot now? Have you had one today?"

She shook her head, her turquoise eyes filling and spilling. "The lab was trashed when we got back to it. We looked everywhere for a spare, but everyone kept their supply safe in the lab."

Gabriel frowned at her. "I've told her to keep an emergency supply in her car, since she cannot afford to miss a dose, but it apparently ran out and she never refilled it."

Starla hung her head and shrugged. Wondering how much time she had, I turned to Teren. "Will you go and get her mine please?"

Teren eyed me for a moment. He didn't seem happy about this, but he knew it was the right thing to do. He nodded, then blurred upstairs.

Starla touched my arm once she separated from Jacen. "Thank you, it took a long time to get here and I've already missed my evening shot. Father says I have another couple of hours, at the most..." Emotion locked up her throat and she shook her head.

I smiled and stood up to give her a warm hug. While we embraced, Teren returned with the few vials that I'd brought here for the weekend. He immediately prepared one and injected her in the arm. Starla didn't react to the sting, anymore than I did. After a while of taking daily shots, you just get used to it. When he pulled away, Starla reached out and hugged him tight. Teren blinked at the snobbish vampire's rare display of affection. Being that close to death leaves you with a different view on what's important in life though. A fact that was reinforced when Jacen stepped forward.

He shook Teren's hand, then pulled Starla back into his arms. "Thank God, Starla. I don't know what I'd do if you..." Sighing, he clutched her to him like he was scared she'd vanish at any moment.

When they pulled away from each other and started romantically gazing into each other's eyes, a feeling started to build in the room. It was an uncomfortable one, like we were intruding on a very private moment. Like any second, they were going to lean forward and kiss, quite possibly, for the very first time.

Respectfully, I turned away. Halina snorted. "We have several guest rooms available, if you'd like to consummate this little love fest you've got going on?"

Jacen's eyes widened and he immediately stepped away from Starla. The tiny debutante twisted to Halina, and the attitude I knew and loved, suddenly returned. "Bite me, Grandma."

Halina slowly rose from her chair. Tilting her head, she looked like she was seriously considering Starla's suggestion. Gabriel grabbed her hand when she took a step towards Starla. Halina ran a hand down her forever nineteen body with a smirk on her lips. "Careful, child, you wouldn't want to have an accident...now that you're free to age again."

Starla sniffed and defiantly raised her chin. "I'll ponder my slowly fading youth tomorrow," she raised an eyebrow at the pureblood, "when I'm basking in the bright, California sunshine." Her smirk rivaled Halina's and I heard a familiar growl burrow out of the elder vampire's chest.

I knew Starla was skating on very thin ice, and I was about to whisper at Teren to do something, when Gabriel spoke up. "Enough, Starla. Please take the vials out to the car and wait for me with Jacen."

Starla's eyes sank to the floor as she immediately responded with, "Yes, Father." Jacen took the few vials that Teren was holding while Teren stood between Starla and his great-grandmother. If things had gone down between the two snarky women, I wondered what Teren would have done? If it were me, I'd have run for cover.

After Jacen took the medicine, Starla grabbed his hand and pulled him away. The heavy smell of her hairspray marked her passing. As Jacen left with her, I noticed several emotions passing his youthful face. He seemed a little angry at Halina's comments, a little embarrassed by the moment he'd been caught in, and extremely grateful that Starla was going to be okay. But, over all of that, he also seemed...intrigued. As his eyes firmly locked onto the back of Starla's tight dress while she paraded him out of the room, I thought that they might do a bit more than just "talk" once they got in the car.

Hoping that Gabriel gave them enough time before he went out there, I contained my smile. If he didn't, he might walk into something even more private. Gabriel watched them leave with a frown on his face, and I wondered if he was thinking the exact same thing.

Halina shook her head at the couple, then sauntered over to Gabriel. They smiled at each other as she ran a hand through his hair, but then Halina frowned. "Who trashed your lab?" Her question got the attention of my silently debating husband. Teren sat back down beside me and looked over to Gabriel, his sad eyes turned inquisitive as Halina asked, "Who could pull off something like that, in your own home?"

That was something to consider. Gabriel's home was even more impressive than the Adams' place. It was also packed with purebloods and mixed vampires alike. The lab was a few floors underground, in a soundproof room where Gabriel spent most of his days. Anyone who had gotten down there and destroyed it must have known exactly how to get in and out undetected. Either that, or there was now a fresh pile of dead-vampire goo somewhere in Gabriel's house.

Gabriel sighed and surprisingly looked over at Teren and not Halina. "I believe that someone I've been hunting was giving me a message…to stop." One edge of his lip curled up; it was sort of a menacing gesture on the powerful man, especially with the orange firelight reflecting over his features. "I don't intend to."

I tilted my head at Gabriel. "Who have you been hunting?" I felt myself cringing, not all that sure that I wanted an answer to my question. If he was hunting a hunter, well, I knew what he did with them once he found them.

His cool eyes turned to mine and he started to answer, but Teren beat him to it. "The vampire who stole from you, right?"

A small gasp left me and I twisted in my seat to face Teren. "The one who gave that hunter the botched drug that killed you?" My eyes shifted over to a frowning Gabriel. "Is he right? Is that who you're tracking?"

Gabriel's lips twisted as Halina slipped her arms around him. "Yes. I sent out people to bring him to me for a…conversation, once you filled me in on what he'd done." He frowned deeper, and Halina lightly scratched his stomach. "He's a slippery one, though. He's managed to successfully evade my net for years now, but I have eyes everywhere and we are getting closer." He raised an eyebrow and shrugged. "It's only a matter of time before he's…dealt with. The crime committed against you will not go unpunished, Teren."

I swallowed nervously, knowing Gabriel's form of justice probably didn't involve lawyers. Teren grabbed my hand, but his eyes were still focused on Gabriel's. "He's getting to you, too, though. If he got into your lab, then he can get close to you." Teren's eyes flicked to Halina as concern filled his voice.

Gabriel noticed and looked over at her too. She looked between the two of them and straightened. "I am not afraid of one pissy little vampire." She rolled her eyes. "I think I can handle *one* man."

Gabriel smiled crookedly at her. "I'm sure you could, dear."

As she grinned at his comment, Gabriel's eyes returned to Teren. "I believe he only successfully got into my lab because I was out of the house, visiting a potential patient." He smiled softly. "A girl, twenty-two, looking to start a family. I'd like to give her longer to think about it."

Gabriel shrugged, sighed, and looked down as he sat on the stones in front of the fireplace. Even though the fire was small, more for ambiance than a heat source, I could feel the warmth of it on my sensitive face. But Gabriel didn't seem to mind sitting directly in front of the heat. If anything, he almost curled into it, like a cat enjoying a warm snuggle. The small blaze was enough to warm the dead vampire's chilly flesh. Halina's too, as she sat beside him.

His hands laced with Halina's. He looked at their joined flesh and sighed. "We will be losing so many overage mixed in the next twenty-four hours." He shook his head. "It does hurt my heart."

Thinking about the mass conversions happening soon, I started thinking of my own; it made my heart speed up. Teren squeezed my hand harder, then leaned over and kissed my cheek. I knew he sensed my unease. It had to be apparent to every vampire in the room. There was no stopping the reaction though. My nerves were spiking as I started thinking about dying.

Gabriel studied me, his eyes analyzing. Wiping a palm on the edge of my flirty dress, I swallowed nervously again. "How long do you think I have?" I asked in a trembling voice. Clearing my throat, I more steadily added, "How long until I die?"

Teren sighed and rested his head against mine. I fingered the locket around my throat while I tried to put on a brave face. Teren had done this, so surely I could too. Gabriel tilted his head while Halina narrowed her eyes, almost like she was waiting for me to keel over. "You had your shot this evening?" Gabriel asked calmly.

I nodded. "Before we headed out. I usually take it around bedtime every day, between eight or nine."

Gabriel nodded as the facts entered his brain. I could nearly see his brilliant mind calculating and formulating, printing out an answer as fast as any computer in the world. "Your consistency has acclimated your body to the drug. It will expect the dosage around that time tomorrow. When it does not receive it, you, like Starla, will have a few hours until your heart gives out." He looked over at Halina, squeezed her hand, then returned his eyes to mine. "I'm very sorry, Emma, but I don't think you'll be alive when the sun breaks Monday morning."

Breathing in slowly, I closed my eyes and clenched my locket in my fingers. So, that was it. I would be a walking, fictional myth by the time I went back to work Monday. I would be heartbeatless and chilly to the touch and wouldn't be able to handle any sort of food. I'd be unchanging to the world around me and would have to be more careful about leaving any loose ends. I'd be fully entrenched in the charade that Teren and his family lived in.

As I silently absorbed it all, Teren's voice cut through the room. "You are sure...that she *will* convert?" An edge of fear was in his voice and I opened my eyes; fear was on his face too. Regardless of Gabriel's assurances that I would make it, that Teren's blood would be enough to finish the conversion, Teren was still worried that I wouldn't.

Gabriel smiled and nodded. "Yes, I see no reason why she should have any difficulties completing the process." He raised an eyebrow. "Assuming she is fed enough, of course."

Teren's mouth firmed into a hard line. "Don't worry about food. She will eat." He looked over at me with determination in his features. "Even if I have to pour it down her throat myself," he added.

I smiled at the love I saw in his expression. Letting the locket swing loose against my skin again, I looked over at Gabriel. "How long will the conversion take?"

Gabriel's appraising eyes shifted to Teren. "How long did yours take?"

Teren shifted in his seat, uncomfortable with even remembering what had happened to him. He shrugged as he answered. "Not long, under an hour."

Gabriel nodded, like it wasn't too surprising to him. "You are essentially his carbon copy, so yours will take roughly around the same amount of time." He shrugged. "The process gets more efficient with each mixed generation, but around an hour is about as quickly as I've ever seen it completed."

I nodded as I leaned against Teren's side. In the silence that followed his last statement, I whispered. "What does it feel like…dying?" Gabriel looked down. Actually, every vampire looked down. Teren released my hand, folding his arms around me, but he wouldn't look at me either, instead, he buried his face in my neck. My heart rate spiked a little higher at their silent confirmation of my fear.

It was going to be…unpleasant.

Hearing my heart, smelling my fear in the air, Gabriel peeked up at me. The firelight glinted off of his eyes, turning the emerald into an eerie shade of bronze. "I'm so sorry, Emma, but I have no words to describe it." He looked over at Halina. The two of them shared an understanding that only undead vampires knew. "Dying," he whispered, "is different for every creature on this earth."

Halina sighed as she looked at me; her ageless eyes were filled with a compassion that I wasn't used to seeing on her. I think that terrified me more than Gabriel's next sentence. "In the end, death is something we must all face alone."

I woodenly nodded while Teren kissed my neck. The stubble of his jaw scraped against my skin, but I barely felt it. Wiping my hands over and over, I prayed for the tears stinging my eyes to not fall. Honestly, I had no reason to be afraid. I would survive death, just as my husband had. I had no reason to fear it. Now, if I could only convince my body of that.

Gabriel gracefully stood, and Halina stood with him, then Gabriel walked over and squatted in front of me. Exhaling slowly through my mouth, I tried to stop the light tremors that I could feel zinging throughout my body. He placed his chilly hands over mine, and stared unblinkingly into my eyes. Even though there was no glow emanating from them, his ageless eyes had a calming quality about them and I found my body relaxing.

Teren rubbed my back as he felt me easing as well. Smiling softly, Gabriel quietly said, "You will survive this, Emma, and you will be reunited with your family." He closed his eyes briefly, a small smile on his lips. I thought that maybe he was taking a moment to mentally check in on his family. While everyone in his nest was genetically a stranger to him, he did have two blood children out in the world, and he could feel their presence in his head, the same as I could feel mine.

"Thank you, Gabriel," I said softly, folding my hands over his.

He opened his eyes and stood. "No, thank you, Emma…for saving Starla. I know she can be exasperating, but she is family to me." He looked through the home to where we could all hear the very obvious sounds of heavy breathing and lip smacking. Gabriel frowned while I grinned. Jacen and Starla were indeed celebrating her survival. Sighing, Gabriel shook his head. "And I am apparently not the only one who would have missed her."

As Teren kissed my cheek again, Halina wrapped her arms around Gabriel. "You could stay tonight? Let them connect in a guest room while we connect in my room?" She suggestively raised an eyebrow and Gabriel smiled.

To give them a moment of privacy, visually at least, I wrapped my arms around Teren and buried my head in his neck. I could still clearly hear Gabriel softly kiss her, and then sigh. "I wish I could stay, my dear, but I have too many conversions happening or about to happen. I need to get back home, to be there for them."

I peeked up to watch Halina bite her lip, nod, and then kiss him. Gabriel kissed her once more then reluctantly shifted to leave. Teren and I stood and followed Halina to escort him out. As the fresh night air hit my face, I inhaled a deep breath, letting the crispness settle the last of my nerves. It would be fine, I would be fine, and now, Starla would be fine.

Smiling as we approached the sleek, black sedan they'd driven up in, I tried to not listen to just how "fine" Starla currently was. Gabriel approached the door just as Jacen murmured that she was beautiful. As Starla giggled and told him that she already knew that, Gabriel jerked the door open. I bit my lip to hold in the laugh at the look on Jacen and Starla's faces. Clearly absorbed in each other, the high maintenance vampires hadn't heard us coming towards them. They both looked shocked and rumpled.

Gabriel cleared his throat and motioned outside. "Can you think clearly enough to drive us home, Jacen?"

Lying on top of Starla, her arms and legs firmly wrapped around his body, Jacen immediately stammered, "Yes, Father," and tried to disengage himself from the young woman beneath him.

Recovering from her shock, Starla frowned and looked up at Gabriel. Popping a bubble with her fresh piece of gum, she twisted her lips in dismay; the mint smell of her breath hit me from where I was standing with Teren. "Father," she said coyly, her arms cinching around Jacen, who was still struggling to get up, "do you think you could drive us back?" She smiled with just one edge of her lip. "So Jacen and I can…talk?"

Gabriel cocked an eyebrow at her while the laughter I'd been struggling to hold in bubbled out. Shaking his head at her, Gabriel let out a soft laugh as well. While he seemed unsure about two of his "children" hooking up right under his nose, he didn't seem to be able to refuse the woman who'd been so close to death anything. "All right." His eyes locked onto Jacen, "but you will act in accordance with your age, Jacen."

Jacen nodded, his face serious. Well, his expression was serious. It was a little hard to take his face seriously with his hair sticking out every which way and faint streaks of lipstick across his mouth. "Yes, Father."

Giggling again, I tried to block out the fact that Gabriel was correct in pointing out Jacen's age. Even though he didn't look it, Jacen was older than Halina, which made him considerably older than the twenty-something Starla. But to vampires, age was irrelevant after a certain point. Gabriel himself had a huge age gap with his own girlfriend…by hundreds of years.

When Gabriel moved to the driver's side, Teren touched his arm. "I'll drive you to my place. We can pick up the rest of the vials." He looked over at me, a sympathetic sadness in his eyes. As much as Teren wanted forever with me, he knew what I was about to face and wouldn't wish it on anyone. I smiled and nodded reassuringly. This was the right thing to do.

Gabriel nodded and cracked open the car door.

"Gabriel?"

He looked up at Halina as she stepped up to the car. Maybe it was a trick of the lights coming from the spacious windows of the home, or the mixing of everyone's dimly glowing eyes, but Halina seemed nervous as she approached him.

Maybe sensing that too, Gabriel closed his door. "Yes, dear?"

Looking over at Teren and me, then Starla and Jacen, Halina lightly grabbed his hand and pulled him towards her. "May we…talk for a moment, before you go?"

Gabriel smiled, then nodded. "Of course."

They walked towards the house and wondering if Halina was about to break up with him, I watched them with unabashed curiosity. While Halina had seemed like she'd decided to let him into her heart, the woman was a free-spirited enigma and could have easily swung herself the other way. Maybe, since we no longer needed his assistance with me now, she felt this was a good time to end things. I hoped not. Regardless of her worries, I knew that she loved him and love should be celebrated, not pushed away.

Teren and I watched Halina separate from Gabriel, then take a running leap to the top of the house. She effortlessly landed on her hangout, the covered section of the roof where we'd had our girl talk not too long ago. Gabriel looked up at her, smiled, then took a couple of steps and jumped. He landed as effortlessly as she had. I frowned that my attempt at that jump hadn't been nearly as graceful as the two of theirs.

Beside us, Starla giggled and I heard the rear car door slam shut. The sounds of lip smacking resumed in the dark car. I shook my head at the eager girl, and Teren chuckled then slung his arm around me. "I could tuck you in before I go?" he whispered in my ear.

I shook my head. "I don't think I'll be sleeping anytime soon." My hand covered my stomach, where a tension knot was forming. There was just no way to fall asleep after being told that you only had twenty-four hours left to live. Teren's pale eyes tracked the movement and he nodded. Sighing, I leaned into his side and murmured, "I just want to stare at our children for a while."

He nodded against my head, then led me into the house. As we silently walked up the stairs to the twins' room, conversations from the roof drifted down to me. I didn't really want to listen, it being a very private conversation and all, but blocking out sound wasn't always possible, and I *was* curious if Halina was going to end their relationship.

Climbing up the steps with my arm around Teren's waist, I heard Halina casually state, "I just wanted to tell you that I've…grown fond of you." I smiled and looked over at Teren; also listening, he smiled too. Halina sniffed and I pictured her standing tall and straight with her chin held high as she reluctantly poured her heart out. "I enjoy your company and miss you when you are gone."

I heard Gabriel's light steps as he approached where I sensed her. "I miss you, too," he said quietly, a warmth in his voice that I didn't usually hear.

As Teren and I reached the top step, Halina's voice lost some of its casualness. Sounding much more like the teenager she resembled, she told Gabriel, "I may…have feelings for you."

Teren smiled wider and shook his head. She *may*? I was pretty certain that she did. Gabriel seemed certain too. "You may?" he asked softly. I pictured him cupping her cheek. I pictured her with tears in her eyes. Of course, she may have been smirking for all I really knew.

"Maybe…possibly…"

I smiled and bit my lip to not laugh at the normally confident woman. She would hear it, and I didn't want to disrupt her outpouring by embarrassing her, even though she wouldn't think twice about doing the same thing to me. She delighted in my embarrassment.

Approaching the door that my sleeping children were behind, I listened to Gabriel say with a laugh, "Are you trying to tell me that you are in love with me, Halina?"

I paused with my hand on the doorknob and looked up to the roof. Teren looked up as well as we both waited for her answer. In true Halina fashion, she scoffed at his question. "Of course not." I frowned at her stubbornness, but then I heard the distinct sound of a kiss. After that, she muttered, "Maybe...I don't know."

Teren looked over at me, smiling as he nodded at the closed bedroom door. Silently, I twisted the knob. A patch of light from the hallway highlighted the sleeping bundles in the large bed they shared. Spike had come with us again this trip and he was in his favorite place, huddled between them. He lifted his head at us as we stood in the doorway, then lowered it; his bushy tail started wagging at his master's return.

Teren sighed in contentment as he watched the chests of our children rising and falling, almost simultaneously. Blissfully unaware of just what had transpired tonight, they held hands across Spike's body. Tears sprang to my eyes as I watched our tiny miracles slumber. Whatever price I had to pay to remain with them, I would. Teren clenched my hand tighter, kissing my head as we gazed at the lives we'd brought into the world.

From up above us, I heard Gabriel say to Halina. "I have developed feelings for you too, feelings I never expected to feel again. You have taken me by surprise, Halina. I do believe that I am in love with you."

A wide smile broke out on my face as I looked at Teren. He smiled and tilted his head, listening for his great-grandmother's response to an outright declaration of love. I nearly wanted to cross my fingers that she'd finally admit it back to Gabriel.

"I...I..." She paused for so long that I would have sworn she'd just jumped off of the roof, if I couldn't still feel her up there. Sighing, she finally said, "I will miss you. I wish I could help you clean up the mess you've been left with."

I shook my head at her and Teren shrugged. Some things Halina was just not ready for. Admitting love was one of them. Gabriel lightly laughed, not at all bothered that she still couldn't say it. If anything, Gabriel was exceedingly patient. "It is nearly dawn, my love, you cannot come with me. But, as soon as I...settle some things, I will return to you."

I heard light kissing, then Halina murmured, "I suppose I should stay here anyway, at least until Emma is safe. I wouldn't want her to die on my watch." I frowned as I looked up at where she was. Teren let out a soft chuckle and I switched my frown to him. Halina's seeming indifference to me was sort of a joke around the house. But I understood enough about Halina to not take offense to it anymore. Well, most of the time anyway.

Returning my gaze to my children, I heard Gabriel laugh and kiss her again.

Chapter 9 – One Last Supper

When Halina and Gabriel finished up with their touching moment on the roof, Teren blurred down to drive Gabriel to our place. A smile was plastered to my face as I listened to Gabriel break up Starla and Jacen's canoodling. Halina tenderly wished him a safe trip home as he started his car, and then Gabriel and Teren were gone.

Halina sighed with contentment, and in the silence of the sleeping household, I told her, "I'm glad you didn't break up with him. You two are good together." I smiled as I thought about how similar they were. Both had been alone for a long time, having lost their respective loved ones ages ago, Gabriel even longer than Halina. Both were the protectors of their families and both could be ruthless when they needed to be. Yet, in this, in falling in love again, they were equally new and inexperienced. Almost…innocent.

Halina scoffed as she blurred into the doorway beside me. "Well, I do enjoy having intercourse with him." She sniffed. "I wasn't ready to give that up yet."

Like I said…*almost* innocent.

I rolled my eyes and shook my head at her as I continued staring at my children. I could feel Teren pulling away from me in my head and, sighing softly, I hoped he hurried back to me. The warmth of our reuniting would help ease the growing knot of anticipation in my belly. My head couldn't stop mentally ticking off the moments. Every heartbeat I had, every breath I took, every second of time I felt passing by, was one less that I'd have…alive.

Silently watching me, Halina tilted her head; her dark hair flowed down her bare arm in the strapless dress she was wearing. "Are you freaking out?" she asked, curious.

Frowning, I shook my head and crossed my arms over my belly, subtly pressing in that ball of tension. "No, of course not. I know I'll be fine."

I lifted my chin, but even I felt the lie in my declaration. Surprising me, Halina put a hand on my shoulder. "My own transformation was different from what you'll be facing, but after having watched Imogen and Alanna go through the torment, I would be fearful of it, if I was about to experience it."

My eyes widened as the ball in my stomach grew considerably larger. Was that supposed to make me feel better? Noting my features, my accelerated heart, she shrugged. "I don't believe in coddling you. This will be painful." She raised an eyebrow. "But it is *only* pain and you have overcome far worse. I know you can do this, Emma."

Nodding at her, I actually did feel a little comforted. Gazing at my children, she smiled. "I'm going down to my room." Looking back at me with a serious expression, she said, "Enjoy every moment of your last day as a human. You won't get another."

Even though she didn't look to be asking for one from me, I gave her a swift hug. When we separated, she languidly headed down to her rooms below the earth. Once her presence was settled downstairs, I walked into my kids' bedroom. Needing to feel connected to the people who made this scary process worth going through, I crawled into bed with them.

Spike shifted to lie at our feet when I nestled in-between the twins. I temporarily disturbed them, and Nika murmured, "Hi, Mommy," as she wrapped her little arms over me. Julian muttered the same as he wrapped himself around me too. Closing my eyes, I inhaled their scent: the grass, the dirt, the baby shampoo, and the distinct essence of them. It calmed me, and that horrid knot melted away.

The next morning, Teren and I filled the rest of the family in on what had happened the evening before. Imogen and Alanna were sympathetic, each giving me long hugs as we discussed my fate over breakfast. Trying not to worry, I watched my children build houses out of their French toast. I wasn't hungry, but I made myself eat. I knew that this was the last breakfast I was ever going to have, so I wanted to enjoy it. I savored every bite that I made myself take.

Jack sighed and put a hand over mine as I popped a slice of bacon in my mouth. "I'm very sorry for what you'll be going through, Emma." His warm brown eyes clearly showed that while he adored his vampiric family, he had no desire to go through the process. He had no desire to become one.

148

I rested my hand over his, locking in the memory of how similarly warm our skin was. "Thank you, Jack."

He nodded, his eyes glassier than normal. Shifting his gaze to his wife, he asked her, "Should I stay the night somewhere else then?"

Alanna immediately nodded, her eyes suddenly protective. She didn't look at me, but I wanted to vow to her, on my very soul, that I would never hurt him. I couldn't, though. Having watched Teren suffer through it, I knew there was a very good possibility that I might go after Jack. I hung my head at the thought. My next one immediately brought my head back up. "The children!"

My panicked eyes flew to them. I could clearly hear their heartbeats, even from across the table. Surely, they would seem appetizing to a creature literally dying of thirst? Hadn't Halina confessed that she'd nearly killed Imogen? The thought of harming them made bile rise in my throat. My trembling hand covered my mouth just as Teren rubbed his hand over my back. The combination gave me chills.

"We'll get them away, Emma," he said softly, soothingly. I looked over at him, irrationally worried that I could somehow hurt them no matter how far away they were from me. That would be my worst nightmare, my absolute worst. As I heard other voices telling me that it would be all right, Teren's sky blue eyes drew me in. "I won't let you hurt them, Emma. I'll keep them safe."

I nodded and he gave me a soft kiss. The kids giggled, not understanding the seriousness of the situation, only knowing that Mommy and Daddy were kissing. With a faked not-a-care-in-the-world smile, Teren twisted to them. "How would you two like to spend the night with Grandma Linda?"

My kids erupted in loud cheers, clapping their hands. Spike, sitting behind them in case they dropped anything edible, barked and thumped his tail, almost like he'd understood the question and wanted to go see my mom too. I laughed at the trio and slapped on my fake smile. "Okay, but you need to go easy on Grandma Linda. She's not as quick as your other Grandmas."

They both nodded, their little faces alive with yet another upcoming adventure. "We know, Mommy," Julian informed me.

Til Death

"Grandma's not a vampire." He stumbled a bit on the word, pronouncing it more with a W sound than a V. The innocence made my smile genuine. Soulless, bloodthirsty monsters? I didn't think so.

I frowned as I rethought that. For a moment, just a moment tonight, that was exactly what I would be. Driven by pure eat-or-die instinct, I'd be the epitome of every late night horror show I'd ever seen. It was not a good weight to carry around, and I was relieved that my children wouldn't be there to witness it. Even though they would go through it themselves one day, they shouldn't have to see one of their parents acting that way. It would be unsettling for them. And I wouldn't exactly be setting a good example.

Teren looked back at me while they laughed around their mouths stuffed with spiced bread. "I'll call and make arrangements for them and Spike."

I leaned into his side with a sigh. "Don't tell her about me, okay?"

He kissed my hair as his arm slinked around my waist. "Are you sure? She would want to know what you're…going through."

Resting my head on his shoulder, I looked over at Imogen and Alanna talking together in a bright patch of sunlight. Even though they were in their own conversation, about which cows should be given up for my conversion, I knew that they were partially listening to Teren and me. "No, my mom would insist on being here, and it's not safe."

Into my hair, Teren whispered, "We could make her leave when you…fall asleep." I smiled and looked up at him. He meant when I died, but he didn't want to scare the children with that word. They still weren't entirely informed on what went down during a conversion. We weren't about to tell them either, not at three years old.

Frowning as I thought over the scenario he was referring to, I shook my head before laying it back on his shoulder. "No, I haven't told her about that part of this yet and…" Sighing, I watched Alanna twist to look at me. "No parent should have to watch their child…fall asleep."

Alanna smiled at me as her eyes shifted over to Teren. Imogen grabbed her hand and Alanna looked back at her mom. I wondered if Imogen had watched her daughter die. As the youthful but grandmotherly vampire smiled sadly and cupped her daughter's cheek, I figured that she had.

Pulling back from Teren's shoulder, I peeked up at him. "I wish you didn't have to see it." Twisting his lips, he shook his head. Before he could speak, I quickly added, "But don't leave me."

His eyes watered and he shook his head again before resting his forehead to mine. "I'm not going anywhere, Em. Nothing could tear me away from you right now." He leaned down to kiss me again, but a piece of toast sailing across the table distracted him. Straightening, he looked over at Nika and Julian sword fighting with sticks of toast. "Don't play with your food."

Knowing the seriousness of our conversation, knowing the seriousness of my upcoming demise, I couldn't help my reaction at the look on his face as he instantly shifted from a sweet lover to a stern parent, scolding our children for improper table manners. I started laughing. In my anxiousness, I started belly laughing. Tears were streaming down my face and my children joined in on the gaiety.

Knowing I was disrupting the discipline that we usually tried to instill in them, but needing a release, I grabbed a slice of my toast and chucked it over the table at them. Their little eyes widened, but giggling, they started throwing food right back at me. I dodged half eaten chunks of bread while I tore up tiny chunks of food to glob over at them. Teren sighed, but didn't deny me my moment of fun. Softly chuckling, he eventually joined in, grabbing some fresh sticks from a platter in the center of the table. Only Teren started chucking them at his mom. It was about three seconds after that when a full-on food fight was in progress.

I laughed until my sides hurt, and Spike happily cleaned up the mess.

Picking stray pieces of food out of my hair all afternoon, I spent the bulk of the day with my children. We did everything that they loved to do. We colored, we read books, we put together puzzles, and Teren and I each grabbed a child and did the vampiric version of piggyback rides, meaning we were mere streaks rushing through the house. We wore them out so hard that they crashed in my arms at naptime. I stayed cuddled with them on the couch, listening to our hearts beat in unison. I tried to imagine never hearing that unison again, but I'd become too accustomed to it; I couldn't.

Teren stayed close to my side throughout the day, holding me when he could, kissing me as often as he could. I knew he was offering whatever support and encouragement he could, and I loved him all the more for it. We didn't speak of what was going to happen to me anymore. It was too hard to talk about around the children. I didn't want to worry or scare them. I would come out of this fine. I was pretty sure, anyway.

After naptime, Alanna started preparing the most elaborate meal I'd ever seen; it rivaled Christmas dinner. When I asked her what she was doing, she would only tell me that she was making something special for me. It twisted my stomach at the same time that it warmed it. She was literally making me my last meal. After today, I'd be on the same all-liquid diet that Teren was on. While he told me all the time that food didn't even sound appealing anymore, I had a really hard time wrapping my head around it. How could hamburgers, fries, pizzas, pasta and ice cream, suddenly not sound mouthwateringly good?

While the children played with some floured dough balls, getting the white powder all over themselves in the process, I helped Alanna cut up vegetables. From across the house in the library, I could hear Teren calling my mother, and asking her if she'd like the kids for a couple of days while he whisked me away on an impromptu birthday getaway. She exclaimed her joy at the idea of having them overnight and I sighed as I watched Julian help Nika squash her ball flat. It wasn't exactly the situation I'd imagined for their first night away from me. I wasn't sure how I'd handle them not being around, but I knew I needed to be away from them, for their safety.

When Teren told her that Jack would be bringing the kids by, since we were leaving shortly, I sighed again. I hated that he had to lie to my mother, but it was for the best. You just couldn't tell a parent that your heart would soon stop beating and not expect them to rush out to you. I'd always meant to tell Mom that it would happen to me someday, but I'd never found the time…or the courage. Like most things that happened with me, I would have to tell her after the fact. I felt a little guilty about that.

Alanna gave me a brief, sympathetic pat before returning to the feast she was preparing. Teren hung up with my mother and immediately called Hot Ben, both to fill him in on the situation and to talk over his own stress with a friend. He didn't outright mention his fear, but I heard it in the tenor of his voice. I tried to stop listening, to give him some privacy, and shifted my attention to Alanna; she was lightly humming, also giving her son privacy.

"Mom?" I asked softly. She twisted to me, a warm smile on her lips at being addressed as family. Lifting her eyebrows, she waited for my question. Curious if Alanna would have done what I'd been doing for the last few years, up until last night actually, I asked, "Would you have taken Gabriel's shot? Would you have wanted to keep aging?"

Alanna leaned back against the counter as Imogen walked into the room. Running a hand over the button-up shirt tucked into her jeans, she paused to rub her empty stomach. "I would have loved to give Teren a sibling." She sighed and Imogen slipped an arm around her. Looking between the two was like watching twin sisters, not a mother and daughter. Shaking her loose, black hair, Alanna shrugged. "It was hard for me to get pregnant. I would have loved to have had more time to try again."

Picturing Teren with a brother or a sister made me smile. He would have loved that. Imogen's free hand skimmed over the long skirt she was wearing. "It was difficult for me as well." She squeezed Alanna tight. "You were my only miracle." Alanna smiled up at her while Imogen looked at me. "Gabriel says that it is harder for a female vampire to conceive, than it is for a male vampire to…" She cut off as she glanced down at my curious children.

Filling in the part she didn't want to say in front of my impressionable youngsters, that it was easier for vampire men to knock up humans, than vice versa, I let her know that I understood. "Oh, I didn't know that."

Imogen shrugged and a strand of dark hair fell from her loose bun. "If we'd known that with Teren, we probably wouldn't have pushed him so hard." She smiled as she listened to her grandson laughing with Ben as his friend eased his mind. "He just seemed so disinterested in settling down, we were worried that he wouldn't want children...until it was too late."

All of us looked at the twins. They each smiled at the sudden attention, swinging their legs back and forth on their stools as they poked holes in the dough with their fingers. Alanna handed them some pretzel sticks and showed them how to make animals with the sticks as legs. I walked over to Imogen and she looped her cool arm around me. "We shouldn't have pushed him, I know, but look at those two..." her eyes drifted back to Nika and Julian. "How could we not pressure him for them?"

Alanna peeked her head up from in-between them and her lineless brow furrowed. "But I raised my son properly, and he knew that he had to find the right woman first, before he brought children into this world with her." Her face relaxed as she looked over at me. "Actually, I think Carrie taught him that," she whispered.

I nodded. Yes, his ex had taught him a lot about responsibility. But then, all exes teach us something about who we are, about who we want to be. Alanna smiled as she went back to making dough animals with the kids. "He just took his time finding you, is all."

"Says who?" Teren said, finally walking back into the room. Smiling with confidence, he slipped his arms around me and nuzzled my neck; the roughness made me laugh. "I think I found you just when I was meant to."

I leaned back into his arms and closed my eyes, nodding. "Yes, yes you did."

The kids started getting anxious to leave shortly before dark. They waited until Halina was awake, so she could see them off, but they'd been bouncing off the walls for most of the afternoon. Spending the night at my mom's house had never happened for them and it created an excitement that was nearly palpable. Especially when Teren told them that my mom had fresh blood in her fridge.

I frowned at him while the kids clapped their hands. "Where would she...?" My eyes widened as I remembered something about her getting a chicken coop a couple of days ago. "Did she get those chickens just...for that?" My eyes drifted down to my kids hugging Halina goodbye. Teren bought live chickens so he could drain them before cooking them. I knew my mom was okay with what the kids were, but her going so far as to provide a food source for them was pretty startling, especially since they really didn't need that much blood.

Teren held me tight and shrugged. "She said she didn't want to deny them what they needed."

I sighed, recalling her saying that to him earlier when they'd spoken. I remembered Teren's response; it was the same as my own. "She doesn't need to do that. We give them all the blood they need," I said.

He shrugged again. "I know, but she's a proud grandma." Laughing softly he added, "I think if our kids breathed fire, she'd have them make her s'mores. Anything to make them feel special." He laughed again and kissed my neck.

I shook my head at my mom's ability to adapt. She had embraced the twins in a way that I hadn't anticipated. I hoped her level of acceptance stretched to me as well when I came back…different. With how much she constantly surprised me with them, I was pretty sure she would take me in whatever form she could get me.

When Jack came down the stairs with his overnight bag, a pang went through me. This was really happening. He was spending the night at our house while our kids stayed with my mom. I watched him walk over to his wife and gently kiss her goodbye. She put on a brave face but my enhanced sight saw the tremble of her lip, the moisture in her pale eyes. She probably hadn't spent a night apart from him since her own conversion. Guilt washed through me that I was forcing them apart, if even for just one evening. I knew he couldn't stay though. It was too risky. And I knew Alanna wouldn't leave me until she knew I was safe. That just wasn't her way.

I turned away from them, to give them as much privacy as I could while they whispered words of love to each other. Our children detached from where they were saying goodbye to Imogen and darted to Teren and me. We each knelt down to enfold a child in our arms. Nika shivered as she held her daddy. Julian melted into me as I held him. I closed my eyes and swallowed, knowing I'd feel different to him the next time he held me.

"Love you, Mommy," he said, not a trace of fear or worry in his voice.

I choked up, my eyes almost to the point of overflowing. "I love you too, baby."

Nika separated from Teren to trade places with Julian. Resting my head on her hair, I felt my tears fall and heard them splash on her body. She peeked up at me, and her fingers came up to touch my cheek. "Why are you sad, Mommy?"

I smiled as even more tears fell. "I'm not, sweetheart. I just love you…so much."

Julian broke free from Teren to rush back to me. I crushed him to my body, suddenly not wanting to let them go, even though I knew I had to. "Don't cry, Mommy," he murmured as his little hand stroked my back.

It was too much for me and the few tears were now a torrent. I kissed each head as I sobbed out, "I'm just so happy to be your mommy. I love you both so much."

Just when I felt myself really starting to lose it, and my emotional turmoil started reflecting in my children as they clung to me, like I was leaving them forever, Teren pulled them back. "Okay kids, time to go. Grandma's waiting." His voice was light, soft and carefree, everything mine was not.

Not wanting them to know anything was wrong, I wiped my eyes dry and threw on the happiest smile that I could. "Daddy's right. You guys have fun, okay?"

They both nodded, then rushed over to give Alanna a final hug before heading out the door with Teren, giggling. He glanced back at me with apologetic eyes and I mouthed, "Thank you," so he would know that I wasn't upset with him for disengaging them from me. He was right to break the tension. I didn't want them to feel anything but joyous about what was happening.

He nodded and left. Their presence in my head shifted to the parking lot as Teren transferred their car seats to his dad's truck. Jack and Alanna gave each other one long, last hug before separating, and then Alanna handed him a bag of the supper that he would be missing. Jack walked over to me while I held in my stomach, anxious, nervous, and sad that half of my family was forced to flee from me. Looking down at me for a second, he shook his head and then swept me up into a hug. I blinked and fiercely hugged him back.

He wasn't super affectionate, unlike Alanna and Imogen, so I knew that he was truly feeling concern for me. Patting my back while he held me tight, he whispered, "You come back now, all right?"

Swallowing, I nodded. "I will, Dad." The word still tore my heart. Having lost my father at such a young age, I'd had a hole in me that Jack had helped fill. I loved him as the surrogate father that he was, and was very grateful that he wouldn't be anywhere near me tonight.

Pulling apart from me, Jack sniffled, then headed out the door after Teren. I made myself stay in the house, but I heard my children laughing and barking with Spike. Jack said his goodbyes to his son, wishing him well with the conversion. I could hear them hug, then car doors started shutting. I turned away after that, not really wanting to hear my children leave me.

Surprisingly, I turned into Halina. The vixen said nothing, only wrapped her ice cold arms around me. Sniffling into her shoulder, I held in my tears. She rubbed my back as she soothingly murmured, "Don't worry, they will all be safe." She hugged me a little tighter. "As will you."

She said something else after that but it was in Russian. I caught a little of it, and from what I could make out, she was saying that I would finally be a sister of the night, and we would celebrate with a slaughter, bathing our bodies in blood. Or she could have been wishing me an early happy birthday. My Russian still wasn't that great.

Teren swished back into the room as the sound of tires crunching down the driveway filtered back to me. I was handed off from one vampire to another as Halina passed me to my husband. Clinging to his shirt, I thought that I'd probably never needed him as much as I did in that moment.

Sensing my turmoil, perhaps sharing it, Teren scooped me up as I laid my head on his shoulder. Too exhausted to keep standing, I was grateful for the assistance. Kissing my head, he sighed. "This isn't exactly how I pictured our first overnight date without the kids."

Blinking, I peeked up at him. Smiling, he shrugged. "I'll do better next time."

I laughed and he gave me a soft kiss. Alanna walked up to us, and gently placed her hand on my back. "Hungry, dear? Dinner is ready."

She looked at the door, and I knew she was thinking of her husband. Reaching out to her, to give her some comfort for her own loneliness, I nodded. "I'm starving, Mom. I would be honored." She smiled and started walking towards the kitchen. Even though my stomach felt too knotted to eat anything, Alanna loved providing for her family, and I knew it would lift her spirits to accept the meal she'd worked so hard on. A small sacrifice for her much larger one.

We all sat down to a feast fit for a king. Alanna had prepared all of my favorite things. Adams Ranch steaks, the best in all of California if you asked me, roasted chicken, mashed potatoes, macaroni salad, and even a lasagna. It was way too much food for only one person to eat, but I appreciated the sentiment. She piled my plate with a little bit of everything, then kissed my head as she tucked me under the table.

I thanked her and stared at my plate as the blood was doled out. I wasn't the tiniest bit hungry. It made me a little sad that I wasn't, since this would be it for me, food-wise. But really, eating was the last thought in my head; even the blood I could smell wafting from the carafe didn't sound good.

Handing Teren his steaming glass, Alanna patted my back. "Eat, Emma, it will help ease the…discomfort, if your stomach is full."

My eyes widened, but I picked up my fork and did as she said. I trusted her advice; they all had a lot more experience with this than I did. Teren drank with his arm around me, cool and comforting. A silence settled around the table as the meal extended; it seemed to take about three times as long as a typical meal at the ranch. Probably because I was picking at my food. They all watched me, too, like they were waiting for my heart to beat its last beat right there in front of them. I wanted to tell them to stop, that I wasn't even late for my shot yet, but as the time went by, I started to do it too. Like my heart was inescapable, aggravating elevator music, I couldn't stop listening to every steady, wet thump.

Bedtime for my kids rolled around as Alanna brought out a cake. I smiled at the chocolate treat and made myself take some. My thoughts were on my kids, though. I imagined my mom reading stories to them. I pictured them holding hands and telling each other goodnight. It hurt my heart that I was missing it. While I frowned, Teren kissed my head; he was also aware of what time it was.

As I finished eating all of the food that my body could handle, the time finally passed by when I typically took my shot. It felt strange to not take it. A warning bell was dinging in my head that I had to consciously ignore. It was hard to. I'd been taking the medicine for so long now that my body was nagging at me, constantly reminding me that I was forgetting to do something. Only I wasn't forgetting. I was not doing it on purpose.

Swallowing a nervous lump, I leaned into Teren's side and stared at all of the curious ice blue eyes watching me. Anxious, I turned my head to Teren. "If we go to Utah, what would we do for work?"

Surprise lightened Teren's expression. Obviously, he hadn't expected me to ask that. "You want to talk about that...now?"

I nodded as I rubbed my full stomach. "Yes." My eyes drifted around the table. "Waiting around to die is starting to kill me..." I narrowed my eyes as Halina smirked at me. "You know what I mean," I muttered, swinging my eyes back to Teren. "Distract me...please."

Teren smiled and shook his head. "Well, I'll get a job writing somewhere, maybe another monthly magazine, or maybe a newspaper." Smiling wider, he hugged me tight. "You can get a job at another accounting firm, or...really, we could get you a job anywhere you want. Feel like changing careers?"

Pulling back from him, I scowled. "How are *you* going to get me a job anywhere I want?"

He was about to answer, but Halina, across the table, got my attention by giving me a sly smile and a wave. My mouth dropped open when I understood. They compelled their way into jobs.

Turning back to him, I sputtered, "That's cheating." Helping someone get their job back that they'd lost because of compulsion was one thing, trancing people into *giving* you a job was completely different.

He shrugged. "The job market is competitive. Sometimes an edge helps."

I shook my head with a scoff. "An edge...really."

He chuckled and shrugged again. As I looked around the table, I took in the opulence that the family gathered around themselves—gold cutlery, crystal goblets, fine china in a pantry against the wall. And this was just one of their ranches. Even for a successful business, it seemed a little over the top.

Looking back at Teren, I cocked an eyebrow. "Okay, I know a few things about finances." My hand swirled around in the air to indicate the luxury around us. "And a few ranches scattered across the country could not have possibly amassed the amount of money you guys have." I pointedly looked over at Halina. "This can't all be from ranching...so where did it come from?"

I heard Teren scratch his stubble, and Alanna and Imogen exchanged a look. Only Halina kept my gaze. "Do you really want to know?" she asked.

Taking in the reluctance around me, I sighed. "I'm going to find it unsavory, aren't I?"

Halina grinned widely and sat back in her chair. "That depends on your definition of unsavory. I call it survival."

Twisting my lips, I sighed, "Okay, hit me."

She smirked. "Well, in my many years on this earth, I may have crossed paths with a millionaire or two. They may have felt...compelled to donate some of their wealth to my well-being." She shrugged again as Teren shifted uncomfortably as he watched me. He probably expected me to start throwing things.

"You stole it?" I asked, surprised but then again, not surprised.

Tilting her head, her youthful face turned contemplative. "Well, that's where the savory-unsavory line comes into play." She shrugged causally. "I asked...they gave."

I raised an eyebrow at her. "Did they have a choice?"

She grinned. "No."

Sighing, I leaned back in my chair and took in the "stolen" wealth around me. "So, all of this isn't really yours?"

Imogen leaned forward, her expression concerned. "Emma, it was just to get us up and running." She smiled. "I'm pretty good with finances, too, and I make sure that we have sound investments, so mother doesn't have to...do that."

I shook my head. "But if those investments ever dried up?"

Imogen raised an eyebrow, clearly confident in her abilities. "They won't."

I leaned forward. "But...if they did?"

Halina snorted and crossed her arms over her chest. "They won't." Her tone was definite; she clearly meant it in the literal sense. If they lost everything they had, money-wise, then she'd find another person with an abundance of wealth and "ask" him or her for a charitable contribution, one that they wouldn't be able to refuse.

Shaking my head, I murmured, "Now I sort of wish I hadn't asked."

I really wasn't sure how comfortable I was with the way they'd made their fortune. Teren squeezed my shoulder and looked about to speak up, but his great-grandmother beat him to it. Leaning over her arms on the table, Halina shook her head as she spoke. "Try to understand the situation, Emma, before you condemn it solely on principle."

Hanging her head, she lowered her voice. "I was turned when I was nineteen. I was alone, in a foreign body, with a newborn infant. My husband was dead. My creator was dead. And every day, I worried that I might turn on my own child." She peeked up at me; the wisdom in her eyes betrayed the youth of her body.

Tilting her swirling mass of black hair, she indicated the land around us. "My husband left me with a fraction of this ranch that you see now, and no one here to help me with it during the day." Sighing, she looked over to the window, out to the fields where dark shapes were standing still in the distance, sleeping. Every vampire in the room was stone silent as they listened to her story; no one besides me was even breathing.

Shaking her head, she muttered, "I fed on cattle and what other animals that I could find nearby. I was too scared to approach a human. Too scared that once I did, a bloodlust would take me, and I wouldn't be able to stop killing humans." She looked back at me with her eyebrows raised. "Believe it or not, but I didn't want to be that kind of creature."

Shifting her gaze to her daughter, she sighed again. "But eventually the cows started to dry up. Eventually I didn't have any left to get milk for my child. Eventually, I *had* to go into town, to feed her." Her eyes saddened as she returned them to me, and I didn't see the sultry vixen who liked to ceaselessly tease me anymore. I saw a concerned mother, same as me.

Imogen rested her hand on her mother's shoulder as Halina continued. "I fought against my hunger. Imogen was my priority." Her lip quavered as anger filled her voice. "She was screaming she was so hungry, and out of fear and desperation, I begged a man on the street to get her food." The anger fled her voice as wonder replaced it. "To my complete surprise, he did."

She smiled as she looked down at the table. Shaking her head, she said, "I watched him walk across the street, not even bothering to move out of the way of the cars on the road. I watched him break into a closed store and come out with bundles of food—rice, bread, and bottles of milk." Looking back up at me, she shrugged. "He walked right over to me, dropped it at my feet, smiled, and then left."

I felt a shiver run through me, thinking about what she'd made that man do. It was so much power for one person to hold. I wondered what I'd do with her abilities? Would I use them for "good" as Teren had once teased me?

Tilting her head, her ageless eyes in awe, she added, "I had no idea that I had that kind of power until that very moment. I tried it out on others, getting the things that I needed." Smiling, she looked around the home, her home. "Soon, I had food, I had cows, I had help with the ranch," she returned her eyes to me, "and most importantly, I had a way to keep my child healthy, happy and alive." After a second, she grinned. "I even compelled someone to take care of her during daylight hours, when I couldn't be there."

I marveled at the woman before me as I watched her lean back in her chair and raise her chin in defiance. "Now, given my options, Emma, what would you have done differently?"

Shaking my head, nearly speechless with awe, I could only get out, "Nothing…"

Halina gave me her trademark smirk, then swirled her hand around the room, similar to how I'd done it earlier. "So, now, this may seem opulent to you, but I'm providing for my family, *all* of my family, however many generations of us may come along." Looking around the room at her family, she met and held each pair of pale eyes. Teren smiled when she got to him.

In a low, passionate voice, she continued, "None of them have my abilities and once I go…they are all on their own. I won't leave them destitute, penniless." She swung her eyes back to me; a fire was in the icy depths. With a snarl of determination she spat out, "No child of mine will ever scream for food again."

Blinking back the tears, I shook my head. "You…really are an amazing woman," I whispered.

Slapping on a casual crooked grin, she rested her leather boots on the table. "I like to think so."

Chapter 10 - The Death and Life of Emma Adams

After dinner, I still had quite a few hours to kill before I died. Not really knowing how to spend the last moments of my life, I alternated between pacing, stressing and restless twitching. As the minutes marched on and on, each one bringing the sun just a fraction of an inch closer to rising again, my heart started accelerating. I wasn't dying yet, just anxious. While I knew the actual act was going to be a bitch, the waiting around for it to happen was probably worse. The mind was a cruel weapon at times, imaging every ache before the body even had a chance to feel it.

Teren squatted in front of me when I started biting my fingernails. Smiling, he cupped my cheek. "Come with me?"

I looked around the room. All of the vampires were watching me, all with expressions of anticipation that matched the jumble of nerves in my belly. "Where are we going?" My nerves made my voice hitch.

As he spoke in a soothing voice, his cool thumb stroked my cheek. "Just for a walk, just to get your mind off things."

I looked back at him, raised an eyebrow and laughed in a bubbly, anxious way. "You think that's possible?"

His smile turned sad as he shook his head. "No, but I'd like to try."

I nodded and stood. Everyone in the room stood with me. It was almost like I'd suddenly become royalty and they were all following my every whim. It made me giggle inappropriately; none of this was funny.

Halina smiled at me, but Alanna and Imogen only looked even more concerned. They all started to follow Teren and me as we headed towards the slider leading out back, but Teren shook his head at them. "I'd like a moment alone with my wife." They all nodded, and only Teren and I stepped through the glass doors.

I shut my eyes as the cooler night air blew across my face. I could smell the awakening of life in the wind—new plant shoots, pollen, freshly cut grass, blossoming night flowers. It gave me a sense of renewal, grounded me with the power of nature.

Teren had told me once that he felt more connected to the world after his death. I already felt more in tune with it, with just my enhanced senses. I wondered if that would change even more.

Grasping my hand, Teren led me to the edge of the flat rocked patio. I smiled over at the chlorine filled pool as we walked by it. I had a lot of memories in that pool—diving in on a hot summer day, teaching the kids to hold their breaths, getting in a water fight with Teren, trying to race him and losing miserably. But mostly, that softly lit water reminded me of getting married. We'd said "I do" over those shimmering-in-the-moonlight ripples. Dead or alive, it would always hold a special place in my heart.

Stepping off of the back end of the patio to a trail of granite steps that led down to where the equipment was kept, I felt the distance of the other vampires in my head. My children were the farthest, sleeping peacefully with my mother back in the city. Halina and the other girls were just where we'd left them, in the living room, probably watching me through the windows as I disappeared with my husband down the back of the hill. I knew they'd be able to find me once I gave out. Locating me was never a problem anymore, not since I gave off a GPS signal to them too.

Heading down a light trail in the tall, tan grass, Teren started swinging my hand like we were on a first date or something. I smiled over at him, grateful for his calming presence. "Thank you for doing this."

He looked over at me, and a small smile was on his handsome face. "I only wish I could do more." He shook his head, his eyes glowing brighter the farther away we got from the lights of the ranch. "I wish I could take the…"

His voice trailed off and he looked down. I filled in the blank. "The pain?"

Glancing up at me, he sighed. "Yeah, I'm sorry. I'd experience it all over again if I could, just so you didn't have to."

He sighed again, his face forlorn, and I cuddled into his side, ignoring the shiver that went through my body when I pressed against him. "Hey, how bad can it really be? I mean, I've had two kids, it can't be worse than that."

I expected him to laugh, but he only looked at me with a raised eyebrow. Swallowing, I muttered, "Right…"

Gathering my courage, I briefly closed my brightly glowing eyes and laid my head on his shoulder. We walked along in silence, our eyes highlighting the vague trail from repeated passings of the Jeeps. We walked through one of the empty pastures. The ranch hand's house was visible to my left, but the large home was empty. The family brought in help a few times a year, but this luckily wasn't one of those times.

As we moved away from the empty home near the barn, I thought about leaving my family behind in a year or so. Suddenly lonely for them, I squeezed Teren's hand. He kissed my head as I sighed, "I wish my family was here."

"I know," he whispered.

I'd called my sister after dinner, not able to stand not talking to her, but she hadn't been home. It had concerned me at first, until I realized that she was probably with my mom, helping to entertain my children. I couldn't call over there and tell her what was really happening without clueing in my mom. I was pretty sure Ash would cry, freak out, or demand to come over here, and Mom wouldn't buy Teren's cover story after witnessing my sister going into hysterics. Ashley would just have to be told after the fact as well.

Watching the moonlight glint off the lightly waving grass, I rested my head on his arm. "I'm scared," I whispered.

Hearing me, he wrapped his arm around me and kissed my head again. "I know," he repeated.

Peeking up at him, I picked out the strong lines of his features with the light I produced. He really did know what I was feeling; he'd gone through it himself. Only his had been worse, so much worse. He'd had to wait to die, knowing that he'd probably kill me when he woke up. He'd waited around to feel excruciating pain while he'd already been in excruciating pain, having had both of his legs beaten to pieces. I couldn't even imagine how terrified he'd been and I'd truly seen none of it. For me, he'd put on a brave face.

Stopping in the grass, I reached up to stroke his face. "Have I ever told you how amazing you are?"

He smiled and nodded in my fingertips. "Yes, once or twice." He chuckled then leaned down to kiss me.

Resuming our walk, we headed down to one of the ponds that Teren and his dad frequently fished from. Some small animals darted away as we approached. A low growl escaped my chest before I could stop it. The heartbeat I heard retreating was a small one, but it still revved up the vampiric part of me. I suppose that was just my body getting ready.

Teren slid his hands down to my fingers and sat near the edge of the water. I sat with him, a little embarrassed at the primal part of me he'd just witnessed. He smiled and softly laughed. "Don't worry about it. It's just a part of who you are." He leaned in to kiss the scar on my neck, a spot that he usually avoided, but it was sort of prevalent in the air tonight.

I smiled that he understood so much about me. Being married to someone who had gone through everything I was going though was very comforting. "Will that finally be gone?" I asked as he pulled away from the constant reminder of my attack.

Peeking up at me, he nodded. "Yes, you'll heal," his eyes scoured my body, "everywhere."

I smiled that my stretch marks would be fading too, then. Slinking my hand over his propped up knee, I slowly exhaled. "What is it like…waking back up?"

I knew he wouldn't tell me about dying, but surely he could warn me about coming back to life? He looked away from me, his eyes shifting to glow on the empty fields across the stream. Finally he said, "You won't feel like you. You'll be pure…animal. Nothing about who you are will feel familiar…not even your own name."

He looked back at me with a sad exhale. "And you'll be hungry. So hungry," he whispered. I swallowed but didn't look away. His fingers came up to touch my cheek, to tuck a lock of hair behind my ear. "I want you to embrace the animal, to let it take over. It will help you fight through the pain, it will help you live. Don't fight the instinct…okay?"

His brow bunched as his face shifted into concern. I saw the fear in the depths of his pale eyes and knew that he was, again, holding back how afraid he truly was. I nodded, cupping his hand to my cheek. "I won't hurt you?" I whispered.

He shook his head. "No, I don't have a heartbeat. I won't be…interesting to you. You'll be looking for pumping blood, the harder the better. And you won't have to look far. I'll have it right there for you." He calmed his features as best as he could. "You have nothing to fear, Emma. I'll take care of you."

I inhaled a big breath and held it for ten seconds as I absorbed his words. I knew he was right, I knew that he'd die again before he let me go, but it was human nature to fear the unknown, and death was a pretty big unknown. He held me close as we sat along that bank. The light of our eyes highlighted each other's features as we talked about less frightening things—whether or not we would put the kids in a public school, when or if my sister would find someone, my mom's health, his dad's, Hot Ben and Tracey's upcoming nuptials.

I could feel time passing by, but as Teren made me laugh, kissed me, or made me smack him with some smart aleck remark, everything in the world seemed to stop. I wasn't about to die. My kids weren't a worry in the back of my mind. Halina's struggles weren't playing on repeat throughout my brain. For a moment beside that pond, Teren and I were just a couple in love. It was nice to go back to that simplicity.

But eventually as the night wore on we decided to head back to the ranch. Teren stood first and, always the gentleman, he held his hand out for me. With a smile on my face, I reached up to grab it. I was halfway to standing when the smile fell off my face. My heart missed a beat, like it did sometimes when I was really nervous or anxious. It was an uncomfortable feeling and I rubbed my chest. Teren's brows furrowed as I straightened my legs.

"Emma? Are you feeling…okay?" he asked tentatively.

I started to take a step forward, telling him that I felt fine, but my body had other plans. My half-step towards him brought me right back down to my knees. I looked at myself confused; it was an odd feeling to have your body do something that you didn't tell it to do.

Before I could worry about it too long though, my heart missed another beat. This time it hurt.

Knowing it was happening, knowing that I was minutes away from dying, I felt my heart shift into overdrive. In my anxiousness, my breath picked up to panic level. Looking around myself, I felt the world constrict around me, suffocating me. I wasn't ready.

Immediately Teren's calming eyes filled my vision. Strong hands grasped my face as he forced me to focus only on the hypnotic depths of his eyes. Oxygen flooded through me as my panic attack subsided."I'm right here, Emma, I'm not leaving you."

I started to nod, but my heart stuttered. My hands feebly went to my chest, like I could somehow externally help the organ along. My smooth running engine was sputtering, part of it wanting to keep going, the rest of it too tired to even try. Like my toddlers tripping over their own feet, my heart couldn't get back up again.

Fire erupted through my chest and down my arms as my heart surged and stopped. It was a different sort of pain than I'd ever felt before. Sharp and intense, dull and aching, and all the more terrifying because it was laced with a razor sharp edge of fear. I knew what was happening, and being aware made it ten times worse. I suddenly envied the cows that would probably be dying tonight as well. At least they had no idea it was coming.

As Teren clutched me to him, his calming influence keeping me sane, I struggled to not cry out with the pain. I bit my lip so hard I tore right through it. My fangs dropped as the taste of blood filled my mouth, but I couldn't even care.

Teren's eyes watered with sympathetic tears as he watched me. Oddly, a part of me wanted to comfort *him*, but the majority of me was too scared. I grasped his face, my body shaking as my heart struggled to keep going. "Promise me," I choked out.

He shook his head, looking like he'd agree to wrangle the moon if I asked. "Anything."

Tears stung my eyes as a sudden, sharp pain felt like it was splitting my chest in half. My voice heavy with held back agony, I sputtered, "Promise me this is forever." Feeling a rush of strength as the wave of pain ebbed and flowed, I quickly rambled, "Promise me that you won't wake up one day, sick of me, hating the fact that you're stuck with me for all eternity. Promise me that you won't ever stop loving me. Promise me that you won't leave me for someone else in a couple hundred years. Promise me that we'll feel this way for the next ten thousand years." My sobs finally broke free as my panic kicked in full force.

His arms wrapped around me. "I promise. I promise, baby. You never have to worry about that. It's you, it's always been you. It will always be you...forever. You're it for me, for eternity. I love you, I love you so much."

I nodded in his arms, embarrassed that I'd verbally doubted him. I knew he wouldn't ever leave me, no sooner than I would leave him, but fear and panic can make you do and say stupid things.

"I love you," I managed to get out...then the real pain started.

Screaming as I jerked against his body, I felt him lay me down. As my heart sped up to an unnatural pace, he leaned down, and his cool hands brushed over my fevered face. "I'm here. I love you, Emma."

I wanted to respond with something other than pain-filled cries, but I couldn't make any other coherent noise. Aside from the discomfort in my chest, it felt like pins and needles were pricking me from the inside as my vampiric blood prepared itself to take over. I couldn't believe that Teren had ever felt this level of pain; he'd hidden so much of it from me when he'd died.

My heart raced as I started convulsing, then, as if someone had flipped a switch, it stopped. I heard myself stop screaming, felt my body stop shaking. I smelled my own blood and fear in the air, but mostly, I felt relief. I was dying and all that meant in the moment was that the pain would finally be ending. As my vision faded to pinpoints and every muscle in my body relaxed, my hearing was the last thing I retained.

It brought a different sort of ache and the part of me that could still think, sort of wished that sense had left me first. Sobbing into my shoulder, Teren was repeating over and over that he was sorry, and that he loved me. I couldn't move any part of my body to comfort him. As my consciousness slipped from me, the last thing I heard him say was, "I'll see you on the other side, Emma. Ya Tebya Lyublyu."

There was nothing about dying that met my expectations. I didn't know if that was because I hadn't fully died, or if I was just completely wrong about my preconceived notions. There was no bright light, no awaiting family members. My long dead father didn't welcome me into his arms during my brief visit to his realm. Ironically, nothing supernatural happened to me while I was transforming into a mythical creature.

But there was peace in the void. A peace that was so warm and safe and welcoming that I could have wrapped it around me and stayed in it for all eternity. No thoughts accompanied the peace. My mind was, perhaps for the first time ever, relaxed. I was a blank slate—no nags or worries intruded on my well-being, only peace. I would have sighed with contentment, if I could have.

But then a feeling started breaking through that serenity. It was uncomfortable, and jostled the calm I'd found in death. Growing stronger second by second, it slowly awoke me, changing me. Everything I knew washed away as the feeling burned through my body, emanating from my stomach. Some fundamental part of me knew the feeling enough to give it a name—hunger—intense, burning, all-consuming hunger. A low, feral growl erupted from my dry throat as the uncomfortable feeling tightened and strengthened.

Slowly, and I had no idea how long it really was, the hunger started reawakening my other senses. Last to recede, my hearing was the first to reawaken. All I heard was chirping, like ten thousand crickets were circled around me, serenading me. My own body was oddly silent, but other rustles and murmurs filled my ears. The glow of my eyes kicked in, highlighting the darkness. It wasn't the comforting peace of the darkness that I'd left behind, and I instantly hated it. Hazy shapes flitted past my vision, tilting my stomach, and I shut my eyes as nausea filled me.

But it wasn't really nausea that I was feeling. It was stronger than that, and ten times as painful. My stomach contracted as a ripping ache seared through me. I knew enough about my foreign body to recognize the danger. I was starving on an eat-or-die level. A stronger growl ripped from my throat as an inborn desire to live filled me. I was an animal, an animal that needed to be fed.

As the hunger constricted my body, forcing me to action, all of my other senses dropped by the wayside. I didn't care about the crickets. I didn't care about the peace that I'd awoken from. I didn't care about the blurry shapes and indistinguishable rustling sounds.

I cared about blood.

A painfully, raspy hiss erupted from my parched throat as the creature within me demanded out. My mouth was forced open by my fangs. They were uncontrollably long, longer than I'd ever thought possible. I wanted to spring up and blur towards a food source, but my body was slow, tired.

Fighting the pain tearing through my abdomen, I opened my eyes again and flexed my aching body. My limbs responded to my silent commands, but they were heavy, sore. Some small part of me wanted to close my eyes again, to desperately find that peace that I'd left behind, but the fire in my throat wouldn't let me go back to that slumber. It was excruciating, worse than dying.

A creature crouched before me; it had no heartbeat and I ignored it. Words hit me, but I didn't recognize them. All I felt was pain, all I knew was thirst. Nothing else existed to me but quenching that thirst. There was nothing else I wanted, nothing else I understood, but wanting blood coursing down my aching throat. I couldn't even swallow. It hurt. Everything hurt.

I stood, stumbling on my feet. The creature before me moved to standing as well. I managed a deep growl, warning the irritant away. It didn't stop moving though, arms raised as if I might attack it. I didn't have the strength. I could barely keep standing. I could barely see. All I knew was it was lifeless, and I didn't want it. I instinctively inhaled for the scent of blood, using my unnecessary lungs for the first time. The warmth of a living creature filled my nostrils, burning them. My dry throat made a cracking groan and my body stumbled forward of its own accord.

A heartbeat, heavy and fast, filled my ears. It was all I heard, all that made sense to me. I stumbled towards it. I had no idea who or what it belonged to and I didn't care. It surged with blood. I wanted it. I needed it. Nothing but death would stop me from taking it.

Hearing words that sounded like encouragement coming from the walking dead creature beside me, I dropped to my knees at the source of the pleasing heat. Something large and black was lying on the ground before me.

Its head moved and the creature tried to bolt, but other heartbeatless creatures held it down. Someone knelt beside me as I leaned over the struggling creature. My movements felt slow to me, my eyes felt heavy. I was so tired, but so hungry. I wanted to lie down and rest, but the drive to eat wouldn't let me.

"Eat, Emma. Drink, baby."

The words the undead creature spouted didn't make sense. Emma? I didn't know what that meant. All I knew was pain ripping through my stomach up to my throat. My entire body felt like acid had been poured inside it. I growled painfully as my lips achingly slow found the furry beast. It was so hard to concentrate. Hard to keep moving. I wanted rest. I wanted food.

"Emma...please, eat." The silent hearted creature beside me seemed concerned. I paused, a desire in me welling to comfort the creature. I had no idea why. I blinked and the beast below me hazed in my vision. My throat burned, my eyes were heavy. I wanted to close them. I never wanted to reopen them. I wanted my peace back. Everything hurt. My entire world was pain. I wanted it to end.

"Emma, baby, no...you need to eat. The pain will stop, once you eat."

Emma? That word again. A growl issued from my chest, weaker this time. My head rested on the beast, the heartbeat thudding in my ear as I laid my cheek on its rough surface. My mouth opened wider, my fangs already as far as they could go. I was so close; I could feel the heat of the animal below me, but couldn't find the strength to make my mouth pierce the flesh. My teeth brushed the creature. It tried to buck me away, but the other undead beings around it kept it still.

I was so tired. I was in so much pain. I just wanted it to end. I started to close my eyes.

"Teren...she's fading..."

The creature at my side cursed, then darted to where my lips were. It sunk its teeth into the beast beneath me. The animal cried out and tried to jerk away. The creature ripped its mouth away and the scent of fresh blood ignited my senses. My aching throat squealed in protest. My partially closed eyes flew open. A rush of blood made it to my lips and my tongue darted out to lap it up. It was warm, sweet, heavenly. It was life, and I wanted more. A fire drove my tired body and my mouth attached to the gaping wound the creature beside me had made. The animal struggled but the blood flowing down my dry throat gave me strength, and I held it down.

As the vitality of the animal flowed into me, I felt myself coming back to who I was. I was not a bloodthirsty creature of the night. I was a person. My name was Emma. Teren was my husband. Teren had just saved my life by exposing fresh blood into the air, forcing the instinct inside me to take over. And taking over it was; I drained that animal, its frail movements slowing, then stopping.

Wiping my mouth with a lightly shaking hand, I sat back on my heels. Feeling dizzy and lightheaded, my throat still ached with thirst and my belly still burned with need. But I felt out of the woods—I no longer felt like lying down and never waking up again. Meeting Teren's concerned gaze, I managed to mutter, "I'm still hungry."

He smiled, sighed softly, and nodded. "Well then, let's get you some more to eat."

As my vision cleared, I saw Teren's features become more distinct. He looked as tired as I felt; heaviness was in his glowing eyes. His arms wrapped around me as we huddled beside the beast I'd devoured. Sighing, I forced my fangs back up and buried my head in the comfort of Teren's neck. It was then, as he helped me to stand up, that I finally noticed something odd about him.

Blinking as I wobbled on my feet, I looked over his body. "You're not cold?"

He smiled and kissed my head. "Yes, I am, but you are too."

Grabbing my hand, he laced our fingers together. He wasn't warm, by any stretch, but the icy shiver wasn't there. Touching his skin was like touching my own. For the first time in a long time, we were the same temperature. I marveled at that fact as he helped steady me. Smiling down at me, he patiently let me explore his face, his silent chest. It was so odd for him to feel the same as me.

Tired, I snuggled into his chest and closed my eyes. He nudged my shoulder as he started me walking. "Not yet, Emma. I know you're tired, but you can rest after you eat some more, okay?"

I nodded against his body, then felt a different lukewarm hand reach out for me. I opened my eyes at Alanna smiling at me. Imogen was next to her, with Halina standing behind them. Halina's bright eyes took in my blood soaked shirt, my stained mouth, and she smiled wider. "Ready to hunt, Emma?" she asked, her fangs dropping down.

My stomach rumbled at the idea. I was still so hungry. The ache in my belly felt better, but I knew it would make a reappearance if I didn't satisfy my needs soon. Taking a step towards her, I eagerly nodded. "Yes," I whispered.

Halina growled. Ducking into a crouch, she twisted to where I could smell the warmth of life in the fields.

None of the other cows had reacted negatively to one of their companions dying; they were all still standing around, waiting to die too. Surprisingly, a part of my body wanted them to run, wanted the chase, but I was too tired to really care. Imogen grabbed my other hand and she and Alanna pulled me after Halina. Teren followed us; a low rumble escaped his chest as his fangs lowered as well.

I let myself become what I was now, a hunter, a killer, an animal. I pushed back the human part of me that objected to what I was doing, and focused instead on what really mattered—getting through this transformation so I could spend an eternity with my husband and children.

The girls made a wide circle around the beasts that had been corralled just for this very purpose. They weren't the best of the best, like Teren had had when he'd died. His family hadn't had the time to get that kind of livestock for me. Instead, they'd used this opportunity to thin the herd of the sick and fragile ones. I'd heard them say *mercy killings* when they'd been talking about it.

As Teren followed the women, his eyes flicked between me and the beasts. He wanted them, too, but he was going to let me make the first move. I crouched down, letting the instinct and the residual pain of thirst lead me. A low growl burrowing out of my chest, I found the strength to blur over to the largest one. I wrapped my arms around its neck, and the scent of bovine overpowered me as I flung it to the ground. My teeth were sunk inside it seconds later—it didn't even have a chance to cry out. Snarls from the other vampires filled the air. Out of the corner of my eye, I saw Halina dart for one. With a wicked smile, she took it down just as efficiently as I had.

Other thumps and cries signaled the other vampires eating. Teren wasn't gorging yet though. He was still watching over me. Grinning when he saw that I was finished, he indicated a cow in the back. I smiled, wiping my mouth as vitality coursed through me. Each cow's life seemed to strengthen my own. We both twisted to look at the doomed beast, then darted towards it together. As soon as we brought it down, we sunk our teeth in. As hot, pulsing blood flowed down my throat, easing every ache I'd ever had, Teren's fingers came out to clutch mine. Holding hands over the fading life beneath us, I embraced the rising life within me, and clasped him back just as hard.

At the tail end of the slaughter, Halina frowned and looked up at the sky. My enhanced sight could see the edge of the sun along the base of the horizon. Sighing, she grumbled that she had to go hide away for the day. Imogen went with her when she blurred away, and both girls chuckled about how entertaining it was to hunt as a group.

Alanna smiled as she watched them streak off to the safety of the house. As Teren and I stepped away from the last cow in the field, Alanna walked over and encased me in a warm hug. "Welcome to the family, dear." She patted my back as she held me and I felt my tired eyes start to water. I guess being dead didn't put an end to being emotional.

Smiling as I clasped her back, I whispered, "Thank you, Mom."

When Alanna was done with me, she wrapped Teren in a hug as well. "I'm so happy for the both of you." Her eyes were watery with pink tears as she looked between the two of us. She flicked a quick glance towards the house before returning her eyes to our faces. "I'm going to go call Jack. He would want to know that you're safe, Emma, and that he can come home."

A brilliant smile brightened her face as the first rays of light hit her hair. Then she streaked back home, to tell the love of her life that they could be reunited. I twisted to bury my head in the chest of the love of my life, my eternal life. His arms wrapped around me; they were warm against my skin. Glancing down at myself, I stared at my silent chest. I kept expecting to hear my heartbeat, but it didn't happen. If I had been purely human first, I probably wouldn't have noticed the lack of a beat, but I hadn't been entirely human in a while, and my enhanced ears had gotten used to the familiar rhythm. It was shockingly odd to not hear it anymore.

Teren's fingers lifted my chin so I'd look up at him. Brushing my jaw with his thumb, he smiled. A shaft of light hit his eyes, making the gray flecks in them leap out at me. I smiled at the distinct clover shape in the right one; it was adorably beautiful. "How do you feel?" he asked.

Sighing, my hands drifted over the wet blood on my ruined shirt. Unlike Teren, who didn't have a spot of red on him, I hadn't exactly been a dainty eater. I was pretty sure my face looked like I'd just filmed a horror movie. My fingers resting on my silent chest as I locked gazes with him, I crooked a smile. "Dead tired."

He grinned, and a soft laugh escaped him. All the tension seemed to release from his face as he scooped me up. The uncertainty of that situation had been just as terrifying for him as it had been painful for me. The memory of that pain tried to intrude on my happiness, but I blocked it out. Much like childbirth, some pains were worth going through.

When I rested my head on his shoulder, I felt him kiss my head. "Come on, I'll tuck you in."

Yawning, I reached up and kissed his neck. Through the cool warmth of his skin, I felt the river of ever-flowing vampire blood coursing through his veins. The same blood now flowed through me—self propelling, no longer needing the extra effort of a circulatory system. I was now one level up on the food chain, but I was still the same person I was before. Now that I'd gotten through that moment of insatiable hunger, I knew I would be able to control it; I wouldn't be out munching on the townsfolk or anything.

In fact, Teren's skin was the only skin I'd ever consider

puncturing. And he would live through any playful attack I made on him. As would I now, when he took nibbles from me. Self-healing, I'd never die a natural death. That was an intimidating thought, but I knew that I'd have Teren by my side for all of it. We would face the daunting endless life in front of us, together.

Blurring us back to our bedroom, he helped me clean up and change clothes, then he tucked me under our covers. He held me until the exhaustion overtook me. Before completely caving into it, I muttered, "I want to see the children soon."

He nodded as he held me to his chest. "As soon as you get some sleep, we'll go get them."

Exhaling, feeling the pleasure from making the movement, but not the need to feel the air through my lungs, I vaguely nodded. "M'kay."

Chuckling, he kissed my hair. Before silencing my unnecessary breath, I heard him whisper, "I'm so glad you made it. I don't know what I would have…" Exhaling a quick, shaky breath, he held me just a bit tighter. "I love you, Emma."

I wanted to respond, to tell him that I understood his fear and I loved him more than anything, but dying was an exhausting experience and sleep crept up on me. Mumbling something unintelligible, I once again slipped back into the darkness, if only for a little while.

Chapter 11 – Emma 2.0

I had odd dreams while I rested. Odd dreams that I couldn't quite remember, although when I woke, the sounds of distressed cattle were echoing in my brain. I had a feeling that my dreams were mainly about the feasting that had happened last night. Not wanting to think about the carnage, I instead focused on my deceased body.

My eyes still closed, I listened for any sound coming from me. Usually, there was something—a heartbeat, the wind whooshing through my lungs, the food in my stomach digesting…something. But as I lay there, not even breathing, everything was completely silent. Forcing myself to not instinctively inhale, I waited for the accompanying discomfort that holding my breath would have given me had I been alive. I waited for the rising panic shouting at my body to stop playing games and take the breath it needed. The feeling never happened though. I could have peacefully held my breath for hours on end.

I inhaled deeply anyway, enjoying the expansion and contraction of my lungs, even if I didn't need the oxygen. Scents rushed in on me when I did. From inside the room, I was barraged with the creosote from the cold fireplace. From out in the hall, the familiar scent of Freesia filtered in to me. Farther away, I could pick out candles, furniture polish, and the unmistakable smell of bacon. Yesterday, the bacon scent would have had my mouth watering. Today, I immediately discarded it, and moved on to the one scent overriding everything else in my world. Blood. Somewhere downstairs was fresh blood; I could practically smell the heat of it.

My eyes flashed open. If my stomach could have rumbled, it would have. I remembered Teren having to eat continually the first few days after his conversion and thought my hunger was due to my newness. My fangs started slipping down, but I pulled them back up. I was still me. I could control the cravings until they subsided into the more normal range.

I was lying on my side, perfectly still and straight, when a face suddenly filled my vision. I smiled as Teren's pale eyes locked onto mine. "Good morning, sleepy. Or should I say, good afternoon?" He half smiled as his hand came up to brush some hair off of my cheek.

I nearly purred at the pleasing feeling of his soft, room temperature touch. While there were some aspects of him being cold that I would miss, mainly in the intimate part of our relationship, it would be nice to hold him without shivering.

Wondering if his mouth would no longer be icy either, I murmured, "Good afternoon to you, too." My words registered as I said them, and my eyes widened as I sat up. Shock and worry flew through me, and I waited for my heart to start racing; naturally, it didn't. "Afternoon? I'm seriously late for work. They're gonna can me."

Teren smirked. "Do you really think I'd let you get fired? After everything you did to get back there?" His face was peaceful as he shifted to his back. Propping his hands behind his head, he crossed his ankles.

Taking in his relaxed posture, I relaxed as well. "I guess not. What did you tell them?"

He laughed; his eyes were playful. "I told Tracey that you were feeling a little under the weather after your weekend and you'd be missing a few days. I think she thinks you're still hung-over."

I smiled, then sighed. I'd have to go back sooner or later, and when I did, I would face the same obstacles Teren had faced when he'd gone back. But he'd managed it pretty simply, I was sure I would too. Aside from being cold and not ever able to eat around humans, I'd be essentially the same as before.

Hearing my sigh, Teren sat up and rested his hand over mine. "It will be okay, Emma. You're through the hardest part. The hunger will be more and more manageable every day." He leaned in to kiss me, and his lips were as warm as the rest of him. "Speaking of that, Mom's got some blood ready for you, if you're hungry now."

Feeling a discomfort in my belly, the same sort of discomfort I would get before my alive stomach growled, I nodded. "Starving." My mouth felt parched to me, too, and it was bone dry when I swallowed.

I didn't have to say more than that before Alanna was standing in my door, steaming thermos in hand. "Here you go, sweetheart." Her smile was peaceful when she handed it to me, and my ears picked up the sound of Jack humming outside. I figured her joy was as much about being reunited with him as it was that I was safe.

Thanking her, I watched Imogen causally standing at my doorway. Taking a much needed sip of plasma, I waved her into the room. Smiling as widely as her daughter, she walked through a bright patch of sunshine. She cringed slightly before stopping herself. I supposed it was still an odd feeling for her, being in the sun when she'd avoided it her entire life.

Leaning down, she placed a warm, grandmotherly kiss on my head. "I'm so glad you made it, Emma."

Taking only a fraction of second to pause and thank her, I continued downing my soothing treat. It was hotter than I recalled it being, and the heat flowed all the way down my body, warming me from the inside out. It only made the experience more enjoyable, as the liquid satisfied the burn of thirst and the discomfort of hunger. I couldn't imagine anything ever tasting better and I had no desire to have anything else.

The very idea of consuming food suddenly sounded about as appealing as eating the mud pies that I used to make as a kid. I hadn't understood how Teren had suddenly lost interest in food after his change, but now I did. Anything that wasn't *this* was suddenly a little nauseating. Just the thought of having a piece of the bacon that I could smell lingering in the air from downstairs made me feel a little ill. It gave me a whole new appreciation for the time Teren had forced food down his throat for me.

After finishing my drink, I stared into the thermos and considered licking the rim. Laughing, Alanna asked, "Would you like another, Emma?"

Cringing, I looked up at her. "If that's okay? I know I've taken a lot...lately."

Shaking her head, she patted my shoulder. "You're an Adams, Emma. You may have as much as you need."

Walking at a normal pace, Alanna and Imogen headed back down to the kitchen. Along the way, they talked about how surprising things had been around the ranch lately, what with Gabriel's light blocking windows being put up, Starla's sudden need for all of my shots, and my unexpected conversion. As they entered the kitchen they started debating what other surprises might be in store.

Teren listened to them with his head tilted, then settled in to kiss me again. Pushing back the extra conversations, I focused on the one thing that always grounded me, my constant, him. Feeling his lips move over mine, his hands clenching my hip, I started to understand what he'd told me once about seeing the world differently. I felt every molecule of air against my cheek. I heard every brush of noise in the room. Through my slotted eyes, I saw variations of color that had never existed to me before.

But instead of it being overpowering, it made everything seem more...real. Like I'd been living in a sepia-toned silent film my whole life. At the time, that had seemed rich and full to me. Then I'd been bitten, and thrust into the world of Technicolor. That had seemed miraculous, and I'd wondered how I'd never noticed how flat the world was before. But now, now I'd been immersed into a high definition 3D film. It was beyond anything I'd ever imagined, and as Teren had correctly told me once, I felt connected to the world, more a part of it than I had ever been before. I felt the very pulse of life washing over my unblemished skin.

My half-closed eyes sprang open as I pulled away from Teren's mouth. His tongue had just reached out to flick me and he seemed a little disgruntled that I'd made him miss. Ignoring how sexy his lip looked, curved into curious displeasure, I brought my hand up to my neck. The spot that had forever been marked with a strange man's teeth was now smooth. Not feeling the rigid bumps of poorly healed skin made me giggle.

I tried to look down to see the spot, but my eyes weren't suddenly detachable or anything; there was just no way to see that angle myself. Teren chuckled at me as I hopped off the bed. "What are you doing?" he asked.

Rushing over to the vanity, I stared at myself in the mirror. "Is it gone?" He walked up behind me as my wide brown eyes searched for any disruption of my smooth, creamy skin. "Is the scar gone?" My HD sight didn't see any imperfection, but I still couldn't believe it. I'd been carrying around that reminder for so many years now.

Teren grinned as he leaned down and kissed the arch of my

once-wounded neck. "It would seem so," he whispered. Resting his chin on my neck, the course stubble familiar and comforting, his pale, playful eyes watched me explore my skin.

Closing mine, I laid my head back and sighed. "Thank God, I was so sick of looking at that."

Sighing as well, he kissed the tender skin again. "Me too," he whispered.

Lowering my head to look at him in the mirror, I reached up to run a hand through his pitch-black hair. Closing his eyes, he leaned in to my caress. My next words made his eyes pop open again. "Bite me," I whispered.

Pulling back, he locked eyes with me in the mirror. "Emma, I don't think I should…you just went through something really…" He shrugged, looking torn.

I shook my head, and my eyes started watering. "You never bite me there, not since that vampire…" I swallowed; a bit of thirst crept back into my throat. I could hear and smell my blood being prepared downstairs, but right now, I wanted this more. "I need to replace that memory with a different one." Moving my hair away from that shoulder, I completely exposed my neck to him. "Please, Teren?"

His eyes flicked between mine, unsure. Sighing, he looked down at my neck. Opening his mouth as he stared at my skin, I watched him in the mirror as his fangs dropped down. My breath picked up and I was overly conscious of the absence of my heartbeat. Normally, that would have picked up too.

Perhaps noticing the loss as well, his eyes flicked up at me. Our gazes unwavering, he opened his mouth wider and bared his fangs. Even with all we'd been through, all the time we'd had together, it was still hot when he did that. The parts of my body that still worked exactly the same as before reacted. Sensing the desire in me, his mouth curved into a cocky, self-assured grin. Lowering his head but maintaining our eye contact, he sunk his teeth into me. I gasped, then groaned. He'd done it with more force than he usually did. Since he didn't have to worry about scarring me or killing me, it gave him some freedom when it came to biting me.

His eyes rolled back before they closed. I kept mine open,

watching him devour me. Everything about it was a little different than I was used to. His mouth and tongue were mildly warm as they worked over my skin; his hands massaging my hips were equally chill-free. There wasn't a pulling sensation as my blood left me. Since it moved on its own now, he didn't have to put in any effort when he fed from me. I knew what that felt like, since I'd bitten him before. It was like turning on a faucet and sticking your head underneath it. And with our super healing skin, you only had to pull your teeth out to stop the flow.

It was still pretty erotic though, especially with the clear delight on his face. It made me smile that he still enjoyed my blood, even though it had to taste different now, or at least it was colder than it once was.

Scrunching my hand in his hair as I let out another soft moan, I watched as he finally gasped and pulled away. His teeth and tongue were tainted red, but the twin holes on my neck healed right before my eyes. It was so weird to see that happening to my body. Breathing heavier, he grinned like he'd just had the best meal on the planet, or the best sex. It actually relieved me that my blood still made him feel that way.

Squeezing me tight, he licked the last remnant of red from my neck. He made a purring noise in his throat as his warm tongue lapped at me. Smiling as I ran my hand back through his hair, I murmured, "Do I still taste good?"

Ignoring the sensation of Alanna and Imogen walking at a slow pace in our direction, since we were obviously…finished, I sighed as he paused to nibble on my ear. "Unbelievable," he whispered.

Smiling as his lips made their way back to mine, I twisted in his arms so I could sling mine around his neck. "Am I different, taste-wise?"

He grinned against my mouth. "It's not hot like before, but that's okay, it's still the best thing I've ever tasted." Pulling back, he ran his tongue over his lower lip. His eyes were so smoky with lust that I almost asked his mother to give us a minute. But, knowing she was bringing me a second cup of blood, which my stomach was starting to ache for, I said nothing.

Maybe seeing the hunger in my features, Teren released me and walked over to our bags on the dresser. Digging through them, he raised an eyebrow at me. "You *are* a bit different to me in one other way."

Torn between the alluring look in his eye and the food coming closer and closer, I frowned and crossed my arms over my chest. "Oh?"

Grinning, he pulled out a light sweater that I'd packed. "Yeah, you aren't nourishing for me anymore." Shrugging, he pulled out some pants, while I wondered what he meant. Handing me my change of clothes, since I was still in the pajamas he had put me in this morning, he chuckled at the look of confusion on my face.

He leaned into me. "You're sort of...vampiric candy." Pausing, he closed his eyes for a second and seductively inhaled me; I stopped breathing. Opening his eyes, he glanced down my body. "Sweet...but essentially void of all nutritional value."

"Thanks." I smirked and smacked his arm right as his mom reappeared in the doorway. She laughed at his remark but didn't say anything about it.

She also didn't mention the dopey, fulfilled smile he had on his face as he watched me down my cup of nutritionally packed blood. I wanted to whisper at him to not look so...satisfied, but it really was kind of pointless. Both Imogen and Alanna had already heard him drink from me, and really, they'd heard much, much worse from us before. I had accepted the embarrassment of the situation a long time ago. Living around vampires, you just learned to give up things like privacy.

Since I was still in an adjustment period and blood was going to be one of the top things on my mind, right under my children really, we decided to stay at the ranch for a few more days. Teren had stayed for several weeks after his conversion, but I didn't feel like I could take that much time away from work. Besides, Teren's break had had as much to do with the mental recovery of our abduction as his physical recovery. Truly, we could have gone back after the first week.

Feeling more like myself once my stomach was topped off,

Teren and I decided to go get the kids. Well, really, he'd wanted me to stay behind with the girls while he went and got them, but I missed them so much, I couldn't just sit around and wait. Besides, I had some things to talk about with my mother. Things she probably wasn't going to be too thrilled about.

I played with the zipper of my jacket on the way over. I was anxious to see my children and nervous about what to say to my mom. Teren eyed me while he drove. Noting the telltale signs of restlessness, he asked, "Do you have any idea what you'll tell her?"

Sighing, I looked over at him and shrugged. "No, any suggestions?"

Grabbing my hand, he pulled it to his thigh. "Hmmm, I suppose 'hey, Mom, I died last night,' would be a little harsh, huh?"

I smirked at the playful look in his eye, the conversation he'd just put in my head. I could just imagine the freak-out if I told my mom like that. But really, what else was I supposed to tell her? Either way, she was going to have a mini coronary. There was just no way to ease a person into a conversation that involves the phrase "my heart stopped beating." I remembered my reaction when Teren had told me his life was going to end. Hopefully my mom didn't start chucking things at me.

Sighing as I leaned my head back on the seat, I closed my eyes and started tapping my foot. "No, I'll think of something better than that." I just had no idea what.

Sooner than I would have liked, Teren was pulling up to her drive. I stared at the quaint little house, suddenly wondering if I should have stayed at the ranch. But I could feel my children inside and their pull was stronger than my anxiety. Forcing myself to do it at human speed, I cracked open my door. Teren followed suit; his smile was just as wide as mine. While we'd been preoccupied with other things in the past twenty-four hours, being reunited with Nika and Julian reminded me how much I'd missed them. And with the ordeal I'd gone through, I couldn't wait to hold them again.

I didn't need to announce my arrival, since I could hear the kids doing it for me. As soon as my foot was on the top step, the door was swinging inward. My mother's warm, loving face filled my vision and I nearly wept at the way my newly-enhanced eyes saw her. It was almost like I could see the way she cared for me, like it was a physical trait, as apparent as the strikingly similar shade of chin length brown hair.

Her eyes flicked between Teren and me as she erupted into a huge grin. "Hey, you two. How was your trip?"

Containing a sigh as I slipped past her into the house, I only managed to get out, "It turned out …well." Teren had told her that he'd taken me away for a surprise birthday getaway. He'd made it sound like we were going to have fun. It hadn't been nearly as much fun as my mom had been led to believe.

Hearing the odd, elusiveness in my sentence, she raised an eyebrow in question as she shut the door behind Teren. I had no time to confess to her what had really gone on, though. Before I could even twist around to face her, two tiny beings threw themselves at my legs. Letting go of my hard conversation for a second, I dropped to my knees and wrapped an arm around each child.

Closing my eyes, I finally felt whole. "I missed you guys…so much." Pulling back, I cupped each smooth cheek; they felt hot to me, almost feverish, but I knew that was due to our temperature difference. It made me wonder if that was how I'd felt to Teren all this time, burning hot to the touch. "Did you guys have fun with Grandma?"

My voice was sunshine and light when I asked them, no strain or tension in me at all, but they both frowned. Nika reached up to touch my face, while Julian clasped my hand. "Mommy, you're…different." Nika said slowly, stumbling on the longer word.

My smile froze in place as Julian's pale eyes searched my face. "You're cold…like Daddy." His eyes shifted to my silent chest. "You're quiet."

Nika brightened, and her fingers on my face urged my vision back to her. "Did you get your magic, Mommy?" With the glow in her brown eyes, this seemed like the best news in the world to her, like we'd finally caved and gotten her that pony.

I swallowed and looked up at Teren beside me, then over to my mom. She had a frown on her face as she tried to decipher what my children were talking about. Knowing that I couldn't keep them in the dark, which meant I couldn't keep my mom in the dark, I briefly closed my eyes before bringing my attention back to them.

"Yes, yes Mommy did get her magic." I felt tears stinging my eyes. Mom wasn't going to like this next part. I had to say it though. My children had to know what had happened to me, because it was going to happen to them too one day.

Pulling back, I allowed my expression to turn serious. "Mommy stopped taking Grandpa Gabriel's medicine. Mommy's heart stopped, but it's okay, because Mommy has her magic and doesn't need her heart anymore, just like Daddy. Now Mommy will always look like this and now we can all be together forever." I said it as light and cheery as I could, but I heard my mom gasp. My children, however, squealed in delight and hugged me tight.

"Good job, Mommy," Nika congratulated me, hugging my neck.

Julian laughed as he tried to get his arms all the way around my body. "Yay! I'm glad you'll be our mommy forever."

I squeezed them tight as Teren knelt down and wrapped his arms around all of us. I knew they didn't really understand anything that had happened to me. Nothing but the only part that really mattered to them—I was going to be around forever. But my mother…knowing a little more about vampirism, well, I was pretty sure she understood.

I cringed as I slowly twisted to look at her. Even though I only felt hollowness in my chest where it would have been pounding before, the icy anticipation still washed through me. My mom had her hands clasped over her mouth. She was shaking her head and tears were beginning to form in her eyes. Seeing her start to lose it, I transferred the children to Teren. He gave them quick hugs then scooped them up to take them out to the car. They didn't need to witness their grandmother going through hysterics.

After they left, I tilted my head and put a hand on her arm. "Mom?" I slowly said.

Her eyes widening, she looked at my chilly hand in disbelief. Slowly shaking her head, she lowered her hands from her face.

"You…died?" she whispered.

Hearing my husband loudly singing nursery rhymes with the kids, so they would be too distracted to hear, I nodded. "Yes…I'm sorry."

Her tears finally fell at my words. *"You're* sorry?" Her voice quavered as she stared at me. Whispering, "Come here," she engulfed me in a hug. Patting my back, she rocked me side to side. "Why are you sorry? You're the one that had to go through it." Pulling back to look at me, she shook her head again. "Did you know this was going to happen when you asked me to watch the kids? Why didn't you tell me?"

Tears dripped down my cheeks and I sniffled. "It wasn't safe for you." She furrowed her brow and I shook my head. I didn't want to go into the specifics with her. I didn't want her to think of me that way, me or my extended family. Mom had been surprisingly open to what we all were, but I was pretty sure that was mainly because she never saw us acting like vampires. If I told her all the gory details about me slaughtering a small herd of cattle, well, she might see the whole thing differently.

Clasping her tight, I buried my head in her shoulder. Feeling her shiver, I told her, "You would have wanted to be there, and…you'll just have to trust me when I say that it wasn't safe for you."

She pulled back to look at me again, but I couldn't meet her eye; I had to look at the floor. Sighing, she kissed my forehead. I knew I was chilly to her, and wondered if that grossed her out at all. If so, her face didn't show it when she tilted my chin up with her finger. "There is so much about you…about this, that I don't understand." She smiled sadly and shook her head. "But if you say you were trying to protect me by not telling me, then I'll accept that."

Another tear rolled down my cheek as my lip quivered. I hated that I couldn't tell her everything, but most of it would only worry or disturb her. The bottom line for her was my happiness though. If I had that, then I had a feeling she would overlook everything else.

Folding me in another hug, the heat radiating from her warming me, she murmured, "I love you, Emma, no matter what."

I exhaled in relief and gripped her back hard. A little too hard.

Squirming some, I heard her squeak out, "Em? I still need air."

Laughing a little, I pulled away from her. "Sorry."

My mom wanted to know what my life would be like now, and I told her that I'd pretty much be just like Teren. She seemed a little sad for me that I wouldn't be partaking in human food anymore. I assured her, just like Teren had always assured me, that I wouldn't miss it, that it didn't even sound good anymore. She felt my forehead and my cheeks, like she was checking to see if I was injured, then she put her hand over my heart. We both looked down, but neither of us felt the thump that should have been there.

As an odd tension filled the room, Mom shook her head. "You really are dead."

Grinning like Teren did when he was trying to assure me by teasing me, I shrugged. "Just my body, I'm fine."

She looked up at me with furrowed brows, but then she managed a soft laugh. Shaking her head she muttered, "Vampires." Exhaling a long breath, she quickly hugged me again. "The kids had a blast staying overnight. Anytime you and your husband feel like transforming into bats and sailing through the sky, I'd be happy to have them again." She gave me an impish grin.

I could hear Teren chuckling out by the car while I rolled my eyes. "Don't be ridiculous, Mom. Stuff like that isn't possible."

She eyed me up and down like everything about me wasn't possible in her eyes. And I suppose to most it wasn't. Heck, a few years ago, I wouldn't have believed in me either. "Sure, honey."

As I laughed, I heard my kids break into a chant of, "Can we fly, Daddy? I want to fly! I'm gonna try right now." Teren and I both broke out into fits of laughter and my mom looked at me with an even stranger expression.

Shaking my head at her, I let her know that my kids were now trying to phase into bats in the back seat. Her face turned a light shade of pink as she laughed. "Gosh, their hearing is good. How do the two of you ever…?" She didn't finish her question, but her heart picked up and her face filled with a bright red flush.

Tears springing to my eyes, I started belly laughing as I hugged her tight. She was referring to the challenges Teren and I faced in our love life, and she was horribly embarrassed for bringing it up. If I were still able to do so, my cheeks would have been flaming hot too. Unlike Teren's family, mine was a little more closed off about discussing each other's sex lives. "I love you, Mom."

My laughs subsided while I gave her one last hug. I tried to imagine living thousands of miles away from the warm, open woman, but I couldn't. Mom and Ashley were my family, my rocks. I couldn't picture them not being a stone's throw away from me. Of course, I couldn't imagine the vampires being more than a stone's throw away, either. I just wanted everyone to stay where they were, centrally located around me. I felt horribly guilty for feeling that.

Pulling away from Mom for the final, final time, I thought of my sister. Blinking, I looked around the house that I knew she wasn't in; I couldn't hear her heartbeat. "Did Ash stay the night too? Did she already leave?" I asked, as I started heading for the door. I needed to tell my sister everything that had happened, maybe somewhere away from the kids, so I could go into more detail with her.

Mom shook her head. "Ashley didn't come over last night. She's been pretty busy at work lately. I actually haven't seen her much this past week." She frowned, and I figured Ashley would have a visit from Mom in her near future.

Nodding, I put my hand on the door. "I called her last night, but she wasn't home. I just figured she was with you."

Mom shrugged and shook her head. "Nope, sorry." Eyeing me, she narrowed her eyes. "She doesn't know that you...?"

I shook my head. "No, which is why I need to talk to her."

Mom looked thoughtful as she nodded. I smiled and wished her well, thanking her for watching the kids as I opened the door. Before stepping out into the bright California sunshine, I twisted back to her. "You don't have to do the chicken-thing, Mom. Teren and I take care of the kids' needs."

She smiled in that way that clearly said, *I'm a grandma, it comes with the territory.* "I know, Emma, but I couldn't resist giving them a special treat." She looked out to where she could see them in the car through the window. "They're so special."

She smiled while I shook my head at her. "You're going to spoil them."

Looking back at me, she winked. "That's my job, honey."

Laughing at her, I finally stepped out to rejoin my husband and my children. He'd turned the stereo on, and Russian folk songs were playing through his speakers. He leaned over the hood as I stepped up to the passenger's side; I could still hear my kids debating on whether or not they were part-bat. Smiling at me, he tilted his head. "That wasn't so bad, right?"

I shook my head and laughed. "One family member down, one to go."

He nodded and opened his door to get in. Hopping in myself, I shifted around to ask my kids all about their stay at Grandma's. As they went on and on about all the things they got to do, I realized my mom was right; they'd had a blast.

Knowing what I needed, Teren took me directly to my old Victorian townhouse. I smiled at the adorable, blue milk carton of a house that my sister now lived in. I had a lot of good memories of this place; I sort of missed it.

Teren left the car running as he pulled in next to Ashley's compact. When I frowned at him, he shrugged and answered my unasked question. "I thought I'd take the kids to the…" He looked back at them before looking back to me. "P-a-r-k," he finished in a whisper; he spelled it out so they wouldn't scream in joy upon hearing their destination. Shrugging again, he nodded towards the house. "I figured you'd want some privacy for this one."

I swallowed as I followed his gaze to my sister's door. This was going to be a little harder, since Ashley knew everything. Looking back at him, I leaned in for a light kiss. "Thank you," I whispered.

He nodded. "I'll come back in an hour."

I nodded and moved to get out. The kids started complaining that I was leaving, then seeing where they were, they started complaining that they couldn't go see Ashley too until Teren finally revealed where they were going. Then they couldn't have cared less about visiting their aunt. They waved me off with bright smiles, cheering the whole while about going to the park with Daddy. Nika was especially excited to have Daddy push her on the swings; Julian told me so.

I blew my husband a kiss as I watched him pull out of the drive, then I twisted back around to my old door. Feeling nostalgic, I ran my hand down the rough grain of the shocking-red beauty. It felt like coming home, but a little different, too, since Teren's home had been my real home for years now. As the sun glinted off the red rubies surrounding the flawless diamond of my wedding ring, I finally knocked.

I heard Ashley mutter that she was coming long before she made it to the door. Luckily, she'd been downstairs. The steeply angled staircase was a little uncomfortable for Ashley, so much so that Mom told me that she sometimes slept on the couch in the living room. I felt a little bad about it, like maybe she should move somewhere easier for her, but Mom insisted that she loved the house, and loved the independence of living there alone.

She smiled when she saw me, but my enhanced vision watched her cheeks fill with a rosy flush, almost like she was embarrassed. "You all right?" I asked, stepping into my old entryway.

Biting her scarred lip, she nodded. "Of course. You?"

Her tone was polite, so I knew she hadn't spotted anything odd about me…yet. "Well, that's why I'm here actually." I looked away as she shut the door. My sister had repainted the atrocious living room so it no longer resembled split pea soup. It was now a pretty almond color. She'd done it pretty recently too; I could still smell the fumes.

As she bunched her brow at my statement, I pointed to her walls. "That's new. It looks nice." I shook my head as we walked into the room. "Why didn't you call me? I would have helped you do it."

Ashley grinned as she sat on my old couch. "Because you cheat." Remembering how I used to blur around her while I painted, I laughed. With a shrug, she added, "Besides…I did have help."

Leaning back against the cushions, she smiled as she played with a stand of her hair. It was the same sort of satisfied contentment that Tracey got on her face when she talked about Hot Ben. Relaxing into the cushions with her, I raised my eyebrows and asked, "A boy?"

Her cheeks deepened in color and she looked down at a button coming loose from the couch. Laughing at her reaction, I placed my hand on her thigh. Her head snapped up and her eyes widened. I stopped laughing, as I remembered why I was really here. Ashley tentatively touched my cheek. "You're cold…really cold," she whispered, her alive brown eyes glossing over with tears.

Sighing, knowing that even my breath was chilly now, I said, "I tried to tell you last night, but you were…out." I paused, wanting to ask her where she had been, and if her painting friend had anything to do with her absence, but her eyes were filling as she watched me, and I knew this wasn't the time for girl talk. Cupping my hand over hers, I whispered, "I died last night…well, this morning."

Both of her hands moved to cover her mouth. As she gasped, her eyes flicked down to my silent chest. I sighed again, wishing I could make the defunct organ beat again, if only just for Ashley. Shaking her head, she brought her fingers to my neck. I exposed the skin to her as she searched for the scar that was no longer there. Her rough fingers felt along the artery in my neck after her visual inspection. I knew those veins were thick with blood, but they streamed, not pulsed, so Ashley's human fingers wouldn't feel them. To her, all she would register was that I didn't have a heartbeat. I was a walking, talking contradiction.

"Oh my God, Emma." Her eyes came back to mine as the tears finally spilled down her cheeks. Wrapping her arms around me, she brokenly whispered, "Were you scared?"

Feeling my own tears, I let down the wall of bravery that I'd kept up for my mom and children. "I was terrified. If Teren hadn't been there…I think I would have gone mad."

She held me tighter, and the hand rubbing circles into my body slightly warmed my dead skin. "I'm so sorry, Em." Pulling back, she cupped my cheek. "Did it hurt?"

Watching her beautifully imperfect face twist in sympathy for me, I thought over the years of abuse she had suffered since her accident. Especially in the beginning. Her recovery had been excruciating, a fate I would never wish on anyone. Shaking my head, I told her, "It was nothing…piece of cake."

She watched me examine her body and she nodded, like she knew I would never complain about pain after everything she'd gone through. Then she smirked at my answer. She also knew that I had a severe aversion to pain. She'd tried for years to get me to pierce my belly button with her. I'd adamantly refused. It was just one of the reasons that she had been surprised that I let Teren bite me. But that was just...a different sort of pain.

Shaking her head, she reached out to hug me again. As I inhaled the soothing scent of her, she asked the one question that my mother would never think to ask. "What did you eat?"

I closed my eyes. I'd told her every part of Teren's conversion. She knew the side effects, she knew the risks. She was well aware that a starved, maniacal need to eat was the price for everlasting life, and that if I hadn't caved to that need, I wouldn't be sitting beside her right now. Sniffling, I pulled back and held hands with her. "Cows. Teren had some ready for me." I peeked my eyes up at her as she tilted her head, maybe picturing my "feast."

Smiling, the scarred skin slightly buckling, she curiously asked, "Was it gross?"

Grinning, I shook my head. "No." Thinking back over that first kill, I remembered the sweetness, the relief. It was like being in a hundred and ten degree heat and having someone crack open a nice cold carbonated soda. It had been anything but gross. Just thinking about it made me a little hungry again. But then, the human part of me considered the whole situation. I was on my knees, in the dead of night, sucking the lifeblood from an animal that mindlessly munched on grass that had probably been pooped on at some point in time. Wrinkling my nose, I laughed out, "Yeah, a little."

She laughed with me, then sighed and clenched my hands. "God, I'm so glad you made it. If you had died," she paused, blinking, "well, died-died, I mean, I don't know what I'd do." Her voice cracked as she choked up.

"I'm fine, Ash, better than ever." I once again considered leaving my family as I gazed at her. She was my best friend, aside from Teren. I couldn't imagine her not being near me every day.

"So, tell me, what's different now. No food?" She raised her eyebrows, curious again.

I sighed. "Just the liquid type."

She frowned, then laughed. "At least I'll always know what to make you when you come over for dinner."

I laughed at her finding a silver lining in what could be a very hard reality to accept. But Ashley had accepted Teren years ago, and really, I was just an extension of him. Nearly identical now. She knew what to expect because she'd been watching him for years. She didn't seem to want my life, a life I'd stupidly tried to force on her once, but she was open to whatever the details of my existence were now.

I'd said it before and I was sure I would say it again. I loved my sister.

Chapter 12 – Dead and Well at Thirty

After finishing up with some of the details about exactly why I'd decided to not take the shot, the hour was over and Teren was pulling into the driveway again. My sister couldn't hear the light hum of his car or my children exclaiming that they wanted Auntie Ash. With her hands folded over her lap, she silently absorbed everything that I'd told her about Starla's fate. As her head tilted to the side, her eyes became unfocused while her mind wondered. Staring at her, I could pick out the flecks of gold in her irises, like someone had sprinkled fairy dust in her eyes. It was remarkably beautiful.

Shaking her head, she refocused and looked over at me. "Poor Starla. I'm glad you could help her."

I smiled at my sister's warm heart. Starla had never been overly friendly to either of us. Not rude or anything, but definitely not welcoming. Mostly she always seemed put out when she came around, like she'd rather be sunbathing at some resort where hot, oiled men delivered bottomless glasses of fresh blood, complete with little umbrella straws in them. "Yeah, she's…different, but I couldn't just let her die."

Twisting her lips at me, she let out a humorless laugh. "So you offered to kill yourself." She raised an eyebrow. "Kind of dramatic of you."

I laughed and slung my arms around her, squeezing her tight to me. She shivered against my chill, so I eased off a bit. Then she rested her head on mine, and I relaxed as I held her. Hearing Teren unbuckling my kids, telling them over and over to calm down, that they would see Ashley in just a second, I quietly said, "We're just sitting in the living room, bring them on in."

Ashley lifted her head with a bewildered expression that I knew I'd used on Teren a time or two. I started to explain that Teren was here, but the door swung open and I didn't need to. Ashley's eyes flicked over to the squeaking contraption right as two tiny beings dashed through it.

"Auntie Ash!" they both exclaimed in unison.

Ashley grinned and held her hands out as the twins dashed into them. She placed warm kisses on their giggling heads while Teren wrapped his arms around me. Leaning back into the loving safety of his arms, I watched my sister asking Nika and Julian all about their stay with Grandma. As they told her everything that they'd already told us, Teren whispered, "Did I give you enough time?" His voice was soft, his breath in my ear barely audible on a human level.

Hearing him just fine, I nodded against his chest. "Yeah…we talked."

He squeezed me, and placed a soft kiss on my cheek. "And? How did she take it?"

Peeking up at him, I shrugged. "Like she handles everything." I looked back at the disfigured woman tickling our toddlers. "With a strength I hope to have some day."

I felt him chuckle against my body, and I twisted around to look at him again. Smirking, he raised an eyebrow. "I think you underestimate yourself." Watching my face, he smiled. As my sister amused herself—she was making Julian laugh by blowing raspberries on Nika's stomach—Teren furrowed his brows in concern. "How are you? Getting hungry?"

I started to say no, but the second I focused on it, I could feel the dull ache in my stomach, the slight dryness in my throat. Teren raised an eyebrow and I shrugged. "Maybe, a little."

Nodding, he seemed well aware of how I really felt, and I suppose he was aware, since he'd gone through this already. "It gets better after the first couple of days. Then you'll only need to eat once or twice a day."

Feeling a little tired, I leaned into him. "Back to the ranch then?"

Sighing, he kissed my head. "Yeah, it's just the best place for you to be right now, while you adjust."

Disengaging the kids from Ashley, I stood my sister up and gave her a final hug. Her hand brushed over my face, feeling my chill, and she shook her head. "I wouldn't have pictured your life turning out this way," she said.

Smiling sadly, I ran a finger across some of her scars; they were rough to my sensitive touch. "You either," I whispered.

Her eyes filled with an emotion that seemed more like joy than regret as her lips curved into a small smile. Shrugging, she cheerily said, "Well, at least we're both happy."

I nodded, then grabbed Nika's hand while Teren grabbed Julian's. "No, Mommy, we don't wanna go." Nika's small eyes filled with huge tears at the thought of leaving my sister. Staring down at the tiny version of myself, I could clearly see the exhaustion in her features. Julian voiced his agreement and tried to squirm away from Teren; he scooped him up and slung him over his shoulder.

While I considered slumping Nika over my shoulder like the potato sack Teren had just turned Julian into, Ashley stepped in front of her. Kneeling carefully with her stiff joints, she cupped Nika's cheeks. "We'll hang out real soon, baby girl." Leaning into her, she brushed her nose together with Nika's; Julian giggled. "Miss you, love you."

Nika kissed her nose. "Love you too, Auntie Ash." Her lower lip extended into a perfect pout. "I wanna stay."

Her voice quavered a little on the end, but then her mood completely reversed and she started giggling near uncontrollably. Both Ashley and I blinked at her reaction. Then we looked over at Teren and Julian. Teren had slipped him down his back and was now holding him by his ankles. Julian was grinning ear to ear as all the blood rushed to his little face. Teren chuckled as he gently swayed him back and forth.

Between giggles, Nika got out, "Julie likes that, Daddy."

I watched the father and son, awed and amazed at Teren's natural ability to avert potential meltdowns with a little fun. Laughing herself, my sister walked over to Julian and blew more raspberries on his exposed belly. Both the kids were howling after that, and we managed to get them out of the house and into the car with smiles instead of tears.

Heading back to the ranch, I again pondered not being around my family. It seemed a little unfathomable to me. Especially with Ash. I hated to leave her alone. Not that she was truly alone here. She had Mom, and friends from work and school, but still, she was my baby sister and I adored her and felt the need to protect her for the rest of her naturally appropriate life.

Lost in thought, I was slowly brought out of it by Teren softly laughing to himself. Curious, I looked over at him. He had one hand on the wheel, and one casually draped over my thigh. His head was tilted as he absently stared at the road with a soft smile on his lips. He seemed absorbed in his own thoughts and they seemed much more pleasant than mine.

Lacing our fingers together got his attention. When he smiled wider as he peeked over at me, I raised an eyebrow. "What are you laughing about over there?"

He bit his lip and shook his head; he seemed a little embarrassed that I'd caught his amusement. Even more curious, I leaned over to look at him closer. "What?" I asked, smiling wider as he laughed again.

Flicking a glance at our children falling asleep in the back seat, he looked over at me again. A familiar gleam was in his eye this time. "I was just remembering the last time the two of us drove along this road."

He bit his lip again as his eyes raked over my body. Taking in the heat of his expression, I quickly glanced at the stretch of road we were on. Shaking my head, I murmured, "I don't..."

Somewhere in my hazy memory of the last couple of days, I recalled being on this abandoned stretch of highway in the middle of the night, drunk, and feeling a little promiscuous. Eyes wider, I glanced back at him. Seeing that I remembered, he laughed. "That was definitely a moment I'll be thinking about on this road for a while."

Smiling, I waited for my cheeks to heat, but of course, they didn't. They couldn't anymore. Oh well, I supposed us experiencing each other while driving was a better memory for this road than when we'd stopped to help the man who had attempted to murder us. I was a little happy to push that memory back a notch as well. Sucking on my lip, I stared out the window. "I suppose that's the last time I'll ever be drunk?"

His thumb brushed over the back of my hand, and I looked back at him. He sighed and shook his head. "Yeah, unfortunately."

From the backseat I heard a sleepy Nika ask, "What's drunk mean, Mommy?"

Peeking back at the child I'd thought was conked out along with her brother, I shook my head at her. "Something I hope you never are, sweetheart."

Teren laughed over that one for a while.

Both kids were sound asleep by the time we got back to the ranch. Teren and I whisked them away upstairs, smoothly putting them into their bed without waking them. Placing a kiss on each slumbering forehead, I smiled over how much they enjoyed being with my family. If we moved them, they'd lose a large part of that.

I sighed once we closed their bedroom door, and Teren looked back at me. "You all right? Want me to get you some food?"

Listening to the light breaths on the other side of the wood, I shook my head. "I'm fine, but yeah, a little hungry."

With a playful twist of his lips, Teren scooped me into his arms. Content, I nuzzled my head into his warm neck. One perk of moving or not moving—Teren would be with me either way.

Jack was downstairs with Alanna when Teren walked me over the kitchen threshold. They both looked up at us and smiled. "Son, want to help me fix a fence tomorrow?" Jack asked as Teren set me down.

Teren's face brightened as he leaned against the counter. Having heard that I was thirsty, Alanna automatically started prepping a glass of blood. "Sure, Dad."

Jack smiled then sipped on a mug that held some very strong coffee by the smell of it. The aroma turned my stomach a little bit, which was an odd sensation for me; before dying, I'd adored coffee. While some things hadn't changed at all, some were completely different.

When Alanna was finished with the liquid that didn't tightened my stomach in disgust, I leaned back against the counter with Teren. Thanking Alanna, I shifted my gaze to Teren's father. "Jack?"

His warm eyes pulled away from his wife to look over at me. The kindness in the depths of them always brought a smile to my lips. Teren may have learned a lot about being a good man from the strong, vampiric women in his household, but he'd learned a lot from the man before me, too. "Yes, Emma?"

Clearing my throat, I looked at Teren and took a quick sip of blood. "Well, it's no secret around here that Teren and I are unsure what to do...about the move." My eyes came back to Jack's. There was a thoughtfulness in his expression. I shrugged. "Teren would like to stay with all of you, as would I...but, I'm having a hard time with the idea of leaving my family. Was it hard for you, to let everyone you knew go?"

Jack sighed and looked down. Alanna's arms immediately went around his waist and his arm immediately slipped around her shoulders. After a moment of silent deliberation, he looked up at me. "I won't lie, Emma, it was difficult." His thumb stroked his wife's shoulder as he gazed down at her. "Worth it, but difficult."

I leaned into Teren's side; he put his arm around me much like his father had with his wife. Jack looked between the two of us and smiled at our connection. "My situation was different than yours though, Emma. My family never knew what Alanna and the girls were."

I blinked, wondering how they'd managed to hide that from them for so long. Smiling at my face, he shrugged. "I was an only child, and my parents weren't the type to ask questions. We successfully hid the truth, and when we left to start our ranch," he glanced at Teren, "and our family, Halina wiped their memories."

Considering Halina doing the same to my family, I averted my eyes. "So, they never missed you, because they didn't remember you..."

Jack separated from Alanna and walked up to me. Feeling my eyes start to sting, I stared into my blood. Even though Teren had assured me that my family could remember, I wondered if it really would be like that. At the bare minimum, what I was would probably be taken from their minds. It left me with a dull ache of loneliness that they wouldn't truly know me anymore. I suddenly had a newfound appreciation for Teren's desire to leave a memory of him…in someone.

"Of course they remembered me, Emma." Lifting my chin with his coarse fingers, he encouraged me to look up at him. Smiling, his aged face deeply sympathetic, he added, "She wouldn't make them forget *you*, just the situation, just what you and Teren are."

I nodded and blinked back the tears stinging. Glancing at Alanna's equally sympathetic face, I asked, "So they never remembered that you married, that you had a child?"

Dropping his hand from my face, Jack looked over at his son. "They remembered Teren. He grew and aged at a normal pace, so there was no reason to keep him from them." Swinging his gaze back to Alanna, his smile dropped. "For my wife…" he sighed and shook his head, "they were only left with a vague memory of her after every visit."

Alanna's smile turned sad as he continued. "Right up until their deaths a few years ago, they believed the cover story, that Teren's mother had died and I remarried a younger woman. As soon as Alanna's never-ending youth became apparent, Halina took away anything about us that might have made them suspicious, and they were fed the lie from then on."

Letting out a soft laugh, he shook his head. "They even met Alanna again when I got 'remarried.' They had no idea that they'd already met her, multiple times. And when we left, Alanna's details left with us. Even though Alanna and I have been remarried several times, on their death beds my parents wouldn't have been able to pick her out of a crowd."

Alanna walked up to him, slipped her arms around him and rested her head on his shoulder. Thinking about how misinformed his parents had been, I shook my head. "Wow, that's kind of…sad." I peeked up at Teren behind me. "I don't know if I want my mom forgetting you..." I blinked as I considered how my situation was a little different from Jack's; I didn't age either. "What about me? If she doesn't know and I never get any older, I'll never be able to visit again."

Teren squeezed me tight. "No, no that's not true. Of course you will." Twisting me in his arms, he gave me a warm smile. "My grandparents were a different situation, Emma. It wouldn't have to be like that with her. She already knows, and she's already accepted us. As long as she continues to stay silent, she could keep her memory of what we are."

He kissed my forehead as Jack patted my back. "It was just the easiest way with my parents, Emma. They…wouldn't have understood the real situation."

I nodded and looked back at him. "But all of my friends?"

Sighing, he glanced at Alanna and then back to me. "Unfortunately, yes, they would all forget the specifics of you and Teren. Otherwise, it's just too many loose ends. Once we move on, we prefer most people's memories of us to be hazy at best." He shrugged, looking very apologetic. "It's the best precaution we have."

Nodding, I conformed myself to Teren's body. He stroked my hair and rubbed my back. "I know what you're feeling, Emma. I don't want to give them up either."

I understood what he meant. He'd sort of made a mess for his family by repeatedly trying to keep ties with other people, first with Carrie, then with Hot Ben. Come to think of it, he hadn't batted an eye over telling Ashley the truth, either. Of all of them, Teren enjoyed hiding the least. He wanted to be normal. He wanted to be accepted. He wanted to be a part of society, not stay in the fringes of it. With what we'd gone through, he understood more why we had to hide, but it was hard for him. He completely understood my dilemma because he was constantly experiencing it, too. Every day I understood just a bit more about him, and every day I loved him a little more.

Cupping my cheek, he stroked my skin with his thumb. "We have time, Emma. We don't have to decide anything today." He kissed my head, and we both sighed at the same time.

I called Tracey early the next morning to let her know that I wasn't coming in for the rest of the week. I had an idea all thought out as I snuggled under the covers with Teren. I was going to convince her that I'd caught that swine flu bug thing that was going around. Surely the entire office would insist I stay away after that.

I heard her pick up the line. "Neilson, Sampson and Peterson. This is Tracey, how can I help you?"

"Hey, Trace, it's me." I practiced my raspy voice and coughed a couple times into my cell phone.

"Emma! Happy Birthday!" She immediately began singing the birthday song to me. It caught me a little off guard; so much had happened recently that I'd nearly forgotten that my birthday was today. I tried to interrupt her a few times, but she ignored me until she was done. Teren started chuckling into his pillows. "Are you coming back today?" she asked merrily, post-song.

Sighing dramatically, I coughed again. "Actually, that's why I called. I'm still pretty sick. The doctors think I got that new virus going around."

Tracey's voice was instantly sympathetic. "Oh, that sucks, Emma. And on your birthday, too." There was a pause in the line while I exaggerated a cough. "Wait, didn't you get the vaccine? We all got that company flyer about it."

My mind replayed back to laughing with her about the seriously written HR memo urging all employees to protect themselves against the epidemic that would surely wipe out all of mankind. "Uh, well…I hate needles, so, no."

Teren started laughing in earnest, covering his head with the pillow so Tracey wouldn't hear him. I bit my lip to not laugh too. Me, afraid of needles? Not anymore, not after injecting myself daily for years.

Tracey, not knowing about that part of my life, sighed. "Well, I bet you'll think twice about waiting next time."

I let myself laugh a little. "Yeah, definitely."

She sighed. "Well, get some rest, drink lots of water, and I'll let everyone here know that you were a procrastinating idiot."

Teren laughed a little harder, and I smacked him on the back. "Thanks, Trace."

She laughed. "Just kidding, Em. Feel better…Happy Birthday."

I smiled, then remembered to cough. "Thank you, I will."

Shutting the phone and setting it on the nightstand, I instantly began tickling my husband. "Quit making me laugh when I'm trying to act. You know I suck at that!"

Still laughing at me, he twisted and grabbed my wrists. "I'm sorry, Tracey's funny." I frowned at him, but he deadweight lifted me on top of him. Holding my wrists behind my back, he brought my face right down to his. "Happy Birthday."

Forgetting my irritation, I leaned in to kiss him. "Thank you," I murmured against his lips.

Releasing my arms, his hands wandered up my back to thread through my hair. Our kiss deepened, and I thoroughly relished our similar heat. I also enjoyed the fact that I was now sharing in a perk of undeadness that I'd enjoyed from him for a while. Let's just say he never needed mouthwash in the morning. He always tasted great, and now I would, too.

Pressing my hips into his, I felt every fiber of my body start to tingle with anticipation. His breath increased as he sensed it too. Flipping us around, so my back was to the mattress, his hand started sliding up the shorts I'd slept in.

"Can I give you your present now?" he breathed in my ear.

Gasping, I grabbed his hand and slid it farther up my skin. "Yes," I panted.

He chuckled as he removed his hand. Frowning, I watched his lean body stretch over mine and open his nightstand. Realizing he'd meant an actual present, I smiled...and reached down to squeeze his butt. Twisting his lips as he looked back at me, he pulled out a small, wrapped gift.

I shifted to my side, and he handed it to me. Furrowing my brows, I shook my head. "When did you find the time to get this?"

Smiling, he brushed a stray lock from my forehead. "I always find time for you." With a laugh, he added, "Even when you're busy giving me an ulcer."

Sighing, I stroked his face. "I'm so sorry you had to watch me die."

Shaking his head, he murmured, "I would never let you die alone." My eyes started stinging and he nodded at the gift. "Open it."

Swallowing the sudden emotion blocking my throat, I started unwrapping the blood red packaging. Inside the shiny paper was a long rectangular box. It felt feather light, like nothing was inside it. As Teren sat back on an elbow to watch, I lifted the lid. Expecting jewelry, since my husband was fabulous in that department, I was surprised to find a piece of elaborately scripted paper.

Confused, I looked over at him, but he only smiled wider and nodded at it. Picking up the thin parchment, the paper smooth as silk under my fingertips, I started deciphering the fancy font. It took me a second to read it, then I re-read it. My mouth dropping open, I stared at Teren in shock. "You're having Gabriel soundproof our bedroom? Like, vampire-proof soundproof?"

He laughed at the look on my face, then sat up and propped an arm on his knee. "I tried to think of something you wanted, really wanted, and all I could come up with…was privacy." Tilting his head, he smiled down at me. "I asked Gabriel if he could make our bedroom like his lab, and he said he could."

More than a little floored, I sat up with him. "We'll be…alone?"

His fingers traced my cheek as he nodded. "For the first time in a long time, we'll be alone."

I shook my head as I imagined that possibility. We always had to be so careful around the impressionable children who could hear us in every corner of the house. Smiling, I let out a soft laugh as I hugged him. "Thank you, I love it."

Something else popped into my head as he held me. Pulling back, I raised an eyebrow at him. "Is this really a gift for me…or a gift for you?"

Laughing at the playful look in my eye, he shook his head. "A little of both, I suppose." Sighing, he lowered his forehead to mine. "It's a gift for *us*, so we have somewhere to just be ourselves. Somewhere to talk about things without waiting for the kids to be asleep, without worrying if they are hearing conversations that maybe they shouldn't hear."

Both eyebrows raised now, I flicked my gaze over his face. "Talk? You did this so we could...talk?"

Laughing, he glanced down at the sheets. His hand came down to rest on my hip, and he murmured, "Maybe other things too." Peeking up at me, his lips curved into a devilish smile that halted my breath. "I didn't think 'hey, I made us a sex room' sounded nearly as romantic."

Laughing, I pulled him to my mouth for a scorching kiss. Romantic or not, I couldn't wait for our "sex room" to be finished. As he lowered me back down to the pillows, the elegant gift certificate he'd made for me dropping to the floor, a drawback struck me. While his hand slid up my thigh, I exhaled, "What about the kids though? I don't want to not be able to hear them."

His breath heavier, he ran his stubbled jaw up the side of my neck as he whispered, "We'll always open the door, once we're done...talking."

I let out a soft laugh, a snarky response to that on my tongue, but then his fingers dipped between my legs and I couldn't think coherently. Biting back the groan I wanted to make, I arched my back and clenched his hair. God, I couldn't wait to not ever have to hold back with him.

That evening, I celebrated my birthday by cuddling with my family and watching a movie. My mom and my sister came over, and once the twins were put to bed, we plugged in a cheesy B-movie. Because I thought it was funny, we watched an old vampire flick.

Halina rolled her eyes and let out a dramatic groan at every ridiculous plot twist in the so-bad-it-was-good film. She got particularly riled up over the myths that she considered dumb.

"Why can't vampires go into people's homes without their permission? Are we suddenly polite, or something?" She snorted as yet another vamp was deterred from their prey by them simply closing the door.

Thinking about that, I looked over at Teren. "I guess that one's not true. You've never needed an okay to go anywhere."

Teren grinned but Halina threw a pillow at the TV, softly,

otherwise it would have gone right through it. "Why would silence bar me from entering a home? I could rip down that cottage plank by plank if I wanted to get inside it."

My sister chuckled while my mom's eyes widened; the full vampire in the family still sort of freaked her out. Wondering how that myth had gotten started, I shook my head. "I don't know."

Halina looked over at me; her pale eyes were fiery, like we were suddenly having a debate. "And how would that work anyway? What if I went to a business? Whose permission would I need?" She leaned forward, her short skirt riding higher up her thighs. "And what if more than one person owned the house? Would I need both? Is the power granted to anyone staying there? And how long do you have to be there to get that sort of power? Would squatters have that kind of magical ability?"

She leaned forward even more, and her hair swished over her exposed thighs. As she punctuated her points with hand gestures, her voice got even more heated. "Or is it the physical act of signing the mortgage papers that seals the deal? Or maybe it's filing the title with the state that starts the process?" Tilting her head, her voice turned incredulous. "What if you inherit the house? Do I need to ask the dead person? Can I enter in the interim, or does the magic automatically shift to the new owner? What if the house gets foreclosed? Do I need to ask the bank?"

Rolling her eyes, she paused to let out an irritated exhale. I took her moment of silence to try and end the debate I wasn't really having with her. "I got it, it's a stupid myth."

She smirked and leaned back on the couch; my mom visibly relaxed and I patted her thigh. Halina shook her head as she crossed her arms over her chest. "That one riles me up. It's right up there with vampires not casting a reflection in a mirror for some odd reason." She rolled her eyes again at the idiocy of mankind. "Do we suddenly stop solely existing in this world when we changeover, and that's why no reflective surface can capture our image?" She raised an eyebrow at me, but I wisely said nothing. Not having anyone to whine to, she muttered, "And don't even get me started on cameras."

Twisting to Teren again, I murmured, "Should we put in Twilight next?"

Halina dropped her head back to the cushions. "Oh my God! What self-respecting vampire...sparkles?"

Every vampire laughed at her comment; the humans joined in as well. Cuddling into Teren's side, I peeked over at Halina muttering about how those vampires didn't even have proper fangs, and I wondered if maybe Halina was just jealous of their sun-walking abilities.

As the deliciously bad B-movie wrapped up, I heard the sounds of light crying upstairs. Immediately in Mommy-mode, I blurred up to where I heard my children rustling in their bed. Quietly stepping into their room, I sat on the edge of the low mattress.

They both twisted to look up at me, then Nika crawled over to cuddle in my lap. Julian sat up, patting her back in sympathy while she cried in my arms. Hugging her tight, I kissed her head. "What's wrong, sweetheart?"

She was crying too much to answer, so Julian softly spoke for her. "Nick hurts, Mommy," he patted his chest, "right there."

I pulled her back to look at her, and the glow of my eyes highlighted her pajamas. Aside from crocodile tears rolling down her cheeks, she didn't look injured. Shaking his head, Julian looked frustrated that I didn't understand. "No, Mommy, inside."

I pulled Nika to my chest again, finally getting what he was saying. She wasn't physically hurt, she was emotionally hurt. Julian, feeling her pain, patted her back again. I soothingly shushed her, and asked her again what was wrong. I asked Julian too, but he didn't know. He could only feel her turmoil; he didn't know the reason for it.

Teren silently opened the door and stepped through. Sitting on the other side of the bed, he placed a palm on Nika's back. "What's wrong, princess?"

Starting to sob in earnest, she looked up at him. The glow of his eyes washed over her, drawing her in. He held her gaze, using the hypnotic side effect of our eyes to calm her tears. When her crying had softened to hiccups, she finally answered him.

"Are we bad, Daddy?"

He blinked, looking up at me before swinging his eyes back to hers. I twisted her face to make her look at me. "Of course not, baby. Why would you think that?"

She rubbed her eyes and sniffed. "Movie said vampires bad." Huge tears lit her eyes as her lip trembled. "We're vampires."

I pulled her tight to me, kissing her head. "Oh, baby, no." Tears stung my eyes as I considered what that awful movie must have sounded like to children who had no idea that the world thought of them as evil. Shaking my head against hers, I rocked her in my arms. "No, Nika. You're not bad."

Pulling back, I cupped both her cheek and Julian's; his eyes were sad too, as he finally understood what had upset his sister. "You two are the most incredible little people I know. You're the best and there is nothing wrong with what you are. You are absolutely not bad. Okay?"

They both nodded, and Julian crawled into my lap and hugged me along with his sister. Teren ran a hand along their backs as he gave me a warm smile. Feeling those tears dangerously close to falling, I shook my head at him. "Soundproofing sounds like a great idea."

He nodded and his finger came up to wipe the moisture from under my eyes. "I'll tuck them back in," he murmured, taking Julian from me. I nodded and gave him Nika, who was already falling back to sleep in my arms.

Kissing each member of my family a final time, I hastily made it out the door before my tears truly began. Leaning against the wall while Teren started humming a lullaby, guilt filled me. I'd never imagined that I'd be the indirect cause of my child's pain. As I ran my hands down my face, I wondered if Nika would need therapy when she got older because of me.

Alanna breezed into the hallway as I listened to my children yawn and my husband comfort. With my eyes closed, I felt her step before me and place a hand on my arm. When I peeked up at her, a tear fell on my cheek. She smiled as she wiped it off. "Not as easy as it seems, is it?"

I shook my head. "It's so strange. I want them to see the world, and yet I never want them to leave my sight." Tilting my head at her, I sighed, "I don't know how you did it. How did you ever let Teren go?"

She raised an eyebrow at me and glanced at the door that her son was behind. "Did I?" She laughed and I considered all of the mothering that Teren had put up with from her, sometimes grudgingly.

Chuckling myself, I pulled away from the wall. "I want to give them every opportunity, but I never want them to feel pain." I shrugged. "With what they are though...that just isn't possible. How do you deal with knowing what they'll be facing?"

Alanna shook her head and shrugged. "You find a way. Raising a child isn't easy. You beat yourself up over every mistake, every tiny little thing that goes wrong. But you do the best you can." Sighing, she swept me into her arms. "And if you fail...you try again tomorrow."

Chapter 13 – Soundproof

After a week, I felt okay enough to head back to my life. Besides, I didn't want to miss any more work. Not for unplanned absences, anyway. If I was going to get away from the office, it was going to be for that never-got-around-to vacation that Teren and I had vaguely planned together years ago. Preferably somewhere hot and muggy, since the temperature extreme would feel amazing on my cool skin.

I was a little nervous about what I'd chow on in the city, since cows weren't exactly walking around in most people's backyards, but I should have known better. Alanna sent me out the door with enough chilled or frozen packages of blood to last me practically until the next decade. And I was pretty sure that she'd be swinging by for the first few months to resupply me if I did get low. Alanna was an innate caregiver, incapable of neglect, and now that Teren's thirst had diminished, I was the lucky recipient of her first-class nurturing.

As I was getting ready for work on my first Monday back from my "illness," Teren gave me some tips that he'd used when he'd gone back to work. Cocking an eyebrow at him, I whispered, "Are you serious...the bathroom? You told me you never needed to eat at work."

Smiling as he buttoned up his dress shirt, hiding his glorious skin with each fastening, he shook his head. "Need, no, but it did...take the edge off. And yes, the bathroom. It's the most private place to do it, trust me."

I shook my head, incredulous at what he'd done, at what he was asking me to do. "So, when you got hungry at work, you took a small thermos of blood into the restroom and took a sip in a stall, where people...do unpleasant stuff?"

Chuckling at me, his shirt completely fastened, but loose over his slacks, he sat beside where I was sprawled out on our bed. Leaning over, he brushed aside some hair from my forehead; I could smell the soap from his shower on his fingers. "It's more secluded than your car or an empty office. And people generally leave each other alone in there...so long as you don't take too long."

He laughed while I sighed. I was *not* relishing the smells that would be mixing with my bloody lunch. Looking at the disgust on my face, he tapped my nose with his finger. "Don't think about it. Just do what you need to do to get through the day."

Reaching my arms around his waist, I sighed again. "And you're sure the temperature thing won't be noticed?"

Shrugging, he kissed me. "No one ever questioned my sudden change." Pulling back to look at me, he lifted an eyebrow. "The average human isn't looking for a supernatural answer to life's little oddities. If you act completely normal, they will think you *are* completely normal." He smirked and shrugged. "As Great-Gran said, they're sort of like the cattle…easily herdable."

I grunted at him and pushed back on his chest. "Please don't start quoting Halina."

He kissed my head as he stood up. "I'll have my phone close all day, just text me if you're having any problems."

Exhaling nervously, I shook my head. "Yeah…okay."

Love in his eyes, he watched me as he tucked in his shirt. "You'll do great, Emma, like you always do."

I nodded as he quickly finished. Giving me one last hug, he made to leave for work. Striding through the door, he suddenly stopped and looked back at me; a serious expression washed over his face. "Most people will ignore it…but not all." His eyes flickering over my body, he shook his head. "Please try and be cautious of the *not* normal human beings."

I bit my lip and nodded. Yeah, the last thing Teren and I needed was another hunter on our tail.

Pulling into the lot after dropping off my kids at Mom's, I breathed in a deep, unneeded breath. I could do this. After all, I'd already handled dying, how bad could this be?

Walking in through the front doors, the smell hit me first. I'd never noticed it before, but a building full of warm-blooded humans smelled like warm blood. It was everywhere. It seeped from their pores.

Smiling, I listened to the thumping heartbeats all around me. It was like walking through a chocolate factory—everyone just smelled so good. On the way to the elevator, I found myself lingering to talk to people that I usually didn't talk to on a regular basis. I just wanted to listen to their hearts. Recognizing that I was noticing people in a way that maybe I shouldn't be, I forced myself to stop enjoying the flow of blood around me and concentrate on getting to my office.

Digging through my purse, I texted Teren as I stepped out of the elevator and onto my floor. *'Everyone smells good...is that normal? Am I okay to be here?'*

I hadn't taken two steps before he responded. *'Yes, it's normal. You're more attuned to them now and you'll notice them in a way you didn't before. That will fade as you get used to it. You are still in control of your actions. Duck to the bathroom if you need anything.'*

Cringing, I placed a hand over the conveniently sized thermos in my mammoth purse and typed back a thank you.

Ignoring how the mailman was a little mouthwatering now, I kept my head down and hurried to my desk. It wasn't as if I suddenly wanted to chow down on my coworkers or anything, I definitely did not, but they were just about the yummiest things I could think of, all clumped together like...well, like cattle.

Laughing a little, I nearly ran right into Tracey. I instinctively inhaled in surprise, and her particular scent hit me. She was more familiar than my coworkers, since I'd spent a decent amount of time with her pre-death. It calmed me down some. Tracey placing her fingers on my upper arm did not. Wanting to pull away, but knowing that Teren was right and casualness was the key to inconspicuousness, I remained where I was under her grasp. Her dull senses wouldn't be able to feel my temperature under my blazer anyway.

Glancing between my eyes, she raised a pale eyebrow at me. "You all right? Back to human?"

My eyes widened at her words, but then I realized she was referencing the flu I'd supposedly been getting over. "Yeah, much better, thank you." I coughed a little, hoping for space. It worked like a charm; she dropped her fingers and took a step back.

Grinning, she shook her head. "Well, glad you're better."

Ducking into my old cubicle, she absentmindedly admired her engagement ring as she sat down. Murmuring at a level she wouldn't hear, I wryly said, "Yeah, all back to normal."

Hearing Clarice grunt in disapproval at me standing outside our joint office, wasting valuable time talking to someone Clarice considered a subordinate, I sighed and shook my head at Tracey. "Duty calls." Tracey blinked at me. She had a lot of things going for her—great job, great fiancée, amazing looks—but she didn't have my super hearing.

With no one else coming anywhere near as close to me as Tracey had earlier, my Monday morning went by pretty uneventfully. But around lunchtime I did start to feel a little peckish. When my throat dried up and my stomach tightened, I figured it would be prudent to stay on top of this, lest I cave and take a bite out of Clarice's pudgy, judgmental ass.

Waiting for Clarice to leave for her standard forty-three minute lunch break, and faking that I was swamped with work when Tracey asked if I wanted a bite with her, I felt real hunger pangs by the time I carefully pulled the container out of my bag. Still not thrilled over drinking where people peed, I wished I could down the plasma treat right there in the office. But, it wasn't worth the risk of someone seeing me.

Sighing, I texted Teren a quick message. *'Going in, wish me luck.'*

His reply was immediate. *'You'll be fine. Wash your hands afterwards...bathrooms are disgusting.'*

Laughing, I put the phone away and tucked the warm mug under my blazer. It heated one side of me and just the thought of that warmth sliding down my starting-to-ache throat, made me want to growl in pleasure. I had more control than that, though.

Walking down the hall with something that I knew would freak out every person in the building made my nerves spike. By the time I was in the bathroom, triple checking under every door, my hands were shaking. As I closed a stall door, I knew my heart would have been pounding, if I were still alive. Even without it, my icy veins felt even icier. I felt like I was doing something nefarious, spying or embezzling or stealing office supplies.

Then I took the lid off my drink and inhaled. Unhindered by bone, flesh, skin and clothing, the direct smell of blood was overwhelming. I let my fangs crash down to where they wanted to be and immediately tilted the cup back. Euphoria flooded through me, and I had to put my hand against the door to steady myself, the taste was so amazing. Sweet, tangy, heady, it was better than any martini lunch I'd ever had; worth every damn germ in this place, not that germs really mattered to me now anyway.

Feeling proud of myself, I contained the satisfied growl that I wanted to make. I also saved half the drink for later. Having several more hours of sitting in a room with Clarice, I was pretty sure I'd need a pick-me-up before the end of the day. Especially when her last comment to me before lunch had been to ask if I'd had all my shots for the rest of the year, like I was a dog or something.

Feeling full and warmed from the liquid in my belly, I almost skipped back to my office. Excited to tell someone that I'd pulled it off, I texted Teren. *That was so incredibly amazing! I should have been doing this ages ago. I'm so satisfied right now...'*

His response was quick, as usual. *'Stop...you're turning me on.'*

Giggling in my joy, my phone beeped at me before I could type back. *'I'm glad you got something to eat. I was a little worried.'*

Shaking my head, I reassured him that I was great and that I loved him very much.

By the end of the week, I felt like I'd successfully adjusted to the undead life. Eventually the newness of being deceased wore off, and I truly began to enjoy how alive the world was to me. Colors, sounds, textures, everything was more distinct, clearer. It was like Teren had said once, the senses seemed to swap around with each other. I could hear color in music, I could feel silkiness in sound. It was something unexplainable that only other vampires understood. It was a world I wished I could have shared with my family, but it wasn't a fate I'd wish on them. The constant worry, the never-ending charade. There were sacrifices to being what I was...like dealing with people eating food all the time.

I'd never realized how much eating and drinking was a part of our society until I'd been taken out of that part. It seemed like nearly everything humans did centered around food somehow. Movies equaled popcorn. Baseball games equaled beer and hotdogs. Even walking through the park involved a stop at the churros stand. It was everywhere. It churned my stomach at first, the sight and smell of so much food, but after a while that reaction faded. It was like watching people eat dog food. I had to forcefully make myself not cringe.

And I had to come up with ways to excuse myself from eating. Being a girl, I had the "I'm on a diet" thing going for me, and it worked for most places where food wasn't the main attraction. But going out to eat was something else entirely. I avoided outings with my friends, but my family and I still got together once a week for meals.

Thankfully I didn't have to hide it from them, but the staff had known me for years and brought me my sandwich without me even asking. I discretely gave pieces to my kids and made my sister eat the rest. Because she was the most awesome person in the world, she did, doggy-bagging half of her own meal if she couldn't finish both.

While Teren's excuse that he was severely allergic had worked well enough for him that he could sit with nothing and our longtime waitress left him alone, I couldn't exactly develop the same rare problem that he'd suddenly developed. That would have just been weird. So with my family's help, I got through our weekly meals with a sham.

On the third week of faking it, my mom sighed and set her fork down. "This is ridiculous. Half of the table isn't eating." She indicated where Teren and I were sitting, watching everyone else eat.

Holding Teren's hand under the table, I shook my head. "It's fine, Mom. We'll eat later." Since I really didn't want her to think about how we ate, I usually left that topic pretty vague. Mom didn't ask either.

"Well, we could do something else when we all get together, something everyone would enjoy?" She said, looking between Teren, me, Ashley and the twins.

Nika grinned when Mom's eyes swept over her; a chunk of my sandwich was hanging out of her mouth. Mom smiled, but then frowned when she returned her eyes to me. "You guys shouldn't have to be bored, just sitting there."

I laughed as I leaned into Teren's side. "We're not, Mom. We're here for the conversation…not the food."

Mom shook her head, picking up her fork again. "All right, well, if it's okay with you guys, who am I to complain, I guess?"

My sister giggled as she ate my sandwich for me. Glancing over at her, I could see creases in her scars that hadn't been there a few months ago, or maybe my poor vision just hadn't noticed them before. Either way, I noticed them now, and what they were made me smile—laugh lines. Crinkles of happiness. The skin so used to the act of smiling that the body had permanently etched the shape of that joy into her young skin. I instantly wondered what the source of her joy was.

Pulling apart the last remaining segments of the meal I wasn't eating, I tilted my head at her. "Ash?" She looked from Mom to me, her face curious. "What have you been up to lately, sis?"

She flushed a little as she looked around the table. "Nothing much," she muttered, digging back into her food with gusto.

Raising an eyebrow, I leaned in "Really? Because I know you're holding something back. I can smell it." I couldn't, but Ashley didn't know that. Her eyes widened as she looked me up and down.

Teren chuckled and shook his head. Ashley's eyes went to his face, then back to mine. "You cannot, Emma. " She rolled her eyes while I frowned at my fib-busting husband. Laughing harder, he shrugged.

Sulking at him destroying my ploy, I dropped his fingers and played with my meal scraps with both hands. Rolling up a piece of my bread, I handed it to Julian. "Then what's going on? Really?"

Mom looked over at Ashley; her eyes were curious now too. Ashley looked between us, then sighed. "Okay, but you can't say anything." I smiled and nodded; secrets were sort of my specialty.

Looking around, Ashley leaned in. "Some of the doctors that I know have been doing a lot of work with cultured skin." I gave her a blank look and she smiled. "Skin that's been grown in a lab. Anyway, they've been letting me assist them in my free time, and I just watched them successfully grow skin with hair follicles." Her eyes widened as her face lit up. "It had sebaceous glands and everything! Do you know what that means, Emma?"

I shook my head. "Not really. They grew hairy skin? It sounds kind of creepy."

My sister giggled and shook her head. "It means that they could potentially do skin grafts for patients on areas of the body that grow hair." She pointed to her bare head, as if to emphasize what had just been made startlingly clear to me. "Baldness, burns, cancer? It's a breakthrough."

Growing skin in labs had been too new of a thing to help Ashley, but she'd told me once before that it was being practiced more and more as the science was perfected. Since her accident, numerous patients had avoided having healthy skin sliced off their own bodies and painfully relocated to cover damaged areas. Ashley had had more than a few of those kinds of surgeries. Now she was telling me that they were on the cusp of grafts that could help patients regain their natural head of hair. My eyes watered at just the thought.

Ashley's did, too. "Can you imagine what this could do for people? The normalcy, the hope?" Her eyes got dangerously close to overflowing as her smile widened as far as it could go.

My mom threw an arm around her as Teren placed his hand over hers. They each offered support and praise while I stared at her, amazed. Everything about her defied the odds. Her living through the blaze that took our father. Her fighting through the painful battle of recovery. Her ability to ignore the taunts and jabs directed her way, to be able to walk proudly in her own skin. Her desire to turn her setbacks into inspiration, to help others like herself. And even now, hearing of a treatment that could potentially help her one day too, her first thought was of how it could help others. Once again, I wanted to be my sister when I grew up.

I was still thinking of my sister's revelation the next day. Sipping my bathroom beverage, and trying to ignore the toilet flushing going on around me, I contemplated what her life could be like if her mentors were successful. Having a full set of hair wouldn't make her completely normal looking, but it would cut back on the stares she received. If just that small thing could be changed, she and others like her wouldn't be the instant elephant in the room, something everyone notices, but most try to avoid talking about.

I wanted that for her, but I'd come to realize that my sister wanted life on her own terms, and hiding her disfigurement had never been something she'd desired. If it were just a matter of hiding herself, she would have purchased a wig years ago. But she hadn't. While gracious and patient with most people, she sort of had an *I'm here, deal with it*, approach to life. Sort of like Halina actually, just on a much, much nicer level.

Teren was all smiles when he greeted me in our driveway when I got home. I felt the lingering joy of our connection completing as he squeezed me into a hug, but I didn't think that was really the cause of his smile. Pulling back to look over his features, I tilted my head. "Something up? Besides being happy to see me?"

Nodding, he pulled my hand. "I have a surprise for you."

Now I was grinning ear to ear. Teren's surprises were usually pretty good. Simultaneously greeting our pet and children, since all three greeted me at the door, I looked around for a big box with a shiny bow or something. Not seeing anything, I frowned.

Teren laughed at my face and started tugging on my hand to get me to follow him. Two excited little bodies were holding me in place though. Jumping up and down, Julian and Nika were both animatedly repeating, "It's quiet, Mommy!"

Confused, I glanced up at Teren. Sighing, he pointed up to our room. "Secret's out, I guess. Gabriel was here, he finished the room."

I blinked and then smiled. Our sex room was complete. Okay, that wasn't entirely the reason for the soundproofing but still, it was definitely a perk. Teren grinned at my response, then successfully yanked me away from the kids.

All of us laughing, we walked upstairs to the end of the hall, where our bedroom was. Running past us, Julian and Nika darted into the room and started screeching at the top of their lungs. It was loud, and I cringed. Then Teren closed the door.

I blinked in disbelief. I couldn't hear them, not a peep. I knew they were still making as much noise as they could, but even if they were whispering, I should have been able to hear them. It was a little disorienting.

Teren opened the door after a second. The sound of screaming instantly filled my ears. Giggling, the twins took turns being the noisemaker and the door shutter. As the sound of Nika yelling her ABCs shifted in and out of my mind while Julian opened and closed the door, I turned to stare at Teren. "Wow, that really is amazing."

Nodding, he pointed to the seal around the door. It was different than before and even though I could hear it swishing across the carpet with each opening and shutting, no sound came past it once it was locked into place. "He installed the seals and changed the insulation in the walls." Chuckling, he added, "He even added several layers of Kevlar, so we're bulletproof now." I smiled at him; we were already bulletproof. Kind of.

Shaking my head as I stepped into the room with Julian, who had taken Nika's place as noise maker, I looked around. Everything was picture perfect, just as I'd left it this morning. You'd never know that the walls had been torn up and replaced. The toxic smell of paint was sharp to my sensitive nose, but really, that was the only clue that anything had happened in this room today.

Ushering Julian outside with his sister, Teren closed the door as he stepped in with me.

Their giggling was instantly silenced, along with every car horn, dog bark, screeching neighbor, and telephone conversation nearby. The quiet intruded on my brain, like a physical thing that could seep in and envelop me, and all I heard for once was the sound of Teren and I breathing.

"It's...so quiet," I whispered, suddenly feeling like I was in a sacred place.

Teren came up to me and grabbed my hands. "I know. It's kind of nice, isn't it?" He shut his eyes, and his face relaxed. "Not having to block the world out, just so you can hear yourself think."

Smiling up at him, I laced my arms around his neck. "It feels like we're the only two people on earth."

Opening his eyes, his lips curved into a warm smile. "We could be, for just a little while."

His gaze flicked down my body and I instantly felt the heat of it. It was all mental of course. My body didn't actually heat up anymore, but the fire of wanting him was still within me, mentally if not physically. He leaned in to kiss me, backing me up to the bed in the process. As his fingers removed my blazer, mine threaded through his hair.

I sat on the bed, and he used his body to force me to lie back on it. I kept a mental tab on the kids. Feeling that they were safely playing in their room, I indulged in not having to hold anything back for once. It gave me a little bit of a high to be with him like this, during waking hours, with sunlight streaming through the window.

My legs wrapped around him as his hands drifted up my lacey camisole. Grabbing his back, I pulled him where I needed him most. He groaned in my mouth. Smiling, I relished the sound, then his hand slid under my bra and I made a moan of my own.

Our breaths heavy in the quiet room, his lips traveled up to my ear. "That sounds so nice. I've missed hearing you let go." His hand coming down to unfasten my slacks, he whispered, "I want to hear you beg for me. I want to hear you scream."

My eyes rolled back as his words tumbled around the room. My hand came up to his cheek, forcing his mouth back to mine. "I want to hear you, too," I muttered, our lips frantic as desire revved up the pace.

Getting lost in him, my fingers busy grasping his shirt, I didn't notice something I really should have noticed. Pressing into me, his body as ready to go as mine was, Teren didn't notice either. We both noticed about five seconds later.

"Mommy, I hungry."

Teren immediately sat up and snapped his eyes to the door. Standing there with pure innocence in her eyes, our daughter calmly watched us as we struggled to breathe. Letting out a soft laugh, Teren looked down at me. "We do still need a lock on the door though."

Laughing, I covered my face. I couldn't believe that we'd nearly been walked in on by our kids. Locking the door had been on our to-do list for a while; I vowed to bump it to the top of that list. After setting the kids up with some graham crackers and chocolate milk, Teren was back in our room moments later. He swished into the room and shut the door. The noise of our young ones eating instantly cut off.

I sat up on my elbows as he grinned and crawled on top of me. "Now, where were we?"

While he nuzzled my neck, not bothered in the least by the disruption, I struggled to stay in cautious parent-mode. "Uh, the kids?"

"Downstairs, watching cartoons," he murmured, his lips wandering up my neck as his hand resumed caressing my breast.

I closed my eyes as a soft moan left me. "A cartoon? Will they be all right, down there all alone?"

Nodding, he moved over the top of me. "Everything is locked up tight. There's nothing dangerous they can get into. They'll be fine." His hands slid down to my slacks, unzipping them. "Besides, in about twenty minutes, they'll come looking for us."

Feeling them safe and secure downstairs, I let go of worry and enjoyed the gift that my husband had arranged for me. Not wanting to waste what precious time we had with foreplay, we blurred out of our clothes. As the tip of him pressed against my entrance, that body part as lukewarm as the rest of him, he paused and looked down on me with lust and love in his eyes.

Groaning at how close he was, at how much closer I needed him, I watched the corner of his lip lift. Needing him so much I wouldn't have even cared if our room *wasn't* soundproof, I pulled at his hips. "Please, take me, Teren."

He closed his eyes as he pushed into me. I let out a cry that ordinarily would have had the kids huddled in a corner. As Teren took long, slow strokes, murmuring, "Yes," into my shoulder, I let him hear every sound he made me feel. I contained nothing and it drove him into a near frenzy. His pace quickened with every sound I made.

Wrapping my legs around him, my fingers digging into his back, I begged, "I want to hear you, too, don't hold back either."

His forehead rested against mine as he sucked in a quick breath then let out a noise that was beyond any erotic sound I'd ever heard. Somewhere between pain and pleasure, it ached with the need to release. I found myself muttering, "Yes," and, "More."

As we drove against each other, I felt the buildup in me but heard it more from him. He swore, and dropped his head back to my shoulder as the intensity of our connection rose. "Yes, oh…God, yes, Em."

Throwing my head back, I screamed out his name just as euphoria burst through my body. His hand came out to clench mine, and his wedding ring dug into my skin as he cried out. I gasped at the sensation of feeling his release, and my own. My undead body felt everything more intensely, orgasms included.

Panting as we both came down, I took a second to locate our kids. They hadn't moved. Collapsing on top of me, Teren let out a deep groan. "I think I'm going to love this room."

Chuckling, I smacked his shoulder. "I knew it. I knew this was more a present for you."

Lifting his head, he raised an eyebrow. "You didn't enjoy that?"

Grinning, I wrapped my legs tighter around him and rocked my hips. "All right, maybe I did." As I continued moving my hips, he closed his eyes. He was still inside me, and I felt him responding again. Groaning at my husband's endurance level, I again let him know how much I appreciated his gift.

Thank goodness the children's cartoon was a long one.

Once we were as spent as we could be for one evening, Teren opened the door while I threw on some comfy clothes. The sounds of the world instantly assaulted me, spoiling the peaceful sanctuary we'd found. Being able to hear my kids again made me smile though. They were watching a cartoon that was asking them questions, and they were diligently responding where they were supposed to.

Teren dressed in some lounge pants and came up to snuggle beside me on the bed. Throwing a leg and arm over me, he sighed in contentment. I kissed his head as I stroked his back with my fingernails. His lips barely moving, he said, "We'll have to send Gabriel something as a thank you."

Smiling, I laid my cheek on his head. "I doubt there's anything he wants." Frowning, I considered how untrue that sentence was. I knew exactly what he'd love to have—full access to my kids.

Maybe feeling my body posture change, Teren lifted his head. His pale eyes searching mine, he shook his head. "He knows we won't ever let him test them. He wouldn't even ask."

Sighing, I nodded. "He stills studies them though. You notice how he watches them?"

Teren looked down. "Yeah, I've noticed." His eyes came back up to me. "But he's only observing, and mainly from a distance. It won't go any further...ever."

His lips firmed into a thin line, and the factualness of his statement was apparent in his features. No, Teren would never let Gabriel do anything other than watch. And really, he only got away with that because we couldn't do anything to stop it. But they were children, not experiments, and neither one of us were going to let him treat them as such.

Pushing my concerns to the back of my head, I ran my fingers through the hair over his ear. "Speaking of Gabriel, how has he been doing with the multiple conversions?"

He smiled softly. "Good, he tells me they all made it safely through." Teren didn't specify what they'd eaten to make it through. I didn't ask either.

Stroking the stubble of his jaw with my thumb, I frowned. "Who do you think the vampire was who trashed Gabriel's lab? Why would he do that?"

Teren propped himself up on his elbow. "Gabriel won't really talk about the vampire who stole from him." He shrugged. "He keeps saying it's a family matter. Even Great-Gran doesn't know a whole lot." He sat up and wrapped his arms around his legs. "From what I've gathered, his name is Malcolm. He was apparently Gabriel's assistant, ages ago, when he'd first started developing the shots. After a while, he took off on Gabriel, and he hasn't seen him since."

I sat up too and looped my arm through his. "Oh…and now that Gabriel knows what he did, he's tracking him?"

Teren nodded, his face grim. "Yeah, and they're getting close. I have a feeling that it won't be pleasant when Gabriel does find him. But, that's Gabriel's problem, Gabriel's decision, not ours." He smiled slightly. "Our family has nothing to do with…any of that."

I sighed and leaned into his side. From downstairs, I heard the kids' show end. Thinking I should go down and make the kids something more substantial to eat than crackers, I heard Nika say, "Press the button, Julie."

Smiling, I listened to the two of them rustling around with something. Then I heard channels being flipped on the television. Teren patted my thigh while I laughed at my kids' attempt to find something else to watch on TV.

"Ready to exit our love nest?" he asked.

Looking up at him, I shook my head. "Not really…but all right." While flipping TV stations echoed in the background, Teren hopped off the bed, then pulled me to my feet. I stumbled a little as he yanked me all the way into his body, wrapping my arms around him.

Holding his arms behind his back, I asked, "Hungry?"

Nodding, he slid his fangs out. He immediately brought them to my neck, like he was going to bite me right then and there. Letting him go, I smacked his chest and pushed him away from me. "Uh-uh." Smirking, I playfully added, "No vampiric candy before dinner."

He rolled his eyes as he grabbed my hand and led me to the open door. "You're no fun," he mumbled.

Laughing, I kissed his shoulder. "I said no candy *before* dinner. I didn't say anything about afterwards."

He looked back at me with an adorable smile as we entered the hallway. The television sounds stopped changing as our kids found something that held their attention. While Teren shook his head at me, I heard Nika exclaim, "Ooh, pretty."

Cocking my head, I listened to what had enraptured them. Oddly enough, it sounded like the news. Of course my kids would find the news fun; I hoped whatever they were reporting on was innocent, a piece about adopting puppies or something. Shoving Teren so he'd move faster, I tuned into what the reporter was saying.

"...fire sweeping over the hills has many Los Angeles residents fearing that they may have to evacuate..."

Teren glanced at me then blurred downstairs. I was right behind him. I didn't need our kids terrified over the fires that seemed to spread over the countryside each year. The one that they were talking about now had been blazing for a while, and showed no signs of stopping.

A pace ahead of me, Teren had the remote in hand just as the reporter said, "...the body was found among the debris. It is believed the woman had been out hiking when she unfortunately got caught up in the disaster. Burned beyond recognition, dental records have confirmed the identity as..."

The television flashed a picture and my hands flew to my face in shock.

"No..." Teren muttered, dropping the remote. Staggering, he looked like he was going to sink right to the floor. His wide eyes swung to me just as the photograph of the person who had perished in the flames was identified.

"...thirty-one year old Carrie Davids. Hailing from a small town in northeast Maine, friends and coworkers have confirmed to us that Miss Davids made an impromptu decision to fly out to California back in April. Not leaving anyone with a clear idea of when she would return, it would seem that Miss Davids set across the country to discover herself. A journey of self-discovery that ultimately led to her tragic demise..."

Chapter 14 – Bad News

Teren was shaking as I grabbed the remote and shut off the details of poor Carrie's death. I couldn't believe what I'd just heard. It seemed surreal, like I was in the middle of some bizarre dream I couldn't wake up from. Teren had turned back to the screen, watching it intently like the image of her face was still blazed across it. I thought that if I was having a weird dream, he was having a nightmare.

Tentatively, I touched his shaking arm. "Teren?"

Not reacting to me, his face was still glued to the television, his mouth still parted in disbelief. As his pale eyes glassed over, I knew he was moments away from breaking down. Sliding my hands up and down his arms, I gently whispered his name again. "Teren?"

Nika whined that I'd shut off the pictures of the fire that she'd thought were pretty; she didn't understand what had happened in that fire. "Mommy, I want to watch."

She hopped off the couch and darted over to the TV, her finger extended to touch the power button. I had a warning on my lips to tell her that TV time was over, but Teren snapped out of his stupor. "No, Nika! No more TV!"

She paused at the harshness in his tone, and her bottom lip trembled. Teren didn't usually raise his voice to her. Still sitting on the couch, Julian frowned, his lower lip sticking out. "Daddy, you scared Nick." Raising his chin, he added, "Inside voice, Daddy."

Teren closed his eyes and swallowed. With a forced exhale, he slapped on a perfectly realistic fake smile. Opening his eyes, he sank to his knee and held his arms out for Nika. She grinned and instantly flew over to him.

"I'm sorry I scared you, sweetheart, but we've had enough television for today." Pulling back, he cupped her cheek. In a surprisingly bright voice he told her, "Why don't you and Julian go upstairs and play with your blocks? You could build Mommy a castle. She'd love to see that." His voice started to shake as he spoke, and my heart broke watching him try and contain his feelings from his children.

Nika nodded and dashed off to her room. Julian hopped off of the couch and patted Spike so the lounging dog would follow him. I watched Teren as he watched the kids head upstairs. The tension in his body increased with every step they took away from him. When they were finally up in their bedroom, fighting over who got the red blocks and who got the green blocks, Teren let out a heavy exhale.

"I need air," he whispered.

He blurred away from me right after he said it. Blinking, I stared at the open space in the seamless wall of windows where he'd opened the nearly invisible slider to get outside. Feeling where he was at the edge of our property, I looked at the TV and sighed. I'd never in a million years have anticipated that happening.

Giving my husband a few moments of space, I slowly walked out after him at a human pace. The backyard sloped down. Standing on the patio was like standing on the edge of a small cliff. The view of the water here was breathtaking, along with the sunsets. Teren and I had spent many nights, pre-kids and after, watching the sun slowly slink below the horizon, bathing the world in colors ranging from burnt orange to pale pink. And there was nothing quite like witnessing a sunset through vampiric eyes. I was grateful that I still got to have that.

Avoiding tricycles, balls, and broken chunks of sidewalk chalk, I walked to the edge of the patio and headed to the lawn. Stepping around the landmines of outdoor toys that our kids had accumulated, I followed the hill to the base, where I could feel Teren. Walking around the shed we stored our lawn care equipment in, I found him leaning against the back. He was hunched over, hands on his knees, inhaling and exhaling as deeply as his dead lungs would allow him to.

Biting my lip, I slowly stepped towards him. Without looking up at me, he shook his head. "Did I do this? Is she dead because of me?" His eyes snapped up to mine; his face was a mixture of guilt and rage. "Is she dead because she came out to see me?"

His voice trembled as his conflicting emotions shook him to the core. Rushing over to him, I grabbed his head and pulled him to my chest. His arms immediately wrapped around me, cinching me tight.

"No, Teren, she died in an accident. That could have happened to anybody, anywhere. You aren't responsible for something like that." My eyes started stinging as I held him, wishing, as he'd once wished for me, that I could take his turmoil, that I could feel it for him.

Clenching his jaw, he shook his head. "She wouldn't have been here if it weren't for me. She wouldn't have been anywhere near here, if I had done what I was supposed to do, if I had wiped her when we were kids. I did this. It's my fault."

Running my hands back through his hair, I whispered, "I'm so sorry, Teren. I know what she meant to you. I'm so sorry you lost a friend."

Teren's rage shifted to sadness as he nodded, and a tear ran down his cheek. Unbidden and unwanted, images of Carrie's last moments on earth leapt into my head. Fire was a horrible way to go...I knew that from experience. My mind scoured open the scabbed wound of my father's passing and poured Carrie's on top of it. My tears started in earnest as my fresh grief mixed with my old grief.

We held each other in the backyard for long moments, Teren comforting me as I comforted him. Between our tears, I listened to my children playing upstairs. They were so involved in the project that Teren had assigned to them that they weren't paying any attention to us.

Kissing Teren's head when he laid it on my shoulder, I listened as Julian and Nika started telling a story about their completed project. The story involved Daddy rescuing a princess from an evil king. As they told the story, it quickly became apparent that Daddy was a superhero who could do anything, even shoot laser bolts from his eyes. How they saw him made me smile. He was sort of my superhero, too.

Teren raised his head as he listened to their story. Looking at me, his face remorseful but composed, he smiled. "It's funny how they see me," he whispered.

I shook my head, running my thumb across his cheek to dry his tears. "No...it's not. Kids see the truth."

He laughed once as he looked down. Then with a long sigh, he shook his head. "I don't understand what she was doing in Los Angeles." He lifted his head and looked south, to where L.A. lay, miles below us. His brows bunching, he shook his head again. "Great-Gran told her to stay in the city and then go home." His eyes shifted to me, and his confused expression didn't leave him. "Why would she have been down there? It doesn't make any sense."

I shrugged. "I don't know. Maybe she decided that she wanted to see Disneyland?"

Teren sighed. "I should have kept a better eye on her, made sure she got home safely. I just...with Starla showing up and your conversion...Carrie slipped through the cracks." Sighing again, he met my eye. "She was supposed to be home by now, asking her boss out."

Exhaling softly, I gave him a light kiss. "I know...I'm so sorry."

"Thank you," he whispered, resting his head on my shoulder. "We should go check on the kids."

Once back in the house, Teren paced until sunset. He wanted to speak with Halina, to see if there was anything they'd messed up on when they'd given memories and suggestions to Carrie. He called his great-grandmother as soon as the last rays disappeared from the sky. She was at our doorstep fifteen minutes later. Imogen and Alanna were a few minutes behind her.

While Imogen and Alanna taught the children how to play Chopsticks on the piano, Teren and I talked it over with Halina in the kitchen. Leaning against the counter, her svelte body wrapped in head to toe leather, she shook her head. "I told her to stay in the city..." she frowned, "she would have been compelled to do so."

Teren sighed as he ran a hand through his hair. "We didn't specify which city...maybe that's why she left?"

Halina looked up at him, shaking her head. "I'm sorry, Teren, I don't have the answers you're looking for." She furrowed her brow, clearly upset that her powers hadn't worked like she'd expected them too. "I don't know how this happened."

Crossing her arms over her chest, she had a look on her face that I had never, ever seen on her before. She seemed...unsure of herself.

It was an unsettling expression to see on someone who was typically so confident. But she relied on her abilities to protect her family. To raise money, if needed, or wipe minds, if needed. If she wasn't as in control of her powers as she believed...that could lead to all sorts of problems in the future.

Looking up at the two of us, she shook her head. "I'm going to head to Gabriel's." She shrugged, sighing. "See if he knows why I couldn't..." Pausing, she bit her lip. "See if he knows why this happened."

We nodded at her as she started to leave the room. Stopping in the doorway, she looked back at Teren. "I'm very sorry. I know she meant something to you." Her eyes were sympathetic towards her grandson as he nodded at her. I smiled at seeing the genuine feeling in her. It would seem that being in love with Gabriel was somewhat softening up the powerful vampire.

After a brief goodbye to the children, Halina streaked away towards her boyfriend. I didn't know what Gabriel could possibly tell her about this, but I hoped the mixed genius knew something.

Not long after Halina's exit, Imogen and Alanna gave Teren compassionate hugs and soft condolences, then helped me tuck the children in before they darted back home. After they left, Teren called Ben. Clearly hearing that his friend was distressed, Ben showed up at our house, too.

Arriving with one bottled beer, the gorgeous man frowned. "I thought you'd want to share a drink, but I didn't have any blood. Sorry."

Teren laughed once, smiling at the sentiment. Swinging the door open wide, he nodded him into the house. Hot Ben stepped inside and gave his friend a brief hug. Pulling apart from him, he turned and gave me a hug too. Shivering as he pulled away, Ben gave me a lopsided grin. "Brrr, Em. I'm still not used to feeling that with you."

Seeming like the entire concept of me dying recently was hard to wrap his head around, he shook his head. I understood; it was hard for me sometimes too. Aside from no longer having a heartbeat, I felt fine.

Giving Teren a warm hug goodnight, I left the men to their

bonding. Once I was upstairs, I listened to Teren warm up some blood; the smell hit me all the way in our bedroom. Sitting down at the table, Hot Ben sighed and popped open his beer. "I'm so sorry, man. I don't really know what to say. I've never had anyone that I know die. Well, no one but you and Emma, I guess."

I smiled at Ben's comment as I got ready for bed, then frowned. Carrie's death wasn't really funny. A chair squeaked as Teren sat down. "It's all right. Thanks for coming over. It's surreal...like I'm having a bad dream. I keep waiting to wake up."

Ben sighed and shifted in his seat. "How about a toast? To Carrie Davids, a life lost too soon."

Teren sighed. "Yeah."

Hearing them clink glasses, I closed my eyes and gave her my own moment of silence. After a couple of long gulps, Ben swallowed and smacked his lips. Then he started talking with Teren about inane off-the-wall subjects that were probably meant to take Teren's mind off of what had happened. Sighing softly, I got ready for bed. As I did, sadness that Carrie's life had been tragically removed filled me. And right after Teren had cut her loose too. The universe had a cruel sense of humor sometimes.

Teren was pretty quiet for the next few days, coming to terms with the horrible accident that had cut short Carrie's life, and hoping her death didn't have anything to do with her coming out to see him. I knew he still felt responsible, no matter how many times I tried to reassure him that people got caught in horrible situations all the time. Something similar to this could have easily happened to her at home. Sometimes, it was just your time to go.

Gabriel came out one evening, to give Teren his condolences. Teren grilled him over and over for information on how a compulsion could go wrong. Sighing as he sat at our kitchen table with a cooling mug of blood, Gabriel shook his head. "I have never heard of such a thing. Once a suggestion is implanted, it stays until it is completed or removed."

For the hundredth time, Teren leaned back in his chair and ran a hand down his face in frustration. "Maybe it was removed, then?

Maybe another vampire compelled her to go down there?"

Gabriel shrugged, his emerald eyes appraising as he looked over Teren's frustration. It was almost as if he was cataloging the effects that guilt and anger had on a person. "It is possible that another vampire superseded Halina's orders, but there haven't been any purebloods in the city for a while."

He raised an edge of his lip and a chill went through my dead body. Teren's past experiences with questioning reluctant vampires in the bay area had pretty much cleared out the city. Gabriel kept a tab on any that had lingered behind, just in case they thought to start something with us. Hopefully those people were more cautious over angering Gabriel than they were about getting back at Teren.

Putting a hand on my husband's thigh, I said, "Don't forget that what happened to her doesn't have to be supernatural. Humans outnumber vampires—by a lot—and we're not exactly a docile species either. Maybe she just found herself in the wrong place at the wrong time. Maybe she was taken down there against her will, against her compulsion?"

Teren lowered his head, nodding as he considered that possibility too. Gabriel tapped his finger to his lips; his emerald eyes were contemplative. Hating that everything bad in our lives always seemed to revolve around some psychotic person, I added, "You know what, maybe it wasn't even as bad as what we're thinking? Maybe she met someone and went to L.A. to spend time with him? Surely she'd be allowed to alter her plans if she wanted it badly enough? Then maybe she got trapped in the woods, hiking, just like the news said. Not everything that happens in life involves foul play."

Teren gave me a humoring smile, clearly not believing my cheerier version of events. Squeezing my hand on his leg, he exhaled sadly. "Either way, I did this to her. She was here because of me."

"No, she wasn't."

Teren and I both looked over to Gabriel. A small but sad smile was on his beautiful face. "She was here because I had her entranced to be here." He raised a perfectly arched eyebrow. "She was here because of me, so I am responsible for this. And I am very sorry, Teren. I never meant for any harm to come to your friend." He respectfully lowered his eyes.

Looking unsure of what to say, Teren only nodded.

Teren was lost in thought, studying the table when Gabriel stood to excuse himself. Teren briefly looked up at him, nodded, then went back to studying the rings of color in his cold cup of blood. Concerned over my husband's mood, I stood with Gabriel.

"I'll see you out, Gabriel."

Smiling at me politely, he nodded. Hearing him leaving, my children blurred down to say goodbye to their pseudo-grandfather. "Walking feet, children," I automatically reminded them.

Gabriel bent down to scoop them up, and both twins laced their arms around his neck. "Bye, Grandpa Gabby," they exclaimed together.

Gabriel smiled at them in turn. "Goodbye, Nika, Julian." He gave each one a kiss on the head, then set them down. His emerald eyes tracked every movement they made as they shifted their attention to the family dog. When Nika rubbed a spot on Spike's back that made his leg twitch, Julian got a face full of tongue. Nika was the one that giggled, though.

As Gabriel shook his head at their shared emotions, I could almost see his mind logging the information. Placing myself between him and my children brought his attention back to me. Stepping towards him, I lowered my voice to near inaudible. "Are you studying them?"

I tried to keep the question polite, casual. Our family owed Gabriel too much for me to risk offending him. He smiled though, his head tilting as he answered. "Studying…watching, it's all one and the same to me."

A frown crept into my features that I couldn't stop. "Teren and I don't want them examined like rats in a lab."

Gabriel blinked at my answer. "I'm sorry if it bothers you. It was never my intention to upset you." Looking around me at the twins playing with Spike, he stepped forward. His voice laced with excitement, he murmured, "I can't help my interest though. Their bond is such a fascinating one. I've never seen anything like it. They feel what the other feels." He shook his head, his eyes wondrous. "Will that bond fade with them, or will it be passed to their children?" His deep green eyes returned to mine. "They could completely change the nature of vampirism. Aren't you the least bit curious about that?"

I was about to answer him when Teren stepped into the room. "We don't want them examined," he whispered. "They are children, not experiments."

Gabriel straightened as he looked over at Teren. Sighing, clearly disappointed, he nodded. "Of course. They are your offspring. I will honor your wishes regarding them."

Teren walked over to me and slung his arm around my waist. Gabriel's eyes flicked between the two of us, then down to the twins starting a game of fetch with the dog. "Have a good evening, Emma, Teren. Again, I'm sorry for your loss." His tone was polite and respectful, but detached, too. I had no idea how he really felt about us denying him access to our children. But some things we would just have to risk his disapproval on.

As the days passed, and my husband silently healed from his emotional wounds, I filled my sister in on everything that had happened. She shared my feeling that it wasn't necessarily something bad that had been done to Carrie. Of course, my sister understood horrible accidents all too well.

Sitting on my back patio, I enjoyed the views of the water with Ashley while Nika and Julian played tag on the lawn. A gust of wind blew across the yard, and the smell of salt water was strong in the air. My sister also inhaled a deep breath. Looking over at her, I saw the slight frown on her lips as she absorbed the situation Teren was dealing with. But seeing her as well as I could, I saw a sparkle of happiness in her eyes that didn't match her mouth.

Anxious to talk about anything other than death for a while, I twisted my lips into a wry smile. "Seriously, what is up with you lately? I know you love your job and all, but it has to be more than that, right?"

Blushing, she glanced up to the slight overhang of the patio above us. The much smaller deck was accessible through a bookcase lined hallway that led to Teren's office, a loft over the kitchen that looked down into the vaulted living room. The spiral staircase in the corner of the living room that led up there was a constant source of amusement to my children, who loved tossing bouncy balls down it.

Teren was home, working, so my sister assumed that he was upstairs in his office. He wasn't, though. He was finishing up an article in our soundproof bedroom. He did that sometimes, when he was working on something meaningful. He said the quiet helped him think. Curious about what she was going to say that she didn't want Teren to hear, I assured her, "He's in the soundproof room. He won't hear you."

She blushed even more and swung her eyes to the kids giggling in the far corner of the yard. "I can't believe you guys had a sex room built."

I smacked her shoulder and she laughed before taking a sip of her wine. "Quit calling it that. You make it sound like we had chains installed in the walls or something." I rolled my eyes and she coughed on her wine a bit. "It's just for privacy," I sullenly muttered.

Still looking horribly embarrassed, she whispered, "Well, I get it now, why you would want the...privacy."

I wondered what she meant as I took a sip of my version of wine. Drinking was a little tricky to do outside, since the act of blood on my tongue naturally dropped my teeth down. I had to forcefully pull them back up after each sip. Wouldn't want the neighbors to accidentally catch a peek of those.

Ashley looked at my confusion and smiled. Glancing at my kids in the yard, she whispered, "I finally tried that...thing that you and Teren do together so much, and I have to say...it's pretty incredible."

I had to slap a hand over my mouth to not spit blood all over her pretty white blouse. She meant sex, but she didn't want to say it again in front of my super-hearing kids. Swallowing and sputtering, I finally got the liquid down. "What? When? How?" I wasn't even aware that my sister was seeing someone, let alone sleeping with someone.

Ashley laughed as I wiped droplets of blood off my chin. "Well,

I'm pretty sure you know the how part. As to when, a couple of nights ago."

Shaking my head, I smiled at her. "I didn't even know you were seeing somebody. Who's the guy?"

Smiling as she looked down into her glass, the embarrassment in her cheeks shifted to the rosy flush of love; my eyes could easily tell the difference. "This guy at work, Christian. I've been seeing him for a while now. We've been taking things really slow, but the other night it just felt so right, so..."

She shrugged and looked up at me; there were slight tears in her eyes. They were in mine too as I set my blood down and hopped out of my seat to give her a hug. It wasn't that my sister had finally had sex. Really, if that was all she cared about, then she could have easily found someone. It was that my sister had finally found love. That was infinitely more important.

Squeezing her as tight as I could without breaking her, I whispered, "I'm so happy for you. Why didn't you tell me about him?"

I pulled away from her, finally letting her breathe, and she sighed. "Well, I wasn't sure where it was going and then..." She bit her scarred lip as her eyes darted over my face. Shaking her head, she shrugged. "I wanted to make sure he was in love with me before I introduced him to you."

Sitting back down, my eyes went to my glass of deep red blood on the table. My finger absently reached up to stroke a retracted fang. Suddenly I wondered just how freakish my sister saw me. But even if I wasn't a monster in her eyes, she would have to be careful with anyone she brought into our family. Just like with Tracey, that person would probably never be allowed to know the truth.

"Oh..."

Seeing my contemplative expression, she chuckled. "No, not because of the fangs, Emma." I looked up at her and she shrugged again. Shaking her head, she whispered, "Because you're...beautiful."

Guilt flooded through me. "Oh, Ash..."

She smiled again, tears in her eyes but joy in her expression.

"Don't, it's fine, Em." Beaming, she let out a happy sigh. "Besides, I'm great, and he adores me...for me. He doesn't even see the scars." Smirking, she tilted her head. "Well, that's not true. It's sort of why he first noticed me."

I blinked, confused again. "Huh?"

She laughed, then took a sip of her wine. "Christian's a doctor in the burn unit. He's one of the doctor's working on the artificially grown skin I told you about." She smiled as she thought about her man. "He's pretty confident that he can someday even out my scar lines, make my face less...noticeable." Shaking her head, her tears got even more evident. "But he says it doesn't matter to him. He says it doesn't bother him. He says I'm beautiful," she whispered.

Holding her hand across the table, I felt my eyes water too. "Ash...you scored yourself a doctor?"

Laughing, she wiped away a stray tear. "I did." We both chuckled for a moment as we watched my kids toss clumps of grass on each other. With their giggles bouncing around the yard, Ashley quietly said, "I know you worry about me, Em, but I'm happy...really happy." She paused for a long moment, then added, "Even being just a human."

The way she said it brought my attention back to her. With the way her lip was twisted into a wry grin and the remnant of her eyebrow was arched, I knew that she knew what I'd asked Teren to do to her, so very long ago, when I'd been very naïve. "Oh...you know about..."

Both her eyebrows rose as she nodded. "Yeah, I know that you asked Teren to change me. He told me a while ago."

My eyes flicked up to where my usually secretive husband was hiding away. Vowing to speak to him later about the unspoken agreement that things between a husband and wife were sacred, and not repeatable, even if they happened before marriage, I grimaced. "Ash..."

Her hot hand squeezed my cold one tight. "No, I get it. You wanted me to be beautiful, like you." She shook her head; the hair swirling around her shoulder was identical in color to mine. "I'm touched by the offer, Emma, but I don't need it." Smiling, she looked to where the ranch was, to where I could feel the rest of Teren's family. "As much as I like Halina, I don't want her life." Her matching brown eyes came back to me. "I like mine. I like the work I'm doing. I like the man I'm seeing. I love my mutant sister—"

I straightened and my mouth popped open in protest. "Hey."

Ashley laughed and squeezed my hand. "I love her undead family." Her eyes shifted to the yard, where my tired children were laughing, panting, and covered in tiny blades of grass. "And I absolutely adore my niece and nephew." Looking as satisfied as her words made her seem, she shrugged. "My life is wonderful, Emma."

Smiling at her, I again wished for her wisdom, patience, and acceptance. "Yeah, yeah it is."

Feeling my husband reemerge from his cave, Ashley and I raised our glasses in a toast. "To wonderful lives," I said softly. She nodded, touching her glass to mine.

Teren stepped on the patio right as we finished with our sip. His face tired, his expression worn, he looked between the two of us. He shook his head. "What are we celebrating?"

I was about to tell him that my sister had a boyfriend, but Ashley beat me to it. Maybe seeing that Teren needed a pick-me-up, her answer was more...descriptive than usual. Smiling, she exclaimed, "I lost my virginity."

Teren smiled genuinely and looked away. I grinned at seeing a natural smile on him again and mentally thanked my sister for forgoing her own embarrassment and saying it that bluntly. Chuckling, he swung his eyes back to her. "Well...congratulations."

Seeming a little embarrassed himself, he gave her a warm hug. Well, warm in sentiment. To her, he was actually quite cold, cold as me. Exhaling like a weight was releasing from his shoulders, he sat down next to me. "Tell me all about him," he said encouragingly, like he also wanted to talk about something that had nothing to do with death.

Ashley nodded and started going over how she'd first met him. Feeling Teren's melancholy finally starting to lift, I stood up and shifted over to his lap. His arms wrapped around me as he laid his head on my shoulder. Threading my fingers through his hair, I closed my eyes and listened to my sister's voice. My sister's and my children's.

In a whisper that only Teren and I could hear, I heard Nika ask Julian, "What's vir..gen..ty?"

Biting my lip, I tried not to laugh. Teren couldn't stop himself. He laughed so hard he made everyone else around him laugh too. Feeling the stress release in his merriment made me love my sister all the more.

Chapter 15 – The Message

Once the shock and guilt of Carrie's accident stopped stinging so much, Teren returned to his usual cheeriness. He dealt with it in his own way—writing an article on wildfire prevention for the magazine he worked for, making a sizeable donation to the United States Forest Service, and even sending anonymous condolence flowers to where Carrie had worked. But after all that was done, he let her go.

Watching him with our kids, you'd certainly never know that he'd recently lost an old friend. Smiling, I watched him wrestle around with them on the living room floor. Lying on his stomach, he was laughing while Nika bounced on his back. Julian sat behind her, facing the other way while he bounced on Teren's lower spine. The two kids were alternating their jumps so Teren was getting constantly bombarded; a normal human would have had trouble breathing.

He didn't need the air to breathe, but he was having a little trouble getting enough to laugh. Teren didn't stop them though. For a long time, he let the hop-on-pop continue. Amused, I watched them from the safety of the couch. Groaning when a kid kicked him in the ribs, Teren twisted his head to look at me. "A little help?" he asked, his voice pitiful.

Shaking my head, I smirked at him. "You look like you've got it under control."

Nika stood up and practically body slammed him when she sat back down. He groaned again. We might be nearly indestructible, but we still felt pain. Laughing at the look on his face, I raised an eyebrow at my daughter. "Gentle, Nika. Don't break Daddy."

Both Nika and Julian thought that was funny and hit him just a little bit harder. Spike wagged his tail and barked. He looked ready to jump on his master too. Grunting at the abuse, Teren frowned at me. "Thanks."

Grinning, I shrugged. "Just trying to help out the big, bad vampire."

Narrowing his eyes, he lifted himself to his hands and knees.

Nika giggled as she rolled off his back. Julian held onto his jean pockets. Laughing, he rode Daddy backwards. Careful to not knock our son off, Teren slinked his way over to me. The look in his eye made me wary; it was mischievously playful. While I preferred that look to the forlorn face he had a couple of weeks ago, I was beginning to wonder just what he was up to.

When he got close enough, he removed Julian and set him beside our giggling daughter. His full attention was on me now, and I narrowed my eyes and pulled my legs farther up the couch. "Teren, what are you doing?"

Still on his hands and knees directly in front of me, his impish grin turned devilish. "Nothing."

Pulling back from him, I had a warning ready on my tongue. I never got a chance to say it though. Faster than humanly possible, he grabbed my legs and yanked me off the couch. Within seconds he had me trapped on the floor, and his body was pressing me down. While we were fairly similar strength-wise, Teren had more mass than me. And more importantly, he currently had better leverage.

Holding me down tight, he glanced over at the kids. "Okay, guys, get her!"

My eyes widened as his plan instantly became clear to me. Teren moved away right as they attacked. Julian flopped on my chest while Nika sat on my stomach. And as if that wasn't bad enough, Teren started tickling me.

With tears streaming down my face, I gasped in breaths so I could laugh. Teren laughed as I tried to smack him without hitting our children. It really wasn't very fair. He was using our kids as a buffer so he could freely torment me.

Nika and Julian eventually grew weary and crawled up to rest their heads on my shoulders; their heat cascaded around me, like soothing hot water bottles. I exhaled in relief when Teren stopped tickling me. The twins slung their arms around my neck, and Teren hovered over me.

"Thank you," he whispered, smiling.

I shook my head. "For what?"

"For...being you." He smiled wider for a second, then his grin faded. "Thank you for helping me through," he glanced at the kids snuggled in my arms, before returning his eyes to me, "...stuff. Thank you for giving me space. Thank you for your comfort. Thank you...for being here."

Stubborn tears pricking my eyes, I shook my head. "I'm your wife. Where else would I be?"

Smiling, he lowered his lips to mine. The twins giggled while we kissed between them, until eventually they reached out for Daddy and pulled him down. Chuckling, Teren shifted Julian around so he could lie in the crook of my arm with Julian on top of us. Slinking his arm under me, he shifted all of us so we were laying on him.

All four of us exhaled contentedly. One happy, vampiric family.

Time heals all wounds they say, and a couple of weeks later our family seemed a shining example of that. I'd adjusted to dying. Teren had put his guilt over a friend's death aside. And the twins had come to terms with the fact that they were never going to get that pony. Our lives quietly fell back to the routine we'd become accustomed to—trying to balance work and kids and time for each other. It was a tricky multi-level scale, but we did the best we could. We even managed to spend some time with our friends.

Dropping the kids off at my mom's, we met up with Hot Ben and Tracey for a movie. Teren helped me out of the car once we found a spot near Ben's SUV in the lot. I instinctively smelled the air when I got out. There was something in it besides the overwhelming stench of popcorn. Looking around, I sniffed. Teren watched me, then looked around too. The odor was familiar, but foreign.

Teren grabbed my arm and gently squeezed me. "Over there." I turned my head and looked over to where he was pointing—the edge of the movie theater. Standing at the corner, leaning against it, was a man who was clearly watching us. Ice flooded my veins as Teren moved me slightly behind him. Meeting up with strange people usually didn't end well for us. His scent was light on the breeze, but it had the distinct zing of vampire to it. Full or mixed, I didn't know.

A low warning growl burrowed up from Teren's chest, cutting

through the empty space around us. I knew I was more resilient now than the last time I'd met up with a strange vampire, but that didn't mean I wanted to test out my healing abilities tonight.

The vampire across the way smiled at the display, and slightly shook his head. Shrugging, he lifted his hands up as if to show he didn't mean us any harm. Teren stopped growling, but made no move to head towards the man.

He smiled wider at our reluctance. He seemed mid-twenties to me, not that that was any real indication of his age or lineage. His hair under the lot lights was sort of an orange shade, but I was pretty sure it would be a dirty brown in daylight, assuming it ever saw daylight. Skinny for a guy, he had a homely look about him, like he hadn't lived in any one spot long enough to repair the rip in his jacket or replace the denims that were badly frayed at the knees. While not unattractive, there was a layer of dirt that permeated him and his clothes. Human eyes probably wouldn't notice, but mine could easily pick it up. All and all, he looked...worn.

Holding up a finger, he reached inside his jacket pocket. Actually thinking he was going to pull out a gun and shoot us, I pulled Teren back a step. The man sniggered at my reaction, then pulled out what looked like an envelope.

Confused and surprised, I watched him set it on a nearby garbage can lid. Then he made a gesture like he was tipping his hat. It was old-fashioned and a little odd, since he wasn't even wearing a hat. After that display, he blurred away.

Teren and I stood stone still, staring at that piece of paper like it was going to explode at any moment. Finally, Teren exhaled in a rush. "It's just paper," he muttered. Looking back at me, his blue eyes stern, he pointed to the ground. "Stay here...please?"

I twisted my lips, but nodded. I didn't smell the vampire in the air anymore and really, if he'd wanted to harm us, he wouldn't have made such a show of staying away. Obviously, harm wasn't his intention. Obviously, he wanted us to retrieve that letter.

Holding my breath, I watched Teren thrust his hands deep into his jacket and casually walk over to the corner of the building. The anticipation was killing me. I wanted to yell at him to go supersonic, but I had enough sense to know that I couldn't do that. We were smack dab in the middle of a parking lot and while not crowded, a few people were coming and going. Teren even nodded at a couple as he passed by them.

A few long moments later he made it to the trash bin. Looking around, he sniffed the air a few times before he picked up the envelope. He stared at it for a second before he made his way back to me. Not able to stand it anymore, I met him halfway. He pursed his lips when we connected. "I told you to stay put."

"You can ground me later. What does it say?"

He shrugged as he held up a plain, ordinary envelope. "I don't know."

Looking around again, he slowly opened it. Pulling out a tri-folded slip of paper, he frowned. I frowned too. The scent wafting from the parchment was unmistakable to a vampire. Whatever was written on that paper was written in blood...human blood.

Anxious, I bit my lip as he unfolded it. Reading what was written there, Teren exhaled a slow and deliberate breath. Pulling it over so I could see it clearly, I gasped and peeked up at him. "Teren?"

Twisting his lips, Teren looked back at where the creature had fled. "Yeah, I know."

Completely thrown, I stared after him too. That lean, homeless looking vampire was the one person on this earth Gabriel wanted to get his hands on, but couldn't seem to. The man who had been calmly standing against a movie theater, staring at us, was on just about every vampire's most wanted list. He was the one who had been indirectly responsible for my husband's death. He was the one who was, in a way, responsible for my own death. And he'd been right in front of us.

Glancing at the paper elegantly scrawled with some poor human's blood, I read it over and over again. It was a message to Gabriel. A message that was all too clear; it chilled my already chilled bones.

My dearest Gabriel,

I understand that you wish to see me. I have no wish to be seen. I've given you several warnings to stop hunting for me. This one will be my last. I believe I've already proven that you are not untouchable. I can harm you, and I will, if you leave me no other choice. Back off, or this will end in bloodshed.

Sincerely yours, Malcolm

Teren ran a hand down his face while I shook my head and read it again. Bloodshed? That sounded a bit…drastic. Of course, I was fairly certain that Gabriel wasn't going to let him off with a stern warning to never do it again. This Malcolm person had been responsible for several mixed vampire's deaths. Children as well as adults. He may not have wielded the stakes, but he was responsible nonetheless. And he seemed well aware of the consequences that he was facing.

"He knows who we are, Teren. He knows that we know Gabriel." My hand clutched his arm as I dropped my hold on the letter.

"I know." Looking over at me, he frowned but said nothing else.

Just as I was about to tell him that we should call…someone, Tracey bounded out of the theater. Teren looked up at her and shoved the bloody note in his pocket as she waved at us. "Hey, you're here! Come on in, the movie's starting soon."

We looked at each other and Teren shrugged. "He won't do anything until we deliver his message." He nodded his head to the doors. "Let's go watch a movie with our friends, make Tracey believe that nothing is wrong, then we'll call Great-Gran."

I nodded as he smiled nonchalantly and waved back at Tracey. As we quickly walked to the building, I mentally tracked every member of my family. The pins were all exactly in the same space in my head; nobody had moved. Our kids were at my mom's. Alanna and the other girls were at the ranch. Feeling better that all the vampires in my life were stationary and still spouting life affirming GPS to me, I tried to match his effortless smile as we stepped up to Tracey.

Smiling, she grabbed my hand and pulled me to the ticket line. I halfheartedly followed her, not really wanting to watch a movie anymore. Twisting to look at me as we approached the counter, she exclaimed, "Dang, you're cold." Smirking, her pale eyes glanced down my body. "Maybe you should put some of that baby weight back on you?"

Faking a scowl of displeasure, I subtly pulled my hand from hers. So used to being a warm blooded person, I sometimes forgot that I wasn't now. Especially since my husband didn't give me chills anymore. My little twin heat boxes were my only real reminder of my temperature.

As Teren and I got our tickets, Hot Ben walked into the lobby. A bag of popcorn was in one of his hands, the other was running through his bleach-blonde highlighted hair. "Hey, glad you made it." He stopped talking as he looked between the two of us, and his brow furrowed to a point. Muttering below his breath, in a whisper that his fiancé wouldn't hear, especially as she noisily munched from the popcorn in his bag, he asked, "Something up? You two looked spooked."

I adjusted my causal smile as we grabbed our tickets and headed to Theater Five. Teren slung an arm around my waist while discretely handing Ben the note as we walked past him. As Tracey walked beside me, telling me that she hoped she didn't scream too loudly, I heard Ben behind us un-crumpling the paper.

Quite clearly to me, but inaudible to anyone else but Teren, I heard him mutter, "Oh...man. Is this the vamp who stole that stuff that killed you?" Teren looked over his shoulder at Hot Ben and nodded. Ben sniffed in a disgruntled way that matched Teren. "We hunting?"

Forgetting that the three of us were having a silent conversation that Tracey wasn't aware of, I stopped in my tracks and looked back at Ben behind me. "No! Absolutely not." My already strained nerves added volume to my voice and Tracey clearly heard me. The person at the end of the hall probably heard me.

Tracey looked between Ben and me, completely confused as to why I'd seemingly told him *no* for no apparent reason. The last thing she was aware of was asking me if I'd share the popcorn with her; my reaction was a little strong for her question, but I hadn't considered

Teren and Ben jumping into the middle of this.

Teren's hand around my waist moved to my arm. Glancing at Tracey, he muttered under his breath. "He killed me, Em."

Not caring how it looked to a clueless Tracey, both my hands clasped his arms. Managing to keep my voice nearly incoherent, I whispered, "No, Teren, no. Let Gabriel deal with this. It's *his* mess, remember?" Teren narrowed his eyes but looked down. I squatted to meet his eye. "Please? You have a family now."

Hot Ben, seeing a conversation he couldn't hear and guessing what I was saying, stepped forward and laid his hand on Teren's arm. "If he gave this to you, then he knows who you are, Teren. He could be a threat." Ben held up the offending note, like just that evidence was proof of ill intent towards us. "We should make sure that he's not."

Ben said all of that at a normal volume and Teren sighed that our private conversation was no longer private. Sticking her hands on her hips, Tracey asked, "What the hell are you guys talking about?"

Giving her just a second's glance, I turned my attention over to Ben. "Gabriel is handling it, Ben. I don't want the two of you involved." My heart would have been hammering if it still could. Just the thought of Teren picking up another stake made me feel ill, worse than the fumes of popcorn all around me. I didn't think I could handle that stress again. I squeezed Teren's arms painfully tight. "I can't deal with you knocking on stranger's doors again. I can't. I won't."

Teren flinched under my grasp and moved to unclench me, right as Ben started in on his opinion. While he spouted that our family's safety came first, Tracey finally got sick of being left in the dark. She snatched the note right out of Hot Ben's hands.

We all three moved to snatch it back, but Tracey swirled around at the same time. It was so ingrained in me to never use our abilities in public, that I couldn't grab it back quick enough. She stared at it, and her blonde hair shook back and forth as she tried to understand what it meant. Twisting back to us with her face comically twisted in confusion, she asked, "Is this a joke?"

Hot Ben put a soothing hand on her arm while Teren and I each took a step towards her. Her ice blue eyes darted between the three of us, like she suddenly didn't know us. My dead heart dropped at seeing the fear on her face. I'd never wanted her to look at me like that. "What the hell is going on? Who is Malcolm? Who is Gabriel?"

Ben cupped her ghost-white cheek before running his hand back through her hair. "I can explain, babe."

I couldn't help but wonder what the heck he was going to say to explain all of this. Tracey seemed to wonder that too. She batted his hand away. "Bloodshed? You can explain bloodshed?"

Her voice rose and warbled as color filled her cheeks. Seeing a couple of people walking past, staring, Teren grabbed Tracey's arm and pulled her into an empty theater. She struggled with him while Ben and I followed, but no human gets out of Teren's grasp unless he wants them to. Shutting the propped open door behind myself, I let out a weary sigh.

"Let me go, Teren. You let me go or I'll, I'll…I'll scream." She inhaled to create the sound and Teren slapped his hand over her mouth. Her eyes widened and she struggled more.

Teren held her close to his body while Ben and I each put a comforting hand on her shoulders. "I'm not going to hurt you, but I don't want you to scream right now," Teren said.

She struggled more, inhaling and exhaling frantically as Teren held her in place against his chest. Hating this, I tried to turn her head toward me. She finally peeked at me out of the corner of her eye. "We're not going to hurt you, Trace, calm down."

She shook her head at me and clamped down around Teren's fingers with her teeth. I could see Teren flinch as she pierced his skin, but he didn't let her go. Ben, trying to rub her back around Teren's arms, sighed. "Trace, don't…just relax."

Her eyes narrowed to fiery points at Ben. Letting out a frustrated grunt, Teren looked her in the eye. "If I let go, do you promise not to scream?"

She looked at the three of us, then reluctantly nodded. Teren tentatively let go, his hand ready to slap back into place if she made the wrong move. As he gently released her, her breathing steadied.

Her eyes locked on Teren and she glanced down to his blood smeared fingers. She couldn't tell, but I could clearly see that he had already healed from her chomp.

Glaring at all of us, she held up the note again. "What the hell are you three involved in?"

Not sure what to tell her, I slowly said, "It's…just a joke. You were right…April Fools," I tried weakly.

Her eyes narrowed at me. "It's May, Emma." Her gaze flicked between the boys. "Who's a threat to you? This Malcolm guy? Why, what did you do to him?"

Teren grabbed the note from her hand. "Nothing, Tracey, this means nothing."

Ben looked away. He was gritting his jaw like he disagreed, but he wouldn't openly contradict Teren's lie. Tracey didn't notice her fiancé's face, though. Her eyes were darting from Teren's fingers to the ink on the paper. Her own fingers flew to her mouth. "Oh my God, is that written in blood? Like, actual blood?"

Teren closed his eyes, then put on an effortless smile. "Of course not, Tracey. Why would we have a note written in blood?"

Tracey pointed a finger at him. "Exactly! Why? Is this some kind of *I Know What You Did Last Summer* thing? Did you guys kill someone, and this Gabriel guy knows and is hunting you down?"

I inadvertently giggled; I did that at odd moments sometimes. Biting my lip, I managed to say, "You watch too many movies, Trace."

She put her hands on her hips while Ben tried to approach her again. He backed off at her warning glance, and she bit out, "No, something is off with you three. You're all hiding something." She pointed at Ben. "You are always so secretive about stuff." Her finger came to me. "And you never let me just pop over to visit."

Her finger finished its circle to Teren. "And you…you are…I don't know, you seem perfect." Teren blinked and Tracey raised her chin. "Too perfect." She gasped and took a step back. "You're the murderer, aren't you? You wrote this! You're Malcolm! It's always the nice, seemingly normal guy that ends up being the serial killer who stores body parts in the freezer! You did it, didn't you? You killed someone!"

Ben and I rolled our eyes at the exact same time but Teren flinched and looked down. He didn't mean to, but I saw the moment of guilt cross his face. While it wasn't exactly what Tracey was accusing him of, he had killed someone before, viciously, and a small part of him still carried around the guilt of doing it, self-defense and self-preservation or not.

When Teren didn't contradict her, Tracey brought her hands to her mouth. She stared at all of us in horror, and then turned and ran. Watching her dash for the emergency exit, I knew I had plenty of time to catch her. Teren grabbed my arm, though. "Let her go," he said to me and Ben, who was starting to run after her at human speed. We both halted as she slammed the door open.

Placing my hand on his, I shook my head. "Teren, we can't just let her think you're a murderer." Even just saying the words, a small giggle came out of me. I just couldn't help it. Teren, some psychopathic killer? Yeah, maybe to the bovine world. Although, Tracey was sort of right in one way...he did have blood in his freezer.

Sighing, Teren reached into his jacket and grabbed his cell phone. "Don't worry, she won't." Flicking it open I heard him press a speed dial button. Immediately upon connection, he sullenly muttered, "Hey, Mom, it's me. I need to talk to Great-Gran."

Luckily for us, Tracey didn't have the keys to Ben's SUV, and it was still parked in the same spot when the three of us finally made our way out of the empty theater. Ben looked around for Tracey while Teren and I smelled the air for her perfume. It was a heavy fragrance, to my sensitive nose at least, and it lingered on the currents. I shifted to look down the main road that led out of the area, back towards Ben and Tracey's place.

Teren's healed finger lifted to point in the direction I was already looking. "She went that way, Ben."

Hot Ben sighed, following our direction. "She only had a couple bucks, she's probably walking home." Looking back at us, he said, "I'll go pick her up, take her home. Meet us back there with Halina."

Teren nodded as he grabbed my hand. In my head I could already feel the eldest vampire coming towards us. Once we got back to Teren's car, we gave Ben a few minutes to calm down Tracey enough to collect her, then we started making our way to his place. Teren drove slowly, clutching the wheel. I bit my lip. Feeling us moving, Halina shifted her direction to follow.

It bothered me that someone I knew was about to get erased, but there was really no way around it. We couldn't explain the note to any real satisfaction, and unlike with Ben, Tracey hadn't discovered the truth. No, she was convinced that Teren was a multiple murderer. Shaking my head, I rolled my eyes at her conclusion. I wanted to laugh at the situation, but the note tucked away in Teren's pocket wasn't at all funny. It sort of put a damper on Tracey's fanciful imagination.

We pulled into the drive, and I twisted to Teren before he could crack open his door. Taking in the faint glow of his eyes as he watched me, I inhaled a deep breath. "Promise me that you and Ben won't go searching for this guy."

Teren looked away from me, his jaw clenching. "Ben's right. He knows who I am."

Placing my hand on his arm, I shook my head. "Let Gabriel clean up his own mess. It doesn't involve us." He looked back at me and I saw the glint in his eye. I knew that Teren felt a little invested, since the vampire *had* prematurely ended him. Touching his cheek, I amended with, "It doesn't involve us *anymore*. You did your part already. You let Gabriel know what was going on. Give Malcolm's message to Halina, and then let's be done with this."

Teren sighed, then nodded. "Okay."

I raised my eyebrows. "Promise?"

Giving me a soft smile, he shook his head. "I promise, Emma. I won't go looking for this guy."

Exhaling softly, I rested my head against his. "Thank you," I whispered, kissing him.

As we lightly kissed in the car, the window was rapped on. Teren and I broke apart and looked out the driver's side to see Halina standing with her hands on her hips, watching us. Having felt her approach, I wasn't startled at seeing her there, and I gave her a smile while Teren opened his door.

Frowning, Halina's slightly glowing eyes shifted to the home where I could hear panicked voices conversing. Tilting her dark head, Halina worried her lip. "Do you think this will work?" she asked Teren, her voice and face oddly unconfident.

Slinging an arm around her shoulders, Teren nodded in reassurance. "Whatever happened with Carrie was a fluke. Your abilities have never let us down before." Squatting, he met and held her eye. "And they won't fail us tonight."

Halina smiled slyly, her general air of "I'm-a-badass" returning. Twisting on her booted heel, she strutted right up to the front door. Teren and I were a few steps behind her. From inside, I could hear Tracey screeching about all the little mysteries she had about Ben. I hated that most, if not all, were directly because of my husband's secret. Hot Ben had been a lock box when it came to Teren, never fully explaining certain things. And he'd never satisfyingly explained the period of time when he'd been out doing reckless things with Teren, hunting vampires for instance. Tracey had a lot of questions about it now, and felt like that mysterious time had something to do with the letter.

Maybe figuring that she was going to wipe her anyway, so politeness didn't matter, Halina walked in without knocking. Teren and I glanced at each other, then followed her. Tracey and Hot Ben were renting a cute little one bedroom house near Golden Gate Park. They wanted something bigger someday, but for now, this worked for them. Bridal magazines and fabric samples were strewn everywhere as Tracey made preparations for her big day. Even though they hadn't picked out a date yet, Tracey had already finalized her flower choices and from what Ben had told Teren, she'd even started on wedding cake samples.

Wading through the sea of Tracey's hope for her upcoming future with the love of her life, I prayed she was able to let Ben's oddities go. For one, I didn't want her to ever find out what Teren and I were. And secondly, I wanted my good friend to be happy, not always questioning whether her husband was a good man or not. He was. Aside from the secrets he was forced to keep, Ben was loyal, honest, and entirely devoted to Tracey.

Hearing the conversation emanating from the kitchen, our trio headed that way. Tracey was leaning back against the counter with an open champagne bottle clenched in her hand. In between questions, she was chugging. Seeing three more bottles behind her, I figured she was also sampling wines for the nuptials.

Finally hearing us, she turned her head mid gulp. She didn't finish the process and wine sputtered everywhere. Coughing on the harsh liquid, her eyes widened. "What are you guys doing here?"

Her gaze flashed over to Halina, and her eyes narrowed to points. Tracey had always thought the vixen had messed around with Ben. And it was sort of true. Halina had thoroughly enjoyed messing with Ben, just not in the way Tracey pictured. She'd once gotten a kick out of tormenting a terrified Ben, chiding him for a fear that she'd loved to provoke. That had ended the day Ben had staked a vampire, though. Ben was now a fellow bad ass in Halina's eyes.

Her sight not leaving Halina, Tracey said to Ben, "What is *she* doing here?"

Halina smirked and stepped forward. Teren sighed and stepped forward too. Tracey's eyes immediately locked onto Teren, foolishly believing that he was the true psychopath in the room. I had to bite my lip to not smile. Tracey's caution over Halina was way more on the mark than her analysis of Teren.

Tilting her head, Halina stepped in between her and Teren, breaking Tracey's connection with him. Hot Ben put a hand on Tracey's arm, but directed his comment to Halina. "Don't take too much," his brow furrowed in an attractive way, "and let her think we all had a good time tonight."

Halina rolled her eyes as Tracey's gaze snapped to Ben. "What the holy hell is going on around here?"

Halina's fingers snatched Tracey's chin, dragging her attention back to her. The blonde started shaking with the contact as she held gazes with the intimidating vampire. As I stepped forward, to offer whatever comfort I could, Halina began to speak. "Relax."

Tracey instantly stopped shaking as she turned into putty in Halina's hands. Halina's fingers ran back through her blonde hair, and curled a long strand between them. In a soothing voice that she often used on the children, she told her, "Tonight, you went to a movie with your friends. You had a wonderful time, and then you came home to spend the remainder of your evening with Ben." Flicking a quick glance at him, she added, "He rocked your world for hours, giving you multiple satisfying releases."

Tracey smiled as Hot Ben turned bright red. Teren, beside me, dropped his head and shook it back and forth, a wry smile on his lips.

Halina continued while I tried not to laugh. "You will remember nothing of a note written in blood. You will not think your fiancé and friends are hiding anything from you, and you will not believe that Teren is capable of murder." As Tracey stared at Halina, I whispered something to the vampire. Giving me a crooked grin, she twisted back to Tracey. "And you will choose the teal bridesmaid dresses over the obnoxious pink ones."

I smiled and Teren shook his head at me in disapproval. I shrugged; he hadn't seen the god awful cotton candy color she'd been leaning towards.

After Halina was done with her, Tracey was calm, collected, and slightly dazed. Recognizing the same look of hypnotic peace from when Halina had altered Carrie's memories, I figured it had worked. That, and the fact that Tracey was no longer yelling at us. Ben smiled and kissed her and Tracey virtually ignored the three of us. She quite possibly didn't even see us, since Halina had told her that she'd come home with Ben alone to...finish off their evening. As their kiss started deepening, I started to think that that part of their evening might not just be a suggested memory after all.

Teren and I physically pulled Halina away from the pair when Tracey starting lifting up Hot Ben's shirt. Once out of eyeshot of Ben's very nicely shaped body, Halina focused again on what really mattered to her—Gabriel.

Her expression tight, she held her hand out to Teren. "Show me."

Teren grabbed the note from his pocket and handed the

distressed paper to her. Her eyes flicked over the page, her brows furrowing as her lips compressed. When she was finished, her gaze lifted to Teren. "You saw him? He gave this to you?"

Teren nodded, then shrugged. "He never approached us, but he clearly left it for us to pick up."

Halina hissed, then looked up at the sky. Feeling how much time was left before the sun reached her, she shifted her gaze down south. "I have to get this to Gabriel. I have to tell him what happened."

She made to immediately blur away, but Teren grabbed her arm. Her pale eyes swung back to him. There was fear there, buried under the bravado. "Be careful around him," Teren said." I don't want you to find yourself...in the wrong place at the wrong time."

Halina nodded, but seemed torn. I could see that she wanted to stay near her family, stay safe for their sake. I could also see that she'd willing throw herself in front of a stake if it meant saving the man she loved. Having to choose was starting to make her face show its true age, emotionally if not physically.

Placing a hand on Teren's arm and then my own, she looked between the two of us. "I don't see why he would bother you again, since he's gotten his message through loud and clear, but..." she bit her lip, "be careful."

Teren nodded and squeezed her tight. She hugged him, twisted to quickly hug me, then dashed out of sight.

Chapter 16 – Full House

Teren and I kept a mental tab on Halina as we headed over to pick up our kids a little while later. The full vampire was quickly streaking away from us, running rather than driving. She did that whenever she was in a hurry, since she could move faster than any sports car on the planet. It exhausted her on long journeys, but she'd do it if it was necessary. And streaking to Gabriel was now a necessity to her.

I thought of Halina explaining our evening to him and squeezed Teren's hand tighter. Shutting the car off in my mom's drive, he looked over at me. His jaw, under that perfect layer of light stubble, clenched as he thought about our evening too. Twisting to me, he nodded his head at my mom's house. "Maybe we should have your mom spend the night for a few days…just to help us keep an eye on the kids."

I looked through the warm, cheery glass of my mom's front windows. I knew he wasn't really worried about keeping eyes on the kids. We could sense them. A child of ours being abducted wasn't really a concern for us. But my mom and Ashley didn't spout GPS like the rest of my family. He wanted her close to keep an eye on her.

Twisting back to him, I nodded. "Yeah…Ash, too."

He nodded grimly, then relaxed his face into a smile. "It's probably nothing. Great-Gran is right, we did our part. He has no real reason to come near us again." He glanced at the front door, where we could feel our kids hovering, waiting for us. "He has no reason to come anywhere near our family."

I nodded and kissed his hand before letting him go. We'd probably never see that vampiric thief again, but I would sure feel better with my untraceable family members close enough to hear.

Stepping out of the car, we walked up to the door together. It slowly opened as we approached. I smiled at the angelic face of my daughter in the cracked opening. She flung it wide and rushed out to me. "Mommy!"

Laughing, I nuzzled my face into hers as I picked her up. Julian, a step behind her, flung himself into Teren's arms. "Daddy!"

Teren and I looked at each other as we squeezed them tight.

My mom showed up a moment later, her face, while not surprised to see us since the twins would have alerted her to our return, seemed confused as to why we were back so early. "That bad?" she asked.

She meant the movie that we'd been heading out to see. It seemed like a lifetime ago, so much had happened to deter us from what was probably a horrible remake anyway. I still would have rather seen the movie than what we had seen. I frowned as I walked into her house. "Yes and no."

While I vaguely explained to her what had gone down, mainly that a nice man had given us a message to give to Grandpa Gabby, Teren sped-wrote her a note. He handed it to Mom while I bounced Nika on my knee. Her deep brown eyes widened as she read it.

Teren and I both kept up calm, comforting smiles, not wanting to spook the kids, and Mom sputtered a few times before throwing on a no-care-in-the-world grin. Teren had asked her to come over in the note, just as a precaution, and looking between the two of us, she nodded. Kneeling down to Julian standing by Teren's side, holding his hand, she asked, "Julian, would you like it if Grandma came to stay with you for a few days?"

Julian's mouth dropped open like she'd just asked him if he wanted Santa Claus to come early. Nodding and smiling, he broke apart from Teren to clasp her body in a hug. Nika clapped her hands. Exclaiming their joy and agreement with her idea, they simultaneously asked, "Can Grandma come over, Mommy?"

Maintaining my smile, even though it felt a little tight to me, I locked eyes with my mom. "I think that would be a great idea." Standing up, I put my hands on my hips. "In fact, we should make it a party. We should see if Auntie Ash wants to come too."

My mother subtly nodded at me as the kids cheered even louder. Once we gathered up all the kids' various toys and treats and my mom packed up an overnight bag, we headed over to Ashley's. She naturally seemed surprised to see us. "Hey." She looked past Teren and me, to our mom sitting in-between the twins in the car, tickling Julian's belly. "What's going on?"

Sighing, Teren showed her the exact same note he'd shown my mom earlier. Her deep brown eyes widened just like hers had. "Oh, oh, yeah…okay. Let me just get some stuff."

She twisted to head into the house, then paused. Looking back our way, her eyes concerned, she asked, "Should Christian come over too?"

It made me smile that Ashley had someone to worry about. Shaking my head, I shrugged. "This is just a precaution, Ash. Nothing's going on. Your boyfriend's perfectly safe." As safe as any of us were, I guess. I didn't mention that to her, though.

Shutting the bright red door of our grandmother's home behind her, Ashley followed us back to our place in her car. Teren unpacked the kids and helped everyone remove their bags from the cars while I converted one of the rooms upstairs from a playroom to a guest bedroom. Against their wishes, Teren and I immediately put the kids to bed. It took some coaxing, since mom had hopped them up on sugary ice cream not too long ago.

After wrangling my daughter back into her bed for the hundredth time, I finally got her to stay there. It wasn't too much longer that I heard the yawns and goodnights start. Knowing their high was wearing off and they'd be asleep soon, I walked downstairs to where I could hear my husband talking with Mom and Ashley in the living room.

Once I joined the trio, Mom put on her serious face. "Okay, so tell me what's going on. The real story, not the one you water down so you won't worry me." She raised an eyebrow and I sighed. "Who is having you deliver threatening messages, and why?"

I shook my head as I walked over to Teren. "Well, I guess it all started when Teren died." He smiled down at me as I slung an arm around his waist.

Enfolding me in a hug, he looked over to my mom. "I may be a vampire, but I was conceived and born in the same way that humans are. For most of my life, I was just as alive as you." My mom tentatively smiled as she sat on the couch; Ashley rested her hand on her arm. Mom knew some things about mixed vampires, since she'd been around a few of them, but she'd never been sat down and given all of the facts about Teren's and my life.

Tilting his head, Teren listened to the sounds of our children quieting. Letting go of me, he walked directly in front of my mom. He said nothing until the sounds of breathing upstairs were light and even. While we didn't try and hide our history from our kids, we didn't need them having nightmares either. Squatting in front of her, he quietly continued. "Emma and I were taken by a man who," he paused, twisting his lips, "who didn't believe that my kind had a right to exist."

"Taken?" My mom's brows bunched together as she flicked a glance at me standing behind Teren. I smiled reassuringly but she frowned. "You were kidnapped by a man who wanted to kill vampires? When did this happen?"

Teren and I both looked up when we heard the children stir. Knowing we were hearing things that she couldn't, Mom followed our gaze. "Teren, maybe we should continue this upstairs," I whispered.

Teren nodded, then stood and extended his hand to my mom. Smiling at her as she stood up, he cocked an eyebrow and playfully asked, "Want to feel a rush?"

Mom narrowed her eyes at him, then slowly nodded. He scooped her up and streaked her upstairs. Her earlier trepidation gone, I heard Mom laughing while I helped Ashley stand. I grinned at her. "Want to try it?"

She looked at our matching height and weight. "Can you lift me?"

Snorting, I easily tossed her over my shoulder and blurred up to where I felt my husband. Both my mom and Ashley were laughing when Teren shut the door. They stopped when they noticed the sounds of traffic and city life stopping. Mom looked around. "Wow, it sure gets quiet in here."

Teren shrugged. "We had it soundproofed so the kids wouldn't hear us."

Ashley started giggling and I poked her ribs. "When we want to talk, Ashley."

My mom flushed and looked anywhere but our bed. Ashley bit her lip to stop laughing and Teren ran a hand through his hair; he was avoiding looking at the bed too. Rolling my eyes, I dragged Ash to the edge of the mattress and made her sit down. Once the embarrassment filtered out of the air, Mom sat down on it too.

The seriousness of our conversation returning, Mom asked, "So…you and my daughter were kidnapped. How did you get away?"

Teren sighed and looked down. He shuffled his feet, seemingly unsure what to say. Not wanting him to admit his part in it, I turned to my mom. "The man was going to kill us…so I killed him first."

Her mouth dropped open and her face paled. Tears sprang into her eyes as she looked between Teren and I. Teren looked about to object, and I gave him a glance that clearly said, *Don't say a word.* As awful as it was to admit to her that I'd taken a life in self-defense, I didn't want Teren to admit that he'd drained the man of his life-force. I wasn't sure how much truth Mom could take in one sitting…and I didn't want Teren to think about it anymore than he already did.

Ashley reached across me to pat Mom's knee, and Mom looked over at her. "Did you know about this?" she whispered.

Ashley shrugged, then nodded. "I knew most of it." She looked back to me. "The rest I…pieced together."

I looked down, and Ashley and Mom wrapped their arms around me. Closing my eyes, I savored their comfort for a moment. Even though the event had happened a while ago, I still had nightmares every now and again.

Teren walked up to me and cupped my cheek. He lifted my chin, bringing my attention to his eyes. Smiling, he warmly said, "She was amazing. She saved my life." He looked back down at my mom. "Well, sort of. The hunter injected me with something that killed me, and forced my conversion." Mom gave him a blank look, and he explained. "Turned me from a living vampire to a dead one."

Reaching her hand up to clasp Teren's, she softly said, "I'm so sorry, Teren."

Dropping his hand from my skin, he clasped her hand between

his. "Thank you, Linda." Shaking his head, he continued. "Anyway, what the hunter injected me with was stolen by the man we saw tonight." He raised an eyebrow. "He stole it from Gabriel...and Gabriel would like to speak with him about it."

Mom twisted her lips. She'd heard all about Halina's boyfriend from the twins. While Mom had never met him herself, she was aware that he was pretty powerful and pretty smart. After the birth of the twins, we'd told her about the shots that were keeping my heart beating, shots that Gabriel had created. Mom looked between Teren and I. "This man won't survive a meeting with Gabriel...will he?"

Teren bit his lip. "Most likely not, no. And Gabriel is getting closer to him, he's getting a little desperate. His message to us was to give a warning to Gabriel, so Gabriel would leave him alone. I don't think Gabriel plans to." Tension filled the quiet room, and Teren threw on a carefree smile as he glanced at everyone. "But, whatever bad blood is between those two doesn't directly involve our family, so you really have nothing to worry about." He patted Mom's thigh and then my sister's. "Staying with us is just a safety measure, so we all know where the other is until this blows over. All right?"

Both my mom and my sister woodenly nodded, each looking thoughtful. Seeing the fear in their features, I slung my arm around each of them; they both shivered as my cold touched them and their heat leached into me. "It's just for a few days. Gabriel is close, I'm sure he'll have him soon," I said.

Teren nodded, his hands coming up to rest on his hips. "Especially since he stupidly popped up on Gabriel's radar. Now that he knows he's in the area...it's just a matter of time before Gabriel catches him."

I exhaled in a long, steadying breath. "Then this will all be over with."

Having my family close, being able to constantly hear them in my home, was a tremendous relief to me. I stayed up late into the night once Mom and Ash turned in, just to listen to everyone breathing. Still awake as well, Teren squeezed my hand. "Get some sleep, Emma." Laughing into my ear, he added, "You're going to need your strength with a full house."

I twisted in our bed to face him, and his arms slipped under me as he held me close. "Maybe we should all go out to the ranch? Maybe it would be better if both our families were together?"

The glow of his eyes washed over my face as he considered that for a second. "We'll see what Gabriel says tomorrow, after Great-Gran has talked to him." Leaning in, he kissed me. "I don't want to disrupt everyone's lives if he is right on Malcolm's tail." He shrugged. "Who knows, maybe all this will be over by the morning?"

Nodding, I curled into his body and hoped he was right. Even still, I listened to everyone's breaths for quite a while longer.

Gabriel called right as Teren would have been getting ready for work; he'd decided to work from home, so he could stay in the house and keep an eye on everyone. Shutting our door so he didn't wake our super-hearing children, Teren sat beside me on the bed as Gabriel started asking him questions. After inquiring about every detail of our encounter with Malcolm that a person could think of, Gabriel assured us that we would be of no further interest to him.

"You've served your purpose, I don't suspect that he'll bother you again. Besides, we've narrowed down all of his possible haunts in the area. We've cut off every connection he has. We've already ended his monetary source and he's running out of places to hide. Trust me, Teren, this will all be over soon and the person responsible for your early demise will be brought to justice. You have my word."

Gabriel had a reassuring way of talking, and I felt soothed by his conviction. Before hanging up the phone with Teren, he added, "Just for your own peace of mind, I have sent a couple of mixed your way. Extra eyes are always…helpful." There was a smirk to his voice as he hung up the phone with Teren, and I raised my eyebrow at hearing the humor.

Teren shrugged and patted my leg. Feeling a little better about the whole incident with the mysterious Malcolm and his ominous message, I got ready for another typical day of work. I didn't really want to leave my family, but knowing that some of Gabriel's devotees were already on their way to us made me okay with it. That was, until Teren called me later and I discovered just who Gabriel had decided to saddle us with.

"He what? Are you serious?" Clarice across from me narrowed her eyes and shook her head, like me being on a cell phone during business hours was a sacrilege.

Teren sighed into the phone. "Unfortunately, yes, I'm serious. They're here now...looking through the bedrooms." Sighing again, he muttered, "I think they want ours."

I groaned into the phone and dropped my head into my hands. "I can't believe of all the people he has down there, he sent Starla and Jacen to protect us," I muttered under my breath.

Teren chuckled into the phone. "Well, you know how he loves to kill two birds with one stone. This way, he's given us some extra protection, and he doesn't have to listen to them constantly make out."

I let out an irritated exhale as Tracey popped into the room with some reports. Her face was peaceful and serene, like nothing odd had happened last night. I quietly thanked her as she tapped a picture of her finalized choice for the bridesmaid dresses on the top report—they were the teal ones I'd had Halina implant on her. Grateful that at least Halina's powers seemed to be working fine on Tracey, I said to Teren, "Well, I'll help you deal with it when I get home."

He sighed and in the background I could hear Starla smacking her gum and complaining about the firmness of our mattresses. "Okay...please hurry." Hearing Starla loudly exclaiming that she couldn't believe our sheets were cotton, of all things, he added, "Are you sure I can't go hunting with Ben?"

Laughing, I firmly told him, "Yes, I'm sure about that."

I almost reconsidered when I was sitting at home later in the evening, surrounded by friends and family. Our house was packed. Except for Halina, who was on her way back from Gabriel's, everyone was there—Teren and the kids, my mom, Ashley, Alanna, Jack, Imogen, and even Hot Ben, and then, of course, our vampiric protection...Starla and Jacen. Our home was moderately sized, but it felt about as big as a postage stamp with all the noise and movement bombarding my senses. The sooner Gabriel got this guy, the sooner we could get back to our routine.

I did relish having everyone close and safe though. Imogen and

Alanna talked with my mother over recipes. Alanna loved cooking, even though Jack and the kids were the only eaters left among us. My sister kept the kids in a constant state of laughter, tickling them or playing hide and seek, which was really unfair when it was the kids' turn, since they could hear the specific thump of Ashley's heart anywhere she hid, even in our packed house.

Teren spent most of the night in his loft office with his dad, discussing details of transferring everything to the new ranch. Jack wanted Teren to go, naturally, but he wasn't going to push him on the matter. Even though they'd all moved together in the past, things were different now. Teren had a family of his own to consider.

Jacen, the blond near-twin of his girlfriend, Starla, was walking the inner perimeter of the home with Hot Ben, discussing strategy if we were ever infiltrated. Jacen talked with the air of a Secret Service agent assigned to protect the President or something. Ben eagerly listened to his advice like we were about to have World War III explode on our doorstep.

Jacen would have seemed more credible about his protection plans, if his girlfriend didn't take every opportunity to grab his butt or suck on his ear. It always affected him too. He'd pause mid-sentence and close his eyes before telling her that he had important work to do as he triple checked every point of entry. With his attention to detail, I was a little surprised I hadn't been frisked at the door when I'd come home.

After being dismissed for the third time, Starla sat beside me on the couch and folded her legs up on the soft leather. Staring at me, she popped a bubble in my ear. I held my breath as the swirl of mint mixed with floral hairspray. Sometimes, I didn't know how Starla could stand the smell of herself; everything about her was so strong.

"Father says this dude's as good as toast, so I'm sure we'll be gone by the end of the week."

I nodded at her, hoping that as well. Starla sighed, like *she* was the one being inconvenienced. Propping her head in her hand, she moaned, "I miss my room at the house." Her eyes closed as she began to reminiscence about the luxury she'd left behind in L.A. "I have the softest European sheets you'll ever find." Her eyes binged open. "One thousand count." Not really knowing what that meant, I only blinked.

Starla looked over at Jacen standing near the elaborate, wrought iron front door with Hot Ben. "Jace and I share a room now, so we'll be sharing one here too…for however long we're stuck here." Her eyes lit up as they traveled down his body. The heat in them was unmistakable. It made me really uncomfortable and I averted my eyes. But not before I caught the equally prissy male vampire look over at her. The heat in his eyes was unmistakable too.

A little irritated, I wondered if I'd have to have the "no sex in the house" speech with her. I really wasn't prepared to give the birds-and-the-bees speech to Julian and Nika just yet, and I doubted Starla would think twice about the tiny, super-hearing children who were just a few rooms away from them.

Standing to put my kids to bed, I muttered, "Well, the sooner this is over, the better for all of us." Starla wholeheartedly agreed with me as I walked away from her steadily thumping heart. The heart I'd decided to help keep beating.

But, lying in bed later, I smiled at hearing the living heartbeats in my home—safe and secure—even Starla's.

A few more nights of family togetherness however, had me longing for the serenity of just the four of us. Our house was in a constant state of flux—someone always coming or going. The Adams clan popped in for a few hours every night, sometimes staying very late into the evening. Hot Ben usually checked in before heading home to guard his fiancé. My mom never left our place, sticking to the kids like glue, but Ash came and went for work and to see her boyfriend. She even chose that crazy time to invite the man over to meet all of us.

As Ashley paced while she waited for Christian to arrive for "family movie night," since the entire clan was at our house again, she went over the rules. "Okay, no freaking him out with inappropriate talk." She pointed at Halina, who had stuck pretty close to our house most evenings since returning from Los Angeles. Halina shrugged and smiled.

Ashley sighed and looked over at Jacen and Starla. Starla had made a couple offhand remarks about my sister's looks when she'd first shown up, mainly that she knew some really great plastic surgeons. From what was now family lore, Teren had blurred over to Starla, tossed her on the front lawn, and wouldn't let her come back into the house until she apologized. The sprinklers in our yard had been on when he'd done it. Starla never said another disparaging word about my sister. I constantly kicked myself for missing that little showdown.

She gave the two lovebirds a stern glare. "No, sucking face, either." Starla bounced on Jacen's lap, crossed her arms over her chest and pouted. Biting her lip, Ashley reminded everyone to act like regular human beings, so the love of her life wouldn't flee in terror.

Seeing her nerves, I stood up and put my arms around her. "It will be fine, Ash."

She nodded, leaning into me. "I know. I just really want him to love you guys." Peeking up at me, she tilted her head. "Maybe this should wait until things are less crazy around here?"

Teren stood up and circled his arms around my waist. "If we always waited for the craziness to die down, we'd never do anything." He patted her arm. "Everything will be fine."

Ashley nodded as Alanna, Imogen and Jack stood up. "We'll leave you to your evening with your boyfriend, Ashley," Alanna said, giving my sister a hug. My sister started to tell her that it wasn't necessary for them to leave, but Alanna shook her head. "I know how intimidating it can be to meet the entire family at once. You introduce him to just yours."

Alanna inclined her head at Halina, silently asking her to leave with them. Halina frowned as she looked around our house, then she nodded. Happy that our home was just slightly less crowded for one evening, I looked over at Starla and Jacen. They'd tuned out everyone and were making out again. Tossing a throw pillow on them, I said, "Why don't you guys go with them? You could have...a little privacy."

I grimaced as I remembered walking in on them "testing" out my soundproof room last night; I'd nearly tossed them out on the lawn myself. Starla smiled like it was the best idea she'd heard in a while. The grin spreading across her lip-glossed mouth was the exact opposite of Jacen's. While she nodded, bouncing in his lap again, he frowned and tried to still her hips.

"Father told us to stay by your side." He shook his head, his demeanor serious. "He wouldn't approve of us leaving."

Starla looked down on him, and her lip twisted into an adorable pout. "Babe, it's just one night." She wriggled in his lap, making him cringe while his eyes fluttered. "Besides, you talked with Father this morning. They're doing that raid thing tonight." She bent down to kiss his neck and his mouth dropped open. "Malcolm is probably already lighting up the sky," she breathed in his ear.

Swallowing, Jacen's eyes refocused on mine. "Perhaps you're right. One night wouldn't hurt anything." Shifting Starla off his lap, he stood and adjusted the obvious discomfort in his jeans. I bit my cheek to not smile. Sniffing, he causally tossed out, "Besides, Father wanted us to protect all of the Adams."

His pale eyes shifted to Halina. A worried look from hearing the word "raid" instantly evaporated off her face. Crossing her arms over her chest, she leaned back on her hip. "I don't need your protection." Her gaze flicked down Jacen's body; he was no taller than her. She lingered on his personal area and a smirk drifted across her face.

Starla stepped in front of her boyfriend. "Hey, Grandma. Eyes up."

Halina's expression shifted. She looked like she was about to verbally rip off Starla's head, but Ashley intervened. "Hey, this is exactly the kind of stuff that I don't want Christian to see." Her hand flicked over to the twins lying on the floor, heads propped up in their hands as they watched the multiple vampires in the room. "Or them," Ash muttered.

Starla lifted her chin. Pulling Jacen's hand, she led him from the house. Alanna and Jack said their goodnights to the twins and then followed after the pair that I could hear continuing their make out session in the driveway. Ashley exhaled in relief as a few otherworldly beings left the area. She was fine with what we all were, but she wanted Christian to feel comfortable. I understood.

Halina and Imogen said their goodbyes to the kids, tickling them into laughing fits, then twisted to leave as well. Halina paused with her daughter at the door. Looking between my mother and sister, she frowned. She glanced up at Teren, and her dark hair swirled around her as she shook her head. "Are you sure about us leaving?" She shrugged. "I could...stay close."

Teren slung his arm over Ashley; she shivered a bit, but smiled. Grinning, he said," I've got these girls." He nodded his head out the door at the rest of his family. "You go protect them." Halina twisted her lips, then nodded. Looking over at me, Teren added, "Besides, it sounds like Gabriel is making his move tonight. This should all be over soon."

Halina sighed and Teren swung his gaze back to her. "Right, the raid. I should be there. I should be helping secure that...creature."

Teren frowned as Imogen laid her hand on her mother's arm. "Let Gabriel handle this, Mother," Imogen said softly.

Halina looked back at her, her eyes torn. Sighing again, she shrugged. "It's probably too late, anyway." She looked back to us. "It's probably over with." Halina sighed forlornly, like she'd missed out on the party of the year.

Smiling, Imogen waved goodbye and pulled her from the home. As I heard the gaggle of vampires dive off, I exhaled a long breath. With only my mother and sister left to visit, the house seemed three times as big.

When Christian showed up an hour later, we'd already put our two yawning youngsters to bed. When Julian's last words to me were, "Starla and Jacen always kissing," I was extremely grateful that everything was going to be over soon.

My sister's entire being brightened when Christian stepped into our home. He was tall and lanky, with a fuzzy beard and graying hair, but his eyes beamed at my sister like she was the most beautiful woman he'd ever seen. Grasping his hand, Ashley pulled him farther into the entryway to introduce him to a part of our family.

Mom was the first to officially meet him. Pleasantly plump, Mom was sort of what Ash and I would have looked like in the future, if life hadn't deviated us. Now, I was un-aging and Ashley's scarred body put her on a different path. But Christian's smile widened as he shook Mom's hand, like he saw the resemblance to the woman he loved anyway.

I got a little nervous when he approached Teren and me. Sure, I'd been dead for a while now, but I hadn't had too much practice touching people I didn't know. Christian stepped in front of me, and his aftershave tickled my nose. Tilting my head, I could clearly hear his racing heartbeat over my mother's and sister's. I listened to it for a second, fascinated, and maybe a little hungry. While his face didn't betray it, he was extremely nervous to meet Ashley's family.

Extending my hand to him, I prepared myself for his reaction to my skin. "Emma Adams, nice to finally meet you, Christian." My gaze flicked over to my sister before returning to him.

He didn't hesitate to grab my hand, and he shook it warmly. As his heat traveled up my arm, I watched his eyes widen, just fractionally. I sniffed for any trace of fear coming from him, but didn't sense any. "Emma...nice to meet you."

Before his skin could linger too long on mine, Teren extended his hand. "Teren Adams, we're glad to have you."

Christian dropped my hand and clasped my husband's. His eyes shifted between my hand and Teren's, but he didn't comment on our temperature. Some people were naturally cold; Teren and I were just colder than most.

Ashley grinned as she pulled her honey away from Teren. Christian smiled and looped an arm around her and we moved our meeting to the living room. All of my sister's worry about him meeting me was pretty unwarranted; it was clear that his eyes were only for her.

Mom sat next to Christian on the couch, and grilled him over the technical aspects of his job. Smiling at my mom ferreting out my sister's potential husband, in her eyes at least, I leaned into Teren's side and only half listened.

Under the human's range of hearing, my husband whispered, "He seems nice...genuinely in love with her."

I nodded discretely, whispering, "Yeah, he seems to really like her." I looked back at him. "I'm glad she has her own version of you to love."

Teren smiled and kissed my forehead. As my mom laughed over a joke that Christian had made, Teren laughed as well. "It's nice, not having so many bodies to block out, isn't it?"

I grinned, also laughing at something Christian had said. In appearance anyway, in truth, I was laughing at my husband's comment. "Yes, Starla and Jacen have been driving me crazy."

Looping his fingers over mine, he murmured, "I know…and I thought we were bad."

I laughed louder than the current conversation warranted and my mom gave me an admonishing look before asking Christian about his family. Teren chuckled at me as Christian started explaining that his brother was a teacher and his parents had passed away a few years ago. Seeing the flecks of white in his speckled hair and the lines of wisdom in his features, I started wondering just how much older than Ashley Christian was. Not that I'd call them on it. Lord knows Teren and I weren't exactly in a typical relationship.

When Ashley started explaining Christian's scientific breakthrough, Teren wistfully sighed in my ear. Knowing his mind wasn't really following the conversation in front of us, I asked, "What are you thinking about? Cellular degeneration?"

He smiled as he looked at me, then minutely shook his head. "No…the raid. Just hoping that everything is truly over."

I discretely searched his face, seeing the hope there as well as the longing. Like Halina, a part of Teren wanted to be in on the action too. Squeezing his hand, I reiterated, "I'm glad you stayed out of it. I'm glad you stayed by me, even if it was hard for you." His eyes flicked over mine before shifting back to Christian and my sister. While he asked Christian a technical question on his research, he nodded at me.

I suppressed a smile at the duel conversations going on and stroked Teren's hand with my thumb. Once Christian had answered his question, his face just as excited as Ashley's when she talked about the hope his work could give people, Teren spoke only to me again. "I'll be glad to have you all to myself again. I've missed you."

Feeling a little saucy, since Teren and I really hadn't had any sort of alone time since Malcolm had shown his haggard face to us, I nestled into his back. Where my sister and her boyfriend wouldn't be able to see it, my hand floated down to rest on Teren's inner thigh. "I've missed you too. I think we'll be testing out the soundproofing tonight."

Teren stiffened a little, adjusting in his seat as he struggled to act like he was paying attention. Under his breath, he muttered, "You're about to give me Jacen's problem."

I let out a throaty laugh. Luckily Ashley had just told a funny story and it was an appropriate moment. To my husband, I whispered, "You have no idea how difficult I'm about to make your...problem."

Teren groaned a little, shifting it to a cough when my sister noticed. Her brown eyes narrowed in warning as she glanced between us. I threw on a causal smile and dropped Teren's hand to innocently curl a piece of hair around my finger. My other hand though, the one invisible to her, shifted farther up Teren's thigh.

Christian asked Ashley a question and she ignored us for a moment. Making it seem as if he was only interested in seeing everyone better, Teren shifted me slightly in front of him. My hand slid off his thigh as he angled me up his lap. From what I could feel pressing into me, I knew he was already sharing Jacen's earlier discomfort.

"I can't wait to get you alone," he muttered. "How long do you think we have to fake that we're paying attention?"

Tilting my head, I wished he would place a kiss on the tender spot of my neck; maybe some fangs too. We couldn't exactly hide that though. Sighing softly, I told him, "We have to wait until he leaves...it *is* our house."

His hand clenching my hip, he groaned under his breath. "Damn..."

Wanting to tease him a little, I rocked my hips, just once, just a tiny little bit. To our sensitive bodies though, I may as well have reached my hand around and stroked him. He stopped breathing, and his hand on my hip tightened and released, encouraging me to do that again. I waited a few minutes before I did.

"Keep breathing," I muttered, reminding him to keep acting human.

His breath started up again, a little faster than necessary. "Sorry...you're distracting."

Leaning back into his body, I laughed and asked Christian what he thought of the stem cell research controversy. Both he and my sister lit up at what was a passionate topic for them. My mother leaned in, fascinated, and Teren groaned. Normally he'd be just as interested, but we hadn't been together in a while, and as I discretely rubbed against him, I knew I was driving him crazy. It drove me a little crazy too, knowing he was going to rip my clothes off the first chance he got.

It was at least two hours later when he shoved me against our closed bedroom door. The sounds of my mom and Ashley gushing about how sweet and intelligent Christian was suddenly stopped as the soundproofing cut off everything outside our room. I finally let out the groan I'd wanted to make all night.

Teren's hands were everywhere as he shed clothes off me. "God, Em, you were driving me crazy."

My hands were all over him, loosening his belt, popping open his buttons. I laughed in his mouth. "I know...it drove me crazy, too." His hands ripped open my slacks and ran down my thighs as he pushed them off. I leaned back against the door as his lips followed his hands down my legs. I groaned again. "Oh God, it's been too long..."

Standing up, Teren twisted me around and pushed me towards our bed. "I know," he muttered, ripping off his shirt. Bouncing on the bed, I slipped my underwear off while he pushed down his pants. True, with our gift from Gabriel we could have been silently enjoying each other every night, but we'd been a little too preoccupied to think about it. That, and it was sort of an advertisement to every visiting vampire in the house if we suddenly closed our door.

When Teren was as naked as I was, he crawled over me. His lips dragged against my skin, and his teeth nibbled my flesh. I shuddered as I dropped my head back and arched my back. His mouth stopped at my hips. "God, smelling this for hours just about killed me," he groaned.

I was about to respond but his mouth was suddenly right…there. I clutched his head, crying out as the wave of intense satisfaction washed over me, stoked over and over by the soft repetitive motion of his tongue. He moaned into my skin as he savored the desire only he created in me. His hands clenched my legs, pushing them farther apart as my cries grew in intensity and volume. It had been even longer since his miraculous mouth had been on me like this.

Just as he drove a finger inside, I released, gasping as I held him to me. He waited until I came all the way down from the euphoria he'd given me, continually brushing his tongue over me. When the wave passed, he lifted his head and slowly continued up my body. By the time he was at my mouth, I wanted him again.

"I love you," he muttered as he slid into me.

"God, I love you too."

I held his body as close to me as I could, listening to the only things I could hear—our bodies, our breaths, our voices. He dropped his head to my shoulder as our movements escalated. Groaning, his body flexed in preparation. Our hips smoothly in rhythm, I flexed my body too, wanting to climax again, but with him this time. I was right there, and together, we cried out in unison, clutching each other tight as his body flowed into me and my body clenched around him. Two beings melding perfectly, even if we were deceased.

As the bliss of the moment mixed with the exhaustion of the last few days, I felt the peace of sleep creeping up on me. Teren felt it too; he shifted to my side and then he passed out. Just as I thought to get up and open our door, slumber pulled me under too.

Chapter 17 – Gone

I dreamt I was falling. Plunging from a great distance, it was both exhilarating and terrifying. The wind rushing past smelled of the sea and for a moment it seemed like I was falling though the ocean. I even saw a few starfish floating past.

As I alternated between wanting to scream in terror and wanting to laugh in delight, I heard my son. Searching around the deep blue space I was plunging through, I found him below, looking up at me.

Sunlight bounced off the jet black hair that marked him as a bone fide Adams. His pale eyes glittered with delight as he extended his arms like he was soaring. I smiled at him as he laughed. Just as I was wondering where my daughter was, he shook his head. "Don't worry, Mommy. We're magic, remember?"

I tilted my head at him and then he was gone. A bat hovered in his place and I laughed out loud that my son had finally mastered the impossible trick that he and Nika practiced so often.

"Mommy?"

A voice back in the real world slowly started bringing me to awareness. Unlike my dream, this sweet, high-pitched tremble belonged to my daughter. I could smell fear in the air along with something faintly familiar, but my hazy brain was phasing in and out of consciousness, and I couldn't focus on anything for longer than a couple seconds.

I felt the end of the bed compress and heard and smelled the sweetness of my daughter crawling up to me. Adjusting the sheets around my naked body, I automatically reached down for her and pulled her up to me. Her entire body was shaking. Thinking she was cold against my dead flesh, I pulled the quilt off of Teren's body and wrapped it around her; he didn't need it anyway.

My daughter's shaking didn't stop any once she was bundled. She clung to me, not wanting the barrier even though she seemed cold. "Mommy?" she whispered, her voice trembling too.

Sleepily, I patted her back and kissed her head. "It's all right, Nika, go back to sleep." Teren shifted beside us. He inhaled for the first time in hours as he woke up a little.

Nika shook her head under my lips. "Mommy...monster."

Half in and out of sleep, I pulled her tight and mumbled, "Shhh, baby. It was just a bad dream. Go to sleep, honey."

She shook her head harder and I cracked open my eyes. My glow highlighted her quivering lips, her wide eyes. Seeing me more awake, she shook her head again. "No, Mommy...monster in my room," she whimpered, still scared.

Teren yawned, fully awakened by her distress. "It's okay, Nika, you're safe, Daddy's here," he mumbled, flipping over to put an arm around where she was huddled in-between us.

Seeing Teren's peaceful face returning to a place of rest, my eyes started fluttering closed. I nestled my head in my daughter's hair. "Daddy's right, baby. You're safe. There are no such things as monsters."

Somewhere in my hazy brain I noted the irony of me saying that to her, considering what we were. Floating back into sleep, I heard Nika's sniffles growing louder, along with her tremors. "Mommy...wake up."

I popped an eye open as I fought against the desire to just ignore her and let that peace wash over me. Maybe she'd pieced things together about why so many people had been camping out with us lately and it had frightened her. She did seem genuinely scared.

Her little heat-pack hands came up to cup my cheeks and I opened my eyes wider. Studying the dark depths of hers, I saw the sheer terror in them and felt a hot tear splash on my arm. Fighting through the fog of waking up, I frowned. "Baby, you're safe. Mommy and Daddy have you." Teren's arm around her tightened as he silently agreed with me.

In a whisper that even I could barely hear, she said, "Monster took Julie."

I opened my mouth to automatically tell her that monsters weren't real, when I finally felt it. Teren and I sat bolt upright at the exact same time. We looked at each other for the briefest fraction of a second as fear washed through every part of me. Nika was right—

Julian wasn't in the house.

We sprang out of bed, blurring on any clothes we could find nearby while Nika watched us. Tears on her cheeks, she sat small and alone on our bed. I ended up in Teren's work shirt and a pair of my lounge pants that I'd tossed in the corner a couple of days ago. I couldn't have cared less though. My son was no longer in my sanctuary. Pure ice flooded my body, my soul.

"Stay in the house with her, I'm getting Julian," Teren said, tossing on some pants and immediately phasing from the room. I could sense him streaking towards the front door, and I scooped up Nika and followed him. Seeing her parents in action, Nika started to sob. Her terror mixed with mine, amplifying it.

The blurb on my personal radar that was Julian was moving fast, away from us, in a southerly direction. I had no idea why Julian would leave his bed in the middle of the night. I had no idea why he'd go outside, much less run away from us. When Teren was at the entryway and I was at the top of the stairs, I felt something change. Julian's position turned around, started coming back to us. Holding my breath, I locked eyes with my husband as he looked up at me. "He's coming back," he muttered.

I nodded. "Go get him." He had the door open before I even finished nodding. I heard yawns and whispers from my mom and sister as I felt my husband streaking to meet up with my son. I was still holding my breath. Nika was still sobbing uncontrollably. Staring at the door below me, I felt my mom and Ashley stumble from their room to enter the hallway.

"Em? What's going on?"

Ashley reached out for a distraught Nika and I woodenly handed her over. I couldn't pull my gaze from the door as I waited for Teren to burst through it with our wandering son. I could feel him closing the distance as Julian's slower blurb sped towards his.

My mom put a hand on my back and asked what was wrong. I couldn't speak, and only Nika answered. In between sobs, she got out, "Monster took Julie."

My stomach tightened at her words. No. She must have been having a weird dream, like the dream I'd awoken from. Kids were rarely taken from the homes, from their beds, especially vampire children. That just couldn't have been what happened. Julian must have heard something and wandered away. With his super ears, he could have heard something blocks from here. Maybe he'd drifted farther than he'd intended and was streaking back to us because he was scared. Feeling Teren almost on him, I closed my eyes. Nika's wailing in the background amplified my stress. For the first time since my death, I felt a phantom thumping in my chest. A fake heartbeat.

But just as Teren was almost on him, everything I'd ever known...changed.

My eyes flew open and I choked on the air suddenly suffocating me. "No," was all I got out before I lost the ability to stand up straight. Falling to my knees in front of the railing, I gripped it with every ounce of strength I possessed; it snapped in two.

My mother's arms were instantly around me as I clutched my stomach. "What's wrong, Emma?"

Her warm, pudgy body gave me no comfort as I rocked back and forth on my heels. Shaking my head, I could only mutter, "No," over and over, like it was the only word I knew.

From somewhere in the night, a yell ripped through the quiet streets. I knew my husband's voice and covered my ears. No, this could not be happening. Even my mother heard his scream and started shaking. Maybe not registering that he'd made that sound, she asked, "What's out there?"

I had no answer for her; I had no coherent words at all, only the beginnings of a long grief-filled wail of my own. Hearing my daughter's pained cries behind me, I clamped my hand over my mouth and forced myself to not scream. It was hard. I felt like my entire body had shattered into a thousand pieces. Tears stung my eyes while a face in my memory filled my watery vision.

My son. My first born. My carbon copy of the man I loved...was gone.

Sucking in breaths, trying to not scare Nika anymore than she already was, I ignored my mother and sister's concerned questions and panicked voices. I felt my husband's presence stop in my head, felt his location aimlessly jerk back and forth. Julian was gone. The blip of him in my head that told me where he was at every second of the day, had vanished. Like someone had thrown off a light switch, it had stopped spouting his location to me. By Teren's scream, I knew he'd lost him too. That only meant one thing in my mind: Julian was dead.

Hyperventilating on the air I didn't need, I felt cool tears streaming down my cheeks. Staring at everything, but seeing none of it, I started muttering, "He's gone...he's gone."

Nika started wailing my name and I heard Ashley coo something comforting in her ear. I felt Teren start to return to me in a circular pattern, back and forth, searching for our son's body.

I shot to my feet, startling my mother back a step. No...I couldn't stomach my son's lifeless body being brought back to the house in my husband's arms. That would surely unhinge me. I had to find him. I had to see where and how and....why.

I started to streak downstairs, but my mom clenched my arm. I turned back to her, not even seeing her.

"Emma? What happened?" Her voice was clipped, short, her eyes murky with unshed tears. Looking at her for the first time since I'd noticed Julian's absence, I finally heard the hearts thumping around me. All three pulsating beats in the hallway were hard, fast, surging with adrenaline. For an odd moment, I wondered if Julian's heart had been racing...before it stopped.

Not feeling like it was even me speaking, I told her, "Julian left the house."

Her eyes widened as tears flowed down her cheeks and she pushed my body towards the stairs. "Then go get him!"

Looking between her and my sister, I shook my head. "I can't." I shrugged, and pieces of my soul crumbled apart.

Ashley held Nika tight; my daughter wrapped every limb around her as she cried for her brother, her twin. "Why can't you? Where's Teren?"

She looked around for him while I shrugged again. "He's searching, but he doesn't know where to look."

My mother grabbed my face, shaking me from my daze. "You can feel him. Go get him, Emma!"

I blinked as a sob rose in me. "I can't...I can't feel him anymore."

My mother now seemed as dazed as me, and fat tears splashed on her skin. "No... Does that mean he's...?" She couldn't finish saying what I most feared and the unspoken word reverberated in the air.

I nodded, not able to say it either, especially with Nika listening.

Both Mom and Ashley gasped, then choked on their grief. Twisting from the sight of so much internal damage, I made to flee from it—towards my grieving husband who was madly searching where he'd last felt our son. "I need to help Teren...find his body."

I could not believe those words had just left my mouth.

My vision clouded to a point where I couldn't even see the stairs anymore, but I flew myself down them anyway. My hand reached out for the knob of our once beautiful front door; every beautiful thing seemed dull and lifeless to me now. Twisting the knob so hard the metal warped, I nearly pulled the elaborate decoration off its hinges. My daughter's voice stopped me a split second before I streaked away.

"Julie's scared, Mommy."

I immediately twisted around to stare up at my daughter. Her tiny head was resting on Ashley's shoulder, her light hair mixing with my sister's darker shade. Feeling like I was on the edge of a precipice and any second I was going to fall off of it, I took a step back. Staring up at Nika, disbelieving, I murmured, "Do you feel him, sweetheart? Do you feel what he's feeling...right now?"

The hope blossoming in my chest was nearly as painful as dying had been. At that moment, I would have preferred another conversion. Every breath in the house stopped as everyone focused on my daughter, the one person on this earth who would know with absolute certainty if my son was still alive. Ticking the long seconds off in my head, I held my breath. I was terrified of what her answer might be.

Nika swallowed repeatedly, hiccupping with her fading sobs. Finally, she nodded. "He's scared," she whispered.

My hands came to my mouth as a sob broke free from me. If he was scared…he was alive. I felt streaks rushing to me in my head. So many were moving towards me at one time that it felt like my world was imploding. The other vampires had also felt the disconnect with Julian and were racing here, to find out why. I had no answers for them. None but—*he was alive.*

My husband was my main concern though. He believed our son was dead; I couldn't let him continue to believe that; it would eat him alive. Wishing I could call him to me with just the connection we had, I hovered at the door. Torn between flying to him and flying to my daughter, to question her on everything she knew, I debated. Just as I started to move towards Nika, I felt Teren's presence shift towards mine. Our pull kicked in when he did. A dull sense of homecoming started to burn in me but I ignored it. This reunion wasn't going to be our usual sweet one. This one would give me no satisfied peace. I didn't think I'd ever feel satisfied peace again.

Maybe sensing his family approaching, Teren was blurring back to me, to strategize on how best to find where our son lay lifeless. I twisted back to the door, eager to tell him that Julian wasn't gone. He may have vanished, but he wasn't gone.

Looking like nothing more than a trick of the lights to human eyes, he phased into the house. I inhaled him as he went past, and the world danced off his skin as a small rush of reunion washed over me. It was nothing though, nothing compared to the void in my chest. Dirt, grease and garbage filled my senses as he stopped just inside the door. His bare chest was streaked with mud, his hands were dirty, his slacks filthy. I had to assume that Teren had been ripping apart…everything. Anything he could to find our son. Glancing down his body, my eyes watered at the blood smeared across his bare feet. He'd already healed, but he'd ripped his skin apart, searching in vain.

Tears fell from his eyes as he looked back at me as I closed the door; his eyes watched the wrought iron as it ominously cut off the path to our lost kin. "Emma," he croaked out, "I couldn't…I couldn't find him. He's gone. He's not there anymore. I could smell

him, but it's windy tonight...it was faint...and then it just stopped."
Tears ran down his face and he started to breathe heavy, like he was
hyperventilating too. "There's nothing there..."

He didn't mention the disconnect we'd all felt, he didn't need to.
A lonely ache filled my body now that I no longer had a bond with
Julian. It was like someone had severed a nerve, and half of me was
numb and useless. The emotional pain of separation was so great, I
felt an actual pain in my silent chest.

My hands were immediately on Teren's face; tears fell to the
ground in the space between us. "He's alive, Teren."

Teren peeled his gaze from the door to stare at me. I could see
the same painful hope I'd felt earlier blazing in his eyes. "What?"

I twisted him around to our daughter, silently crying on Ashley's
shoulder. "Nika feels him...he's alive."

Teren's jaw dropped as he looked up at the only connection to
our son. "Baby, is Julian okay?" he whispered, his voice warbling.

Hot tears sliding down her cheeks, she shrugged. "He's scared,
Daddy...really scared."

Teren closed his eyes, and moisture squeezed out between his
lashes. Lifting those wet lashes, he narrowed his eyes at Nika. "Is
he...hurt? Does he feel pain right now?"

Nika raised her head, tilted it, then slowly started shaking it.
"No...just scared."

Teren exhaled. Crumpling over, he dropped his face into his
hands. "Oh, thank God," he muttered. Glancing up at me, his voice
wavered as he said, "I thought, I thought he'd..."

Nodding, I tossed my arms around his waist. I'd thought that
too. We clung to each other as I felt his family draw even nearer.
Nika was still crying, so after we separated, we blurred up to her.
Feeling calmer now that I knew Julian was still breathing, that he
wasn't in pain, I pulled Nika from my sister. Her arms wrapped
around my neck as she attached to me. Teren's arms encircled us
both. Just as my mother and sister joined our group hug, the front
door burst open; it cracked the wall it hit it so hard. Both Mom and
Ashley jumped, but Teren, Nika and I only looked down. We'd felt

her approaching.

Halina flew into the entryway, and her eyes were on us immediately; there were blood red tear tracks down her pale white skin. "Teren?" was all she got out before her voice closed up.

Releasing us, Teren shook his head. "He's alive. Nika feels him."

"He's scared," I whispered, tears dripping off my chin.

Halina staggered, and her hands came up to her face as she swayed for a second. Then her head snapped up. "Where is he? Why can't we feel him?"

Teren looked back at our daughter. "We don't know," he whispered. Nika looked over to him and held her hands out. Teren scooped her up and walked her downstairs. As our entryway again filled back up with people, Teren stroked her back. She wrinkled her nose at the smell emanating from him, but didn't stop clutching him. Meeting eyes with his great-grandmother, Teren set his lips into a hard line. I could feel tension building in the air as I stepped beside him.

Imogen and Alanna flew into the house, both still dressed in pajamas like they'd been aroused in the middle of the night from a deep sleep. I supposed they had; Halina was the only Adams who stayed up all night long. Their questions filled the air as Teren stared at Halina.

"He's alive, just vanished," I told Alanna, enfolding her in a quick hug. She asked more questions, but her eyes were on her son who was having a stare down with the pureblood vampire.

When Imogen and Alanna's questions were answered to the best of my ability, which was mainly that we didn't know anything, we all turned to stare at Teren. His jaw was clenched as he unwaveringly stared at the teenage vixen. She unflinchingly stared back.

My mom ran her arms around Ashley. She asked what was going on, but no one answered her. In the quiet that followed, Teren asked in an oddly calm voice, "Did Gabriel do this?"

Halina blinked, pulling her head back in surprise. She eyed Teren up and down. "No," she confidently said.

Teren tilted his head. "Before he turned back, Julian was headed down south...to Gabriel."

Halina shook her head. "He did not do this."

Teren narrowed his eyes. "Who else could shut the bond off?"

Halina looked up at Nika, then back to Teren. "He wouldn't," she whispered.

As I held my breath, debating whether or not Teren was right, he leaned into Halina. "He's always wanted to test them, to test their bond. What better way than to take one?"

Halina looked around at all of us watching her. "No, he wouldn't...he couldn't." She added in a whisper. Her head snapped back to Teren. "He was busy with the raid."

Nika raised her head. "Monster, Daddy, not Grandpa."

Teren shushed her and stroked her hair. Not looking convinced, he kissed Nika's head and then twisted back to Halina. "Gabriel knows a lot of people. I wouldn't put it past him to 'ask' someone else to do it. Especially when we all assumed he was 'busy' with the raid. What better alibi could he have?"

Halina bristled, her back straightening. "He is not responsible for taking Julian, and we are wasting precious time."

Teren sniffed, then kissed Nika's head again. "I will end him if we find out differently." He pointedly raised an eyebrow at Halina.

Twisting her lip, Halina crossed her arms over her chest. "If he is involved, you won't get the chance." She raised her eyebrow right back at him, her intent clear. If Gabriel's hand was in any way involved with our son's disappearance, in love with him or not, she would destroy him.

Just then the front door slowly opened. Every vampire in the house turned to the silently swinging door with a growl in their chest. Teren handed Nika to my mom and blurred to the door. His hand cinched around the throat of the person walking through it. Halina joined him. Reaching out, she pulled the person all the way inside.

A scream was stifled as Teren's hand clenched around windpipes, then he was shoved back a step. Hands on her throat, a stunned Starla gazed at Teren wide-eyed. Standing in front of her, crouched down into a low, defensive position, Jacen was growling a warning at Teren and Halina.

The tension in the air grew as Starla rubbed her neck and looked around at everyone staring at her. Twisting her lips, she stepped up and popped a bubble in Teren's face. "That hurt, vamp boy."

His eyes narrowing, he lifted his chin. "What are you doing back here?"

Jacen stepped in front of the debutante. His blonde hair was disheveled like he'd also just woken up, although Jacen and Starla hadn't rushed over quite like the others. "We heard the commotion when everyone left the house." He paused, his sky blue eyes suddenly sheepish. "We're your protection...so...you know, we're here to...protect."

Halina scoffed and rolled her eyes, then she slammed the door shut so hard Nika flinched. Mom rubbed her back as Ashley cooed in her ear. Crossing her arms over her chest again, Halina muttered, "You're doing a great job."

Jacen glared at her as he circled his arm around Starla's trim waist. "We came as soon as we could."

Starla looked down. "We were...busy." Halina scoffed as she flicked a spritzed point of Starla's bedhead hair.

Teren ran a hand down his face as he looked around the assemblage. Focusing on Ashley, he pointed at the phone in the kitchen. "Call Ben," he twisted back to Alanna, "and call Dad." His pale eyes took in every other set of pale eyes, then they lingered on mine. "Tell them to get over here. We need everyone."

Running a hand through his hair, he darted towards the stairs as Ashley and Alanna moved to make phone calls. I watched him blurring up the stairs, and took a step to follow him. Halina grabbed my arm. "How could this happen? How could Julian leave your home undetected?"

I shook my head, guilt and remorse flooding me so fast I felt like I was drowning in it. "We were asleep, we didn't feel him leaving."

Her grip on my arm tightened. "Why didn't you hear it? He was right down the hall from you."

Tears splashed on my cheeks as I shook my head. Not able to hold her gaze, I closed my eyes. "We closed the door...I forgot to reopen it."

I dropped my head in my hands, and a sob broke out of me. Muttering encouragement to my sniffling daughter, Mom took Nika away. Walking into the living room with her, she turned on a movie. Over my sobs, I could hear Teren tossing things around in our bedroom and Alanna and Ashley on the phone. Starla and Jacen stood there forlornly, hands in their pockets and guilt on their faces. The guilt was in mine, too. I'd done this. I'd sent everyone away because I'd wanted an "empty" house for one night. It hadn't seemed like a big deal at the time; now it seemed monumental.

Imogen's arms were around me instantly. "Don't blame yourself, Emma. Accidents happen."

Surprisingly, Halina's grip on my arm turned comforting. "You couldn't have known..." Her voice drifted off as she sighed.

Halina let go of me and tilted her head upstairs. "If Nika was telling the truth, and he didn't wander off...there should be some clues upstairs. Some scent of who took him."

My head shot up as I stared at her wide-eyed. I hadn't really believed that a monster had swiped him. It seemed more rational that he'd wandered off. But if someone had, Halina was right; our advanced senses should pick up...something.

I blurred up the stairs past her.

Teren met us in the twins' room. The jungle play land theme seemed ominous in the dark. Our glows highlighted shapes and animals that were warm and cheery in the daylight, but the tiger crouching behind the tree screamed predator to me now.

Wearing a fresh shirt and sturdy shoes, Teren inhaled deep as he looked around. I instantly smelled the foreignness in the room. It seemed familiar, I just couldn't place it. We looked for anything out of place once Teren flipped the light on, but everything was exactly how we'd left it when we'd put the children to bed. Everything except the beds themselves. The covers were both pulled back, and both children were gone from them.

And Spike. He was different too. Having slept in the room all night with the children, since our bedroom door had been closed off to him, he was huddled under the bed; only his tail was visible. He crawled out when he smelled us in the room, his curvy tail slowly swishing back and forth. Walking up to me, he buried his head in my leg, almost like he, too, felt guilty for not doing a better job. I sympathetically petted the collie.

Teren's brow furrowed as Halina sniffed a stuffed animal on Julian's bed. Imogen smelled the curtains as I bit back the frustrated bile. Scents didn't exactly come with a driver's license. For the first time in a long time, I felt like a regular, unenhanced, helpless human being. I could only sense that someone had been here, but I didn't know who that person was. Teren's theory that Gabriel had "encouraged" someone to drop by was sounding more and more reasonable to me. Anger knotted my stomach, and I considered plunging a stake into the ancient vampire myself if he had.

From downstairs, I heard Jacen beating himself up for neglecting his responsibility and leaving. Starla encouragingly told him that there was no way he could have anticipated something like this, and Jacen told her that it wasn't an excuse. Sighing, he added, "I should let Gabriel know I failed."

Teren's head shifted from staring at Julian's bed to downstairs. A low growl came from his chest as Jacen punched numbers into his cell phone. Halina narrowed her eyes at Teren and seemed about to protest her boyfriend's innocence again, but Teren blurred out of the room. One of Julian's favorite army men fell from his hand and clattered to the floor as he did.

Taking one last look around, my eyes tearing up as I cataloged the strangely familiar scent permeating my home, I followed with Halina. Just as the line picked up and Jacen was about to say hello to Gabriel, Teren snatched the phone from the mixed vampire's hands.

His face contorted in anger, he snarled, "What did you do?"

Rushing to his side, I put a hand on his arm. We really didn't know if Gabriel was involved in this or not; best not to piss him off either way. Teren held gazes with me while Gabriel answered with, "I beg your pardon, Teren. What did I do...about what?"

Teren exhaled slowly, purposely. "Someone entered our home...took my son while we were all sleeping. Would you have anything to do with that?"

A long pause on Gabriel's end, then, "Julian is missing?"

Teren grit his jaw. "Yes," his voice warbled. "Did you have anything to do with it?"

As Alanna and Ashley finished with their phone calls and walked into the room, Gabriel answered matter-of-factly, "No, I did not."

Starla and Jacen kept their matching eyes to the ground, for once, no longer touching each other. Alanna and Imogen put their arms around me while Ash turned to sit with Mom and Nika in the living room; I could hear my mom humming and rocking my distraught daughter. Wanting to hug her myself, but needing to know what Gabriel knew, I stayed beside Teren, and watched his face flex in frustration.

In the pause of Teren gathering his thoughts, Halina stepped forward. Speaking at a normal volume, even though Teren was holding the phone, she asked, "Did you use me to get to my grandchildren?"

Gabriel's voice was immediate through the small device's speaker. "No."

Halina took another step forward. Her hands were in tight balls as she stood in front of Teren. Locking gazes with him, she asked Gabriel, "Did you use me to study my family?"

Again, Gabriel instantly answered her. "No."

Halina closed her eyes and looked about ready to grab the phone from Teren and scream into it. She didn't need to, though; everyone could hear her just fine. "Do not lie to me. If you, in any way, had something to do with Julian's disappearance..."

Gabriel sighed. "It wasn't me, my love. I did not take your grandchild."

Teren took over the conversation when Halina's face softened;

she so wanted to believe him. Teren needed more convincing. "Of course you did, of course you took him! Who else has the power and knowhow to steal him right out from under our noses? Who else knew about the soundproofing done to our room? Who else could shut off the bond so we can't feel him!"

Behind him, Starla and Jacen began to look very uncomfortable, like maybe Teren would think them guilty by association. I watched them intently, curious myself now.

Gabriel was silent as he paused. When his voice came out, it was scientifically curious. "You can't sense him anymore?"

Teren gripped the phone tighter. His eyes narrowed as he stared at our daughter in the other room, still being rocked by my mother. "No…only Nika can feel him."

"Fascinating." Gabriel whispered it, but I still heard him. A growl burrowed out of my chest, but Teren was the one who lost the hold on his temper.

"Exactly!" he yelled, making every vampire flinch. "You think it's fascinating! To you, this is all one giant experiment—which is why you took him!

Halina looked away, red tears stinging her eyes. Alanna dropped her arms from me and went to hold her emotional son. I ran my hands back through my hair, every second believing more and more that Gabriel was indeed capable of this.

Teren was right; he knew about the room. In fact, he'd given it to us. He'd supplied himself with an alibi, making sure his spies told us the raid was tonight, so we'd let our guard down. For all we knew, everything about Malcolm was a lie, a hoax to draw our attention away from him. The man we'd met at the theater could have been anybody. It was possible that Gabriel had already dealt with him, right after the lab trashing. It was even possible that there was no Malcolm. All of it could have been a lie. All for an experiment.

Gabriel wearily sighed into the phone as tension pricked the air. "Honestly, Teren, I did not. I would not separate a family against their will. True, their bond fascinates me, but I would not conduct an experiment of this magnitude on a child." He paused, then quietly said, "Do not forget that I am the reason he even made it to his birth.

I've only ever tried to help your family, Teren."

Teren closed his eyes as he angrily shook his head. "Right, how could I forget? You're constantly reminding us how valuable you are. The shots, the windows, finding Carr…finding people." He swallowed harshly, and his voice was shaking when he continued. "And all for nothing, right?" He sniffed as he reopened his eyes. "I don't believe it. No one does something for nothing. No one is that altruistic."

Alanna stroked her son's arm while we waited for Gabriel's response. Starla and Jacen shifted on their feet while Halina closed her eyes. "Teren, not everyone has ulterior motives," Gabriel said softly.

I watched my husband struggle to rein in his temper; his rational head was combating with his heart. Sometimes it was easier to yell when you were frustrated or scared—Teren was both. In a clipped voice, he said, "But *you* do. You did what you did for access, to study them because they *fascinate* you. You stay close to us to watch them. You've already admitted that much. If you orchestrated all of this to test their abilities, it will be the last experiment that you ever run…you have my word."

Gabriel sighed again. "If you find that I did have anything to do with this, I would let you do what you will with me. But I promise you, I did not." A short sniffle on Gabriel's end surprised me, along with the rare emotion in his voice when he spoke again. "Believe me or don't, but I love your children, Teren."

Teren's hand was shaking along with his voice when he responded to Gabriel's declaration. "Then who? Who else has the power to pull this off?" Alanna stroked Teren's back as she rested her dark head against his shoulder. Her eyes were moist with pink tears.

I clutched Imogen tight as the emptiness in my soul, where my son's presence should have been, hallowed out my heart. The absence of him was beyond any pain I'd ever felt. An ache of surprising dread filled me. If Gabriel really didn't have anything to do with it, then my son could be anywhere, with anyone. As much as it hurt, I almost would have preferred the idea of Gabriel snatching him for some sort of wacked out experiment. At least then I'd know that

Julian wouldn't be harmed. I believed Gabriel when he said he loved them.

Gabriel's voice was dark with heat when he answered Teren's seemingly unanswerable question. "I believe I know who has him, Teren."

Every somber, hanging head in the room lifted. A painful bubble of hope rose up my chest again as I locked gazes with my husband. His eyes were strained as well, and I could see the painful longing rising in him too. "Who?" I whispered, hoping he'd spout out an address for me.

Hearing me, Gabriel said, "The raid did not go as planned. I lost a few good men tonight," he paused and Jacen stepped forward, his face paler. I looked over at him with sympathy in my heart. Gabriel's "men" were Jacen and Starla's family. Starla grabbed his hand and stepped into his side as Gabriel continued. "We were able to wound him, but not grievously enough to stop him from automatically healing." Gabriel sighed, his voice rough. "We almost had him, Teren. None of this would have happened if we'd just gotten there sooner."

Teren started breathing again as he shook his head. "Are you saying...? Did...?"

Gabriel sighed as my husband couldn't complete any of his questions. "Yes...this is my fault, Teren. Not because I planned it, but because I made him so desperate, that he felt he had no other choice. I'm sorry, I really didn't think he'd go after you, and I'm not sure what his intentions are with Julian, but...yes...I believe Malcolm has taken your son."

A deep growl rose from Teren's chest and as his eyes flashed to the front door, I barely recognized my husband. He only spoke one word, but it chilled me to the core. "Malcolm."

The smell upstairs instantly linked with a memory. That man by the movie theaters. His scent had been faint in the breeze and faint on the paper, but now that the two were linked, they perfectly matched. The thief that Gabriel was chasing had somehow, and for some reason, snuck into our home and taken our child. I couldn't see why, and I didn't really care. I wanted Julian back—that was the only thing I cared about.

Eyes still on the door, Teren growled into the phone, "Are you close?" When Gabriel answered that he could be there within the hour, Teren nodded. "Good, get here. We have work to do." Then he snapped shut the phone and tossed it at a remorseful Jacen.

Teren scanned our home. His pale eyes clearly showed a spinning mind. Like a skipping CD player, my mind was shuffling too, thoughts and feelings continually shifting from one to the next; none of them were helpful. A second of silence passed as we all watched Teren, then Halina stepped forward, and everyone's attention shifted to her. "What are we going to do, Teren?"

He twisted around to her. His eyes simmered as determination and righteous anger flooded his expression. Lips curling into a snarl, he growled out, "We're going to get my son back."

Chapter 18 – Three Days

They say the first forty-eight hours are the most critical when it comes to finding a missing person. I wasn't sure if that still applied when the missing person was a vampire who had been abducted by a desperate man with a grudge, but that feeling of time ticking forward still added tension and fear to our house. And we couldn't ask for outside help, either. It wasn't as if I could go on the news, plastering Julian's face and description all over every television in America. That sort of exposure was too difficult to contain. We didn't let people remember our features. How on earth would Halina wipe millions of viewers?

But we did have a home full of eager helpers and we did have a pretty good idea of who'd taken Julian. That was confirmed when Gabriel showed up at our house. Stepping into the twins' room, his nose immediately wrinkled. "Yes, that is Malcolm's scent. He was here." Gabriel's face stormed up with genuine anger and he looked ready to tear apart…something.

Halina's arms slipped around him, and she buried her face in his chest. "I knew you didn't do this," she whispered as he held her.

With Gabriel now in our search party, rather than on the suspect list, Teren started barking out orders. With Hot Ben glued to his side, Teren pointed at Gabriel, Jacen and Starla. "You three check down south. He was headed that way before he turned back. I want to know why."

Starla and Jacen immediately nodded and blurred off. Jacen looked eager to get away from Gabriel's turbulent eyes. While Gabriel hadn't chided him directly, there were more than a few narrowed glances when it became obvious to him that Jacen had ignored his orders and left us alone. The guilt swept over me again. I'd asked and encouraged the mixed pair to leave.

Watching his family depart, Gabriel twisted back to Teren. "He wouldn't have headed south with Julian, Teren. He wouldn't have headed towards my nest." He raised an eyebrow as he crossed his arms over his chest.

Teren sighed as he sat on the couch, his slacks were still filthy from his earlier search for our son. "Then why head that way?"

Gabriel smirked and shook his head. "So you would think that I took him." Looking out the large window overlooking the ocean, he narrowed his ancient eyes. "Maybe he hoped that if he placed you on my tail, you wouldn't suspect him. And that did work…for a second."

I sighed as I paced and Gabriel looked over at me. "His switching direction is the key. He did that intentionally, so when he shut the bond off, you wouldn't know where to look."

Stepping forward, I shook my head. "How did he turn off the bond? I didn't think that was even possible."

Tilting his head, Gabriel's eyes shifted up, as if he were accessing a different part of his brain. "I've never attempted it, but it is possible that he has come up with something that naturally inhibits the beacon, if you will." He shrugged. "Honestly, I don't know. Halting the conversion has been my focus for years, not the bond." He sighed. "But Malcolm was my assistant for centuries for a reason. He's ingenious and resourceful…when motivated to be."

Teren sighed as he looked around at the remaining family members. "So, since he tried misdirecting us before he yanked the bond away…where do we look?"

Gabriel pointed north. "I'll check that direction." He looked over to Halina. "You check east, as far as you can." Halina nodded, confident that she'd be the one to find him. She blurred away to begin her search while Gabriel twisted back to Teren. "You two stay here to protect the rest of your family."

Standing, Teren shook his head; Hot Ben stood with him. "I'm not just sitting around while Julian is alone out there. I can't do that."

Alanna stood with Jack and Imogen. "We will take everyone to the ranch, Teren." Alanna looked over at her husband, then her mother. "Between the three of us, Nika, Linda, and Ashley, will have night and day protection there."

Jack walked over to Teren, his warm brown eyes full of barely contained emotion. Placing his hand on Teren's shoulder, he nodded at the door. "Go find your son." That was all the encouragement

Teren needed. He blurred out without another word.

I gasped as his presence streaked away from me. Looking a little lost as to what he should do, Hot Ben ran his hands through his hair. Since he couldn't move as quickly as we could or follow a scent like we could, he probably felt a little...human.

Placing a hand on his shoulder, I forced myself to smile. He looked over at me, and a sigh escaped his lips when he guessed what I was about to say. "I'm sorry, Ben, but you won't be able to search with us." I cringed. "You're just not...equipped like we are, and we can't wait for you."

He hung his head, and Ashley came up to put a hand on his back. Leaning down to his face, I added, "But we'd really appreciate you looking anyway. If you want to drive around the city, ask around if anyone saw anything...weird recently." My hand came up to stroke his face. "I know Teren would really appreciate that."

Ben's jaw set in determination, now that I had given him a task he could handle. Nodding at me, he said, "I won't let you down, Emma. I won't stop looking."

Tears pricked my eyes as I watched the brave man leave. It was almost hard to imagine a time when Ben had been a shivering, cowardly mess of a man who'd thought Teren wanted to eat him. Saying quick goodbyes, he dashed out after Teren at a much slower pace.

Gabriel put a hand on my shoulder. "I'll be north, Emma, if you need anything." He patted his pocket. "I'll call...if I find him."

I was still nodding when he phased away.

Twisting back to the Adams and Taylors still left in the house, I shrugged and said, "I can't stay either. I need to do...something." I felt my husband's presence drifting away from me, to the very outskirts of the city, and I longed to follow.

My eyes rested on my daughter, though, who had finally cried herself to sleep on my mother's lap. Looking worn herself, Mom lazily stroked circles onto Nika's back. "Go, Emma," she whispered, her eyes locking onto mine. "We'll be safe." Her eyes flicked up to Alanna's and the vampire smiled with her fangs exposed.

Cocking an eyebrow at me, Alanna seriously said, "No one will harm them." Smiling around her teeth, she added, "Don't forget, Halina is a part of me, too."

I nodded and gave her and the rest of my family a hug. I lingered on my sleeping daughter last, placing soft kisses in her hair. She stirred under my cool touch, but remained asleep. Dried tear tracks were clear to me, and I lightly brushed them off her cheeks. A part of me wanted to wake her, to ask her if she could still feel Julian, but I didn't. I let her get her rest, and hoped that whatever the reason was for Malcolm taking our child, hurting him wasn't his intention.

I ran to where I could feel Teren, at the edge of the bay. The smell of saltwater assaulted my nose as I dashed along the sandy beaches. I moved so fast, I barely left an impression in the dunes. I found my husband searching under a pier. His eyes scanned every nook and cranny of the dark wood, looking for any trace of a child, ours or not. The faint glow of his eyes turned to me as the sweetness of our bond announced my arrival. He didn't even crack a smile. He only nodded, his lips set in a hard line. I nodded back, and together, we began the futile search for our son.

It was like looking for a needle in a haystack, we both knew that, but our only other alternative was to sit at home and do nothing. Nothing wasn't an option for us, so we searched. We ran in short bursts throughout the city, searching every hidey-hole that was large enough to place a toddler. We looked through every home and business that was open, and quite a few that weren't. Then we streaked away to the next location. It was tiring, searching and streaking with no real direction.

I checked in with my family often, tracked my daughter and the rest of the girls as they shifted east, to the ranch. It brought me a little peace to know that my loved ones were on high alert now; that meant that another swiping was unlikely, not without a fight at least. But the majority of me was starting to feel despair, and fatigue. The endless searching of hundreds of miles was an impossible task. And our bodies weren't designed to maintain super speed. By the next evening, I had to walk, I just couldn't phase anymore. And I was starving; Teren and I had searched all day without pause.

Feeling aches in areas of my body that I didn't know could even ache, I put a hand on his arm as he shifted to streak to a new location. "Teren, stop, I can't…" Even though I didn't need it, my breath was hard from the exertion.

Teren looked back at me, his breathing was harder too, but determination and a stubborn refusal to give up masked the weariness on his face. "Go home, Emma. Rest."

He twisted and lunged, but I still held him tight. "What about you? You need rest, too."

Glancing down his body, I clearly saw the grime and tear marks of hours of frantic searching. I knew that I was equally disheveled, but I didn't really care, my son was out there in the world somewhere. Teren sighed as he looked back at me. "Go home, get something to eat…I just want to check out one more spot, then I'll be right behind you." He peeled my fingers off of his arm, and then he was gone. I knew he was just as tired as me, but pure love-filled panic was driving him. I had no idea how long it would drive him, before he keeled over.

When two more entire days passed, and Teren still hadn't come back to rest or eat, I started to worry about him. When our forty-eight hour window closed on us, Teren's search had actually picked up pace, and length. Having given up on the city, he blurred up the coast. He hadn't gotten any leads to send him that way. He was just picking a location and doing the best he could. Feeling that my child was closer to home, I stayed in the city. I kept running back home, to see if any more blood written letters had been left for us, but we heard nothing from the kidnapper. For all we knew, he wasn't speaking…because Julian wasn't alive any more. It was hard to negotiate the return of a deceased person. That thought chilled my icy flesh though, so I forced the hope back into my body. There was no point in killing Julian, so he wouldn't.

I repeated that to myself every ten seconds in a never-ending loop.

Finishing a thermos sized glass of blood to keep my strength up, I mentally checked in on my husband. A euphoria building in my chest told me that he was on his way back to the city, back to me. I closed my eyes and felt for him, hoping beyond hope that he'd run home and tell me he'd found…something. I briefly considered calling him, but then his presence shifted east, and I knew he was only picking out a new location. Nothing had changed.

Our son had been missing for over seventy-two hours, and *nothing* had changed.

Feeling so weary that my enhanced body no longer felt real, I wondered what my husband must be feeling. He hadn't slept or eaten. I'd asked. Every time I called him or met up with him, he told me that he just wanted to check out one more place, and then he'd come home and get something to eat. That one place led to one more place, then another and another, and he still hadn't rested. If I was running on fumes, Teren was running on pure will power.

Wanting to help him in some way, I poured some warm blood into the largest sized thermos we had. Our supplies at the house were starting to dwindle. We kept about a month's supply in the freezer, with a couple of days' worth of fresh stuff in the fridge. It had been time to go "shopping" at the ranch when Julian had been taken. We'd just been too busy to think about it since then. I wasn't too worried though. We wouldn't be reduced to snacking on pets when we had fields of fresh cattle under an hour away. But still, keeping a full fridge was one of those little mundane things that had to be done, regardless of the horror we were facing. Like paying the bills, some aspects of life didn't care if my world was falling apart.

Like my job. I'd completely forgotten all about the fact that life was still progressing around me and I was expected to show up to work. Hot Ben had been my saving grace there. He called me when Tracey started asking where I was. I called her back with a fanciful story of a family member suddenly passing and a funeral I needed to go to a state over. I'd sobbed into the phone with Tracey, my depression completely real, even if my story wasn't. She'd offered her condolences and promised up and down that she'd get everything squared away with HR, even if she had to backdate a vacation request. She told me she loved me, and I returned the sentiment while silently thanking her for all the times she'd made me feel better without even realizing it.

Getting in my car, since I was too tired to run, I made my way to where Teren was. I forcefully ignored the back seat. I couldn't look at the car seat where my son should have been safely buckled. I couldn't stomach seeing his favorite truck wedged between the cushions. I couldn't even stomach listening to the radio. My car was silent as I drove along, but I still heard Russian nursery songs in my head. Everything, everywhere, reminded me of him. Every section of my silent heart burned.

When I found Teren, I shut the car off and stared at him in shock. The man before me was not my husband. Walking out of an abandoned building that looked like it had once been a grocery store, he staggered on his feet. He looked like he'd just stepped out of a war zone. While his face was lifted and his eyes were in my direction, I didn't think he saw me. His clothes were torn, streaked with blood and dirt. His walk was haphazard, like he was going to collapse at any moment. But none of that compared to his face. I'd never seen a look of such hopeless desolation on his face before. He'd never looked that way, not even when my fate had been in question.

Even with the space between us, I could see the weariness, the straight-to-the-bone exhaustion. But still, he moved with determination. With a limp of an old man, he trudged out to the parking lot. I blurred over to him, thermos tightly held under my arm. My hands went to his cheeks as he blinked at me with blank eyes, like he didn't recognize me. "Good God, Teren."

"Emma?" he croaked out, his voice sounding dry.

Worried that he really hadn't stopped anywhere to eat, I unscrewed the thermos lid. His eyes instantly fixated on it. "You haven't stopped moving in three days, have you? Have you slept? Eaten?"

He didn't answer me, only wavered on his feet and stared at the drink in my hands. Once the smell of blood hit the air, his fangs dropped down. A weak growl rose from his chest as he snatched the mug from me, and tipped it up to his lips. In his eagerness, he tipped it back a little too far and the blood spilled down his chin, staining his caked-with-mud shirt. Gulping hungrily, he didn't seem to care.

My eyes watered as I watched him. Both hands on the thermos, he didn't stop drinking until it was empty. I suddenly wished I'd brought more with me. Lowering the mug, he swiped his sleeve over his mouth. His eyes more alert, he locked gazes with me. "Thank you," he whispered, his voice a little stronger too.

My hands stroked his cheeks, and my thumbs wiped some soot off of them. "Come home. Take a break, rest, and then you can set off again."

He immediately shook his head, but his body was teetering like he was going to fall over. "I can't."

Biting my lip, I shook my head. "You're no good to him dead on your feet. Rest, sleep…please."

His eyes looked past me, to the infinite places our son could be tucked. The world had never seemed as large to me as it did right at that minute. We could literally search for him forever and never find him, not with the bond shut off. Teren's pale eyes shimmered with tears as he took in the vastness around us. "I can't go home. I can't leave him…alone."

I felt the tears sliding down my face as his eyes returned to mine. "You haven't been eating." I ran my fingers along the soft spot under his eye. "You're running on empty," I whispered. "Just come home and have some more blood." I pointed at the thermos clenched in his hand. "When was the last time you ate?"

He shook his head. "When was the last time *he* ate?" More tears fell down my cheeks as I shook my head. I didn't want to think about that. I wanted to picture Julian full and healthy, even happy…though Nika often told me that he was still scared.

Teren took a step and staggered, and my arms went around him. Holding him tight to me, I summoned all of the strength I had. "You *are* coming home with me. You're eating and resting. You can't search for our son if you can't even stand." He pulled away from me, shaking his head, and I gripped his chin; the stubble was coarse under my fingers. "You could see him and pass right over him, you're so exhausted."

He opened his mouth to object, then shut it. Running my hands back through his hair, I soothingly said, "At least come with me to the ranch to see your daughter. She misses you. Mom says she cries all the time, feeling Julian's fear. Come home, hug her, let her know that we're still here…for her." I kissed his forehead. "She needs us, too," I whispered.

Closing his eyes, tears squeezed out and dripped down his dirty cheeks. "All right, I'll come home," he whispered, his voice breaking midsentence.

I was leading him back to my car when the wind shifted. A familiar scent was on it and my head snapped up. Teren's did too. Across the empty lot a man was patiently standing in a bright shaft of sunlight, watching us. He was lean, lanky, horrible disheveled, slightly bloody, and instantly familiar.

A rumble in my husband's chest was followed by one word, "Malcolm." Then he used the last of his strength and blurred across the lot. The empty thermos crashed to the ground as he dropped it. I was a pace behind him. Fear and anger gave Teren a new reserve of strength and he tackled the man who'd taken our son. By the time I got there, Teren was holding him down, and his hands were clenching his throat tight.

"Where's my son?" he barked, the streaks of blood down his chin only emphasizing the viciousness in his eyes. For a moment, I thought Teren might start ripping limbs off of Malcolm until he got an answer. He'd tortured before for a loved one, and this time, it wouldn't horrify me if he did it again. I might even help.

Not needing the air that Teren was cutting off, the undead mixed vampire in his grasp only smiled. He pointed to his windpipe with a raised eyebrow. Teren eased up on his throat, but leaned over him; his face trembled in his rage. "Where's my son?" he asked again, colder.

Malcolm continued smiling at him. "This is certainly no way to begin introductions. There used to be an art to it. Makes me miss the old days." One thin lip curved up into a devilish grin as he suggestively raised his eyebrows. "And truly, I like to get to know a person a little better before being this intimate."

Teren's hand shoved Malcolm's chin up, exposing his throat. His fangs dropped down as a growl rumbled out of his throat. "You don't want to get to know me. What have you done with my son?"

Malcolm rolled his eyes at the display, then flatly said, "The rugrat is fine, but he won't be, if you don't back off."

Teren eased up a little. His entire body shook with the restraint to not rip the man to pieces. "I will shove a stake right through you if you've hurt him," he growled.

Malcolm laughed. "Oh, big man." His hazel eyes flicked up to me. They were narrow-set, making his face seem as thin as the rest of him. "I bet that turns you on? I bet you find that sexy?"

A growl of my own ripped through the lot as I took a step towards him. Maybe *I'd* start the torture. Malcolm's amusement ended as he snapped his attention back to Teren. "Now, get off me, unless you never want to see your son again."

Teren flexed his jaw. Lifting Malcolm's head up a bit, he slammed it back to the concrete; the crack it made was distinct to my sharp ears. Malcolm flinched and hissed. "Start talking, where is he?" Teren held him down when Malcolm started to genuinely struggle to get up.

His fangs dropping down, Malcolm's eyes blazed with anger. "You will never find the hole I shoved that brat into if you do not get off me right now!"

Teren hissed back at him, his fangs getting longer. "I can make you talk, I've had practice."

Malcolm snorted, his fangs receding. "Yes, I've heard all about your 'talks' with vampires." Teren blinked and pulled back, his fangs pulling back as well. Sniffing, Malcolm looked between Teren hovering over him and me standing beside him. "You probably could make me speak, it's true." His hazel eyes narrowed at Teren while his thin lips hardened into a straight line. "But, can you break me...in time?"

I stopped breathing as I watched the worn vampire under my husband. Everything about him screamed exhaustion and desperation—the bloody tears in his worn clothes, the ratted, dirty light brown hair, the streaks of grime on his deceptively youthful face. As Teren was just as dirty and disheveled, I thought their physical levels of wear might be closely matched.

Teren sat up a little, backing off. Malcolm sat up on his elbows. Glancing between the two of us again, he put on a confident smile. "You see, I was a little quick to stash the child," he focused on Teren, "for obvious reasons, and I didn't really leave him much food or water." Looking up at the clear blue sky that didn't seem to bother him at all, he shook his head. "Come to think of it, I'm not sure when the snot ate last." His cold eyes came back to me. "I haven't been around much."

My vision of a fat, happy Julian was suddenly popped. Now I pictured him in a dark hole, scared and starving. I couldn't remember how long a person could go without food or water. A series of threes thudded through my brain—three minutes without air, three days without water, three weeks without food? Was that it? I had no idea. Even still, I knew dying that way would be excruciatingly painful. I started hyperventilating.

Teren lost it. His fist came around and bashed into the man's face. I could hear the cartilage snap as his nose shattered; blood spurted everywhere. Malcolm cried out, more annoyed than anything, and shoved Teren back, hard. Weak from lack of food and sleep, Malcolm managed to get him off and he blurred to standing before I could stop him.

While Teren started to stand, losing his balance and falling back to the cement, Malcolm adjusted his nose. He sniffed when it was healed. Pointing at Teren still on the ground, he snarled, "You get one, vampire. That was it!"

I helped Teren stand up. Both of us were shaky from the news that we were still trying to absorb. "Why take a child? What do you want?" Teren feebly muttered.

Malcolm shrugged as he adjusted his threadbare clothes. "What do any of us want? A safe place to lay our heads. A few warm blooded bodies to nibble on." His lips curled up into a smirk as he wiped some blood off his chin. "Gabriel's heart, staked to a platter."

Teren and I flicked a quick glance at each other while Malcolm crossed his arms over his chest. "You see, here's the thing." Reaching down, he picked two rocks off the ground. Holding one up, he said, "I have a problem," he lifted the other one up, "and you have a problem." He made the two rocks touch each other as he smiled at us. "Perhaps we can work together to solve both our problems."

Finding the strength to stand tall, Teren grasped my hand; I could feel the tension in him. He took a confident step forward. "My only problem...is you," he spat out.

Malcolm rolled his eyes and sighed in irritation. "Hmmm...well, my problem, since I can see you're so choked up about it, is that I have a very determined vampire on my tail." Smirking, he lifted the grayer of the two rocks. "Picture this, five years ago, I was living my life, minding my own business. I had a lucrative little career that afforded me an opulent home and a small bevy of beautiful human hangers-on." He lifted the darker of the two stones. "But then, some asshole vampire killed one of my clients. Then that same do-gooder ran to my ex-partner and clued him in on the fact that his research wasn't exactly destroyed, like he'd thought."

He took the dark rock and flung it towards the abandoned building; it shattered the front window. Scowling, he looked back at us. "Now, a very powerful, pissed off vampire, is scouring the earth looking for me. And his form of justice is old school—we're talking no jury, no judge, and definitely no lawyers! Only an execution awaits me!"

Teren lifted his chin. I tried to do the same but my entire body was shaking. "We don't want any part in your fight with him. It has nothing to do with us. Let my son go."

Malcolm snorted, palming the gray rock. "He was oblivious to my activities, for decades, until you drew him a path right to me. That makes you a pretty big part of this." He sighed as he bounced the rock from hand to hand. "And now that asshole won't let me be. He's got every spare set of eyes in his cult looking for me. And his influence extends everywhere. For years I've managed to escape him, but he's tenacious and vindictive. I'm broke, and I'm tired," his eyes flashed back to us, "and I'm done running." He snapped his wrist and the other rock sailed away, smashing another window in the abandoned building.

Loathing for the man in front of me gave my voice heat. "You brought this on yourself! You betrayed your own kind."

His eyes slid to mine, and he seemed as cold and unfeeling as vampires were generally portrayed. "I watched him flounder around with his 'miracle' drug for over three hundred years. His pipe dream was never going to work. He was never going to stop conversions...but that didn't stop him from trying." He rolled his eyes and wearily started to pace before us. "All he did accomplish was converting vampires before their time."

Malcolm shrugged. A bloody section of his shirt lifted to reveal a long tear, like he'd been sliced open recently. "And what do I care if vampires convert early? We all have to do it sometime. We are all destined to convert." His hands rested on his hips as he stopped and glared at us. "What do I care when it happens?"

Teren stepped forward, the memories of his own conversion clear on his features. "You sold it to hunters. You let them kill our kind with it." His face twisted into a snarl and he looked like he wanted to spit at Malcolm's feet. "How could you condemn our brothers and sisters?" Teren lifted his free hand into the air; the anger in his face shifted to incredulity. "My God, they used it on children!"

Malcolm only tilted his head and raised a shoulder. "Hey, I'm a businessman. I saw a very small niche with very deep pockets." He raised an eyebrow at Teren as he sat back on his hip. "You would not believe what some hunters will pay for this crap." His hand made a circle in the air while his lips twisted derisively. "They prefer killing us when we're more like monsters to them." A small smirk touched his lips as a light laugh left him. "Killing us with a heartbeat is apparently 'unsavory.' Less sinful if we're dead, I guess." He shrugged.

Teren's mouth set in a firm line while his brow deepened to a sharp point. I felt like walking over and taking a swing at the weary vampire, to smack the sneering grin off his face, but I had to remind myself that he had my son, and only he knew where Julian was. We couldn't afford angering him, so that he left without telling us where he'd stashed him, especially since we now knew that he'd left Julian with practically nothing.

Seeing our silent conflict, Malcolm coldly smiled and resumed his pacing. "I needed to make a living, away from Gabriel and his followers. I found a demand, a very lucrative one." He theatrically tossed his hands in the air as he shook his head. "But Gabriel's shut down every production lab I had." Malcolm flexed his body as he stalked back and forth; his wiry muscles were tight with anger and frustration. "He destroyed every vial I ever recreated," he paused to smirk at us, "so I returned the favor and destroyed his. I sent him a warning—penetrated his sanctuary, trashed his worthless research." He spat on the ground like he was spitting on Gabriel's grave.

My mind instantly flashed to my own conversion, to Starla's situation. Malcolm had almost permanently killed the prissy vampire by destroying all of Gabriel's work. I stepped forward a couple of spaces until Teren's hand held me back. "You idiot! Those actually did work! He was saving lives with his research." I patted my chest while tears stung my eyes. Thinking of my miracle children, alive only because of Gabriel, I spat out, "He saved us!"

Malcolm snorted and Teren pulled me back to stand beside him. Teren's arm went around my waist, twisting me to him, and Malcolm raised his lip in a sneer. "I don't really care about saving people. I care about remaining alive, and if Gabriel keeps this up, I won't be."

He took a few steps towards us; he was so close I could have reached out and touched him. The smell coming off of him was musty, like he'd been in dark, dingy places lately. "Gabriel won't leave me alone, so yeah, I trashed his lab. But that didn't stop him, so I upped the ante, torched his little human bitch." Malcolm's lips twisted on the harsh word, and his green-brown eyes roamed up and down our bodies. "But he still didn't get the message, so I decided to be a little more proactive." He shook his head wearily, and his eyes softened and aged. "I'm tired. I'm tired of running. I warned him to stay away. I warned him this would happen. I told him there would be bloodshed." His aged eyes hardened right back up.

Teren dropped his hold on me. Tilting his head, he stepped towards Malcolm; Malcolm took a step back. "You what? What human?" As I looked over Teren's quickly darkening face, I thought over what Malcolm had just said—torched his little human. Torched? My eyes widened as Teren took another step towards the man who had our son.

Backing up another step, Malcolm shrugged. "Some girl. He had a vampire I was watching compel her to fly all the way to California for him." He rolled his eyes while Teren stood stone still. "I figured she was important, so I followed. I figured he was grooming her for a changeover, maybe even going to attempt one himself. So once I finished with his lab, I snatched the little human and got rid of her before he could convert her—to teach him a lesson."

In a whisper, my husband said, "Carrie? You killed…Carrie?"

Malcolm smirked and shrugged. "Maybe. I didn't exactly ask her

name first. It was more a grab and go, if you know what I mean. "
Teren's jaw tightened and his fists clenched. Malcolm noticed. He
cocked his head in curiosity. "I held her for a while, snacking, waiting
to see what Gabriel would do. When it was clear he wasn't letting up,
I thought about tossing the little imp on his doorstep after I'd
drained her, to prove my point, but then I decided a public fire would
be more...poetic."

Teren's face exploded in anger, and a rush of adrenaline gave his
worn body a second of strength. Striding forward, he shoved
Malcolm, hard. The elder vampire was caught off guard and smacked
onto the ground. I blurred to Teren's side, holding him back from
pummeling Malcolm to pieces; sadly, we needed him alive.

Breathing heavy, Teren hovered over him. "She wasn't here for
him. She was here for me. She was innocent!"

Malcolm spat out a wad of blood; he'd bit himself when he'd
landed so harshly. "Who on this earth is truly innocent?" he growled.
Standing slowly as Teren tried to rein in his anger again, he gave him
a cold smirk. "I saw her on your doorstep, you know. Touching little
moment there. I figured he was sharing his plaything with his 'pet'
before he brought her into the fold." Chuckling to himself, he shook
his head. "Watching her led me to you."

 He walked around Teren while he quivered with restraint. "I
specifically made sure that Gabriel would find out about her, about
what I'd done. Who do you think anonymously led the police to find
her body? And I knew that once she was identified, Gabriel would
figure it out. Gabriel doesn't believe in coincidences."

Leaning in close, so he could whisper in Teren's ear, it was
obvious Malcolm was enjoying taunting Teren. "I fed on her for a
couple weeks, keeping her just on the edge of death. And, just for
him, I left her alive enough that she would feel every lick of the
flames, but weak enough that she couldn't do anything about it.
Message delivered."

Malcolm cocked his head. "How ironic, then, that she was here
for you and I decided to give you the note written in her blood. Kind
of fitting, actually." He laughed and Teren lost his control. He lunged
at Malcolm, but Malcolm was ready this time. He blurred just out of
reach, then raised his hand in warning. "Back off. I said you get *one*,

vampire." His eyes narrowed as he looked between the two of us. "And now that you know I will kill, don't think I won't again." He raised an eyebrow, pointedly. "Only this time, I won't be killing a fully grown woman...I'll be killing your son."

"You son of a bitch," Teren murmured, his hand reaching down to clench mine.

Malcolm shrugged. "Yeah, I'll give you that one." He tilted his head as he walked to the other side of us. "But Gabriel is worse. My warnings seem to make no difference to him." His expression irritated, he studied the ground. "He's cold, relentless and he's after my hide. He won't stop chasing me now. Not until I'm dead...or he is." Nodding to himself, he added, "That's the only way I can disappear. The only way I'll ever find peace again." Looking up, he pointed at Teren. "The only way to get him to stop hunting for me is if I hunt him first."

Teren shook his head, disgusted. "Maybe you should have thought of that before you went up against him."

Malcolm narrowed his eyes. "He went against us first. You think he's so perfect. You think he's some miraculous saint, because he finally, after hundreds of years, got his drug to work on a handful of vampires?" He pointed at Teren. "You probably call him Father too, don't you?" He looked Teren up and down, his face twisting to match the disgust in Teren's expression. "Just like his other mindless drones."

Lifting his hand, he pointed south, to where Gabriel's nest lay. "He's not perfect. He's not a saint. He's a coldly calculating scientist who will stop at nothing to get his end result." Malcolm raised an eyebrow and took a step forward. "Do you know how many I've watched die because of him? Because of his obsession?" He shook his head and his thin mouth tightened. "Unlike human labs, we didn't exactly have rats to conduct tests on." Looking between Teren and me, he lowered his voice to a growl. "He used vampires, living vampires. Ask him how many died before he got to the drug that merely jumpstarted the conversion."

I forcefully pushed aside what he was saying about Gabriel. I knew Gabriel was determined enough to do the things Malcolm was saying, but I didn't believe he was as cold as Malcolm was making him sound. The odds were pretty good that Gabriel had made some mistakes in the past few hundred years, but I was sure he felt badly about them…unlike Malcolm, who only seemed to care about, well, Malcolm.

My eyes narrowed as I took in the weary, chatty man who had one of my reasons for being stored up in a hole somewhere, terrified. Wishing I could shake Julian's location out of him, I sarcastically spat out, "Is that what he did to you? Did Gabriel accidently kill someone you loved and stealing from him was your pathetic attempt at revenge?" I eyed the dirty man up and down. My breath was heavy as anger consumed me. "Is that why you hate him so much?"

Malcolm only gave me a blank stare. "Who said I hated him? No, if I hated him, I'd have tried to kill him ages ago." He leaned into me, and Teren stepped between us, shielding my body. I could nearly smell the desperation leech off Malcolm as he coldly said, "Don't romanticize me. I just wanted away from him." Smirking at Teren's protective display, he took a step back. "This has nothing to do with a woman. This is no he-killed-my-lover-and-I-want-revenge fight." His voice dropped as he narrowed his eyes at us. "He's a power hungry cult leader and I wanted out from under him." He cocked his lip and shook his head. "The drug was my ticket to being on my own with pockets full of cash, nothing more. I saw an opportunity and I took it."

Still in front of me, Teren shook his head. "How sad, that all it took was money for you to stab your species in the back."

Malcolm dryly replied with, "Don't forget the freedom part." Rolling his eyes, he shook his head. "And don't give me that high and mighty crap. Humans stab each other in the back daily, for far pettier reasons." Stepping towards us, he put both his hands on his narrow hips. "But my motives aren't really the point, are they? The point is, I need you to do something for me and you *are* going to do it."

Malcolm held his ground before us, and even though Teren was weak and exhausted, he lifted his chin, holding his ground as well. "What could you possibly want from me?"

A slow smile spread over Malcolm's face, and his eyes brightened for the first time since we'd started talking to him. With chilling coldness, the smile stretched across all of his haggard features before he spoke. And when he did, I wished he hadn't. "You are going to kill Gabriel for me."

Teren and I glanced at each other, shocked beyond words. Malcolm smiled even wider, seeing our stunned reactions. Looking over Teren's startled features, then mine, he shrugged. "You help me. I help you—tit for tat. See how it works? It's a win-win for both of us."

Too dazed to speak, I could only gape at the clearly mad person before us. Teren somehow found a way to still be articulate. "I knew you were off, but I didn't realize you were completely insane."

Malcolm narrowed his eyes. "Am I? You're in his inner circle now. He knows you. He trusts you. He would never see it coming from you. You can get close...and finish him."

His body quivering with fatigue and stress, Teren gritted his jaw. "No, never."

Lifting one corner of his lip, Malcolm leaned towards us and whispered, "Really? Do I need to remind you that I have your son?" Shaking his head, he shrugged again. "And thanks to my own unique, and quite brilliant concoction, you can't track him."

Teren looked back at me. Fear and dread were in his eyes; I had to believe they were in mine too. As we stared at each other, Malcolm let out a cold laugh. "You *will* kill Gabriel for me...because you have no other choice."

Pulling my gaze from Teren, I stepped around him. "Please, let Julian go. He's a child, he's innocent." Teren tried to pull me behind him again, but I dropped his hands and grabbed Malcolm's dusty jacket. "Take me...let him go, and take me."

Malcolm brushed me off as Teren said, "No," and grabbed my elbows. Twisting his lips at me, Malcolm took a step back. "I did consider that, I truly did. But you made it so easy for me to snatch the child, I couldn't resist." He locked eyes with Teren; his arms were now firmly around me. "Soundproofing your room? Brilliant, and kind of," he tilted his head, his smile languid, "how would they say it now...hot."

Raising his eyebrows suggestively, he let that sink in a moment before adding, "Children are more manageable. Plop them in one place and they tend to stay there. That stupid woman was always trying to get away. But you should consider yourselves lucky. I did leave you the girl, after all." He leaned forward, an eyebrow raised. "Do you really need two?"

Teren let go of me, lunged forward, and clutched Malcolm's clothes in his fists. I pulled at his arms, but he had Malcolm tight; the last of his strength was in the effort. "You're dead!"

Malcolm laughed as he calmly placed his hands over Teren's. "Very true, and so are you…" he looked over at me, "and you." Unclenching Teren's hands, he calmly took a step away from us. "You have three days or I snap your son's neck." Cocking his lip, he shrugged. "Or maybe…I'll just leave him in his cubby hole and let him starve." Lifting his eyes to the pale sky that matched our son's eyes, he pondered aloud, "Or maybe, just for fun, I'll raise him as my own…and teach *him* to kill Gabriel." He looked back down at us. "Since I can't successfully turn people and I can't have my own kids, maybe I'll just steal an army of them?"

Teren tried to grab him again, but he staggered and dropped to his knees, all of his energy gone. Malcolm chuckled as he stepped in front of him and looked down on his exhausted body. Placing a hand on Teren's head, he warmly told him, "Think about that. Think of how many lives you'll be sparing, how much needless suffering you'll be stopping, by taking one little life." While Teren glared, Malcolm patted his head, like a dog. "Now, doesn't the good outweigh the bad?"

Chuckling again as he backed up a step, he pointed to Teren on his knees. "Think about it, just not for too long." Drawing his brows together in concern, he looked over Teren's slumped form. "And she's right. You should rest, you look…exhausted." Malcolm's own exhausted eyes flicked between the both of us. "Have a good day, you two." Then he streaked away, leaving only an imprint in our vision of where he'd been standing.

Chapter 19 – Decisions

When Teren had the strength to raise himself to his feet, we searched for any trace of Malcolm's scent. For a second we had it, and thinking to follow him back to Julian, we blindly followed it. It was only when the scent ran through a sewage treatment plant that we realized Malcolm was messing with us; he hadn't been going to back to our son at all. Any trace of him was abolished in the overwhelming stench of the place, and with no scent to track and no idea what direction to go, we tiredly headed back to our family.

Teren was quiet in the car, staring out the windows as the countryside blazed past us. Biting back the bile in my throat from the entire encounter, I watched him from the corner of my eye. His dark head resting against the seat, his eyes unfocused, he was looking at everything while seeing none of it.

"I'm sorry about Carrie," I whispered into the silence of the vehicle. His pale eyes shifted over to me; the normal gray flecks I saw in them did nothing to brighten their dullness. "I'm sorry that she had to die like that. I'm sorry she had to get mixed up in this at all."

Teren nodded, his gaze trailing down to his torn, dirty clothes. Idly playing with a tear in his shirt, he muttered, "No one should have to go that way." He closed his eyes, and his face aged before me. "I wish he hadn't told me." Lifting his face to me, his eyes near tears again, he asked, "Does that make me awful? That I'd rather not know how she died?"

He looked down and I reached over to put my hand over his. "No, it doesn't make you awful. It makes you normal. We don't want to think about loved ones experiencing anything so…horrible." My voice cracked on the word as my thoughts drifted to the dark-haired, blue-eyed little boy I hadn't seen in days.

Clenching my hand tight, Teren sniffled. "He won't hurt him, Em. He won't."

I nodded, and my vision of the bleak highway before me hazed. He really didn't know that for sure, anymore than I did, but he had to believe it to stay sane. Me, too.

Practicing the deep calming breaths I was taught in my yoga class, I struggled to keep a hold of my senses. I couldn't afford to break down into a blubbery mess right now. I needed to hold it together, for Julian's sake. He needed me. He needed me focused.

More in control, I looked over to Teren. "What are you going to do?"

Knowing what I meant, he sighed. "I don't know."

I bit my lip and forced my eyes back to the road. Malcolm wanted Gabriel's head. Too weak and chicken shit to do it himself, he'd maneuvered Teren into such a spot that even Teren didn't know if he should do it or not. I couldn't have been more torn on the matter. I wanted my son back, but I didn't want my husband to commit coldblooded murder. I wanted my son back, but I didn't want to remove the man that Halina had finally let herself fall in love with, even if she couldn't say it yet. I wanted my son back, but I didn't want to sacrifice the person who had saved my life, mine and the kids. But...I wanted my son back.

"I'll support...whatever you decide," I muttered, the speech barely passing my lips.

Teren sighed again. Leaning his head back on the seat, he closed his eyes. He was silent for the remainder of the drive.

We were greeted by a bustle of activity when we arrived at the ranch. Winding my way up the outrageously long driveway, I felt my daughter's anxious energy, her presence darting back and forth. A small smile cracked on Teren's face as he lifted his head and opened his eyes. He'd missed her just as much as she'd missed him. I parked next to Jack's truck and Alanna's sedan, and my daughter dashed out the front doors before I could even shut the car off. Tired but eager, Teren popped open his door and shuffled over to her. Giving them a moment, I slowly stepped out.

As Nika ran to him, Teren sank to his knees. Whether too exhausted to stand, too overwhelmed with emotion, or just sinking to her level, I didn't know. She flung herself into his arms, not caring at all that he was grimy and filthy. Peppering his face with kisses, she squeaked out, "Daddy! Daddy! Daddy!"

His arms squeezed around her tight as he exhaled. By the force of the sound, it seemed like it was the first exhale he'd taken in days.

I could hear the flurry of people inside the house as I watched my husband and daughter bond. My mother and sister were in a heated conversation about hunting vampires. Hot Ben was there too, giving his opinion on the subject. He'd been sticking close to the ranch when he wasn't out searching for Julian. He'd become frustrated with the needlelike search early on, and was itching to start knocking on doors again. My mother was trying to talk him out of it. My sister was being swayed to Ben's side.

As a heated frustration grew in me, I balled my hands, closed my eyes, and counted to ten. I'd told Ben before, and I'd have to tell him again, that we couldn't risk it. Not to bring up the fact that Teren and Ben already had some major grudges out there in the vampire community, they weren't searching for a mysterious, mythical group of people this time. They were searching for one person, one who had my son, one who might kill Julian if we started rattling cages that were too close to his. And now, after meeting the man in question, I knew without a doubt that he'd take Julian's life if it meant sparing his own.

Teren stood on wobbly legs with Nika buried in his arms. Looking over at me with a deep frown on his face, I knew he felt the same about hunting as I did…finally. We just had too much to lose to go stirring up nests again.

Alanna greeted us at the door as we stepped inside. The scent of homecoming hit me—freesia and fresh linens—and I smiled softly at her. She gasped at the sight of her child, then engulfed Teren and Nika in a hug. "What have you been doing?" she asked him.

She tried to remove Nika from Teren, but she was attached too tight. Like a barnacle on the underside of a ship, our daughter would have to be scraped away from her father. Teren kissed her head as he brushed aside his mother's concerns. "I'm fine, Mom, just tired."

Nodding, she started dragging him towards the kitchen.

Imogen rushed out to us. She rubbed Teren's back while he was shuffled forward. Nika cracked her eyes open at me as she rested her head on Teren's shoulder. "Hi, Mommy," she whispered.

Rubbing my thumb over her pale, worn cheek, I smiled. She

looked just as tired as Teren, only all of her exhaustion was mental. Feeling Julian's constant terror was sapping the strength right out of her. It broke my heart. I wanted to give her a break from the stress, but at the same time, I didn't want to lose the connection with my son. "Hi, baby."

She smiled, closing her eyes again, content for once, in her daddy's arms.

Stepping into the dining room, we walked into the argument that I could hear from the outside. Hot Ben was pointing to a map of California spread on the table. He was pointing out locations of old nests that he and Teren had gone to years ago. I knew those nests would be abandoned by now, but Ben still wanted to try scoping them out.

"Teren and I could check these ones here." He pointed to the northeast corner of the map. "They were big last time, there might still be some people hanging around."

"It's too dangerous, Benjamin," my mother said, crossing her arms over her chest.

Ashley looked over at her. "What else can we do, Mom? Look under every rock in the state? The country?"

Teren walked up to the table and every voice in the room quieted as they looked at him. Knowing my husband looked like he'd been on a wild bender, I wasn't too surprised when they stared at him wide-eyed.

Glancing down at the map, Teren sniffed then looked back up at Ben. "We're not hunting." Ashley started to object and Teren sliced his eyes over to her. "It won't help. He's not hanging around other vampires. They won't know anything."

Ben started to walk around the table while Alanna swished into the kitchen to make her son some food. "Teren, man, you never know. He has to have some connections somewhere. If we can find out who's helping him…"

Teren looked over at Ben. "He will kill my son. If we look, if we stir the wrong nest, he will kill Julian." Nika sniffled, clutching Teren tighter as he patted her back. In a whisper, he added, "He's already left him starving and alone...I won't risk it."

Imogen squeezed his arm and Teren looked down at her. "How do you know?" Her pale eyes frantically searched his, the hope in them was clear.

Teren looked at me behind him before shifting to take in every awaiting person. Jack held my mother's shoulders while Ashley started to tremble. Hot Ben looked between Teren and the map, silently weighing the risk. Alanna swished back into the room, her breath held and her hands empty, while she waited for her son to confess what he knew, what he'd found out. Stepping up to him, I put my hand on his back.

He sighed. "We met Malcolm today. He confessed that he left Julian with nothing, and he would let him starve to death if we...didn't do what he wanted."

Gasps and sobs filled the room. I closed my eyes, but I could still hear my mother crying as Jack clenched her tight. I could still hear Ashley heavily collapse into a nearby chair and Hot Ben cursing under his breath as he sat beside her.

Alanna's presence stepped up to us and I peeked up at her. Her face was suddenly as worn as Teren's. Pink tears dripped off her cheeks as she shook her head. "What does he want?"

Imogen's eyes were brimming with red tears. She wrung her hands as she looked around their home. "What do we have that he needs?" She looked about ready to hand him over the deed to the ranch if he wanted it.

Knowing that his needs weren't material objects, I sighed. Teren sighed, too. Closing his eyes for a second, he wavered on his feet. With a quick kiss to his daughter's head, he reopened them and his gaze floated around the room. "He wants me to kill Gabriel," he whispered.

Every standing person found a chair to sit in. As one, all of the vampires looked east, to where we all felt Halina. She hadn't been back either, instead pushing farther and farther away from us in her search. I knew she was probably sleeping under a mound of dirt right now, and I knew she probably hated it, but she was as relentless in her quest as Teren. And now, Teren had to decide if he was going to kill the man she loved....to save our son.

Alanna studied Teren's face. "And what are you going to do?"

Clutching Nika tight, his eyes misting, Teren shook his head. "I don't know," he whispered.

Alanna closed her eyes and nodded. Imogen was shaking her head in disbelief. A ray of sun highlighted the grandmotherly vampire's face but in that moment, I saw a concerned daughter more than a loving grandparent. "You can't," she whispered, brushing a loose lock of hair back into her bun. "Mother loves him...you can't..."

She looked up at Teren with torn eyes. Her expression was the same one that was on my face. No, he couldn't, it was horrible, but if it was our only chance to get Julian back...should he anyway?

Everyone looked between Teren, the location Halina was, and the table. Teren silently watched everyone's reactions as he tilted a bit on his feet. My arms went around him, steadying him. "Go upstairs, rest."

He shook his head. "I can't rest. I can't...with Julian out there."

One of my hands rubbed Nika's back as she clung to Teren, my other hand reached up to brush his cheek. "He gave you three days. Nothing will happen to Julian until then." My voice cracked but I made myself continue. "Go upstairs with Nika and try to take a nap. You're exhausted," I said, knowing I was mimicking Malcolm's last words. "And the next time we meet him...you'll need your strength," I quietly added.

Teren closed his eyes and leaned into my hand. Nika generally fought against the idea of a nap, but her arms around Teren tightened as she buried her head in his neck; she wasn't letting go of Daddy anytime soon. Alanna blurred out of the room while Teren nodded.

He looked around at the remaining people in our home, then looked north, to where Gabriel was also searching for our son. He'd checked in with us periodically, mainly to let us know that every lead he'd gotten so far hadn't resulted in anything helpful. They'd been so close to nabbing Malcolm before, and then he'd all but disappeared. I remembered the torn bloody section of Malcolm's shirt. If only they'd finished the job in the raid…then he wouldn't have slipped away and snatched my son.

Sighing, Teren pulled his eyes from the man he'd been assigned to murder, and started shuffling back down the hall. Everyone at the table silently watched him leave. Not able to stand the oppressive silence in the room, I followed Teren.

Alanna blurred out to us by the stairs with a steaming thermos of blood in her hand. Teren instantly locked onto it, and his hand reached out at the same time hers did. Tilting it back, he hungrily gulped it down, although he didn't spill any on himself this time. I watched his thirst with tears in my eyes. He'd been putting himself through so much, just to keep up the impossible task of finding our son.

Tears in her own eyes, Alanna took back the container once he was finished. "Do you want some more?" she asked, her voice shaky as she brushed some hair off his forehead. The movement was so similar to how I always brushed hair out of Julian's eyes that my throat choked up.

Teren sighed and shook his head. "No, thank you, Mom. I just want to lie down." He staggered on his feet and Alanna nodded. I ran my hand over his back and urged him upstairs. He needed to rest before he simply fell over.

With his head against Nika's, I led him to our room. I thought to help him clean up, but Nika wouldn't disengage from him long enough for me to strip his clothes off. I tried to gently pull her off, but she whined, shook her head, and clutched him tighter. She seemed terrified to let him go.

Teren shook his head at me. "It's okay." He shrugged and sat down on the bed with her. Swallowing the emotion in my throat, I took off his shoes and helped him shift under the covers with the lump of our daughter attached to his chest. She didn't relax her rigidness until they were snuggled together.

I wrapped an extra blanket around her, to counteract Teren's chill. Teren sighed and closed his eyes. Kissing her forehead, he ran a hand down her hair. She peeked up at me when I pulled away from them. "Mommy?" she said quietly.

Threading my hand over the hair above her ear, I murmured, "Yes, baby?"

Teren's eyes cracked open as our daughter responded to my question. "Julie's scared."

My throat tightened as I locked eyes with Teren. "I know, sweetheart, we're gonna bring him home really soon."

Nika nodded and closed her eyes. Her young face was worn, but she completely believed me. She had absolute faith that what we told her would happen; I prayed it did. Teren let out a broken exhale. Kissing his forehead, I whispered, "Sleep. We'll figure it out when you wake up."

He nodded and his eyes fluttered closed. Watching them, I slowly backed out of the room. Nika's breaths were low and even by the time I reached the door. Teren's had completely stopped. Exhausted, they'd both passed out.

I felt my own weariness and considered joining them. I couldn't, though. I heard conversations downstairs over what to do now, and I wanted to be a part of them. Plus, every nap or rest I'd taken in the last few days had ended with me waking from a scream-worthy nightmare. I didn't want to have any nightmares right now; my waking moments were nightmarish enough.

While Teren slept, I took a lightning-quick shower, then changed into fresh clothes. After I was dressed, I streaked downstairs to join the family while they debated our options. There weren't many. Blindly looking for Julian was an impossible task. Knocking on vampire's nests was also an impossible task, impossible and dangerous. The odds of them knowing anything helpful about Malcolm weren't all that great, since he'd been on the run for years. Plus, Gabriel knew several vampires, if it were really a matter of just asking one, he would have done that.

That of course brought the conversation around to Gabriel. No one flat-out said that Teren should just kill him, but the tension of the idea was in the air. It wasn't as if anyone disliked the man, far from it, but he *was* over six hundred years old. He'd lived a full life—several of them. My son's life had barely just begun. The tradeoff seemed fair, in a horribly unfeeling way.

When the sun set, I began to feel Halina's presence stir. All the vampires looked her way as we felt her come towards us. I didn't know if she was returning to the ranch because she was tired and frustrated with pointless searching, or if she just felt guilty for being so far away from her clan. Probably guilt. Halina would relentlessly search if she needed to, but she'd have a problem with completely abandoning her position as protector. Even though she could feel us, she was probably anxious over our safety.

Like Teren, Halina had dashed out to search for Julian on foot. She'd been forced to break her frantic pace during daylight hours, when she had to hide out from the sun, but I was sure she was just as weary as Teren, emotionally if not physically. Since her presence was heading back towards us at a pace that was slower than she was capable of, I figured she had obtained a car during her travels. Knowing her, it was probably a fast one. I wondered briefly what fortunate soul had "gifted" her a vehicle. But, fast as the car was, it was still going to take her some time for her to make it home. A couple of days, since she could only travel at night.

When Hot Ben decided to go out for more pointless searching, Alanna, Jack and Imogen agreed to go with him. They'd been studiously watching over my mother, sister and Nika, protecting them in case Malcolm had decided that he wasn't done abducting people, and they hadn't had a chance to look for my son yet. I wished them luck as they left, but I knew they wouldn't find anything. I understood the need to look though. Even now, knowing that Julian was safely stashed somewhere for at least the next few days, I wanted to look for him. It was hard to stay still, but I did, for my family.

I heard Jack and Alanna get into his truck, Imogen slip into her car, and Hot Ben get into his SUV. My mom and Ash wanted to head out too, but I made them stay behind. Unless you were undead, or had experience dealing with the undead, it was too risky to be out in the night, kicking over rocks. Scary things sometimes lived under rocks.

So we played Parcheesi while everyone else searched for Julian. It was the most somber game of Parcheesi I'd ever played. I felt Teren stir to life not long after everyone had gone. Glancing at my mom and Ashley, who were both looking out the windows more than the game board, I listened to Teren get out of bed and walk to the bathroom.

The sound of running water through the pipes alerted my mom and Ashley and they looked up, to where Teren was above us. Ashley's eyes swung over to mine. "He's awake?" I nodded, noting that my daughter was still asleep; she must have really been exhausted.

Slowly walking to the kitchen to prepare another drink for him, I gave him a few minutes to shower and collect himself. Since I wanted a little refresher, I warmed one up for me too. My thoughts instantly shifted to Julian. It was so unnatural not to feel him, not to be fixing him something to eat, not to be preparing to send him off to bed. I would give anything to go back to when our biggest challenge had been getting the twins to brush their teeth.

Holding the two steaming cups of plasma, I made my way upstairs. Opening the door to our room, I instantly saw my husband. Standing in the doorway of the bathroom, drying his hair with a towel, he was staring at the shape of our daughter snoring away in our bed. The light from the humid room silhouetted his body, casting a shadow of him on our mattress. It almost looked like he was still lying down with Nika, his black form protecting her just as he would.

The scent of body wash tickling my nose, I headed over to him with one cup extended. He cracked a smile as he took it, warmed by my gesture just as much as the return of my presence. Our bond glowed between us, for a second filling the hole that Julian's abduction had created. Tilting back our drinks together, I watched Teren as I swallowed mine. Dressed in rugged denims and a loose, dark blue button up shirt, he again looked clean and fresh, ready to take on the world. I wasn't sure if his spirit was quite there though. I knew he was still conflicted over his decision.

Only stopping when his mug was empty, he sighed softly and closed his eyes. When they reopened and locked on me, they seemed brighter, more alive and determined than I'd seen them in a while. Sometimes rest and nourishment was all it took to give you the drive to start again. We might not know what to do, or where to go to look for our son, but he was alive and he would be for the next three days. There was a surprising amount of comfort in that.

Taking his thermos from him, I watched as his ice blue eyes shifted back to Nika on the bed. His black hair as dry as a towel could get it, he blindly tossed the cloth behind him, into the bathroom. Leaning against the frame, he sighed and shook his head. "I thought a shower would clear my mind. I thought the solution would instantly hit me."

Setting our mugs on a dresser, I came up to him and rested my head on his shoulder. "I don't think there are any instant solutions to this, Teren."

He looked down on me as I slung my arms around his waist. He smelled clean, familiar and comforting, and I allowed myself to indulge in that peace, burying my head in his shoulder much like Nika had earlier. His hand rubbed my back, comforting me, even through his own pain. "You look better at least," I murmured. Peering up at him, I asked, "Do you feel any better?"

His lips thinned as he pressed them together. "I feel like a hole has been punched straight through me. I feel...incomplete."

As I pulled back to look at him, his pale eyes glassed over. His gaze was studiously fixed on Nika, like he knew that if he met eyes with me, those glossy orbs would fill to a breaking point. I palmed his cheek but I didn't make him look at me. He was struggling to remain in control, and I understood. I constantly felt on the edge of hysteria...and that wasn't going to help Julian.

"I know...I feel that way too." I followed his gaze to stare at Nika. Her arms were outstretched on the bed, like she was still reaching out for Teren, or Julian, but her legs were bunched up to her chest, curling herself into a protective ball. My kids sometimes fell asleep in the exact same position. Was Julian right now reaching out for us, for his twin?

My vision hazing, I whispered, "I wish we could feel what she feels." I looked back at Teren, "Just so we could know for certain that he was all right, that he was safe, that he was...alive."

Teren looked down and swallowed, and his arms squeezed me a little tighter. "If I had never told Gabriel about what had been done to me, none of this would have happened."

Sighing, I stroked his cheek and shook my head. "If I'd

remembered to open the door, we would have heard Malcolm. If we'd never soundproofed our room, we would have caught him."

Teren slumped and I squatted to look him in the eye. "But then, if we hadn't met Ben at the gym that night, I wouldn't have been bitten. If we hadn't stopped to help someone that day, we wouldn't have been abducted." I smiled softly as Teren sighed. Shaking my head again, I murmured, "And…if I hadn't spilled coffee down your shirt, we wouldn't have met."

Teren smiled at the warm memory he loved while we both straightened. My arms moving up to slink around his neck, I rested my forehead against his. "We can play the what-if game forever, Teren. It doesn't change anything. This happened. We have to focus on what to do now."

Exhaling steadily, the faint smell of sweet blood on his breath, he rocked his head against mine. "What *do* I do, Emma?"

Intensity in my eyes, I pulled back to gaze at him. "You do whatever you have to, to get Julian back."

Closing his eyes, Teren nodded. When he opened them again, he looked around the room. "Where did everyone streak off to?"

I felt the pings of family members in my head, some near, some very far, and shrugged. "They wanted to search for Julian." His eyes came back to mine, and I shrugged. "They haven't had the chance yet, since they've sort of been on guard duty."

Teren nodded as he looked at the floor, to where we could hear my mother and sister discussing what Teren should do. They seemed just as torn on the matter as we were, both sides having pros and cons, the biggest pro of course being Julian's return. Shaking his head, Teren muttered, "They won't find him."

Hearing him admit that made an ache run through my silent heart. Biting my lip, I nodded, and conceded. "I know…but they want to try."

Teren looked up at hearing me admit defeat. It was a difficult thing to say. Having doubts and fears was one thing. Verbalizing them to another person was quite another. It made the entire situation suddenly seem real…and hopeless.

His hand came up to cup my cheek, and his skin was almost hot against my chilled flesh after his searing shower. "I'll do whatever I have to, Emma, to get him back to us."

Swallowing, I nodded. Nika stirred on the bed, her arms tightening around nothing. Glancing at her, Teren started pulling me towards the door. "Let's go downstairs, let her sleep in peace."

I followed him out after placing a cool kiss on her hot cheek. She stirred, mumbling something that sounded like, "Julie." Then she fell back into peacefulness. I wished her a long rest. Her tired, tiny body needed the reprieve.

Teren was waiting for me in the hallway with a hand outstretched. I grabbed it, and a small smile lifted my lips at the connection. It faded instantly though. Small pockets of joy coursed into me throughout my day, but they were never enough to truly lift the weight around my heart. Teren's lips exactly mimicked my actions and he sighed. Tilting his head to the dual staircase, he started leading me that way.

Expecting us to walk back to the living room to rejoin Mom and Ash, I was a little surprised when Teren twisted us so we left the main building. Walking through an open air breezeway, the scent of cattle stung my nose for a second before we entered one of the side buildings here at the ranch. Each building beside the main one held numerous guest rooms, games rooms, formal dining rooms and laundry rooms...everything a growing vampire family could ask for.

None of the rooms were made available to the ranch hands that helped out a couple times a year. They were relegated to their own home far from the main house. That gave the vampires freedom to be who they were. Not having to constantly rein in their nature. The ranch hands' house was empty, everyone was still being held away. My earlier conversion had thrown everything off schedule, and Alanna and Jack had told Peter Alton, their trusted crew leader for years, to push back everyone's return until after the twins' fourth birthday in a couple weeks. A birthday I prayed they both got to celebrate together.

As we walked down a hallway that I knew well, a hallway that held the room I'd prepared to marry Teren in, that sweeter, purer time filled my head. Our life had seemed so hopeful back then. I had been completely human, recently pregnant. We hadn't known about Gabriel and his expansive circle of mixed and full vampires. Carrie was alive and well, and I'd been oblivious of her past connection to my then-boyfriend. They were simpler times, and they seemed like a lifetime ago now.

Our biggest problem on our wedding day had been Hot Ben walking in on us and discovering what Teren was. Remembering Ben asking Teren if he was going to eat him, a small smile cracked my lips. It fell off my face the moment we stopped before another door that I knew well. A door that held memories that weren't so pure and sweet.

Teren's face was hard and serious as he opened the door into what I liked to call the "war room." I never came in here, not since that day that Teren and I had fought here. He'd been packing up for battle, preparing to do whatever was necessary to find an elusive mixed vampire—any mixed vampire—in the insane hope that someone could help save me. It made me cringe that it had come down to this. That once again, Teren was being forced to do something unsavory to protect his family.

I wanted to pull him back, to forcibly make him leave this room with me, but I couldn't. I knew the risks, and this time…I supported his decision. His breath heavy, he dropped my hand and opened a chest on the floor. In it were all the weapons Teren and Ben had accumulated on their hunting trips. I bit my lip as he rifled through stake after stake. I hated the vision of violence before me—guns, silver knives, even a crossbow. It was all so barbaric, so against who Teren was as a person. The image of him examining an aged, wooden stake, seeing if the point was sharp enough, was so jolting that I felt my stomach rise in protest. I didn't want this…but I wanted my son.

Finally settling on a silver one that shone brightly in the sun streaming through the window, its light refracting around the room, he stood back up. His face was tight as he examined the object in his hands. "I need to call Gabriel, have him come back here. I'll tell him I found something, a clue, and I need his help with it."

My eyes watered as I watched Teren's thumb stroke over the deadly piece. Surprisingly, an intrinsic part of me was afraid to be near it, like my body understood the danger of the weapon. I took a step back from him. Teren's eyes lifted to mine; his face was haunted by what he had to do for our son.

I wanted to scream at him that there had to be another way, that he couldn't seriously be considering murder. But I didn't. I only nodded at him and forced myself closer to the hated object so I could touch him. Exhaling a shaky breath, I wrapped my arms around his neck and held his head tight to mine. I could feel him trembling as he rigidly stood, stake in hand. He didn't want to do this either, but the odds of us blindly finding Julian were impossibly high. We'd have better odds finding Bigfoot.

Holding him close, I whispered in his ear, "I love you."

Chapter 20 – I'm Sorry

Teren's phone call to Gabriel was brief and to the point. He didn't want to give away any of his turmoil to the ancient vampire. Our only chance to make this work was to catch Gabriel completely off guard. And that, of course, was why Malcolm had chosen Teren for this assignment. One, we had something of tremendous value to lose, and two, we could get Gabriel alone. He trusted us, regarded us as family. He would never suspect that we'd betray him, not after everything he'd done for us.

I hated that we would, if we had no other choice.

Teren sat on the bottom step of the staircase, waiting for Gabriel to arrive. I'd heard their conversation. Gabriel was anxious to see what Teren had found and was speeding south to us. He'd been in one of his specially designed cars, so he could drive around without pain in direct sunlight. Even still, he wouldn't be at our door until morning.

Watching Teren finger the stake in his hands, I figured he'd stay in that spot until morning, contemplating. Diverting their attention from the stake in his palm, I saw my mother and sister off to bed. When Teren didn't even acknowledge them as they passed by him on the staircase, I assured them that his distraction was only due to his worry for our lost child. I heard them up in their room later, though, debating if his introspection was because of Julian, or if he was actually considering Malcolm's plan. I didn't let them know that he was. That we both were.

Sitting beside him on the stair, I put my hand on his lap and rested my head on his shoulder. A soft sigh was his only reaction as he continually stroked the weapon in his hands.

My own exhaustion swept over me as I leaned against him, and I fell asleep. I woke up when I heard tires crunching on the gravel of the driveway. Blinking, I lifted my head off of Teren's shoulder; he hadn't moved at all since he'd sat down there, right after calling Gabriel. I watched him as I listened to two cars pulling up. I knew who was in the cars, I could feel them. It wasn't Gabriel yet, it was the evening search party returning, most likely empty handed.

Teren and I both glanced at the front door at the same time, right as it opened. A worn and weary Imogen walked through, shaking her head as she met our gaze. I nodded and swallowed a hard lump; I hadn't really been expecting them to find him anyway. Alanna and Jack came through next, also looking worn and dejected. Alanna couldn't meet our eyes. She only stared at the floor in front of us and muttered that they found nothing—no trail, no clue, no scent.

Even though it was expected, tears still stung my eyes. If only we could find the hole he'd been thrust into, then Teren wouldn't have to do the awful thing he felt he had to do. Jack sighed as he strode into the room, and Alanna closed the doors behind the trio. My un-beating heart cracked at yet another door being closed on my missing baby.

The aging rancher stepped up to the pair of us, looking even more worn than Alanna and Imogen. As I watched the lines on his face seemingly deepen right before me, I suddenly saw the mortality of Teren's father. He was aging, daily, and it was beginning to show. His hair was more touched with gray than it had been the first time I'd met him, and his joints creaked as he sat on the step beside Teren.

I was sure he was still a good couple of decades away from the grave, but still, that was his path. A path he'd chosen. Placing an arm around his son, he exhaled as he stared at the stake in Teren's hands. "What are you thinking, Teren?" he asked.

His question got the attention of Imogen and Alanna, and they pulled their gazes from the sun rising in the east to look our way. Not having Teren's or my ability to walk freely in the sunshine all day, they'd had to call off their search early, and it clearly bothered them. Although, as they noticed what Teren was twisting in his palms, they looked even more bothered.

When they stepped in front of him, Teren shifted his eyes to his dad. Speaking for the first time in hours, he whispered, "I don't know what to do, Dad. I don't know what *not* to do, either." His eyes continuously searched his father's, like he was looking for an answer in them.

Jack sighed, and ran a hand over his mouth. His eyes glassy, he shook his head. "I can't tell you that, son. I don't know, either. For once, this area is just too gray."

Imogen stepped forward. "No, it isn't. Gabriel is a person, ancient or not." She lifted her chin. "And we don't kill people."

Teren looked up to his grandmother; his face was almost as aged as his father's from his inner struggle. I looked up at Imogen, too. I could see her youthful chin tremble as she swiped loose stands of jet-black hair behind her ears. Her statement wasn't entirely accurate, and she knew it. Halina would kill, if the mood struck her, and if she found a victim she deemed worthy of the death. And Imogen herself had even taken a life or two, although she was remorseful for her actions, and wouldn't do it again. I understood her sentiment though. No one in the family wanted to take part in the murder of a good man. And beneath all the power and detached scientific demeanor, Gabriel was a good person. A person who had saved my life. That was what I wanted to believe about him anyway.

Seeing the debate in Teren's features, Imogen shook her head. "Mother loves him. If you kill him...I don't know what she will do."

Her voice was quiet but it seemed to crash around the house. This was something I hadn't considered. Halina could be...fiery when she got upset. Killing the man she was in love with would certainly upset her. How far would she take that anger? Anger she'd admitted to me that she purposely forged to survive. Would she take out vengeance on her own grandson? I wasn't sure...but what other choice did we have?

Teren's eyes slid over to mine. I could see my thoughts reflected in his pale blue depths. He didn't know what Halina would do either, but again, we were out of options.

As Alanna stepped forward, placing her hand on her mother's arm, Teren opened his mouth to speak. He stopped when the sound of more tires crushing over gravel filled all of our ears.

I stood up along with Teren. Alanna and Imogen twisted to look at the front door and Jack, seeing all of the vampires reacting to something he couldn't yet perceive, stood as well.

Feeling Halina still miles away from here, stationary as she hid out the day, I knew that it was Gabriel approaching us. Teren's target was coming within range. He'd never get another chance to take him by surprise like he would right now. Teren took a step towards the door. Shoving the silver piece in his back pocket, he hid it with shirt. Imogen grabbed his arm as he walked past. "There has to be another way," she whispered.

Teren's eyes were dull and lifeless as he shrugged. "If you know of one...tell me now, because I don't see any other option at this point." His eyes swept the room, swept over the faces of the people he'd do nearly anything to protect. "Do any of you?" he whispered.

No one answered him.

Exhaling softly, he twisted to walk to the front door. Without pausing, he opened it with his left hand while his right snaked around behind him to rest on the spike in his pocket. I wanted to hold my breath, I wanted to beg him to stop, I wanted to shout a warning to Gabriel...but I couldn't. My son's life was on the line. And I knew it was wrong, I knew I'd hate myself every day, but if I was being forced to choose between Julian and Gabriel...there was no choice. Julian would win, every time.

Imogen grabbed my hand, clenching it hard while Alanna grabbed Jack. Trying to seem bereaved but not anxious, we all breathlessly watched Teren swing the door open. I was suddenly grateful that my heart was no longer beating. Surely the rapid, thumping beat would have made Gabriel suspicious.

The intrinsic beauty of Gabriel was the first thing I noticed. He was tall and trim, well-shaped, with sandy brown hair and sharply green eyes. His face was flawless among human standards. Among vampires who could see faults and imperfections that humans couldn't, he was still astounding.

Frowning as he stepped through the door, out of the sunlight that would eventually irritate his skin, he grasped Teren's elbow, his right elbow. Teren stiffened and twisted around so his back was to the door as Gabriel stepped into the room. For a moment I thought Gabriel somehow knew, but then he spoke.

"What did you find, Teren? Can I see it?" His voice was rushed, eager, as his jade eyes searched my husband's.

Teren took a step back and regarded him for a moment. Gabriel released his hand from Teren and tilted his head. He watched Teren and then twisted to watch us. "What happened?" he asked calmly, the scientific detachment back in his voice.

Too afraid of answering, of even moving, I bit my lip. Everyone around me was equally silent and still, and the room quickly filled with tension. Before I shut off my breathing, the sharp scent of pine drifted to me from Gabriel, like he'd been out searching forests. I instantly wondered if that was where my son could be, shoved in a cold, dark cave, alone and terrified. My eyes watered, and I hoped this sacrifice was worth it.

Gabriel's eyes slowly swung back to Teren, right as Teren brought his stake wielding hand around. As I clenched Imogen's hand, Teren whispered, "I'm so sorry."

Gabriel's eyes widened as he watched the silver streaking towards his heart. He took a step back, but Teren lunged forward. His eyes wide but unafraid, Gabriel seemed completely thrown. As the beginning of a sob rose up my throat, Teren jabbed the point into Gabriel's chest...and then completely stopped moving.

My cry fumbled in my throat, and I swallowed and scrunched my brows, confused. Everybody else seemed confused, too, and nervous shifting sounded around me. I could see that the sharp stake had cut the expensive fabric of Gabriel's shirt, but I couldn't see any blood. Teren had only pierced his clothing; he'd halted his momentum before slicing through skin and bone. His arm shaking, he held the stake over Gabriel's heart.

Gabriel's eyes flicked to the near-mortal wound he'd almost received then back up to Teren, shaking with restraint in front of him.

His jaw trembling so badly that his words came out stuttered, Teren murmured, "Give me a reason. Give me a reason to not give Malcolm what he wants. Give me a reason to not kill you...please," he added, his face softening.

Gabriel blinked, but didn't move. "Is that what he wants? My head...by your hand?" His lips lifted into a small smile. "Clever, I didn't see that coming." Teren pressed forward with the stake and Gabriel sighed, but didn't seem worried in the slightest that he was a shove away from death. His face sagging, he shook his head. "I have no reason that would be worth the price of your son, Teren." He lifted his shoulders. "You *should* kill me."

Teren bunched his body, the tendons in his forearm straining with his resolve to do it, but still he balked as his eyes frantically flicked over Gabriel. Tilting his head, Gabriel calmly looked at him. "I have lived a long time, Teren. Several lifetimes have passed me by. I would not blame you, if you chose to end my life so your son could live." He raised his eyebrows. "But ultimately, this price will be yours. The question isn't really whether or not I should die. It's whether or not *you* should kill me. Do you want that weight?"

Teren blinked, then dropped the stake. It clanged to the marble floor, hurting my ears. I immediately rushed up to Teren as he slumped, looking a little sick. Throwing my arms around his waist, I helped him stay standing when he looked like he wanted to sink to the floor. Feeling the emotional resolve draining from him, my eyes started to sting. I didn't want my husband to take a life either, but he'd just shut the door on our only chance to get Julian back.

Teren's entire body started shaking. "I'm sorry, Emma. I can't…"

Kissing his head, I squeezed him tight. "I know. I love you because you can't."

He solemnly nodded while Gabriel watched us. Pressing his lips into a hard line, Gabriel stared down at the stake on the floor. "You spoke with Malcolm?"

Gabriel cocked an eyebrow at us, and I nodded. "He found us while we were searching for Julian. He told Teren that he would let Julian star…" I choked and had to start again, "starve to death if we didn't deliver you to him…dead."

Teren looked up at Gabriel, guilt in his eyes. "I'm sorry. I didn't know what else to do."

Gabriel dismissed him with a wave of his hand. "I don't blame you, Teren. If my own children were placed in harm's way, I would have made the same choice." He smiled as his eyes got a faraway look, one I registered with him checking in on his distant family. "Any father would," he said quietly.

Then frowning, Gabriel shook his head. "There is no clue, is there?"

Teren's body relaxed as the turmoil and guilt released. "No, I just needed you to come over."

Gabriel sighed and nodded. Walking over to the fountain of the crying woman, he swiped his thumb over her never-ending tears. "Yes, well, I'm sorry to hear that." He looked up at Teren as we all took a step towards him. "Since taking your son, Malcolm has fallen off the grid I had in place. It's quite possible that the brief moment you had with him was the only time he's surfaced. Wherever he is hiding, it is deep and remote."

Gabriel cracked a small smile. "It must be torture for him. He always preferred living extravagantly, right in the middle of human life. A wolf among sheep." He twisted his head to Jack, the only pure human in the room. "No offense." He politely nodded his head.

Jack's eyes widened but he shook his head. "None taken. I know what we are...to some of you."

Gabriel smirked and shrugged. Teren released himself from me and took a step forward to stand on the other side of the fountain. "Malcolm told me some things about you, about your early research. Was any of that true?"

Gabriel stared at him, his green eyes clearly processing. "I'm assuming he painted me in an unsavory light for you? Told you I slaughtered hundreds of our kind, to develop a drug that, to him, never produced the results I was looking for?"

Teren nodded and looked over at me. Malcolm had made Gabriel seem quite cold, and we knew he could be...distant at times.

Gabriel shrugged. "I won't lie, some vampires were inadvertently killed along the way, although, not nearly as many as he probably made you believe." Smiling, he shook his head. "Several of them were my friends. They all either had something to gain by trying the drug," he looked up at Teren, "or nothing to lose." He shook his head again. "But either way, they all volunteered, they all knew the risks. I forced this on no one, Teren, no one. And each death was respected, cataloged, analyzed and mistakes were corrected. No vampire's sacrifice was taken for granted."

Looking away, Teren closed his eyes. Slowly returning them to Gabriel, he asked, "Then what is it between you and Malcolm? Why did he leave you? Why does he have such resentment?"

Gabriel laughed. "Did he call me a cult leader? That was always his favorite description." His eyes locked onto the fountain and he watched the water twist and slide down the marble woman's body. "Malcolm, at first, wanted to help with the drug, wanted to help our kind." Shaking his head, he fingered the water again. "But whenever I brought in another vampire out of the cold, gave them food and shelter, a safe place to convert, he grew a little...jealous." His eyes came back up to Teren's. "He wanted the attention, he wanted the accolade, but...he was demanding in his attempt to get it."

Gabriel sighed and stepped back. His eyes shifted to absorb the ranch, the ranch he'd altered to help the mixed vampires inside it. "I only ever tried to help. The attention, the adoration, I never asked for it." Sighing, he looked over to me. "Maybe I should have tried harder to dissuade the follower mentality, but, the research was my focus. And if the people I brought in deferred to me, the nest was calm."

Smiling, he looked over to Alanna and Imogen. "And, as you know, a calm nest is a happy nest." Shrugging, he twisted to Teren. "We are a social species. We generally clump together if possible, deferring to one leader, generally the eldest, though not always."

The slight smile fell off his face. "But Malcolm resented the affection that he could not create through force. Over time, that resentment turned nasty...made him bitter." Gabriel sighed. "I think the final straw for Malcolm was when it became clear that I would never charge our brethren for my assistance."

Gabriel looked out the windows, over the fields. "I had money. Whoever joined with me contributed to the wealth of the family, but that wasn't enough for Malcolm. He saw dollar signs with our work. I disagreed."

Swinging his eyes back to Teren, Gabriel shrugged. "When our disagreements disrupted the research, we parted ways. It was mostly an amicable split...on my part at least."

His head down, he said, "I had no idea he stole from me before he left." He peeked up at Teren. "He knew what that version of the formula did. He knew that I never wanted that mixture released…and he took it anyway." His face softened as his usually impartial eyes filled with emotion. "He still saw dollar signs…and our brothers and sisters paid the price." His sad eyes flicked down Teren's body. Teren had paid that price.

Running a hand down his worn face, he sighed. "I studied alone for a while after that, until Jordan came to me. I didn't even let him enter the lab until I was sure that his motives were as," he smirked as he locked gazes with Teren, "altruistic as mine."

Teren smiled at hearing his accusation towards Gabriel repeated back to him.

I stepped forward and timidly put a hand on Gabriel's arm. "So, you really are a good man?"

He looked over at me, and every single one of his years was apparent on his youthful face. "I'm not perfect, Emma, and I am no saint." He gave me a weary smile. "But I do try to be a good man, a good father…to those who need one."

He shrugged, taking in every person in the room. "That is all I have ever tried to do."

Teren stepped forward and put his hand over mine on Gabriel's arm. "I believe that about you." He raised his eyebrows. "So what do we do about Malcolm? How do we get my son back?"

Gabriel shook his head. "I do not know, Teren. Finding Malcolm and bringing him to justice was one thing. Finding him and making him give up the location of your child is quite another." Gabriel shrugged as he looked down to the floor. His words echoing in the large, quiet room, he said, "I've already spread the word that he is not to be harmed, that he must be taken alive, but vampires…"

Shrugging, he looked back up at us. "We can be an emotional lot, purebloods even more so." He scrunched his lips. "A part of me hopes that he stays hidden, so the fool does not get himself killed before Julian can be found."

Teren sighed and rested against the fountain. With a hand massaging his forehead, he sat on the lip of the water bowl, silent. Watching my husband, memories of our meeting with Malcolm flooded through me. Teren's weariness, Malcolm's desperation, his coldly laid out plan to end Gabriel's life, the things he'd already done to warn off the ancient vampire stalking him...

Shifting my gaze to the man who was also staring at Teren, I asked Gabriel, "Did you know that he killed Carrie?"

As the others in the room who didn't know that fact gasped, Teren lifted his head. Gabriel sighed as he looked at me. From the tiredness I saw in the perfectly green depths, I assumed that he had known, possibly from the very beginning.

Alanna stepped forward while Teren straightened from the fountain. "Her death wasn't an accident?" she asked.

Teren sniffed as he stepped up to Gabriel again. "No, Malcolm admitted that he took her, fed on her, and then left her to die in the wildfire...as a warning to you. Did you know that?"

Holding his gaze, Gabriel nodded. "I did. I suspected something was...amiss with the situation with Miss Davids. A vampire's trance would not have let her leave the city so easily. I figured she was taken against her will. Since I don't believe in coincidences, and her being found in my backyard was too...convenient, I started to believe that Malcolm was responsible."

Gabriel paused, appraising Teren before speaking again. "I examined her body at the morgue." He raised his eyebrows at Teren. "There was no trace of soot in her lungs. She was dead before the fire got to her." He smiled a sad, reassuring smile at Teren.

Closing his eyes as grief, guilt and relief crashed through him, Teren nodded. Twisting my head to Gabriel, I spouted something logical, even though I was feeling like all logic had left my life ages ago. "Don't the police know that? Aren't they looking for a killer now? If they are on Malcolm's tail too..."

Gabriel smiled crookedly. "The medical examiner was brought to believe that she died in the fire, a pure accident. Carrie was promptly cremated and returned to the remaining members of her family after that."

My eyes widened before I shut them. Hearing my husband's voice, I opened them again. "Why didn't you tell me back then?

You've known for a while now that she was murdered. Wasn't that something I should have known?"

Gabriel sighed and placed a hand on Teren's shoulder. "No, it wasn't. As you said, Malcolm believed that she was here for me. He believed that he was doing something to harm me. The message was solely intended for me, Teren. There was no good that would have come from you knowing the truth."

Teren straightened his stance. "You have pushed a desperate man into desperate actions. Actions that have involved people that I care about. He has my son! If you had just stopped—"

His face turning stone cold, Gabriel removed his hand from Teren's shoulder. "And let the man who is ultimately responsible for the torture and murder of countless of our species...for numerous children and adults alike...go free?" He raised his eyebrows as he shook his head. "Should I have let him go with only a warning for his crimes? Would that have been fair?"

Teren sighed as he slumped his head. "No," he finally muttered.

His expression softening, Gabriel touched his hand to Teren's arm. "I'm sorry this has involved you so much. I tried to keep the ugliness of it away from you and your family, I truly did. But...obviously, I have failed in doing that."

Teren locked gazes with him, his jaw tight. "Your family matter is now my family matter. That lunatic has Julian, and the price of his freedom is your head. If you know anything else...now would be the time to spill it."

Gabriel smiled at the look of determination on Teren's face, then nodded. "Of course, Teren. I will tell you whatever you wish to know."

Walking through the glass double doors, we all adjourned to the more comfortable living room. As Teren walked through, he reached behind himself to grab my hand. Holding me tight, we stepped into the ski lodge-like room with the rest of his family together. When Gabriel stood before the dormant fireplace, I instantly recalled the last time Gabriel was in this room, giving another speech that involved apologies towards our family. As his deep voice started going into detail about how he and Malcolm first met, back in the old days, the medieval old days, I recalled him telling me that I would die in this room.

And all because of one lone vampire. He had truly done more damage than I'd first believed he could. Gabriel seemed so powerful, so well connected, but Malcolm had slipped through his nets for years. But eventually the noose around him had tightened enough to make Malcolm react violently, and violently he had. As Gabriel went over happier times, when they had started their lab together, I thought of Carrie. Caught in the middle of a war that she knew nothing about, she'd paid the ultimate price. And she'd had no clue why. We'd wiped her clean. She wouldn't have even known who Teren was, let alone what he was. As Malcolm had been feeding off of her, it would have been her first and only experience with vampires. She'd died thinking we were all as evil as the horror movies made us out to be. She'd died not knowing that there were very good vampires too. And she'd loved one, nearly had his child.

It made my stomach crawl. Carrie had died, I'd died, and Starla had nearly died, all over money. It seemed childish and pointless, but to some people it wasn't, I guessed. To some, if they had nothing else, money was everything. Maybe life had gotten stagnant for Malcolm. As I listened to Gabriel gloss over the hundreds of years in their relationship like it was nothing more than a handful of weeks, I began to believe that was a possibility. Were we destined to become cold and unfeeling simply because we were so long-lived? Would humans eventually mean nothing to us, because they came and went as quickly as house flies?

Teren squeezed my hand as I considered our longevity. Glancing over at him, I watched his light eyes flick over mine. Then I turned to regard the other sets of light eyes in the room, all of them raptly listening to Gabriel's life with our son's kidnapper.

Alanna had her arms around Jack, while Imogen had her arms around Alanna. The love and warmth passing between the three people was nearly palpable to me. I thought of Halina, her presence a blip in my head, her actual location still hundreds of miles away. She could seem indifferent at times, but I'd seen her soften as Gabriel's love warmed her. Perhaps it wasn't Malcolm's long life that had dulled his humanity. Perhaps it was just how long he'd been alone.

Even as Gabriel described the times they'd been together, it still sounded like Malcolm had been alone. Jealous, petty, and demanding the affection of others, he'd never actually let anybody in.

I squeezed Teren's hand back as my gaze returned to his. No, the Adams would never fall into the lifeless rut that Malcolm had. We had each other, for eternity, and I knew that the bonds in his family would keep our souls in check.

Now we just had to find a way to get all of our family back together again...alive and intact.

As soon as Gabriel finished filling us in on everything he knew of Malcolm, Teren and I resumed our search for Julian. We knew it was pointless, but we felt like someone in the family should still be looking and we were the best equipped for daylight hours. We drove a lot though, and took frequent breaks. Teren didn't want to become so weak again that he couldn't put up a better fight, should we run into Malcolm. Teren stopped to drink more often in that one afternoon than I'd seen him drink since the night of his conversion. It helped though; he was more animated and alert than he'd been since Julian's abduction.

Gabriel joined us for our search, mostly staying secluded in the safety of his tinted vehicle, but venturing out with us if the location was shaded enough. He gave us better direction, places that would appeal to Malcolm or places he would never go, places that were the likelier targets. It nearly seemed that we had our own criminal profiler along with us, and it made the process feel more streamlined. I finally felt like we weren't just aimlessly looking around.

When he wasn't out traipsing around the countryside with us, Gabriel was on the phone with his vast array of contacts. He'd left a search party up north when he'd blazed back to us, and he kept them in a constant state of movement, much like he was keeping us. He also checked in with his lab, seeing how the new batch of drugs were coming along under Jordan's watchful eye. I remembered the coolly professional, dark-skinned vampire and thought he was probably in hog heaven, taking over while the boss was away.

Gabriel even checked in on Starla and Jacen. Once he'd sent them south, they'd kept going. From their last conversation, it seemed like they were in Mexico. While I'm sure Jacen was taking his task with all seriousness, I was equally sure that Starla was sipping margaritas.

When the sun set, the last Adams member that I could feel stirred and started heading our way again. By how quickly her form was closing the distance, I'd say she'd be in town well before morning. We called her as soon as we could, filling her in on the meeting with Malcolm. We did *not* mention that Teren had nearly driven a stake through Gabriel's heart. That was just something that was better for everyone if she never found out about it.

While we were debating trudging through the sewers, Teren's cell phone rang.

Probably thinking it was one of our parents, he answered it without looking at the ID. "Hello?" he said curtly, popping open a storm cover for Gabriel.

As Gabriel surveyed the dark hole, I heard the caller's response, "I'm not in there, Teren. I don't hide in sewers. That's just disgusting."

Teren's entire body went rigid and he dropped the manhole cover. Gabriel stepped back as the heavy slab clanged down to the ground, wedging sideways in the hole that he'd just been staring into.

Teren twisted around and searched the dark buildings along the empty stretch of road that we were on. I searched too, wondering if Malcolm was close enough to see us, or if he'd just heard something that had given away what we'd been doing.

"Where are you then?" Teren said it calmly, but his eyes betrayed how frantic he felt, darting from location to location, never once resting.

"Not in a hole in the ground," was Malcolm's snide response. "I know I'm early, but I find I'm getting impatient. Have you completed your task?"

I straightened and stopped looking around. Teren did too. As one, we looked over at Gabriel silently staring at us. Teren gave him the hush symbol and Gabriel nodded. Malcolm had just asked if Teren had killed Gabriel yet. That meant he couldn't see us. Otherwise he'd see Gabriel, too. He must have been sarcastically tossing out an idea of where we were, and happened to nail it right on the head.

With a growl of conviction, Teren murmured, "Yes...Gabriel is on his way to me now. It's as good as done. Now where's my son?"

"As good as done isn't done, Adams." Malcolm laughed. "Besides, do you expect me to take your word for it? I want to see the body. I want to hold his lifeless heart...then you get your boy."

Teren closed his eyes. "Fine, then I'll bring it to you. When I've taken it, I'll bring you his heart. Just tell me where to meet you."

"How about the place where this all started? Hmmm, that would be poetic, wouldn't it?"

Teren opened his eyes. Scrunching his brow, he searched my face. I shrugged, not understanding either. "What are you talking about?"

Malcolm chuckled again, his laugh raw, like he was parched. I instantly prayed that he wasn't hungry enough to feed on Julian. "One of my deceased client's favorite haunts was in California, not too terribly far from your home. An old, abandoned farmhouse? I believe you know it, yes?"

A flood of ice ran through me as I remembered that hunter taking us, and locking us up like prisoners in a bad horror flick. We'd been thrown into the cellar of an old farm house. That was where he wanted to meet? Teren's lips pressed into a hard line. "Yeah, I know it. All right, I'll meet you there."

Malcolm's tone got serious as he bit out, "Bring me his heart...along with a photo of the rest of his body. The instant kind...the one that you can't doctor. I want to know that this is real before I tell you where to find your child."

Teren sighed and ran a hand through his hair. "And how do I know you even will? How do I even know that he's still alive?"

Malcolm sighed then a muffled thump came through the phone. Like he was talking to a dog, he said, "Speak."

Instantly a tiny voice filled the line, a voice I knew so well I heard it in my head in the middle of the night. "Daddy? I wanna go home."

My hands flew to my mouth as my eyes instantly watered and my knees threatened to buckle in half. Julian's voice was angelic, the cleanest, purest sound I'd ever head. All the more so, because I was sure I'd never hear it again.

Teren's knees did buckle. Catching himself before he fell, he took a stumbling step and cupped the phone to his ear. "Julian, baby, are you okay? Did he hurt you? Daddy's coming to get you, okay, Daddy's coming—"

Malcolm's voice snapped back onto the phone line. "I will be at the farmhouse at midnight. I will wait twenty minutes. If you don't show, I skip town and never come back. If you try and deceive me, I skip town and don't ever come back. If you try and trap me—"

Teren grit his jaw. "Yeah, I get it...you'll leave Julian to die..."

Malcolm let out a cold laugh. "Good, you understand. Give me the proof, I'll give you your son's location...everybody wins."

"Except Gabriel," Teren whispered, locking eyes with the ancient vampire silently listening, his brow deeply furrowed.

Malcolm snorted. "Yeah, well, as with most things in life, for someone to win, someone else needs to lose. Midnight, Adams. Don't keep me waiting." Then the line went dead.

I started sniffling, my lip trembling. Julian's voice rang through my entire body. I wanted to reach out and hug him, tell him that everything was going to be okay, but I had no idea where he was. His hand shaking, Teren put his phone away. He closed his eyes, inhaling and exhaling as slowly and intently as I was.

"Well," a voice began. Teren opened his eyes and we both looked over at Gabriel. Twisting his lips, Gabriel shook his head. "It would seem that you need a heart."

Teren sighed and shrugged his shoulders. "Yeah, it would seem I do. Any ideas?

Smirking with one edge of his lip, Gabriel slowly nodded. "Yes, I do have...one idea."

Chapter 21 – A Heart

An hour later, Teren, Gabriel and I, were at the hospital where my sister worked. We'd called the ranch moments after getting off the phone with Malcolm and explained Gabriel's crazy idea to her. Ashley had insisted that if we were going to go through with this plan, then she was coming with. I'd wanted to object, but Hot Ben had been out at the ranch and had offered to bring her to us.

With my sister having an escort, I'd felt better about her leaving Alanna and Imogen's supervision. Once Julian had been taken, she'd stopped going to work, stopped going to see Christian. Pretty much stopped having a life. I hated that mine was affecting hers so much, but I wanted her to be safe. I didn't really know if Malcolm would snatch another family member or not, but it wasn't a risk I was willing to take. Ashley, either. She knew the stakes, knew what could happen to her if she crossed paths with a vampire with an attitude. My sister was brave, but she wasn't an idiot.

As she led our band through the halls of the hospital where she worked, she waved and acknowledged several of the people we passed by. None of the people working here gave her looks a moment's pause. They were too interested to hear how the family tragedy that had kept her away was going. Ashley had told the hospital the same sob story that I'd told Tracey: that we'd gone out of town for a funeral. The nurses and doctors that we met along the way all wanted to know if Ashley was okay. It warmed me that she was so completely accepted here. She really did have a second family to fall back on. Well, maybe a third, since the Adams had pretty much adopted her.

Stopping at the doors where the recently deceased bodies were stored, Ashley glanced around the empty halls. "They don't like people being down here that aren't supposed to be, but Christian has me come down sometimes to collect donor tissue, so no one should find it too odd for me to be here." She looked around at the group assembled before her. "Now the rest of you…well, I'm just glad it's getting late. This is just a waiting area, so it should be empty until morning."

Teren sighed. "Yeah, it's getting late. We're running out of time, we need to hurry."

Ashley nodded and opened the doors. Teren paused before going through them, and placed his hand on her arm. "I'm very sorry you got dragged into this, Ashley."

Looking up at him, she shook her head. "He's my nephew, Teren. There's nothing I wouldn't do for him."

Smiling warmly at her, Teren leaned down and kissed her bare scalp. My sister squeezed his arm, then patted him through the door. I came through last, slinging my arm around Ashley as the doors swung closed behind us.

The smell of disinfectant hit me first, then…the smell of blood. Teren had walked over to the cold storage drawers and had found what we'd come here to find. Two freshly killed humans. From what Gabriel had told us when laying out his idea, they'd shot each other in some petty, territorial, gang fight. The hospital had tried to save them, but the damage had been too great and they'd each died on the table.

I inhaled deep. The scent in the air was heavenly and a bit disgusting, since I knew where I was and what I was doing. The human side of me cringed away from being in a cold, sterile room with fresh corpses. The vampiric side of me growled in pleasure.

Hot Ben looked at me, his eyes wide, and I realized then that the vampiric side of me *had* actually growled in pleasure. I shrugged at him as I looked around at all of the people staring at me. "Sorry…it smells good in here." I looked down at the floor. "I'm sort of hungry," I mumbled.

Ben made some sort of disgusted noise as he started digging into his backpack. Gabriel smiled crookedly and nodded, not a big deal, and Teren ignored me completely. His eyes were focused on the two dead bodies lying under sheets on metal slabs in the otherwise empty room. My sister held my waist tighter and whispered, "I could get a blood bag for you, if you need something?"

Embarrassed beyond belief that my sister was offering to steal blood that could be used to save someone else's life, just because I had a hankering, I mumbled, "I'm fine," and stepped up to Gabriel.

"How did you know about this?" I indicated the two men that
Teren had revealed when he'd pulled the sheets away from their
faces. One had deeply tanned skin and dark hair; the other was paler
with sandy hair. I couldn't help but think, staring at them, that to
someone out there, these two were just as important as Julian was to
us…and they'd lost them today. My heart sank as I gave them a
respectful moment of silence.

Gabriel took a second to answer me, almost like he was also
giving them a moment. "It was on the news earlier today. I heard it
broadcasted while I waited in the car." Walking up to the sandy
brown-haired man, he bent over and studied his face. "Then they
were displaying their pictures on a television screen in a house that
we were driving past." He touched the dead man's face, angling him
so he was looking directly at him. "I thought it intriguing that this
one looked a bit like me."

I blinked at Gabriel. He was right, while shorter and slimmer,
the face on the slab was oddly similar, if not as refined as the vampire
before me. He'd caught a split second of a news program as we drove
past and had seen enough to recall the dead man later in the evening?
Gabriel's brain mystified me.

"Oh," was all I could think to respond with. My brain was less
mystifying.

As Ashley stared at the bodies with a blank look on her face, a
purposely held in place blank look, Hot Ben handed my husband a
butcher knife. Teren stared at the knife and then looked back up at
Ben. "It's sort of big, isn't it?" he asked, his lips twisting at what he
had to do with it.

Ben shrugged. "You said to bring a knife so you wouldn't have
to waste time swiping one. You said you had to cut out a heart with
it." He indicated the long blade in Teren's hands. "I figured bigger
would be better."

I shook my head at Ben. My husband told him he needed help
cutting out a dead man's heart, and he only responded with—*How big
should the knife be?*

Teren frowned as he stared down at the sandy haired dead man.
Even though the blood around the bullet holes smelled wonderful, I

didn't relish this act being caught in my mental photo album. Twisting around, I grabbed my sister and made her look away.

She protested at first. "I'm a nurse, Em, this is nothing compared to what I've seen." But then the sounds of bones cracking filled the room, as the boys forced back the poor man's ribcage, and she stopped trying to turn back around. "This was not something I ever pictured myself being a party to," she muttered.

As I inhaled and exhaled the more intense smell of blood in the air, I shook my head. "You and me both, sis."

Hearing Hot Ben mutter, "Oh, God, I'm gonna be sick," I tried not to picture what they were doing in my head. It was a little difficult, since I could hear each squishy sound they made. There was one last suctioning noise, and then the sounds stopped. I risked a glance and turned back around. Hot Ben was a little green as he watched Teren hand a lumpy, red thing over to Gabriel.

Teren popped a finger in his mouth once he handed it over, like he was cleaning off a tasty snack. Hot Ben's hand went to his mouth as he shoved Teren's shoulder away from him. "Dude, I know you're a vampire and all, but that's disgusting!"

Teren stopped sucking on his finger and looked down at his hand a little sheepishly. "Sorry, Ben…I guess I'm a little hungry, too."

He looked over at me and shrugged as he wiped his hand on a towel that Ben handed him from his bag. Gabriel studied the bloody mess before him, then walked over to a sink. My brow furrowed as I watched him studiously rinse the heart clean. Trying not to think about what he was holding, I asked him, "Why are you doing that? Won't a clean heart be kind of…obvious?"

Gabriel smiled at me as he carefully removed any trace of blood from around the organ. "No, dear, a human heart would be all too obvious."

Finishing, he glanced up at Teren. "May I see that?" He nodded his head at the knife in Teren's hand. Teren's looked at it, shrugged, then walked over to him. Gabriel glanced at Ashley. "Do you have a container we could put this in? Something generic, that we could have gotten anywhere?" Ashley nodded and ducked into a cabinet.

Seconds later she was back, handing him a typical plastic bowl with a lid. Smiling and thanking her, Gabriel tenderly placed the organ in it.

Glancing over at Ben as he walked up to us, Gabriel smirked. "You may not want to watch this either, if the blood is bothering you?"

Hot Ben locked gazes with me and lifted his chin. "No, I'm fine."

Shrugging, Gabriel held his arm over the bowl and shoved the knife blade in. Hot Ben hissed as a stream of dark red blood flowed from the knife point, but he didn't say anything else. Teren watched as Gabriel kept the point in his arm so that the wound wouldn't heal. "The heart will smell like you now, not like a human's. I wouldn't have thought of that."

Gabriel twisted his lips. "I know Malcolm. He will test it." Once a convincing amount of blood was covering the organ, Gabriel pulled the knife from his arm; it healed instantly.

When Gabriel was done, the knife was cleaned and put back into Ben's backpack, along with the dead gang member's heart. I hoped that some good would come from the pointless death that had happened today. I hoped that no more deaths happened today. After Teren, Gabriel, and Ben cleaned themselves up, Ben scrubbing his hands until they were practically raw, we all turned back to the body.

Sighing at the mess they'd left, Teren grabbed the last item we needed from Ben's bag. Pulling out a Polaroid camera, he aimed it at the body, trying to get the right angle on the face so that it looked enough like Gabriel to be convincing. Finally happy with the shot, he snapped a picture.

He took a couple more just to be sure, then pointed at the body. "We can't just leave him like this. That would make the national news."

Wrapping the corpse up in the sheet, Gabriel effortlessly lifted him. "I will take care of it, Teren. A missing body will raise less attention than a ripped apart body, at least, until I can get a vampire in here to make some adjustments." Tilting his head at Teren, he seriously told him, "You go out to the farmhouse, and I will meet you there. After Malcolm tells you where to find Julian, I will take him down, and this will finally be over." That was Gabriel's master plan, to convince Malcolm that Teren had indeed killed him, then jump out and bring swift justice down on Malcolm, once Julian was found.

Teren nodded. Gabriel twisted to leave and Teren put a hand on his arm. Gabriel's beautiful face looked back as Teren nodded his head at the body in Gabriel's arms. "Don't just dump him somewhere. Bury him...respectfully. He may have just bought my son's freedom with his life."

Gabriel tilted his head, then nodded. Turning away, he blurred out of the room so fast a human's eyes would have barely registered the movement.

Putting the room back in order, the rest of us walked out of the hospital like nothing weird had just happened. Clasping Teren's hand as we hurriedly walked along, I wondered how my life had deviated so far from the realm of normalcy.

In the parking lot, I put my hand on Ashley's arm. "Go back to the ranch and watch over Nika."

Ashley shook her head. "I want to come with you. I want to help get Julian back." She lifted her chin and I saw no trace of fear in her. She'd seen a lot over the past few years. She'd faced a lot of fears, most revolving around family members. It had strengthened the already strong woman.

I rested my head against hers; she burned hot against my chilly skin. "I know you could handle yourself if you came with us, Ashley." I pulled back to look into her deep brown eyes, eyes that reminded me of all of the moments that we'd shared together over our lifetime. "But I can't handle anything happening to *you*. I'm sorry, I know it's selfish, but I need you to stay away from this."

She twisted her scarred lips as she stared at me, but she didn't have an objection that would work against my need to keep her away from the darkness I sometimes found myself in. As she slowly nodded, I tilted my head back at the hospital. "Besides, I think you've done enough. Most people wouldn't willingly help their sister steal an organ."

I cringed at the thought of what we'd just done and she grinned.

Giving me a soft kiss on the cheek, she nodded again. "Go get Julian back…I'll keep your daughter safe."

Hot Ben tossed her the keys to his SUV, then opened the rear door of Teren's Prius. Teren and I both twisted to stare at him and he defiantly met our eyes. "I'm not hiding away with the women." He held Teren's gaze. "I've got your back, Teren, always have…always will."

Teren smiled, nodding his head as he opened his door. Waving a goodbye to my sister, I watched her in the parking lot as we pulled away. Careful to not draw the attention of any cops, since we really couldn't explain away a butcher knife and a bloody heart, and we didn't have a mind-wiping vampire along, although, she was closing fast, Teren drove as quickly as he could out of the city.

I examined the photos he'd taken as he sped us to the place where he had died. Before heading out to the hospital, we'd talked with Imogen at length about the farmhouse, so she could tell us exactly where it was. She and Halina had been able to find the place that pernicious night, so many years ago, by tracking the scent of the man around where they'd last felt Teren's location, but we'd been sort of out of it that day and I couldn't remember where to go.

Imogen's description had brought back the memory of driving away from there though. Horribly enough, I was certain I could find it again if I needed to. And apparently, I needed to. Malcolm knew about Teren's transformation there. Or maybe he'd just pieced together the facts. If that was a stopping point for his "client" in this state, maybe Malcolm had delivered his supplies there. Since he knew that Teren had killed the man, maybe he'd pieced together that the death had happened there, at the man's favorite location. He was as ingenious as Gabriel after all.

I was stressed enough over our upcoming subterfuge that I wished my heart could thump again. At least the thudding beat would have been an outlet for my nerves. Squinting my eyes at the instant photo, I tried to see Gabriel's face in the gangster. I could see it…if I wasn't aware of the truth.

Sighing, I laid my head back on the seat. I just wanted all of this to be over with. I just wanted to live in peace with my family. I just wanted my son back. I wanted to go back to debating whether or not to move. That seemed an easy task now. Teren's hands gripped the wheel as he sped out of town. We had enough time to make it, but anxious as well, he was pushing himself.

As we neared the property, I felt something that concerned me. Except for my daughter, every blip on my vampire-radar was moving, following our location. Teren looked over at me as he sensed it too. Hot Ben leaned forward in the back seat. "What is it?" he asked, his lips pressed together as he looked between the two of us.

I tucked the photos back in Ben's backpack and grabbed Teren's phone from his side. Frowning, I answered Ben. "I'm not sure." The phone started ringing before I could even dial. I started at the unexpectedness, then answered it as the ranch's number popped up on the screen. "Hello?"

"Oh, hi, sweetie," my mom's voice answered me. I frowned that she was still awake, but didn't say anything; sleep wasn't really easy for anyone lately. Before I could ask anything, my mother started talking. "Alanna wanted me to call and explain?" She said it like she didn't quite understand. The bond we all felt was a little puzzling to her.

Teren answered her, loud enough for her human ears to hear. "Why did my mother and grandmother leave the ranch? Why aren't they staying with you and Nika?"

My mom paused before whispering in my ear, "He can hear me? Through the phone?"

I smiled but Teren frowned. "Yes, I can hear you, even whispering. What happened?"

My mom sighed. "Ashley called the house and let us know that you guys got what you needed." She paused again, then added, "Did you really...? No, never mind...I don't want to know."

Wanting to forget what we'd done, I tried prodding my mom along. "And...?"

She cleared her throat. "Right, well, Alanna and Imogen both decided that what you were doing was dangerous, and they couldn't just sit at home while you were out there...meeting with that man." In a slightly softer voice she added, "Are they right? Are you in danger, Emma?"

Wanting to reassure her, I quickly said, "No, of course not, Mom. He's not interested in hurting us, and we're not alone. Gabriel and Ben are with us. Alanna and Imogen really should have stayed with you. I don't want you left alone..."

Teren sighed in irritation. "I wanted Mom and Gran away from this. I wanted to know that they, at least, were safe."

My mother heard him, and knowing that he could hear her, she answered with, "Teren, Emma, the threat is where you are, not here. Jack, Ash and I will be fine, and we'll keep Nika safe. But, as a parent, it is nearly impossible to stay away when a child is in peril. You, of all people, should understand that. If I were as indestructible as your mother, Teren, you couldn't keep me away, either...and I know your father feels the same."

Teren looked down but didn't say anything. Hot Ben put a hand on his shoulder and Teren raised his eyes to look at him in the mirror. "It's like you said when Julian first disappeared, Teren, when you called me into this...we need everybody."

Teren smiled at him and looked over at me. "All right, then, we'll use everybody."

I smiled that my husband was finally accepting the supernatural help around him instead of trying to do everything himself. Thanking my mother, I told her to give Nika a big hug and a kiss for me. Mom sighed in my ear. "I will. I'll probably be cuddled up next to her all night, worried about how you are."

Sighing softly myself, I looked out the window. "I'll be fine, Mom, and when I come home...I'll have my son with me."

Mom sniffled and wished me luck. Putting Teren's phone back, I grasped his thigh and hoped that what I'd just told my mom was what was really going to happen. Teren glanced over at me, then pressed his foot down even further, pushing his little car to its max.

What felt like hours later, we pulled onto a bumpy, dirt drive. Memories flooded me as each bounce jolted my body. Even though the car was deathly silent, Teren and I not even breathing, I heard the echo of Teren's pain-filled cries in my head. I even saw his blood soaked jeans in my vision. Teren glanced over at me, his jaw tight and his eyes wide; he was remembering too.

"Wow," Ben muttered from the back, "creepy."

In front of us was a decrepit building. Planks were missing, the windows were boarded over, the front door was half off its hinges... It looked like the home a chainsaw wielding serial killer would use. And in a way, I suppose it had been home to an equally deranged man. I glanced down at the dirt-packed ground as we pulled up to the house. Somewhere in the basement levels of this place, that man had lost his life...at my hands. Mine and Teren's both.

Shoving the past aside, I tried to focus on the now. The soft glow of the dash showed that we'd made it a few minutes before midnight; we hadn't missed him. Two of the blips on my radar were already here, their sonic bursts of speed faster than Teren's drive. The third vampire approaching us was closing the distance at a strikingly fast speed. Maybe feeling all of us together and away from the ranch, Halina had realized that something was going down and ditched her slower moving car. I wasn't sure if Gabriel was here or not, but I figured he was. He wanted this over with as much as we did.

As we stepped out of the car, the dusty smell in the air instantly brought the remembered horror of death with it. Alanna and Imogen walked out of the front door, and Ben jumped a little at seeing them stride through the loosely hanging screen. But Teren and I had already felt them, and only looked over, interested at what they'd found.

Carefully stepping around the missing floorboards, Alanna shrugged. "It's clean. No trace of, well, much of anything really."

Imogen shrugged her shoulders. "It looks the same as when mother and I sterilized it." The warm, grandmotherly woman had said that so matter-of-factly that a chill went down my dead spine. She and Halina had cleaned up the incident, erasing all signs of foul play for what the human world would have considered murder. Well, manslaughter at best.

Teren frowned and looked around the empty property. I held my arms to my chest, wondering if my son was close. Did Malcolm bring him here, or leave him where he'd tucked him? Teren stepped forward, sniffing the air. I did as well and I sensed it in the wind blowing our direction—that faintly familiar scent from the movie theaters and the abandoned building's parking lot. Malcolm was here.

A growl burrowing from his chest, Teren stepped forward again. Walking behind him, feeling on edge, I followed as he stepped over to where a fluorescent lamp post was shining a pool of bluish light over the dark ground. It was attached to an equally decrepit barn. The light itself was the only sturdy looking thing on the weathered behemoth.

Staring through the cracked opening of the doors, Teren's growl grew louder. My silent heart wanted to race as nerves flew through me. Was my child with him through those doors? The group of us fanned out in a wide semicircle around the doors, giving Malcolm enough space that he didn't feel cornered. Ben stayed close to Teren's side, his trusty stake in one hand, his heart-containing backpack in the other. Alanna and Imogen stood farther back, near the edges of the circle, closing off any real escape the man had…from their direction at least. Knowing Malcolm was good at evading traps, I figured he had about five other ways to leave this situation, if he needed to.

The look on Malcolm's face as he stepped out of the building clearly showed that he believed that, too. There was no fear of us in the worn vampire's features. Just a tiredness that betrayed how much he wanted this to be over with, too. I hoped that after tonight, it would be, for everyone.

His eyes slowly taking in all of us, he softly muttered, "I see you brought the cavalry." His eyes locked on Teren's as he stepped directly underneath the light streaming from above; the spotlight he'd always craved. "Do I frighten you that much?" His lips lifted into a cruel, satisfied smile.

Teren didn't react to his goading, only stepped forward; his entire face was a stone mask. "Where's my son?"

Malcolm sighed, rolling his eyes. "That's all I ever hear from you. It's so…repetitive." Narrowing his eyes, he raised an eyebrow. "Where's my heart?"

Teren grabbed the bag from Ben and tossed it at Malcolm. He'd tossed it pretty hard and it smacked the vampire in the chest. Malcolm smirked as he clutched the bag to him. "That wasn't very friendly. Not exactly a nice way to treat your business partner, is it?"

He unzipped the bag while Teren gritted his jaw. His eyes darkened as he stared at the man who'd ripped our family in two. Opening the bag, Malcolm met eyes with Hot Ben. Ben lifted his chin, and clutched his stake tighter. A slow smile spread on Malcolm's face. "Well, hello, human. Are you the bodyguard?" He nodded at the stake Ben was clutching so tight his knuckles were white. When Ben didn't answer, Malcolm swung his eyes back to Teren. "Interesting choice."

Exhaling as calmly as he could, Teren forcibly said, "Let's just get this over with so I can get my son back."

Malcolm concentrated on the open bag. "All right, all right. People nowadays...so impatient," he muttered. Reaching into the bag, he pulled out the human heart that we were trying to pass off as Gabriel's. A cold smile lit his face, and the bluish light cast from the lamp made him seem even more devilish. "Ah, hello there, Gabriel. Sorry we had to meet up again this way."

He chuckled then stuck the container under his arm. Reaching his hand back in the bag, he pulled out the knife, then sniffed it. I tried not to tense, to not give anything away, but we'd washed the blade and it only smelled of soap, not human blood. Malcolm tossed it to the ground, uninterested in the weapon. Finally his fingers closed around the Polaroid photos. Snatching them, he dropped the bag to the dirt at his feet.

He raised an eyebrow at Teren as he prepared to flip through them. "Shall we see your handiwork, then?" I made myself not hold my breath. If he didn't buy the pictures...

Focused on the slightly blurred figure of the dead man in the photo, Malcolm's brow bunched together. He held it an inch from his face and I nearly wanted to scream with all the tension pricking my body. After a long moment, he pulled it back and lifted his gaze to Teren. "Remind me to never piss you off, vampire."

Teren growled and I clearly heard his words in the sound—*Too late, I'm already pissed.*

Malcolm smirked at the show. Seemingly satisfied with the photos, he tucked them in his jacket. Glancing around at everyone studiously watching him, he popped open the container. Teren, getting restless and anxious, took another step forward and tossed his hands out to the side. "You got what you wanted. I did it, I killed him. Now, where's my son?"

Malcolm retreated a half step. "All in due time, Adams. I still haven't tested the merchandise." He pulled the lid off the container and the scent of blood hit my nose. It was similar to human blood, sweet and tangy, but with a foreign, comforting note to it. Malcolm leaned down to sniff it, then smiled. Reaching in, he held the wet thing tenderly, just like he'd said he'd wanted to. As Ben made a disgusted noise and looked away, Malcolm ran his tongue over the heart. Even as a vampire, even knowing that he'd basically licked our version of a lollipop, the sight made me cringe. I looked away too.

Malcolm purred though. "Ahhh, vampirically delicious." I glanced back to find him giving Teren an appraising eye. "You did well, Adams. I'm surprised. I thought for sure I'd have to start sending you pieces of your brat to get you to do this."

Teren stepped right up to him, his face heated. "You son of a bitch."

Taking a step back, Malcolm held his hand out at Teren. "Hey, I didn't. We had a deal, you lived up to it. I'll tell you where he is and then we both go our separate ways. Agreed?"

Teren backed off, relaxing his stance. "Agreed," he nodded.

I tensed, waiting for the words from him that would tell us where to go, waiting for him to confess my son's hiding place. Malcolm opened his mouth to speak, the heart straight in front of him, in his still outstretched hand. His eyes narrowing, he closed his mouth. Bringing the heart back up to his face, he turned it over and over, looking for something. My breath hitched and I took a step forward. He knew where Julian was, he had to tell us.

Glancing up at Teren, Malcolm's entire face hardened. "What is this, Adams? Some sort of joke?"

Teren blinked and took a step back. "What do you mean? It's a heart, Gabriel's heart."

Malcolm tilted his head and held up the bloody organ. "Really? This is the heart of the man you murdered, the man you *staked*?"

Teren opened his mouth to speak, then his eyes went wide and he froze. I didn't understand why until Malcolm spoke again. "If you staked this heart, where's the hole?" His brow furrowing in anger, he tossed the thing at Teren's feet. The dirt instantly coated the organ, the perfect, intact, holeless organ. We'd missed something in our charade and he'd noticed.

Malcolm shoved his hand in his pocket and pulled out the photos as everyone in the semicircle tensed. "And don't tell me you took his head off, because I can clearly see that you didn't." He tossed the photos on the ground too. Taking an angry step forward, he poked Teren in the chest. "Did you just walk up and rip it out of his chest?" He pointed back down to the heart, "Because that looks *cut* out to me!"

With both hands, he shoved Teren's shoulders back. "Whose heart is that? What did you do!"

The universe not working with us, the wind shifted. I could smell it, so certainly the ancient vampire before me could as well. Gabriel had indeed shown up. He was behind us, remaining hidden downwind. He was no longer hidden.

Malcolm released his grip on Teren's shirt and backed up a step. "No, no, no...you didn't." His eyes flashed to Teren's. "You tried to trick me, with your son's life on the line?" Shaking his head, Malcolm stepped back again. Teren reached out for him, but Malcolm lunged to the edge of the barn. All he had to do was slip back through the slotted door and pick one of his many preplanned escape routes, and then he'd be gone, along with any hope of finding my son.

Malcolm's face paled when Gabriel finally dropped the charade and let his presence be known. As he slowly stepped out of the darkness, his glowing eyes announced his arrival. "Malcolm," he intoned, "I believe we have a few things to discuss."

Malcolm started shaking. This was probably the closest he'd been to Gabriel in a while. He shook his head as he backed up another step. "I have nothing to say to you, Gabriel." His hate-filled eyes shifted to Teren. "But you! You just signed your kid's death warrant! You will never find where I stashed that brat!"

Malcolm took another step back and everyone took a step forward. Witnessing his worst case scenario happening right before his eyes, Teren ran his hands through his hair. His face was torn. I understood. I was torn myself. Malcolm was either going to escape, or in the struggle to escape, he was going to get himself killed...and then our son was dead, too. He was right, our attempt at deception had just insured Julian's death. A sob started to rise in me, but I held it in.

Teren ran his hands back through his hair again as he looked around at everyone closing in on Malcolm. "Wait," he muttered, his hands coming out as if to hold back his family. "Everybody, just wait," he tried again.

It wasn't working. Everyone was too intent on not letting Malcolm get away. Seeing this, Malcolm twisted to dart through the barn, to his escape. My dead heart lurched with despair, but a sudden streak in my head collided with Malcolm at the door. A wicked grin on her face, Halina crouched low before him; her growl ripped through the night. Malcolm skittered away from her, into the center of our ever-shrinking circle. Panicked, he twisted around inside the circle, not knowing how to escape it. I saw my son's fate tied up with his, and I stepped forward, too. He couldn't escape...he just couldn't.

Teren stayed where he was, on the inside of the circle now as Gabriel filled in his spot along the edge. "Wait, please," he said, his hands still lifted into the air, trying to hold back his family. As he twisted around to look at everyone, he seemed like a mirror image of the alarmed Malcolm.

Now that both of them were inside the circle, Malcolm finally directed his fear at Teren. "You're dead, Adams! You and your son are both dead!"

He grabbed Teren's shirt and Halina lurched forward. Teren held out his hand to her. "Stop, just stop. Everybody stop!" he yelled.

Alanna and Imogen paused along with me, but Ben, Halina and Gabriel still crept forward, hands ready for action. Malcolm squeezed Teren's shoulder. "I hope you find death enjoyable...since you and your son will be experiencing it with me," he hissed.

My hands came up to my face as I saw all of this going horribly wrong. Gabriel was going to kill Malcolm before our son's location could be revealed. Even if he did get Malcolm to spit something out before he staked him, there was no way he'd tell us the truth now...Malcolm would rather die than let Teren have the satisfaction.

Teren realized this too and broke away from Malcolm. He backed up to Ben while pointing at the frazzled vampire trapped between us. "You want blood! Is that what you want!" Twisting, Teren grabbed the stake from Hot Ben's hands. I didn't even have time to wonder what my husband planned on doing with it. Glaring at Malcolm, he yelled, "Then I'll give you blood!" and he blurred over to Gabriel.

Spinning, he sank the stake into Gabriel's chest, as far in as he could get it, then he pushed it a little farther. Gabriel's mouth dropped open in surprise and the front of his shirt immediately stained dark red. He choked and sputtered as he stared at Teren in disbelief. Then he sank to his knees and fell facedown to the ground. Even in the bluish light, I could see the dirt around his chest stain and darken as his life's blood seeped out of his damaged heart.

It was the one thing that even the undead still needed...a heart, and Teren had just taken Gabriel's, for real this time.

Chapter 22 – No Mercy

Everyone stopped moving. Everyone who could, stopped breathing. Even the sound of nature around us stopped. No serpents slithered in the grass, no night animals skittered under the brush, no owls hooted in the air. Everything was silent, either paying their respects for the fallen, ancient vampire, or shocked into silence that my husband had been the one who felled him.

Teren, the only one of us not shocked and silent, panted as he twisted back to Malcolm. "Now, where the hell is my son!" he yelled, his voice breaking the stillness.

Malcolm's hazel eyes were as wide as they could be as he stared at his nemesis on the ground, stone still in death, a true death this time. "Holy shit! I can't believe you actually did it!" His eyes flashed up to Teren's, and a happy smile was on his lips. "That was incredible! I really didn't think you'd go through with it, especially when you brought him here. Way to man up!" He shook his head. "And out of nowhere too. He never saw you coming. Wow…and you think I'm cold."

Teren, obviously done with playing games, blurred over to Malcolm and grabbed him by the throat. As he lifted him into the air, everyone pulled their eyes from Gabriel's corpse to watch what Teren would do next. Everyone but Halina that was. She was still staring at the body of her beloved, her face frozen in shock. I had no idea what she'd do when she snapped out of her daze. Family or not, Teren had just killed the man she'd finally let herself love. I couldn't believe she'd just let that go.

"Do not underestimate what I will or will not do for my family." Through clenched jaws, Teren spat out, "My son…now."

Malcolm fidgeted against Teren's hands. Prying the thumbs free from his vocal cords so he could speak, he said, "Yeah, yeah, relax. It's over now. A deal's a deal. Put me down and I'll tell you."

Teren lowered him, but didn't remove his hands from his neck. Malcolm smirked and shrugged. "Your kid is forty miles up the road. There's a clump of woods a few miles east of the highway. There's a car tucked in those woods. He's in the trunk."

Malcolm shrugged again and smiled, like everything in the world was all right. My eyes shifted to where he'd pointed. My baby was alone in the woods, in a trunk? God, how long had he been there? Anger clouded my judgment, and for a minute, I wanted Teren to cut out Malcolm's heart now.

Teren eyed his mother and then his grandmother. "Go get him." His eyes snapped back to Malcolm's; they were icy cold in the lamplight. "Once I know he's there and...fine...I'll let you go."

Alanna and Imogen instantly blurred away, eager to find Julian. I wanted to go too, more than anything, but I couldn't leave my husband with this psycho...especially when I wasn't sure what Halina's reaction would be when she snapped out of her stupor. She was still staring at Gabriel's limp form, her eyes misted over with blood red tears waiting to drop. It was still sinking in for her that he was really gone.

Malcolm, seemingly exhausted now that the tension was over with, sighed in irritation. "The kid's fine, and he really is there. You'll be able to feel him by morning, if you don't believe me."

I switched from watching Halina to studying Malcolm. "What?" I asked, cautious to feel too much hope all at once.

Malcolm looked over at me from the corner of his eye. "I had to inject him twice a day to block the bond. It's a tricky thing to shut off. He'll pop back up on your radar in a few hours."

I exhaled a relieved sigh. Teren clenched his hands tighter. "We'll be able to feel him? So, if you just lied right now about where he is, I'll be able to find him soon. I don't need you anymore," he whispered, his voice lethal.

Malcolm's eyes snapped back to Teren and he tried with renewed vigor to pry Teren off of him. Teren was well rested now though, and Malcolm was still exhausted and worn. For the moment, Teren was stronger. "Hey, we had a deal. You lived up to your part, I lived up to mine. I've got no further beef with you!"

Teren leaned in, his face centimeters from Malcolm's. "You stole my son from me and kept him locked up like an animal. You murdered a friend of mine. I've got a beef with *you*."

Malcolm bristled and tried to pull back from him but Teren held him tight. Ben walked up and grabbed an arm. I walked up and grabbed the other. He might be exhausted, but fear can lend a person strength. And Malcolm had everything to fear from Teren right now. Teren and me both.

Malcolm looked between the three of us as I ticked off how far away Alanna and Imogen were. Their streaks were still moving, still getting to my son. Malcolm pulled at his arms but we had them tight, even Ben, who was using every ounce of human strength he had.

His eyes wide, Malcolm started sputtering. "I didn't hurt him! I was lying about the food and water thing. He's as healthy as a horse. I just needed a card to play so you wouldn't kill me. I've treated him like a king." His frantic eyes looked between the three of us. "I'm a business man, not a child torturer. I just needed you to *think* he was in danger, so you'd back off. In fact, if you *had* taken me, the daily injections I'd been giving him would have worn off and you'd have found him easily. I was bluffing!"

Teren leaned in close again. "Why should I believe anything you say?" His grip tightened around Malcolm's throat and he winced in pain.

Malcolm's eyes widened as he realized that Teren just might kill *him* as well as Gabriel. Struggling, he managed to squeak out, "Hamburgers!"

Teren relaxed his hands as he tilted his head. "What?"

Malcolm inhaled a deep breath. "Hamburgers. The kid eats them like they're gonna disappear." Teren narrowed his eyes and Malcolm added, "Ketchup! He likes them plain with about a gallon of ketchup." His eyes flicked between mine and Teren's. "He thinks it makes them look like they're covered in blood."

My hands loosened on Malcolm along with Teren's. We stared at each other, our expressions equally startled and relieved. It was true, that was exactly how Julian loved his burgers. I always got the super large ketchup bottle at the store, just for him.

As Teren and I smiled at each other, hope that our child might not be starving filled us. And then a roar of grief and despair pierced the air. My ears rang with the force of it. Before I could even start looking for who or what had made the sound, Teren was yanked away from Malcolm. Malcolm staggered back a step as his neck was suddenly free.

Twisting my head, I watched an enraged Halina pulling Teren to the ground. She immediately ducked down, her short skirt riding high up her thighs, and clenched an iron hand around his throat. With a strength that superseded us all, she easily lifted him into the air.

His eyes wide, he struggled against her. "Stop," he croaked out, his air supply cutting off.

"What did you do!" She yelled, her face in an unrecognizable snarl.

Her eyes filled with hatred and pain as she stared up at him. I wasn't even sure if Halina saw Teren anymore. No, I was pretty sure she was no longer looking at the grandson that reminded her of her late husband. She was letting her normally contained anger explode in her grief, and the only thing her eyes saw now was the monster who had destroyed the man she loved.

My hands loosened on Malcolm as I took a step towards her. After everything we'd survived...*she* might be what finally killed my husband.

"What did you do!" she repeated, louder. Her hand jerked him back and forth, shaking him like she could shake an answer from him. He couldn't get enough air to speak though, so he couldn't answer her.

I watched Teren mouth, 'not now,' and filled in his speech for him. "Halina! Stop it. You can deal with Teren later!"

As if to prove my words, Malcolm took the moment of family strife to break away. Squirming out of my distracted hands, he easily broke free from Ben. My head snapped back around to him right as he shoved me. Not expecting it, I fell to the ground. My hip land on a jagged rock in the dirt field and I gasped as I felt skin tearing. It healed as soon as I shifted, but it still hurt like a bitch.

Hot Ben watched me fall and started to help until he noticed Malcolm making a break for it. He grabbed hold of the weary vampire's shoulders, stopping him from blurring away. Irritated,

Malcolm twisted around and connected his fist with Ben's jaw. Weary or not, Malcolm was still a supernatural being, and a hit from him was as hard as a steel bat. Hot Ben twisted around and slumped to the ground. He didn't get back up.

Halina had her back to the turmoil of Malcolm making his escape. Seeing what was going on, Teren tried to kick his great-grandmother in the shins, but she ignored him. She only batted his legs away like he was paining her no more than the twins would have. Leering at him, she finally lowered him, but only to bring his head to hers. "You…will pay," she hissed.

Teren shook his head and tried pointing at where Ben's lifeless body was, but Halina was ignoring everything that wasn't him. She wanted vengeance and Teren was the only one who could give it to her.

After downing Hot Ben, Malcolm smirked and twisted to flee. I blurred back to my feet, torn between stopping him and helping Ben, assuming the gorgeous man was even still alive. Ultimately, the fear of Malcolm being loose in the world made me go for him. I attached my body to his. If he was going to try and blur away, he was going to take me with him.

Malcolm struggled; he didn't have the strength to hightail it with me on his back. Cursing, he tried to grab me and tear me off of him. Quite unfairly, his main hold on me was my hair. He grabbed a fistful and yanked. My head had no choice but to follow, which suddenly exposed my throat to him. His fangs dropped down as he stared at the surging veins. He might not kill me by feeding on me, but he could certainly weaken me to the point where I couldn't fight back. His arms holding mine down, he sank his teeth into me as far as he could. I screamed. It hurt. It also reminded me of being attacked.

Pure I-won't-be-a-victim-again panic pulsed through me and I kneed him in the groin, hard. Some things still hurt men, even when they're deceased, and he groaned and staggered back a step. Pissed off at yet another creep taking an unwanted bite out of me, I curled my hand into a fist and clocked the bastard. I felt the jolt of it all the way up my arm, but his face whipped around and he looked stunned, so I felt vindicated. Then he snarled and looked back at me like he wanted to tear me apart. No longer intent on fleeing, he growled and lunged for me.

I managed to duck out of his grasp by mere inches. Twisting back to Halina who was still having a stare down with a freaking-out Teren, I screamed, "Halina! Let him go and help me! You're the protector, so stop messing around and freaking protect!"

Irritated, Halina finally looked at me. The heat in her expression cooled as she watched Malcolm successfully tackle me to the ground. His hands firmly on my head, he bashed my skull into the dirt, smacking it into the same rock that had injured me earlier. When I was dazed and more complacent, his palms on the sides of my face started pulling my head away from my body.

Halina snarled and released Teren. She might blindly hate him at the moment, but she wasn't about to let me get my head ripped off...thank God. Blurring over to Malcolm, her foot came out and connected with his jaw. He flew backwards about twenty feet, landing hard on his back. Stunned and not looking like he wanted to take on a pureblood, he stood on shaky legs and twisted to leave. Halina phased right in front of him. Grabbing fistfuls of his shirt, she yanked his face directly into hers.

"Going somewhere?" she seethed, anger apparent in every syllable she uttered.

Malcolm's eyes were wide as he watched Halina's fangs drop. I was pretty sure that if she wanted to, the teenage vixen could decapitate him with those teeth. And her eyes blazed with enough fury that I was equally sure she wanted to.

Teren's arms were instantly around me, inspecting my already healed head. His face twisted in rage as he helped me stand. Behind me I heard a weary groan and looked over to see Hot Ben starting to stand as well. Relief that he was okay, that *I* was okay, surged into me.

As Teren started stalking over to Malcolm, looking ready to assist in his decapitation, something changed.

The blips of Alanna and Imogen in my head started racing back to us. Knowing that they'd only come back if they had found my son, I closed my eyes and imagined that I felt his presence returning too. Quickly opening them, I saw Teren and Halina looking towards the direction of where Julian was rapidly coming towards us. As the wind shifted again, I imagined I could smell him in the faint breeze. Maybe I even could? I wasn't sure if it was real or not, I wanted it so much.

Malcolm took the distraction to disengage from Halina. Successfully breaking free, he wasted no time in blurring away.

I yelled, "No!" as I watched him streak towards the edge of the barn. Everyone's heads turned to watch him zip to the edge of the pool of light…where he ran smack into a wall. Well, it seemed like a wall, with how solidly he'd run into it. But as he stumbled backwards to the ground, I realized it wasn't a wall at all. I blinked and gasped.

It was Gabriel.

My eyes were wider than they'd ever been as they flicked from the spot where Gabriel's prone body had been lying, to the very much alive vampire standing before Malcolm. On the ground, only Ben's bloody stake remained. Gabriel's shirt was dripping with the red blood soaked down the front of it; he'd definitely been staked. He'd been dead, I was sure. I had no idea how he was standing before Malcolm, hands on his hips in displeasure.

Hot Ben staggered to his feet, and let out a low curse while he stared at Gabriel as if he were a ghost. "Holy hell, I thought he was dead?" he muttered while Halina gaped, stunned into silence again.

But our reactions were nothing compared to Malcolm's. He looked about ready to implode from fear and stress. Backing away from Gabriel, he started muttering, "No, I watched you die…that's not possible." His slightly glowing eyes darted over Gabriel's body.

Gabriel frowned down at him. "Malcolm, I'm very disappointed in you."

As Gabriel advanced, Malcolm retreated, scooting right up to bump into Teren's legs. Teren imposingly stared down at Malcolm huddled by his feet, and then he smiled. Turning his head between Teren and Gabriel, Malcolm disbelievingly said, "You? You did this? You tricked me?"

Leaning down slightly, Teren whispered, "I told you not to underestimate me."

Malcolm's pale face seemed to pale even more as he began to

realize that he'd been successfully tricked this time; he'd given up Julian's location. He made a dash for it, but Gabriel reached down and pulled him up by one arm. Halina snapped out of her stupor and immediately grabbed his other arm. Malcolm struggled, but both incredibly strong vampires held him tight.

His head twisting between the two of them, Malcolm started to genuinely panic. "Gabriel, please...let me go. I didn't hurt the child!" Gabriel's only response was to narrow his eyes; they were a dark shade of emerald in the lamplight.

Teren stepped in front of Malcolm and crossed his arms over his chest. Malcolm tried beseeching him, since Gabriel was unmoved. "I did nothing to the kid! I didn't hurt him. Just wait, he's fine, you'll see. When he gets here, you'll see!" His scared eyes took in all of us. "He's fine!"

I took a second to register my family approaching. The faint scent I'd imagined earlier was turning into a real one that was getting stronger. Teren smiled at smelling it too. Seeming more relaxed now that Malcolm was securely held and our son was coming closer, he sneered at Malcolm, and leaned directly into his face.

"My son was terrified...for days," he said in a cold whisper. Teren's hand came out to point back to the ranch, to where we could both feel Nika. "My daughter can feel every emotion that he feels. She felt every ounce of his fear! She was terrified...for days!" His voice gained strength as fatherly anger poured out of him. "We had no idea where he was, no idea where to look...no idea if he was even alive." He lifted his hands to mimic the complete and total helplessness we'd felt. I never wanted to feel that way again. "He's not fine. None of us are fine!" he shouted.

Staring at the river of blood down the front of Gabriel's shirt, Malcolm struggled against his captors. His panicked eyes shifted to Halina and then back to Teren when Teren started walking away. Malcolm shook his head and shrugged. "I didn't hurt him, you have my word. I treated him like royalty. I swear. I didn't hurt anybody."

Teren's eyes flared and the light of the lamp made them gleam in an inhuman way. Turning back to Malcolm, he snarled, "You didn't hurt anybody? You killed a friend of mine...to prove a point."

Malcolm's brow bunched together and he shrugged. "She was just a human…?" He looked lost, like he really didn't understand the problem. Like she had meant nothing.

Gritting his jaw, Teren straightened, but said nothing else. Turning his back on Malcolm, he walked away. As he left him, Malcolm's fearful eyes shifted between Halina and Gabriel. Halina's pale eyes glowed with fury. Gabriel's look was more impassive, but equally displeased. "You betrayed me, Malcolm. You took something that wasn't yours to take."

His voice was detached, unemotional; it gave me shivers. It made Malcolm look like he wanted to pee his pants. He struggled between the two vampires, but he was outmatched between the ancient, mixed's strength and the pure vampire's. Maybe seeing that no one was going to stop this, he started yanking on his arms, trying to free them. I thought he might start trying to gnaw them off soon, if he thought of it.

His gaze flicked between Gabriel and Halina, and he started endlessly repeating, "No! Please, Gabriel, please, no. Have mercy! I was just making money. I didn't hurt any vampires!"

Gabriel's eyes widened as he pulled on Malcolm's arm, holding his body closer. "You didn't hurt them? You sold my drug, Malcolm. You were directly involved in hunters killing our kind." He leaned in, his voice suddenly passionate. "In killing children, Malcolm."

Malcolm swallowed and shook his head. "No…I didn't know about that. You gotta believe me. I didn't know!"

Gabriel shook his head, his impassive expression returning. It didn't matter if he knew or not; Malcolm was still guilty of the crime. Malcolm's eyes widened at seeing Gabriel's face hardening and he again begged for his life. "Please! You know me! Have mercy! Please!"

Gabriel, done listening, ignored him. Looking over Malcolm's struggling body, he nodded at Halina. She locked gazes with him. Her lips in a hard line, she nodded back. Both of them simultaneously prepared their stances, pulling Malcolm taunt.

Malcolm started yelling for help when he realized just what his sentence was. My eyes widened when I realized what they were going to do. I felt like gagging. Deserving or not, it was awful. This was a sight I didn't need in my head. I wanted to close my eyes, but, horrified, I couldn't look away.

Just as Gabriel and Halina used every vampiric muscle they had to pull their portions of Malcolm in opposite directions, and just as Malcolm's yells shifted to pain-filled screams ripping through the night, arms were suddenly around my head, holding me close to a silent heart, and blocking my eyes from the gruesome sight.

My hands flew around Teren. His arms over my ears didn't block out all the noise, but it helped. Running my fingers up his back, holding him to me, I was grateful that he was blocking this image from my sight. My imagination made up for it, though. With the muffled, wet noises and the scent of fresh blood in the air, a lot of fresh blood, I felt like I didn't actually need to see it, to see it.

When the night was silent from the screams and gory noises, Teren loosened his grip on me. Peeking up at his face, I took in his grim expression—his head lowered, his eyes closed. Malcolm might have created a storm of havoc in our lives, but Teren was a good person and he didn't enjoy hearing the death of another, necessary or not. Once again blocking my ears, he'd heard it all. I reached up and cupped his face, silently thanking him. He opened his eyes and smiled down at me, and his face relaxed into a calmness I hadn't seen in days.

"Ugh, now I really am going to be sick."

At hearing Hot Ben's voice, I twisted to look over at him. He was holding his stomach, staring at the dirt-packed field, and his lips were twisted like he'd just seen the grossest thing imaginable. He looked greener than ever, even under the strange lighting. He also had a split lip and the beginning of a nasty bruise on his jaw. I wouldn't be surprised if he'd fractured something.

Following the line of his sight, I instantly wished I hadn't. The dirt was a deep brown in the lamplight, but there were distinctly dark, wet lumps of...something in the space between Gabriel and Halina. They were now standing thirty feet apart, staring down at the clumps of what was left of poor, stupid Malcolm.

Sniffing, Ben recovered his intestinal fortitude and walked over to pick up the stake that had been inside Gabriel's body. Striding over to Halina, he started rummaging around her half of Malcolm, searching the body for something. While I twisted my lips, wondering if Ben had gone a little mad, he suddenly found what he wanted, and jabbed the stake through Malcolm's dead chest...through his heart.

Standing and looking pleased with himself, he smiled and glanced around at all of us, like he'd just saved the day.

Amused, Teren shook his head at Ben. Unless Malcolm's super healing abilities included repairing himself from long distances, there was really no way he was walking away from that. As all eyes shifted to Hot Ben, he started looking a little sheepish, and his smile dropped a little. "What? You can never be too careful, right?"

Teren started laughing then, and the tension eased off of him as he did. Halina joined in as well as she clapped Ben on the back. Then she blurred over to Gabriel, threw her arms around his neck and leapt onto his body, showering him in kisses.

Teren smiled, watching them. Then, still chuckling a little, he twisted back to Ben. "Want to be really thorough?" Ben eagerly nodded and Teren shook his head. "We should burn the body."

Ben nodded and pulled a lighter from his pocket. While he got to work on completing his task, I sank against Teren. Exhaustion, residual fear, and remembered pain washed through me, but it was nothing compared to the joy of knowing that Julian was coming closer. I wrapped my arms around my husband and sighed.

Pulling back from me, he tenderly ran his fingers down my cheek. His eyes searching mine he whispered, "Are you okay? I was so scared..."

He bit his lip and cupped my cheek. Smiling, I put my hand over his. "Julian's coming...I'm great."

Smiling, he nodded, then his expression shifted into amusement and concern. "Did you seriously deck that guy?"

As the acrid smell of smoke hit the air, I shrugged and looked over at the indistinguishable body parts Ben was adding to the growing pile. "I couldn't let him get away," I muttered, watching Ben duck into the barn, only to come out moments later with a gas can.

Soon his timid fire was a raging inferno. Luckily there were no nosey neighbors out here in the middle of nowhere.

Teren's hand on my cheek urged me to look back at him again. "He could have…" Stopping his words, he shook his head. "What am I going to do with you?"

Exhaling slowly, I rested my head against his and nuzzled my cheek over the hardness of his stubbled jaw. "You take me home…me and the kids."

Squeezing tighter, he nodded. "That I can do."

As Teren and I started to drift away from the pungent smell of Malcolm's demise, Gabriel and Halina walked over to join us. Attached to his side, Halina was rubbing his blood soaked chest, and staring at it in wonder. Her fingers poked and prodded for holes in his skin, but I knew she wouldn't find any. Whatever Teren had done to him, he'd already healed from it.

As Gabriel clapped Teren on the shoulder, Halina gazed at him. Her eyes were completely different as she stared up at her ancient boyfriend. No anger or fear remained in them, just an obviously deep well of love. Whatever reservations she'd had about being with Gabriel before, I was sure they were gone now. Thinking someone was dead had a way of making all of the impossible obstacles suddenly seem…possible.

Shifting her eyes to Teren, Halina shook her head. "That was all fake? You were bluffing?"

Teren shrugged. "He needed Gabriel dead. I made him think he got his wish." Teren's smile shifted to a cringe as he met eyes with Gabriel. "I'm sorry I couldn't warn you. He would have heard."

Gabriel rubbed his blood stained chest. "Yes, well, I almost didn't have to pretend. You came extremely close to my heart, Teren."

He raised an eyebrow, and Teren cringed even more. "Sorry, I needed it to look real."

Gabriel smirked and shook his head. "Another couple of inches and it would have been."

Teren released me and put a hand on Gabriel's arm. "Thank you for playing along, for understanding my plan."

Gabriel nodded, then twisted his lips. "I wasn't entirely playing." He looked down at the mess on his chest and shook his head as he rubbed the area over his heart. Peeking up at Teren, he grimaced. "That was exceedingly painful."

Teren chuckled a little as he shook his head. "Sorry."

I squeezed him a little tighter, grateful that Halina hadn't lashed out more aggressively and immediately killed him. Halina seemed to be thinking the same thing. Sighing, she released Gabriel and walked over to Teren. I took a step back from him as she started a long Russian sentence. Teren met her gaze and nodded. When she finished with her speech, she stroked her fingers along the neck she'd been cinching tight earlier, then she cupped his cheek. Shaking her head, she swept him into a hug.

In words I could finally understand, she whispered, "I'm so sorry, Teren. I truly don't know what came over me."

Teren pulled back and smiled down at her. "You thought I staked the man you loved." He shook his head, and his pale eyes shifted to me. "Situations reversed, I don't think I would have reacted any differently."

Halina sighed and rested her head on his chest, and Teren stroked her back. Feeling Alanna and Imogen nearly on us, we all stopped and looked over to the field where they were approaching. I started getting antsy, needing to be with my son again.

Teren and Halina broke apart, both looking antsy as well. Teren's eyes took in the bonfire of destruction that Ben had going. Standing before it, his body highlighted in the orange flames, Ben was tossing bits and pieces of evidence into it, wiping his hands off after every toss. Twisting back to the fields, Teren raised his chin in that direction. "Come on, let's go get our boy."

Not wanting Julian to see what we'd done, I eagerly nodded and streaked off towards him. I could feel the other vampires right behind me as I blew across the empty fields. Whatever had been growing out here was long gone, and only weeds and overgrown tan grass impeded my progress.

Not wanting to collide with the approaching blurs, I slowed to a regular run along with the others. As if we'd planned it, Alanna and Imogen arrived at the same time. Like someone had adjusted the lens on a camera, their hazy streaks suddenly snapped into focus. Beaming brighter than I had ever seen either of them, they humanly ran the distance between us. My vision hazed as what Alanna was carrying in her arms became clear to my enhanced eyes.

My son. My external heartbeat. My carbon copy of the man who seared my soul. Julian.

My legs were trembling so hard I could barely keep running. I watched Julian start to struggle against Alanna, and she set him down and let him run to us on his own. As he shifted into overdrive, I sank to my knees. He collided with me right as I connected with the dirt.

Clenching his arms around me, he buried his head in my neck. Leaning back on my heels, I held him to me so closely that I had to remember to relax so he could breathe. Teren's arms were instantly around him from the other side as he dropped to the ground as well. Holding him between us, sandwiched in the middle of our bodies, we both exhaled at the same time.

"Oh thank God, thank God," Teren murmured over and over, stroking his son's back and kissing his dark head.

Our glows highlighted the shaking child in our arms and I felt the emotion of his homecoming rising up my throat. Holding back a sob, I swallowed repeatedly, kissing Julian's forehead as I did. He nuzzled into me further, and one of his hands reached out for Teren. Holding us both tight, he sniffled. "Mommy, I didn't like that."

A small sob breaking free from me, I clutched him tighter. "I know, baby. I didn't like it, either."

Lifting his tiny face up, his completely glowless eyes locked onto mine. Hoping the hypnotic sensation of my eyes would calm him down, I held gazes with him. His sniffling stopped as he stared at me, his breathing evened out. Cupping his cheek, I tried to brush off the tear-streaked dirt. When he seemed calmer, I studied him head to toe. I didn't see any scratches, no marks of any kind. He didn't have the sunken look of someone underfed or dying of thirst. Just as Malcolm had said, he looked fine. Even so, I wanted to take him home and pump him full of all of the treats that he loved the most. Whatever he wanted…he could have.

As Teren and I gazed at him, searching for injuries, all I saw was a weary-to-the-bone tiredness. When Halina and Gabriel dropped down to touch him, kiss his head, and Alanna and Imogen squatted down to put an arm on mine and Teren's shoulders, Julian blinked at all of us.

His voice worn from days of exhaustion, he looked over at Teren and croaked out, "Daddy…I want Nick."

Gabriel and Halina stayed behind with Hot Ben, making sure all traces of the vampire were hidden away from the world, the world that had no idea what had gone down tonight. Teren picked up Julian and walked him back to our car; he was asleep by the time we got him into it.

I sat in the backseat with Julian, not able to even be apart the space of a few feet. I wasn't sure how I'd ever part from Julian again. It didn't help matters any that I still couldn't feel him. Even sitting at his side, holding his relaxed hand while he snored, I couldn't sense him. It was disorienting, and I hoped that Malcolm wasn't bluffing about the drug he'd given him wearing off soon.

Not wanting to leave his side either, Alanna and Imogen piled into the car with us. Alanna sat next to Teren, her hand over his as he sped us to our daughter. Imogen sat beside me, her arm wrapped around mine as I kept my eyes glued on Julian.

He'd only been gone a few days, really, but it felt like years, and I studied every attribute he had. The shape of his nose, the curve of his lips, the slightly elongated fangs as he slept with his mouth partly opened. There was nothing my eyes didn't notice, didn't memorize. They especially locked onto the red needle pricks on his bicep, where Malcolm had injected him twice a day, every day. As a rage boiled within me, I was immediately grateful that Malcolm was already a pile of ash. Otherwise I would have stopped at nothing to turn him into one.

When we arrived back at the ranch, all of the lights were on. Everyone still being awake so late at night, just an hour or so before dawn, made me frown. But, then again, if I'd been Mom, Ash or

Jack, and I knew what my supernatural loved ones were doing, I wouldn't have been able to sleep either. It just wouldn't have happened.

As Teren pulled the car to a stop, the front doors busted open. Julian snapped awake when they did. Euphoria flooded his face as he looked over to the tiny person who had shoved open the massive doors, and was scrambling to get to him. I hadn't seen that look in so long it made my eyes water.

Screaming at the top of her voice, Nika skipped out to the car. "Julie! Julie! Julie!"

My eyes filled as I immediately unbuckled his restrains. Hopping out of his seat, he opened his own door. "Nick!"

The rest of us piled out of the car while the others hustled out of the house. None of us speaking, we all watched the two empathically joined twins reunite. I was crying long before they did.

Their little bodies collided together, and their arms wrapped each other tight. Nika was giggling, her face as joyous as Julian's. I hadn't heard her laugh in an eternity; it overjoyed me that she hadn't lost the ability to do it.

"I missed you, Julie!" she exclaimed as she laughed.

"I missed you too, Nick," he laughed right back.

Pulling apart, they stared at each other. Nika frowned. "You were scared."

Julian nodded. "You were, too."

Nika peeked up at Teren, standing close beside me, holding my hand. "Is the monster gone, Daddy?"

Teren nodded as he smiled down at her. "No more monsters, baby."

Turning back to Julian, Nika nodded. "Grandma said we can have cocoa. Want some?"

Julian nodded and clasped her hand. Giggling like they'd never been apart, like they each hadn't just experienced something horrifically awful, they dashed into the house. I shook my head, marveling at the resilience of children.

Chapter 23 – What Family Does

Once Nika had her reunion, the rest of the family loved on Julian. As he noisily slurped down a steaming cup of cocoa, Mom and Ashley alternated in planting him with kisses. Jack had tears in his eyes as he clapped Teren on the back.

I could see the rings of exhaustion in Teren's eyes as he smiled back at Jack. I imagined from the look on his face that when Teren did finally succumb to sleep, he was going to stay there for a while. As my hands never strayed far from Julian, I wondered if I'd be able to relax enough to sleep. I didn't want to lose a second with him. I'd lost too many already.

Jack beamed down at Teren. "You did it, son." He shook his head, and weariness was in his eyes, too. "I'm sure I don't want to know all the details of what went down tonight…but I am so very proud of you."

Teren swallowed and looked away, towards his son. "Thank you," he whispered to his dad.

I smiled at the three generations of amazing men in my life, then I wrapped my arms around Teren's waist. He smiled at me, but his gaze didn't leave Julian. I had a feeling that those watchful eyes that I loved wouldn't be straying long from our son for a while. "Are you all right?" he asked, darting a quick glance at me from the corner of his eye.

Laying my head on his shoulder, I waited for the aches and pains that my human body would have felt after a night like tonight. I should have had a bruised hip, a cracked skull and an aching jugular. I felt fine though. Not a trace of pain lingered in my recently brutalized body. Thank God for super healing. Definitely my favorite new ability.

Nuzzling my head in his neck, I murmured, "I'm great…I'm perfect."

"I know," he whispered, smiling into my hair as he planted a kiss on my head.

Clutching him tighter, I felt the emotional drain of the past few days leeching strength from my body. That was one thing that super healing didn't fix—even a vampiric body still needed rest. I yawned, covering my mouth at the last second.

A chain reaction of yawns went around the room; my kids were the last to give in. I laughed at the warmth and peace I felt. Chuckling himself, Teren went over to pick up Julian. Removing the mug that he was now licking clean, Teren propped him over his shoulder. Julian giggled, the long-absent sound squeezing my chest.

Nika laughed too, for once feeling joy from her brother instead of the constant state of terror that he had been in. Clapping her hands, she raised them to Teren. "Me too, Daddy."

Grinning ear to ear, Teren leaned down, lifted her, and easily plopped her over his other shoulder.

"All right," he laughed, twisting the kids around in a half circle, "It's time for munchkins to go to bed. Give everybody goodnight kisses." He started to parade them around the room but Julian squirmed and sat up straight.

Teren adjusted his hold on him, while being careful to not drop Nika in the process. Julian's pale eyes widened and glistened as his arms went around Teren's neck. Confused over his reaction, I stepped forward and rubbed his back. He was obviously upset about something, more than just being told it was bedtime. He almost looked terrified.

Nika, sensing it, raised herself up and put a hand on his shoulder.

His eyes locked on Teren, Julian whispered, "Monsters come when you lay down, Daddy."

He started to breathe heavier, and his heart started to race. My arms were around him instantly, my fingers soothingly stroking his hair as I suddenly understood. He'd been taken from his bed while he'd been sleeping. Then he'd largely been left alone, terrified, and now, now that he was back, he was petrified to go back to bed, afraid that he'd be snatched again. Kids were resilient, but they weren't impervious. My dead heart wanted to break in two. A little bit of his innocence had just been lost, and he wasn't even four yet.

Teren quickly shushed him as Julian started crying. "It's okay, it's okay, Julian. Mommy and Daddy are going to lie down with you."

Julian's little face relaxed, and the terror in his eyes faded. "All night?" he whispered. Teren nodded, tears in his eyes.

I ran soft circles into Julian's back, the way that Nika told me he liked. He looked down at me just when I felt a tear spill from my eye. Quickly brushing it off, I smiled. "All night, baby. All night, every night...as long as you need us."

Nodding and relaxing, he slumped into Teren's shoulder. Nika put her head on his arm in support. I heard vague sniffles around the room but my eyes were locked on Teren's. Leaning his head against his son's, his eyes were glossy as he held gazes with me. "As long as you need us, Julian. We're always here for you. You won't ever be alone again...I promise."

By the time we got the kids upstairs, taking them into our room here at the ranch, they were already asleep. I took Nika from Teren and he gently laid Julian down. Julian whimpered and reached out for him. Teren sat beside him, putting his arm around him and Julian nestled into his chest, his body stilling into peace. As I laid Nika on Julian's other side, her arm protectively wrapping around her brother, Teren looked up at me.

Running a hand over his mouth, he shook his head. "Em..." He shrugged, not able to say anything else.

Nodding at Teren, I lay beside my daughter and stared down at Julian. How much damage had been done in the few days he was gone? Treated like royalty or not, he'd still been ripped from his home. He'd still been terrified. Could we erase that memory by immersing him in love and affection?

Reaching out to rub his back, I watched a smile creep onto his sleeping face. His eyes fluttered, like he was dreaming. I glanced at my daughter and she smiled too, dreaming as well. Looking between the two of them, I saw the same peace and contentment.

Maybe it wasn't too late. Maybe we could erase the one dark spot in an otherwise idyllic youth. Leaning over, I kissed his head. That would be my goal, every day.

We all stayed in bed for a solid day, arms wrapped around each other; nobody wanted to let go. Once the drug wore off, Julian's location started returning to my awareness. It vibrated through my soul, comforting me inside and out, and I focused on the sensation of him in my head for hours on end. The knowledge of where he was, that I could always find him if I needed to, was a blessing that I did not take for granted; I clung to it throughout the day.

I knew we would eventually get back to our regular routine, but I also knew that it would take some time. Julian needed to feel safe again, and getting him to that point was my priority. But I didn't mind. I needed to feel safe again, too. And all of us being together...felt safe. We took the healing in stages. We stayed out at the ranch for a few more days until Julian asked to go home. Then we all dispersed from the ranch, my mother grudgingly going back to her empty nest, my sister anxiously bounding out of there to be with Christian.

When we got back to our place by the bay, Julian looked around. Nika grabbed his hand in the entryway when he seemed frozen in place. "Let's go play, Julie," she said softly, pulling on his arm. He nodded and smiled at her, and the two of them dashed up to their bedroom. Spike barked and dashed after them, eager to play again with the tiny version of his master.

I exhaled in relief that he was okay enough to go back in there. He wouldn't sleep there, though. Every night, he insisted on staying with us. We always let him. Burying himself in-between Teren and me, he conked out pretty fast each evening. Usually his dreams were quiet ones, but occasionally he'd start thrashing and whining. I rubbed his back while Nika sleepily patted him, and he relaxed.

I prayed every night he had a bad dream that it was the last one he'd ever have. I knew that was an impossible prayer, since even I still had the occasional nightmare about my abduction, but I still made the prayer for him. For the first time ever, I wished he wasn't part vampire. Then Halina could wipe him, give him a fresh start. Him and Nika both.

While Nika didn't have the same haunted look that Julian would get at times, when it was getting late, close to bedtime, I could still see a fear in her that wasn't there before. She watched Julian extra close. She protectively hovered by his side. She almost seemed like she was guarding him, like she would never let anything bad happen to him again. She reminded me of Teren. He often had that look of determination on his face when it came to helping his loved ones. Even though I hated the situation, it made me smile that the father and daughter were so much alike.

Eventually though, through lots of love, patience and encouragement, Julian asked to sleep in his and Nika's room. Biting my lip, a little nervous for him, I tucked him into his separate bed. Nika immediately reached out for his hand in the space between their beds. Looking over at her, he clasped it tight. His wide eyes drifted up to the window and I instantly wondered if that was where Malcolm had come in. It had to be. He'd crawled up the wall and into our house like the fictional monster he was. I was so glad he was no longer an issue.

Patting Julian's head, I leaned over and kissed the soft blackness of it. His eyes came back to mine. "Love you, Mommy."

Smiling, I cupped his cheek. "I love you too, baby. Mommy and Daddy are right down the hall if you need anything."

He nodded, his face serious. "I okay, Mommy."

With pride in my heart, I praised him for his courage. After kissing him one last time, I leaned over and kissed my daughter. Her eyes were all on Julian. "Goodnight, sweetheart," I whispered.

She finally looked up at me. "Goodnight, Mommy." I wrapped my finger around a strand of her hair, listening to the silky strands slide against my skin as I pulled away.

Teren immediately took my place, leaning in to give her a big hug and a kiss and then Julian. He held Julian for an extra second, murmuring that he loved him very much, and that he was very proud of him for wanting to sleep in his own room.

Julian beamed up at him, seemingly proud of himself too.

I genuinely smiled. I didn't need to worry about my children's psyches. With Teren as their father, my kids were going to be just fine.

Standing and backing towards the door, Teren grabbed my hand.

I clenched his, almost not wanting to leave. My kids might be a little stronger than me. As Nika and Julian settled into their beds, Teren twisted and pulled me out the door. "Come on," he whispered, "they need this."

Sighing, I followed him out.

Leaving their door open, we slowly walked back to our room. On the way, I heard the sound that reminded me that Julian was never alone, not really. Even if she hadn't been in the room with him, holding his hand, even if they'd been forced apart for a time, he shared a bond with his sister that was eternal. It had probably brought him a great deal of comfort, when he'd needed it most. He was never alone...Nika was always with him, and he was always with her.

"Goodnight, Julie, love you."

"Goodnight, Nick, love you too."

Smiling, Teren and I looked over at each other as we reached our door. Hearing their goodnights lifted my heart, made me feel light again. Kissing the back of my hand, Teren whispered, "It's going to be okay, Emma. Everything is going to be okay."

Once we were on the other side of our door, I reached up and grabbed his cheek. His glow enveloped me as warmly as his heart. Silent or not, his was the most giving heart I'd ever met. "I know," I whispered, leaning my lips up to his.

His kiss was soft, tentative. We hadn't had any sort of intimate connection since the night Julian had been taken. I often wondered if Teren felt the same guilt over that night as I did. We'd both made a mistake. If one of us had opened the door, we surely would have heard Malcolm entering our home. But then again, maybe not. You never know how things might go down...until they do.

I pressed my lips to his harder, needing the residual guilt I felt over being with my husband gone. That would be the final point of healing for us, feeling safe enough to reconnect. And if Julian was brave enough to sleep in his own bed again, surely we could be brave enough to let our guard down for a moment.

Neither one of us moving to shut the door of our soundproof

room, I pulled him backwards to the bed. That had been an unspoken agreement; we wouldn't use the soundproofing. Not yet, anyway. I needed to hear my children at all times, even if that meant that they could hear us too. Teren had gotten through his childhood that way just fine. Surely they would too?

Sliding my fingers down the front of his dress shirt, I slowly popped open each button. Teren had finally gone back to work, waiting until after me, so one of us was with the kids at all times. Mom had nearly jumped up and down when we brought them out to her to watch again. She loved taking care of them so much.

Sliding the shirt off his shoulders, I ran my glowing eyes over the smooth planes of his chest. He was beautiful, and perfect, and eternally mine. His lips came back to me, hungry for more, but he was still holding back. As our breaths increased, his hand on my back slid over my bottom, gently squeezing. I smiled and locked gazes with him. He didn't smile back. His face looked serious, almost too serious.

"I've missed you, Emma."

He glanced over my face, then down my body. My hands left the comforting warmth of his chest, and cupped his cheeks. Tilting his head, I made him look at me. "I've missed you, too...are you okay?"

He shrugged. "I feel...like I...can't protect you, you or the kids. I'm...afraid to let go," he whispered.

My eyes misting, I shook my head. "Everything is okay now, Teren. He's gone...he's not ever coming back. We're safe. Because of you, we're safe." Peppering him with light kisses, I murmured between our lips, "You saved me, you saved Julian..." I kissed his jaw, down his neck. "You *do* protect us. You do whatever you have to do to keep us from harm."

My hands ran back down his chest as my nose ran up his throat; he growled a little, deep in his body. "You could have killed me during your conversion...you didn't. You could have let me die when I was attacked, you didn't. You did the impossible...you found other mixed vampires and saved my life. Mine and the kids."

My mouth trailed over to the other side of his neck, lightly sucking the skin as I worked my way down. His chest was moving harder as his breath increased. Igniting his body, easing his mind, I shook my head as I rubbed my lips over his collar bone. "You could have given up on trying to find Julian...but you never did." Wandering over to the other side of his chest, I placed a soft kiss over where his heart should have been fiercely thumping. He sucked in a quick breath, his hands resting on my hips tightening.

I peeked up at him as I rested my cheek against his chest. "You cut out a heart for God's sake. All for us, all for them." I started placing kisses straight up his throat, forcing his head back. His mouth dropped open a little as another soft growl rumbled around the room. "We're safe, Teren. We're all safe...because of you."

At the top of his chin, I quickly swiped my tongue out, stroking the harsh stubble. His head snapped down, and his eyes were burning with desire now. "And you aren't in this alone, Teren. You protect me, I protect you. That's how a marriage works," I whispered, my breath washing over his mouth. "That's how a family works. We're in this together, Teren...'til death."

His fangs crashed down as he stared at me lustfully...and lovingly too. Always lovingly. Then his mouth was on mine and any tentativeness he'd had flew out the window.

Just like with the other dark spots in our history, we'd get past this and come out stronger...together...forever.

By the end of the next week, all traces of the recent hardships that my family had gone through were faded scars in the background. Still there, deep under the surface, but not noticeable to the naked eye. But I knew that over time they would vanish and we'd be the joyous unit that we were before. It was already starting.

My children were laughing and playing, running up and down the dual staircase of the ranch, chasing Spike, blurring with speed until I reminded them not to, since a not-in-the-know human was in the house. But they were especially giddy today. We were all especially giddy today. Today was the twins' fourth birthday.

Not only was it their birthday, which to them meant tons of cake and tons of presents, but Teren had broken down and gotten them that pony. Not to keep though, just for the day, but they were still bouncing off the walls, waiting for it to get here.

When the screech of tires on gravel announced its arrival, my children bolted to the front door. Teren rustled their hair, chuckling as I held them back. We didn't need to freak out the poor man who was in charge of the animal by our excited children moving faster than humanly possible. I even had to remind Julian to pop his teeth back up, and I rarely had to do that anymore.

Alanna and Imogen tickled their bellies, making them giggle, while Teren, Hot Ben and Jack stepped out to help unload the shaggy little pony he'd lined up. Mom and Ashley were giggling with Tracey in the kitchen, decorating two horse themed cakes for the twins; a blue one for Julian, a red one for Nika. Ashley was sighing that Christian had really wanted to come today, but he'd gotten called into work after an explosion at a warehouse had left two firefighters badly burned. Yes, her hero helped other heroes. My sister had found a man nearly as wonderful as mine. I was over the moon for her, as was Tracey, when she finally heard that he was doctor.

In the rooms deep below the earth, I could feel Halina's silent presence sleeping the day away. I couldn't feel him or hear him, but I knew that Gabriel was down there with her. His darkly tinted sedan parked outside was one giveaway that he was at the ranch. The other two giveaways were busy with the task that I'd assigned to them– Starla and Jacen were currently stringing up streamers, banners, and other birthday decorations around every possible surface. No balloons though, nothing that would frighten Julian.

It was a pointless assignment, since Alanna had already dressed the house accordingly, but whatever I could do to try and keep Starla and Jacen from mauling each other was a good thing. I swear, since giving in to the feelings they had, the two of them were so much worse than Teren and me.

Listening to them in the living room as Starla smacked on her gum and commented on Jacen's cute ass as he tacked streamers to the wall, I rolled my eyes and smiled. Obnoxious as they could sometimes be, they were sweet too. I hoped that Gabriel could someday help the doomed mixed vampire, so Starla could have a long life with her beau. From the longing in Jacen's eyes when he stared at her, I knew he was hoping for that too.

Once the sound of a horse snorting and hooves on cement hit my ears, my kids became uncontainable. Squirming away from me and the other vampiric women, they scrambled out the front door to take a peek. I smiled and followed, happy for their happiness. I might not share in their empathic bond, but their joy today was contagious; we all had smiles on our faces.

Jack and Teren had set up a small area in the closest field and the man led the horse that way. He was going to stake the animal to a pole and have the kids walk it in an endless circle, but Teren convinced him to let the animal be free. The field was fenced, so it wasn't really an issue, so the man agreed. Personally, I think Teren just didn't want Julian to see anything contained in a small space. That was all he would tell us about where he'd been held. It was small and cold. He wouldn't say anything more, and we never pressed him to.

The tiny brown and white horse shook its mane, seemingly happy to have a little more freedom. Barely coming up to Teren's waist, the creature was beyond adorable, and I knew we'd be hearing about getting one every day from both of the kids now. Who knew? Maybe we would get one to keep at the ranch for them. While Halina had a thing for horses, she loved these kids more. She wouldn't harm anything they adored, tempted or not.

Hot Ben plopped Julian onto the beast's saddle, while Teren placed Nika right behind him. Jack took the reins, urging the pony into a small walk. Both kids were instantly laughing. As Teren walked beside the animal, just in case a kid fell off, I walked over to Ben.

Hands crossed over his chest, he watched Julian and Nika laugh together. When he noticed me next to him, he slung an arm over my shoulder in a brotherly way. He shivered a bit as my chill seeped into his skin. Where our bare skin touched on our arms, his pricked with goose bumps. The reaction always surprised me a little, since I didn't feel cold. But he sure felt warm and I leaned into his side.

He smiled down at me, his face finally healed from the vicious blow Malcolm had given him. Luckily he'd only been bruised, not broken. Not able to hide his appearance from his fiancée, he'd told Tracey that he'd been mugged. She'd been appropriately terrified for him, and had even marched him to the police station and made him fill out a report. He'd hated doing it, hated lying to her and the law, but really, what else could he say? I was knocked out by a vampire in a crazy attempt to rescue the kidnapped child of my undead best friend? That wouldn't have exactly gone over well, with Tracey or with the police.

"I'm glad everything worked out, Emma." He shook his perfect head of highlighted hair. "I can't imagine if…" He didn't finish. Biting his lip, he shrugged instead.

I nodded as my eyes misted. "I know…I can't either." We looked back at my pony-riding children, and Teren laughing as he walked beside them. "Thank you, Ben…for everything," I whispered.

He squeezed my shoulder. "Don't thank me, Emma. I'd do anything for you guys. You're family…and that's what family does."

Smiling, I rested my head against his shoulder. For the hundred millionth time, I could have kissed Ben.

After hours of pony enjoyment, the kids were finally shepherded into the house for way too much sugar and way too many presents. They zipped around, playing with toy cars and plastic ponies until well after the sun went down. When it did, the pureblood in the house finally emerged.

Silently slinking into the living room while we all watched the kids play, Halina came up behind Tracey and me. I knew she was there and didn't think much about it, but Tracey had no idea, and nearly jumped through the roof when Halina leaned in-between us.

"Good evening, Emma…Tracey."

She smirked at Tracey as the beautiful girl squealed and pulled back a little. Halina just loved to mess with people. I glared at her while she chuckled at the expression on my face. Gabriel behind her raised a corner of his lip in amusement. He seemed to find her sultry, playful ways humorous. I could only imagine what the two of them did when they were alone.

Tracey found the teenage vixen less humorous and frowned at her. Then her eyes darted to Ben. While we may have wiped away some of her memories, she still didn't like the provocative woman being around her man. Especially when Ben stood up and walked over to her.

Halina and Ben had come to a level of mutual respect for one another. I think they even considered each other friends. While Ben only looked like he was going to shake her hand in greeting, Halina wasn't really a…hand-shaker. She engulfed him in an embrace that even made Gabriel lift an eyebrow. Not easily riled though, that was all the reaction that Gabriel gave. Tracey, however, looked about ready to rip Halina a new one.

Starla across the room laughed at the display and popped a bubble. Below human level, she laughed out, "Nice, Grams, going for the younger boys now? I always knew you were a cougar at heart." Her arms casually flung around Jacen, she didn't look intimidated by Halina in the slightest.

Halina didn't like not intimidating people. She released Hot Ben and started to move towards the mixed vampire who irritated her to no end, but Gabriel intercepted her. Sliding his arms around her waist, he drew her tightly leather-wrapped hips into his. "Let it go, love," he whispered. Halina melted into his body and actually let it go.

Of course the twins darting over to her probably helped. Gabriel released her when they attached to her legs. Teren, sitting on the other couch with my mother and sister, locked eyes with me. He was smiling in contentment, enjoying everyone being together again.

When the kids were nearly comatose from their sugar high, I got up to put them to bed. Teren stood with me, but put his hand over mine when I reached for Julian. Scrunching my brows, I looked up at him. He smiled at me, then lifted his eyes to Tracey. I followed his line of sight, even more confused. The perky blonde met his eyes with a slight furrow in her brow. She didn't know what he wanted either.

Looking back at Teren, I watched as he tilted his head in an adorable way. "Tracey, would you like to put the kids to bed?"

Tracey's eyes widened and her mouth erupted into a huge grin. Standing, she nodded. "Yeah, if you don't mind." She shrugged while Teren shook his head and helped the sleepy kids stand up. Sneaking a peek at Ben, Tracey murmured, "I love kids."

Ben's eyes widened. Containing a smile, I was sure that a baby was soon to follow their wedding night…about nine months after their wedding night. Maybe sooner, if Tracey had her way. Squatting down to Julian and Nika, she ruffled their hair. "What do you say, kiddos, can Auntie Tracey put the birthday boy and girl to bed?"

They both grinned and nodded, and Teren and I gave them warm hugs and kisses. The scent of birthday cake lingered around them and the faintest trace of frosting lined their mouths. It still churned my stomach a little, but not as bad as before. Giving their cheeks dozens of kisses, I reminded Tracey to help them brush well. Hopefully they remembered to keep their teeth up in their tiredness. Well, if not, Halina was right on hand to mentally rewind Tracey if necessary.

Once the kids were loved on and sent out of the room, Teren twisted to face the people left behind. He smiled at each friend and family member while I sat in his spot by Mom. Snuggling into her side, I waited for him to say what was obviously on his mind— something he didn't want Tracey to hear. I figured it was vampiric then, since everyone else in the room knew the family secret.

Mom wrapped her arm around me while Teren cleared his throat. Running a hand back through his hair, he smiled nervously. "Um, well, I wanted to talk to all of you about something…and now seems as good a time as any."

Ashley looked over to me and I shrugged, since I didn't know where his head was at. Teren's smile relaxed as he met my gaze. "We've been through a lot together, and one thing I've learned through all of it…is we work better together. That's how family works," he whispered to me and I smiled, remembering my words to him.

His eyes slowly swept over the rest of the room. "I really don't think we'd have gotten Julian back if…" he choked up, swallowed, and had to try again. "If we hadn't all been on the same page." Smiling at his parents, then Ben, then Halina and Gabriel, he shook his head. "You were all so amazing. I'm so…grateful…to each of you."

His eyes drifted to Mom and Ashley and he sighed, a little sadly. "My family doesn't stay in one spot for too long…and it's getting close to the time when we should leave here." His brow furrowed as he shook his head. "Emma and I have talked about what to do, whether to stay...or go..."

Mom and Ashley both looked at me and I dropped my head. I still didn't know what to do about that one. I'd sort of forgotten about it with everything that had been happening to us lately. I wasn't sure why Teren was bringing it up now, when the actual move was still a ways away. Maybe he was going to plead his case for us to leave in front of everyone. That wasn't really his style, though.

"Emma wants to be with her family...I do too. I love you all, but I need my family, too." He sighed. "But ultimately the choice isn't only ours, which is why I'm bringing this up today." I peeked up at him. He was smiling at me, shaking his head. "This affects everyone, so everyone should get a say." He looked around the room. "Do you want to stay here in San Francisco...or do you want to leave with my parents to Utah?"

I blinked as I stared at him. I hadn't considered giving everyone the option to stay or go. It had just seemed like a decision only for us. I wanted to smile, as I considered everyone leaving the area together...but I didn't know what the others would choose. Listening raptly, I looked around the room.

Everyone looked at everyone else, and no one said anything right away. Teren shrugged. "I guess I'll go first...I want to go to Utah." He said that directly to me, his eyes apologetic.

I nodded at him. I already knew that was how he was leaning. I was about to speak when my sister surprisingly beat me to it. "I want to stay," she whispered. My eyes watered as I looked across my mother to her. She smiled and shook her head. "I know you want me to go, Emma, but my life is here. My work is here. Christian is here. I think he's going to ask me to marry him, and I want to say yes. I want a life here with him. I'm happy...and I want to stay."

I swallowed several times, not sure how to feel. She reached across Mom to lay her hand on my knee. "I'll be fine, Emma." She raised her half brows at me. "It's okay for you to let me go." Smirking she added, "I'm a big girl now. I don't need my older sister looking out for me anymore."

Swiping my fingers under my eyes, I chuckled. "I know."

As I clenched Ashley's hand, my mother suddenly exclaimed, "Well, I've always wanted to see Utah...no better time than now. When are we leaving?"

Shocked, I could only stare at her. I really hadn't expected her to say that. I'd really expected her to stick by Ashley. Her warm face smiled softly, the lines of happiness around her eyes and mouth deepening. "I want to be where I'm needed most, Emma." She twisted back to Ashley and patted her thigh. "I love both you girls, and I'm so proud," she looked back to me, "but out of the two of you, you could still use my help, I think." Sighing, she added, "And I'm not getting any younger, Emma. I think I could use your help, too."

Smiling, she looked up at the ceiling, where I could hear Tracey starting to read a bedtime story to my tired twins. "Besides, I can't be that far away from my grandchildren." The tears flowing freely now, I held her tight to me. Maybe I wouldn't have to completely choose after all. Maybe I could leave *and* keep a part of my family close. I hadn't considered that before.

As light laughter went around the room, Hot Ben stepped forward. Resting his hand on Teren's shoulder, he shook his head. "I'm sorry, man. You know I love you guys, but my life is here...with Tracey." He looked up at the ceiling like my mom had. I could hear the oblivious blonde beauty still reading the kids their favorite story; their yawns were more frequent now.

"I'd love to move with you, Teren, but Tracey wants a life with me...marriage, a big house filled with lots of kids." He shrugged. "I need to put her first. I need to stop lying to her. I need to give her the life she deserves, a normal one."

Teren smiled sadly and clapped his back. "I know." He nodded his head, and his eyes were serious. "It's been an honor knowing you, Ben."

Ben smiled, equally sad. "No, Teren. The honor was mine. You, your family, you're the most amazing people I've ever met and if you need anything, *anything*, I'm only a phone call away."

Teren smiled, and tears glistened in his beautiful eyes. "Thank you. You don't know what that means to me."

Ben extended his hand to Teren. "Yeah, actually, I do." While they nodded at each other, shaking hands in brotherly friendship, I think I started crying harder than when Mom had agreed to go with us. Ben was everything to Teren. But it wasn't like they'd be completely separated. If my sister was staying, then we'd be down here all the time visiting. At least, that's what I hoped.

Letting go of Teren's hand, Ben seemed to wonder the same thing. He pointed at Ashley as he looked back at Halina. "Will we get to remember you?" he quietly asked.

Ashley perked up as she seemed to consider this for the first time. Halina looked between the both of them, then at Teren and me. Tilting her dark head, she nodded in acquiescence. "You have both earned our trust. We will never wipe you, not unless you ask. Your memories will be left intact, you have my word." She shook her head. "You will be the only ones left behind who entirely remember us."

Ben exhaled and nodded at the pureblood, looking relieved. Teren looked relieved, too. He'd sort of bucked the family system when he'd fought for Ben to remember. I was so grateful that Ben had turned out to be the man he was. Teren deserved no less in a friend. Thinking of my friend staying behind, I raised an eyebrow at Halina. "Tracey?" I asked softly.

Halina frowned at me and slowly shook her head. "I'm sorry, Emma, but no. I'll let her vaguely remember, but not really. You'll be a coworker she had once. Teren will be an old acquaintance of Ben's. She won't remember much more. Even your names will be hazy. Everything specific about you, and us, will be blurred away." She shrugged, looking genuinely apologetic. "I'm sorry, but this is the way it must be."

I swallowed several times and tried to be okay with it. Tracey and I had gone through a lot together. Her not remembering any of it was going to…suck, but that was just the fact of my life now. I was immortal. I was a vampire. Tracey was neither of those things. And she had a chance at a normal, happy life with Ben. I smiled as I looked up at him. They both deserved that.

Smiling back at me, Ben shrugged. "It's okay, Emma. I'll take good care of her." He nodded his head at my sister. "Her and Ashley both. I'll make sure they stay out of trouble." Ashley smirked at him and soft laughter went around the room again.

Nearly as one, every eye shifted to where Gabriel was standing. He smiled at all the attention directed his way. "You haven't already guessed my decision?" he asked, meeting every eye.

Halina stepped into his side, and grabbed his hand. "You have a nest...I understand." She swallowed, and her lip quivered as her eyes shimmered bright red.

Tilting his head, Gabriel palmed her cheek as he spoke over her shoulder. "Jacen, I've already informed Jordan of this, but I want you to know as well...he'll be taking over the nest in L.A." His gaze shifted from Halina's startled face to Jacen's startled face. "I'll be relocating to Utah."

I think every mouth dropped open. Everyone's but mine. I'd been pretty sure Gabriel wouldn't let Halina go that easily. I'd been hoping anyway. She'd been alone for too long. Him, too.

Jacen adjusted in his seat. "Father? Do you think that's wise?"

Gabriel lifted an eyebrow at him and Jacen stared at the floor. Starla stood and walked over to Gabriel, her hands on her hips. "Well, I'm going, too. You're not ditching me, Father."

Gabriel smiled and put a hand on her shoulder. "I wasn't going to. The choice is yours, Starla, yours and Jacen's both. If you wish to stay in L.A., then I will leave Jordan with instructions to give you all the medication you need. But, if you wish to go with me...you may."

I frowned at this development but didn't say anything. Starla's eyes moistened as she looked between Gabriel and Jacen. She seemed to be choosing between the two men and it seemed to be killing her. The short, blonde male went to stand by his girlfriend. Encircling his arms around her, he said, "I'm with you Starla, wherever you want us."

She swallowed and looked back at Gabriel. "You saved me. You took me in when I had nobody. You cared for me." A tear dropped to her cheek. "I'm with you, Father."

Smiling, Gabriel brought her in for a hug. Halina sighed but kept her opinions to herself. I sniffled; my emotions were still on overdrive. Gabriel kissed Starla's hair as he closed his eyes for a second. Pulling back from her, he looked between her and Jacen. "I only have one request if you choose to stay by my side. "

They both immediately said, "Yes, Father?"

Gabriel frowned and shook his head. "That must stop. I am not your father and you don't owe me obedience." Sighing, he shrugged. "Please, call me Gabriel."

Jacen shifted his stance but smiled. Looking down he muttered, "All right...Gabriel." The way he said it was awkward, like he'd clearly been calling him Father for dozens of years, maybe a hundred or more, and it was completely unnatural to call him anything different.

Starla snorted and pulled back from his embrace. "No, I won't call you that."

Gabriel narrowed his eyes at her in a way that used to make her lower her head in submission. Making me very proud, she defiantly raised her chin. "My mother is dead. My sister is dead. Even my natural father is dead. You're my family and I love you." Rolling her eyes, she snarked, "I'm calling you Father whether you like it or not, so you may as well get used to it."

Chuckling, Gabriel shook his head and held her tight. "All right, then."

Releasing Starla after a moment, he twisted back to Halina. When he smiled at her, like everything was settled, she shook her head at him. "You're staying with me?" she asked, seemingly dazed that he would.

A blood red tear ran down her cheek as Gabriel placed his forehead against hers. "I have been surrounded by people for centuries, Halina, but I have been completely alone until you. I have no wish to go back to a life of loneliness." He pulled back to stare into her eyes. His green ones deep and soulful, he intently whispered, "I love you...do you love me?"

Halina swallowed and started to shake her head before she stopped herself and nodded. "Yes, yes, I do love you...so much."

Gabriel smiled and kissed her as another bloody tear rolled down her skin. "Then we're agreed," he murmured against her lips.

A small sob escaping from my mouth brought everyone's attentions back to me. Darn emotional vampires. Teren lightly laughed at me as I glared at him before laughing myself. Throwing my hands into the air, I shrugged. "All right, Teren, you win. I want us to go to Utah."

Chapter 24 – One Year Later

I was a nervous, anxious, excited ball of energy. I was pacing back and forth, being careful to not distress my perfectly styled updo or my perfectly applied makeup. While my body was maintaining a human pace, my mind was spinning faster than a normal eye would have been able to perceive. In fact, to a regular person's vision, my brain probably would have seemed to be standing still it was processing so fast. I couldn't help the restlessness…so much was going on.

A little more than a year had passed since everyone had made their own choice on whether or not to stay in sunny San Francisco. Once our lives had calmed down from the horrid mess with Malcolm, plans to head out of state took off in earnest.

Still savvy of the real estate investment of a free-and-clear owned home, Mom put her house on the market as a rental. Her second, since she also still owned the adorable Victorian house that I'd lived in for a time. Mom moved in with Teren and me once her house got rented out. Watching someone else live there was…weird, but with Mom in my home, it was okay. Her home would still have a nostalgic place in my dead heart, but Mom was what mattered, and the warmth that I associated with her old place would follow her to the next place, even if that was her own wing at the new ranch.

And yes, once she moved in with us, Teren and I started closing our soundproof door again.

Mom then proceeded to learn all that she could about homeschooling. She and Imogen were going to teach the children everything they would need to know. Until high school, that was. Teren insisted that they be allowed to join society, once their abilities were tightly under rein. High school was when Teren had come out, so to speak, and he'd immensely enjoyed being around his peers instead of his parents. I wanted to give my kids that too, although, we would be having firm discussions with them about the birds and the bees and how to be safe with their bodies. I didn't need them to have *all* of Teren's high school experiences.

Teren and I decided to keep our place by the bay. It would be convenient to have a familiar home to go to when we came out to visit Ashley and Ben, and really, I was just too attached to the place to let it go. Happy that I loved what was technically his home, Teren warmly told me that we'd keep it forever if I wanted. And I did. I wanted it as our secret getaway spot. People had vacation homes, right?

A few months after Julian was safe and sound, Hot Ben kidnapped Tracey. Well, okay, technically he swept her away to Mexico, where they eloped. He didn't want to wait anymore. I understood. A lot can happen while you're waiting. Being the romantic that I always knew he could be, Ben didn't tell her about it either.

Tracey and I were at work, her diligently copying and collating for me, when he'd shown up in a full tuxedo. And, God…my husband is beyond attractive, but Ben, fully decked out, brought new meaning to the word hot, even I could admit it.

Tracey's mouth had hit the floor as she watched him walk up to her. Every other jaw dropped too…even Clarice's normally scowling one.

Standing before her, Ben dropped to one knee. Tracey's heart had shifted into an unnaturally fast pace when he did. I'd worried for her health there for a second, but then Ben spoke and she calmed down.

"Tracey, will you do me the honor of being my wife?"

Tears in her eyes, Tracey had nervously giggled and looked around. "Uh, Ben, you already did this part…and I already said yes."

I'd had to bite my lip to not laugh at the blush on her face. Smiling charmingly, Ben's only response was, "Will you be my wife…today?"

Her eyes widening, Tracey's gaze locked onto him and stayed there. The entire office held their breaths—I heard the inhales—waiting for her answer. I swear I could hear every person thinking, *Say yes, you idiot.* Eventually, and with tears dripping down her cheeks, she nodded. "Yes."

Shaking my head, I'd waved goodbye to the pair and didn't see or hear from them for a week and a half. From what Tracey told me later, Ben had taken her directly from work to the airport. Having made every arrangement, even packing everything she'd need, a skill Teren must have helped him with since he was a master packer, they immediately flew to Cancun. By that evening they were married...on the beach...at sunset.

Even now it still made me sigh. My daughter wasn't the only romantic in the house.

A few months after Mr. and Mrs. Hot Ben got back, the two of them moved out of their tiny place and started renting the Victorian that Ashley had been living in. Ashley wasn't there anymore, because Ashley had decided to try living with her man. She and Christian moved in together around wintertime.

As I continued my back and forth strut on the thinly carpeted floor, an irritated voice behind me snapped out, "Would you stop moving! You're making me nervous...and I don't get nervous!"

Smiling, I twisted around to look at Halina. She was scowling at me, but with what she was wearing, I laughed; my nerves spilled into the sound. Frowning even more, Halina adjusted the floor length dress she had on. It was the most modest thing I'd ever seen her wear, full sleeves, empire waist, fabric lightly draping along the floor. She looked highly uncomfortable being so well covered.

Scratching her head, she also looked uncomfortable with her hair being secured into an updo as elaborately twisted and pinned as mine was. Adjusting her stance, she muttered, "I can't believe I agreed to this. I haven't been part of a wedding ceremony...for about a million years."

The sound of bubble gum popping shifted our attentions to Starla. She was leaning back in a chair, watching us. Smacking on the obtrusive thing, she laughed out, "Million years, huh? Sounds about right, Grandma."

Already nervous and agitated, Halina stepped towards her; her gown rustled against her body, and the light color clashed with her ebony hair. "If you call me that one more time, little girl, I will end you," she snarled.

Smiling, unafraid, Starla snapped another bubble in her face.

"No, you won't. Father loves me and you love him." Smirking she added, "Face it, you're stuck with me, Grams."

Sighing, Halina rolled her eyes. "Yes, until old age finally claims you," she muttered.

Standing, Starla smoothed the tightly fitted designer dress she had on over her hips, like she was emphasizing the outfit that I knew Halina would have preferred to be in. "I wouldn't bet on that." Tilting her perfectly styled head, she smiled. "Father is brilliant. He'll find a way to help me convert." Leaning into Halina, her small grin turned into a wide one. "Then we'll be together forever."

Halina groaned as she looked back at me. "What did I get myself into?" she pitifully muttered.

I laughed as I resumed my endless pacing. Starla snickered and left the room to find Jacen. Those two didn't stay separated for very long. They were a constant thorn in Halina's side as they stayed at the ranch with Gabriel. She made them stay in a side building, as far from her as she could get them, but with our ears it wasn't far enough. Gabriel found it humorous. After a while, I did too.

Halina had already informed them that they were getting their own place in Utah…preferably miles away from her.

Teren and I were looking for places to live in Utah, too. Just last week, Teren had shown me a three bedroom home that he liked, about twenty minutes from the new ranch. Shaking my head at him, I'd finally asked him what had been rolling around in my mind for a while. "Why don't you just give it up and admit that you like it at the ranch, and you want to live there with your family?"

Dropping the real estate magazine that he'd been holding, he'd shrugged. "Well, yeah, I like it, but…I want us to have our own place, our own lives. Plus, a house near the city would be closer to our jobs."

Shaking my head again, I'd sighed and slung my arms around his waist. "And why don't you just admit defeat and work at the ranch?" Ducking down, I'd met his eye. "I know you love it." If there was one thing that always happened whenever we visited his parents, it was that Teren turned into a cowboy. If we were starting new lives with them, it just made sense to me to finally give in to what he loved.

Looking down and smiling, he'd shaken his head. "Yeah, I do, I'll admit it." Peeking back up at me, he'd said, "I don't know, at first I just didn't want to do the family business. I wanted to see who I was away from *what* I was, away from the others." Smiling wider, he rocked me in his arms. "Then I found something that I loved to do, and Dad does all right running the place with Mom and the girls."

Kissing my head, he'd held me tight against him. "Someday, when my dad can't handle it on his own, then I'll take over." Pulling back, he'd raised an eyebrow at me. "That should make you happy, right?" His smile turned cocky. "Since you secretly enjoy watching me as a cowboy."

Kissing those cocky lips, I'd sighed in contentment. "That I do…but you really do need to buy a hat."

He'd laughed pretty hard, then tenderly kissed me when his chuckles had subsided. "And what about you? Would you want to do what my mom does? Help me run the place?" His smile had been peaceful as his fingers had tucked loose strands of hair behind my ear. The warmth in his words melted me all over, even just remembering them now.

Placing light kisses along his lips, I'd considered that future. Truly, I was still considering it. "Hmmm…although a part of me will miss office life, I think I'd really like that someday." Pulling back, I'd cupped his cheeks. "But whatever I do, whatever we do, my eternity is with you."

Remembering how heated things had gotten between us after those words had left my lips, I paused in my pacing and felt for my husband. His presence was a few rooms over, tucked away in a room with our children and the other men in our extended circle of family. I suddenly wished we had an emotional connection like our twins did, so I could let him feel the level of love I had for him. Not that he didn't already know…I just wanted him to feel it.

As our group was leaving town in the next couple of days, the old ranch was completely cleaned out. All the cows were gone, all the hired help was gone, and a new crew was already waiting at the new place. From what Jack had told me, Peter had everything up and running in Utah. All that was missing…was us.

Teren had finally accepted a writing job for a local magazine. He preferred the small publications, more anonymous that way. I stuck with his pattern and took a job with a small accounting firm. The hours were less, the pay was less, but that worked out fine for us. It was a way to have time for my family but still be regular-Emma too. And for now, I still needed that, and I understood why Teren wanted to keep his day job for a little longer. We would have a lifetime ahead of us of running ranches around the country. For now, having our own lives felt nice.

Tracey bounded into the room while I thought about our upcoming move. A part of me couldn't believe it was here already. This past year had flown by. Luckily, it had passed peacefully.

The blonde's do was as meticulous as mine and Halina's. Her outfit exactly matched ours, too. Beaming at me, she giggled. "Everything's ready, Emma, is she?"

I smiled as the glowing woman stepped over to me. Her hand was instinctively covering the adorably cute, six-month baby bump. She and Ben had indeed wasted no time in starting their family. A part of me was incredibly sad that I wouldn't be her friend by the time the baby was born. I mean, I would always be her friend, until the end of her life, but she wouldn't remember our friendship.

But for now, she did, and I slung my arm around her and listened to the child I could hear kicking in her stomach. Silently thanking the woman for always being there for me, even when she didn't realize that she was being there for me, I nodded at her question. "Yeah, she's ready."

As one, we both twisted to look over at my sister. Sitting in front of the vanity with our mother, doing last minute touches on the half of her head that still grew hair, she was a vision in white. Today was her wedding day. The last thing I had to take care of before we left town was watching her walk down the aisle. I wasn't leaving her behind until I knew for certain that she was safely in the care of another.

And she was. Christian had shown on numerous instances that he genuinely adored her. Not bothered by her looks in the slightest, he lavished her with affection. It warmed my chilly body, knowing that she would have the life I'd always hoped she'd have. And, always the strong one, she'd done it on her own terms.

As Tracey, Halina and I–her bridesmaids—walked over to her, she stood up. Tears threatening to ruin the perfect makeup around her eyes, she smiled at me. "I'm getting married today, Emma," she giggled, clasping her arms over mine.

"I know," I whispered, cinching her in a hug. "And it's about time," I added with a laugh.

Pulling back, she laughed and smacked my arm. Searching my face, she shook her head. "I love you, Emma…I'm gonna miss you."

Swallowing back the huge lump in my throat, I willed my eyes not to water. If I cried, she'd cry, and then we'd both have to get our makeup redone. And she didn't have time for that…she was about to get married. "I'm gonna miss you too, Ash." Carefully dabbing a finger under my uncooperative, watering eyes, I smacked her arm. "Now stop that, it's not like Teren and I won't be bringing the kids down every couple of months to visit with their aunt."

She laughed and pulled me tight. "You'd better."

The small group of us got quiet as we all watched my sister for a moment. Then the sound of a church organ filled the space. Halina glanced over at me at hearing the sound; she was smirking. When Ashley had told us that Christian wanted to get married at a church, in a formal ceremony, I'd asked Halina if she'd be able to go. You know, being a pureblood vampire and all, churches just seemed…forbidden.

She'd actually snorted at me. "It's a building…do we need to revisit the conversation about me being able to go into *any* building I want to go into?" I'd dropped it after that. Apparently that myth wasn't true either.

Ashley let out a quick exhale as she smoothed the white satin over her hips. "I guess that's my cue," she softly said.

Mom hugged her and grabbed her arm. She was already crying a little as she prepared to walk her youngest daughter down the aisle.

Halina smiled at Ashley, gave her a swift kiss on the cheek—a very rare sign of affection from her—and then twisted to face the door. "Let's get this over with then," she muttered.

Her escort, a male friend of Christian's, met her at the door with wide eyes. Halina was intoxicatingly sensual, and men picked up on that, especially human men. His eyes glanced down her modest dress as Halina sashayed through the door. Looking back at us, she winked as she laced her arm though his. "Well, aren't Christian's friends just…edible?"

She grinned slyly and disappeared. Tracey harrumphed, still not overly liking Halina. She hadn't really understood her comment anyway. Mom, Ashley, and I exchanged quick glances. I hoped Halina hadn't meant that literally. Not that she would really take a bite out of a groomsman at my sister's wedding. Well, not before the ceremony anyway…

Tracey was next, meeting up with Teren at the door. It made me a little sad that my husband wasn't walking with me, but I was the Maid of Honor and Teren was only a groomsman. Christian had asked him to be in the wedding as a show of welcome, of melding our families together. I thought the inclusion was very sweet of him. Plus, it gave me the chance to ogle my husband in a tux again.

Smiling crookedly at him, I raised an eyebrow as he extended his elbow to Tracey. She giggled up at him as she took it. His dark hair matched his dark clothes; it was incredibly sexy. Looking back at me, he muttered under his breath, "You look amazing in that dress…I can't wait to get you out of it." His pale eyes were smoldering as he turned and left with my best friend.

I closed my eyes and felt a flush that I knew was imaginary. My body couldn't flush anymore. But Teren's words always made me feel it anyway. He was talented in that department.

Neither my mom nor sister had heard what he said, and they only smiled at his broad back as he left. I carefully bit my lip, hoping this ceremony wasn't overly long.

Eventually it was my turn, and when Christian's brother turned up at the door, I looked back at my sister. She had tears in her eyes, watching me leave with her new family. They were in mine too as the vision of her hazed before me, softening into an angel. "I'll see you up there, sis."

What I could see of her nodded, and I twisted to the middle-aged man holding his arm out in a gentlemanly way. Smiling politely, he led me to the main chamber filled with pews. Each pew had a bouquet of white and pink roses attached to the end; the pale pink flowers matched the shade of the bridesmaid's dresses. Swarms of people were sitting on those benches, eyes trained on me. Some I knew, some I'd seen a couple of times, some I'd never met before in my life.

My mind blanked them all out as I stared at the altar before me. It was decked out in white chiffon, more roses, and a few tall candles. It was simple, yet gorgeous, much like my sister. My eyes drifted to the people assembled there. Halina looked uncomfortable as she held her small bouquet of flowers, while Tracey looked perfectly at ease with her flowers resting right over her baby bump. The minister was waiting patiently in the center, with a debonair Christian standing right beside him. Last in the line of men was Christian's good friend, who was still staring at Halina, and next to him, was my husband.

After being escorted into position next to where my sister would stand, Christian's brother sweetly kissed my hand before sliding over to stand in his appointed spot, between Teren and Christian. I couldn't keep my eyes off of Teren.

Even though we'd already done this before, and even though this wasn't our ceremony, it sort of felt like we were the ones getting married as we stood up there. Teren smiled at me, like he felt the same way. Then his eyes drifted down my body for a second and a rush of desire hit me. I narrowed my eyes at him, trying to stop the sensation. He really shouldn't be turning me on in a church. That was most definitely…forbidden.

He chuckled a little, biting his lip. I shook my head at him, loving him, warmed by the bond that was seeping into me ever since I'd started walking up the aisle. It ached to complete the connection, along with other, more intimate connections, but that could wait until after.

The music shifted and I twisted my gaze from Teren to look down the aisle. Every human in the audience stood and looked back as well. The vampires, of whom the crowd was completely unaware, also stood. Alanna and Imogen were right in the front row, along with Gabriel, Starla and Jacen. For once, Starla and Jacen were managing to keep their hands off each other, as they attempted to be respectful of the environment.

Jack and Hot Ben were on the other side of Alanna, Jack had his arm around his wife as a chorus of, "Aaaahs" went through the crowd. My smile was huge as my eyes glassed over again.

Julian and Nika were walking down the aisle hand in hand. Five years old now, they looked a little more grownup to me. Their fangs had grown longer, their spindly legs were each at least three inches taller, and the slight baby fat that had been on their bodies had all but vanished. They were growing up so fast. Before I knew it, they'd be teenagers, preparing to find their own soul mates. A tear dripped down my cheek at just the thought.

Julian held a basket of flower petals and Nika was reaching in and scattering some along the ground as they walked along. The crowd was eating up the adorable pair, the miniatures of Teren and me. Everyone watched their every move. When they got to the steps leading up to the altar, they stopped as one and looked up at me.

Nika smiled brightly and waved. "Hi, Mommy. You look really pretty."

She said it pretty loudly and a chorus of chuckles went around the room. With a nod and a laugh, I shushed her and pointed in front of me. Giggling, she and Julian stood in their places, and waited as patiently as five-year-olds can. I ran my free hand through Julian's black hair, looking over at my husband again. He had tears in his eyes as he watched the three of us. Oh God, if he lost it, I was doomed.

"She's right, you do look very pretty," he muttered below the music.

Smiling, I swiped under my eyes again. "Thank you…and you're very…handsome."

He grinned at me but then the music changed again. Still standing, the crowd instantly shushed. Within seconds, my mother walked in with Ashley on her arm. I'd never seen my sister so radiant. Slightly shuffling with her walk, she still seemed to glide down the petal strewn aisle. I gave up on holding the tears in, and let them fall down my cheeks so at least my vision would be free to see her. A netted veil was in her hair, coming down over her face to her chin. Beneath it, my eyes could easily see the pure joy and love on her face.

When she finally made the long progression to her near-husband, our mother placed Ashley's hand in his. A calming sigh escaped me as part of my worry over her lifted. She was fine. She was happy. I could let her go.

After the ceremony started, my eyes couldn't leave her. She and Christian exchanged tender vows of love and devotion, and I could clearly see that they both meant them. Christian slid her wedding ring onto her with trembling fingers. She in turn, enclosed him. I idly played with the band around my finger with my thumb, the cool metal not much different than my skin now.

When it finally got to the point where Ashley and Christian could kiss, he almost timidly pulled back the veil covering her face. The older man's fingers came up to brush the scarred skin along her jaw, and only love was on his face. She beamed at him as I clearly heard him whisper, "I love you, wife...always." Then he lowered his lips to hers.

I sobbed as the crowd clapped.

When they twisted to face the audience as man and wife, I finally broke my gaze from her to stare at Teren. I laughed when I noticed his cheeks were wet, too. Shaking my head at him while he shrugged, I muttered, "You're such a softie." He laughed, nodding in agreement.

Watching my sister walk away, I smiled at my husband. Below human level, I told him, "I know you're always telling the kids that I'm the most beautiful woman in the world...but I think you're wrong." He scrunched his brows at me as I looked over to my sister shuffling her way back down the aisle. "She is."

I glanced back at him as he smiled warmly at me. Slowly, he nodded. "Yeah, I think you might be right," he whispered.

Teren and I both turned to watch her walk away, while Julian leaned over to tell Nika that he was going to marry Auntie Ashley one day. Smiling as the wedding party started to disperse, I broke protocol and joined up with my husband to walk back down the aisle.

He kissed my head as I slipped my arm through his. Both kids ran off to their grandparents, now that the formal stuff was over with, and I laid my head against Teren's shoulder.

Happy and content, we both walked off to celebrate the new lives blossoming around us.

After a quick round of congratulations, we moved the celebration to a nearby reception hall, where we could all help Ashley and Christian keep the festivities going until the wee hours of the morning. We all raised glasses in a toast, the undead creatures in the room faking the sips that the humans were taking. We all watched the newlyweds cut the cake, Christian daintily placing a piece of the frosted confection on her tongue. And we all silently watched the couple share their first dance as husband and wife.

The love between them lifted my spirits and reminded me of my own first dance with Teren. Extending a hand out to him, I tilted my head to the dance floor which was starting to fill with people. "Dance with your wife?"

Teren grinned and grabbed my hand. "Gladly."

Pulling me to the middle of the floor, close to my sister, he wrapped one arm around my waist, while holding my hand tight to his chest. We were quickly joined by all the other couples that populated our lives—Jack and Alanna, Gabriel and Halina, Starla and Jacen, Hot Ben and Tracey. Even my mom and Imogen laughingly started twirling around the floor together.

Staring into the depths of my husband's amazing, pale eyes, it took mere seconds for our children to cut in. Giggling, the adorably dressed pair wedged right in between us. Teren and I backed up a step, letting the youngsters hold our waists while we continued to hold each other. As a foursome, we continued dancing the night away.

When the bulk of the partygoers started leaving, Ben and Tracey approached us. I clenched my jaw, knowing that we probably wouldn't see them before the move. Well, I was sure Ben would see us off, but Tracey... We had all agreed that tonight was the best opportunity to give her a clean slate.

Placing a hand on my shoulder, Halina gave me a quick glance before stepping towards the perky blonde. I put a hand up to stop her. "Wait...can I have...just a minute?" I whispered to her. Halina paused, then briefly nodded. Twisting away from me, she stepped into Gabriel's embrace, and slow danced with him even though the song playing was a fast one. Lost in their own world, the couple ignored everyone else at the party.

Glad that Halina was giving me a chance for a final goodbye, I stepped up to where Ben was shaking Teren's hand. Ben looked over at me and nodded his head. "We're gonna head out, Emma. Tracey's beat." Holding his wife's shoulders, he pulled her into his side.

Tracey smiled then yawned; she did look exhausted. Reaching out for me, she pulled me into a loose hug. "I'll call you tomorrow, okay?"

Tears in my eyes, knowing she wouldn't even remember me tomorrow, I fiercely hugged her back. "I love you, Tracey. I hope somehow you always know that."

Feeling my seriousness, the emotion in my voice, she pulled back. "Hey, you okay?" I felt Teren put a supportive hand on my back, but I couldn't stop the tears that were now streaming down my cheeks. "Yeah, I'm great...I just..." I paused as I swallowed. I knew none of this made any sense to her, but I had to say it anyway. "You have helped me so many times without ever realizing that you were doing it, and I want to thank you for that. For being my friend...through everything."

She nodded, her eyes misting. "Hey...are you pregnant or something?"

Teren and Ben both chuckled and I eventually did too. Laughing, I hugged her again. "No, I'm just going to miss you, is all."

Now tears dropped from Tracey's eyes and she sniffled as she pulled back. "Stop that. Utah isn't that far, and Ben and I are going to visit." She rubbed her stomach. "We have to get the kids together for play dates."

I nodded, but I knew that would never happen. I looked back to Halina and Gabriel dancing. "I'm ready, thank you." Halina stopped dancing and looked back at me. She gave me a sad smile, then nodded.

As she began walking towards us, Teren asked me in a barely audible level, "Are you sure you want to do this now? There really is no harm if she remembers you for a few more years."

Looking up at him, I searched his light eyes. He looked at Halina as she joined our foursome. Ignoring Tracey and Ben for a second, I quietly reaffirmed with her. "Can she remember me for a while? At least, until my looks start to become an issue?"

I was, after all, physically unchanging. That was the entire reason the Adams cleansed places when they left, so that their never-ending youth wouldn't start people asking the wrong questions. But I still looked the age I technically was. Surely I could pull that off for a while?

Halina frowned as she looked behind me at Tracey. Hot Ben was taking a moment to distract his wife while we conversed, asking her what baby names she was leaning towards. Loving the idea that I could maybe meet her baby, I placed my hand on Halina's arm. She sighed. Halina didn't like loose ends and she was already conceding with Ben and Ashley. There was already a plan in place for Christian too, one that involved hazing our physical appearance from him after each visit, starting in a few years, when we would need to start hiding our looks. I knew Halina would have preferred the simplicity of just wiping him completely, but he was sort of family now. Tracey...was not.

As Gabriel came up to her, slowly nodding, Halina huffed out, "Fine...for a while, I guess."

Looking a little irritated that she'd been outvoted, Halina rolled her eyes and muttered, "Why don't we just tell her that we're all vampires while we're at it? God forbid someone didn't find out the family secret."

I laughed at Halina's comment, then flung my arms around the teenage vampire. She sighed again as she causally patted my back, probably hoping I'd get off her soon. Sure, she'd lightened up considerably since falling in love with Gabriel, but she was still Halina. "Not forever, Emma...but for now."

I nodded as we pulled apart. "For now is fine," I muttered, feeling the tears in my eyes spilling out again. No, Tracey was not the sort of person who could calmly handle what we were, not like my sister had, or even Ben…eventually. She'd never look at me the same if she knew. She'd always be scared if she knew. I couldn't blame the girl for that…the world of vampires wasn't for everybody. But to hold onto her friendship for a few more years…that was enough.

"Uh, if everything is okay, Ben and I are going to go," Tracey hesitantly said, her hand coming out to touch my shoulder.

Ben lifted an eyebrow, not knowing the outcome of that near-silent debate. I nodded at him, then her. "Yeah, you guys are free to go."

I emphasized that for Ben and he smiled, understanding. Looking over at Halina, he inclined his head in a polite bow. "Thank you," he whispered to her.

She smiled at the show of respect then inclined her head. "You're welcome."

Not long after they left, my sister was ready to go. Christian was taking her to a secluded island in the south pacific, where she could walk up and down the beach in a two piece and not feel an ounce of self-consciousness. I adored Christian already.

Giving her a bear hug, and probably bruising her in the process, I wept my goodbyes. Crying herself, Ashley kissed my chilly cheeks. "You call me when you get to the new place," she whispered, "and I'm coming up to visit the second I get back."

I nodded, giving her a final hug before hugging Christian and wishing them both well. Halina stepped up next. She hugged my sister as fiercely as I'd hugged Tracey. Then she stepped up to Christian and cordially said goodbye to him. Leaning in, she said something to him that shocked me. In a way that I knew was a command, she told him that he would never betray Ashley. He obediently nodded at her. Looking satisfied that her trancing ability had never failed her, and never would fail her, Halina turned to walk back to Gabriel.

Seeing me staring at her with my mouth open, she shrugged. "You can never be too careful with men…especially human men."

I opened my mouth to defend my species, but I sort of couldn't.

I shrugged then, too. I was pretty sure Christian never would have betrayed Ashley anyway, not with the way he openly adored her. A slow peace flowed into me as I shook my head. I guess now I didn't ever need to worry about it.

We waved as they took off in their limo, and Teren held me as I sobbed harder than my mom. I couldn't help it. I'd looked after Ashley for so long, protected her as best I could…even though she'd never needed me too. But now she had Christian to do that.

Leaving the wedding with my husband, kids and mother, I felt that peace stay with me. Ash was going to be just fine. And so were we.

On the evening of our great departure to Utah, Hot Ben and Tracey saw us off. Tracey commented that she thought it was weird that we were leaving at night, and I only shrugged and smiled. I couldn't exactly tell her that traveling during the day with Halina just wasn't possible, and we'd all decided to go together. Even though that meant a pit stop halfway there, so Halina could hide away from the poisonous light she missed seeing on a daily basis.

Jack and Alanna piled into Alanna's car, Imogen and my mother rode with them. Gabriel and Halina stepped into his sleek sedan, and Starla and Jacen giggled as they slunk into the back seat. The rest of the cars had been shipped out to the new place weeks ago, and the ranch looked exceedingly empty as Teren and I piled the kids into his Prius. We waved as the cars filled with vampires pulled away. We'd see them in a few hours, and we'd be able to track them the entire time, thanks to the blood bond that joined us all.

I smiled as I glanced back at the rear seat, where my kids had started a game of cards; Spike was happily nestled in the space between them. I felt our bond with them and let out a happy sigh. It would never be taken away from me again. Teren and I gave the ranch one final, last look—the white beauty encrusted with river rocks, the blood-red tiles gleaming in the moonlight. It was the most beautiful place…I was going to miss it. But I knew we'd be back, the next time it came up in rotation.

Clasping Ben and Tracey a final time, we finally got into our car and left our castle in California behind.

On the second night of travel, Teren nudged me awake. I jerked out of my dream, momentarily confused. Then he smiled and pointed to the home that we were parked in front of. "Welcome to the new ranch...well, new to you and me anyway."

I was in awe. It was one of those homes that you only saw on magazines catering to the independently wealthy, never in real life. We were on the edge of a wide, circular driveway. Low, bright green hedges lined the circle, with a fifteen foot fountain of a crying woman in the center of it. I blinked as I stared at where it glowed, lifelike, under the spotlights surrounding it; it was the same statue that had been inside the other ranch, only a much, much larger version.

We'd passed through a six foot high wall to get into the complex. The gate behind us was made with elaborately twisted wrought iron, and it sort of matched the design on Teren's San Francisco home. Over the top of the gate, large metal letters spelled out ADAMS. The floodlights on either side of the gate were fixed on the family name, warming the bronze letters, even in the dead of night.

A plush, green lawn lined the drive, leading up to one of most impressive buildings I'd ever seen. It didn't even really look like a home. It looked more like an Ivy League University. It was an aesthetically pleasing, multi-leveled home—one story around the edges of the house, but lifting to at least four stories near the center. I had to assume it stretched just as far underground, to accommodate the pureblood in the family. Imagining those underground levels, the shape of the structure reminded me of a diamond. Fitting, for the family it protected.

The house was built completely out of blood-red bricks, and there were several tall, slim chimneys that dotted the roof like castle spires. Long in length and sturdy in appearance, the building had to be just as strong as the vampires who were going to be living inside it. Three sets of dark cherry and glass front doors gave me a peek into the interior of the home. With the lights on, in preparation for the returning owners, it already looked warm and inviting.

My enhanced eyes could clearly pick out the snow-capped mountains in the distance that created an idyllic backdrop for the massive home. I could tell that in the daylight, the pure white peaks would contrast artistically with the dark red bricks and the bright green lawns. It would be a sight to see in the glory of the day. But even in moonlight, it was breathtaking.

Next to the main home, there was a matching two-story building that I assumed was the garage. The home for our vehicles was attached to the rest of the house by a cute, circular breezeway that was just large enough to drive through. As I stared, dazed by my surroundings, Teren drove his Prius to the back of the house. I had been right about the building—there was a long line of garage doors along the back wall. Most of the doors were closed, already filled with the other's cars, but a few spaces were still open, and Teren headed towards one.

From behind the home, I could see even more buildings. Imogen had told us before leaving California that this ranch had an indoor pool, so one of those long, lean buildings had to be housing it. Off to the other side of the home there was a tennis court *and* a basketball court. I smiled as I imagined Julian and Nika growing up here. In the distance, as far as I could see to either side of the main house, were the pastures. I could see the dark blobs where the cows were, and I already felt at home. Of course, the same could be said of any place I went with Teren.

After turning the car to back into an empty space in the garage, Teren paused a moment to lean over the steering wheel and take in the splendor of this very different ranch. Smiling over at me, he cocked an eyebrow. "It's pretty amazing, isn't it?" he asked. I nodded, still speechless. He smiled wider, amused by my stunned reaction. "Yeah, I've seen pictures of this ranch before, but they really didn't do the place justice." With a laugh, he added, "From what Great-Gran told me, the ranch in California is sort of the small one." As he chuckled over that, I shifted my gaze from the home most would consider a mansion to look over at his content face; he was by far more magnificent than any opulent ranch could ever be.

Bringing his head over to rest it against mine, he let out a happy sigh. The sound mixed with the dual snores coming from our children in an appealing way. "I love you, wife…forever," he muttered, his voice deep with peace.

Closing my eyes, I savored the connection we shared, the family we shared, the love we shared…the life we shared…even if we were dead. "I love you too, husband…forever."

The End

About the Author

S.C. Stephens is a *New York Times* and *USA Today* bestselling author who enjoys spending every free moment she has creating stories that are packed with emotion and heavy on romance.

Her debut novel, Thoughtless, an angst-filled love triangle charged with insurmountable passion and the unforgettable Kellan Kyle, took the literary world by storm. Amazed and surprised by the response to the release of Thoughtless in 2009, more stories were quick to follow. Stephens has been writing nonstop ever since.

In addition to writing, Stephens enjoys spending lazy afternoons in the sun reading fabulous novels, loading up her iPod with writer's block reducing music, heading out to the movies, and spending quality time with her friends and family. She currently resides in the beautiful Pacific Northwest with her two equally beautiful children.

Titles currently available for purchase:

The Thoughtless Series (Published by Gallery Books):
> Thoughtless
> Effortless
> Reckless

Collision Course (Published by S.C. Stephens)

The Conversion Trilogy (Published by S.C. Stephens):
> Conversion
> Bloodlines
> 'Til Death

Titles awaiting publication:

Conversion: The Next Generation Trilogy:
> The Next Generation (Book one)
> Book two (Title to be determined)
> Book three (Title to be determined)

It's All Relative

Not a Chance

Thoughtful (Kellan's POV of Thoughtless)

Connect with S.C. Stephens

Email: ThoughtlessRomantic@gmail.com

Facebook: https://www.facebook.com/SCStephensAuthor

Twitter: https://twitter.com/SC_Stephens_

Website: authorscstephens.com

CPSIA information can be obtained
at www.ICGtesting.com
Printed in the USA
LVOW01s1033050317
526180LV00009B/699/P